BAAGH

Tiger - The Inside Story

Abhishek Ray

BlueRose ONE.com
Stories Matter
NewDelhi • London

BLUEROSE PUBLISHERS

India | U.K.

BlueRose ONE.com
Stories Matter
NewDelhi • London

For permissions requests or inquiries regarding this publication,
please contact:
Abhishek Ray
+91 8851382193
officialabhishekray@gmail.com
Instagram @abhishekraywild

BLUEROSE PUBLISHERS
www.BlueRoseONE.com
info@bluerosepublishers.com
+91 8882 898 898
+4407342408967

ISBN: 978-93-7139-047-7

Cover design: Abhishek Ray
Typesetting: Tanya Raj Upadhyay

First Edition: June 2025

ABOUT THE AUTHOR :

Abhishek Ray is a celebrated Indian Film Composer, Playback Singer, Filmmaker and a Wildlife Conservationist widely known for composing music for award winning & superhit Bollywood films like 'Paan Singh Tomar', 'Welcome Back' ,' I am Kalam', 'Saheb, Biwi Aur Gangster', 'Haasil', 'Shagird' and many others.

He is also known for best selling albums with the legendary **Gulzar** Sahab, Shreya Ghoshal, Sonu Nigam, Shaan, Kavita Krishnamurthi, Hariharan and other top singers. He won **the National Mirchi Music Awards** in 2017.

Abhishek Ray has won worldwide acclaim for investing all his savings and creating **Sitabani Wildlife Reserve** by rewilding an entire barren hill close to Corbett Park. Today it is India's first private wildlife haven with wild tiger & leopard presence along with 300 bird species.

He has created, sung & composed **India's National Cheetah anthem** & Tiger Anthem for the **NTCA** (National Tiger Conservation Authority) .

He has alco created the branding anthem & film for the **IBCA** (International Big Cat Alliance) for UNDP & Government Of India.

Abhishek Ray has been conferred with **The Amazing Indians Award** from thr Hon'ble Vice President Of India with a letter of appreciation from the Hon'ble Prime Minister Modi, **Swabhiman Bharat** and the **Forbes —We Serve India Awards 2025** for Wildlife conservation.

"Abhishek Ray's 'BAAGH - Tiger: The Inside Story' is a testament to his profound connection with nature and his passion for storytelling.

As a renowned composer-singer and government bonafide tiger tracker, Abhishek brings authenticity and depth to this gripping wildlife crime thriller.

'BAAGH' is not just a novel; it's a clarion call for conservation, woven into a thrilling narrative that will leave readers spellbound.

BAAGH is the Jungle Book of today — Real & raw — an account of how the tiger survives in an increasingly human dominated landscape dodging deadly threats and poachers.

I commend Abhishek on this remarkable achievement and look forward to seeing his vision brought to life."

Abhishek is a man for all seasons, a true lover of environment who created Sitabani wildlife reserve.

Hope his vision for protection of mother earth is seen and felt by everyone on this planet.

JACKIE SHROFF

(Indian Actor)

Present day jungles are wilderness of the Anthropocene. Human influence is impacting forests and wildlife. Their dynamics are distorted. India is no exception to this global phenomenon. With more than 70% of wild tigers globally, India still has a multitude of tiger forests with assemblage of wild denizens – but not without problems. Our tiger landscapes are amphitheatres of new actions.

The jungle book of today has different contours owing to social stressors. More tigers amidst people and poverty bring in more challenges!

Abhishek, a keen naturalist, has captured it all – tiger forests, tigers and other wildlife in deep sylvan setting, threatened by poachers. The resilient tiger has survived well against all odds.

The book travels from the dusty Deccan to emerald Sal forests, from frantic car chases in the by-lanes of Kathmandu to Yak caravans across the snowy Himalayan passes of the Tibetan plateau tracking the grim, murky world of tiger poaching. Tiger is a collective responsibility and Jaggu's inward journey has a deep spiritual message for all of us.

An erstwhile tiger poacher turns against his clan and becomes a true champion of the wild. This has happened in Periyar tiger reserve, Kerala, India. The author's labour of love is adorable. His passionate description is so realistic and appealing, making us part of the setting. We need champions like Jaggu to save our wildlife and forests. This is a must read for all interested in nature and our life support system.

GTF

Global Tiger Forum

Dr. Rajesh Gopal (Secretary General, Global Tiger Forum)

Abhishek Ray, the composer the person, is a seeker, in all aspects.

Having known him since 2004, and besides working with him musically, I can say I know he is a special soul, in pursuit of something, he doesn't know what, like every other seeker, but he knows he will not settle for the average, the mundane.

I had my first experience of trekking and that too in Nanda Devi Biosphere Reserve thanks to Abhishek way back in May 2005.

His passion for wildlife, and his incredible knowledge of the flora and fauna, especially of India, is very heartening and endearing.

No surprises then that he debuts with this…

A thrilling wildlife crime- action- adventure which takes you on a rollercoaster ride through the magnificent Indian subcontinent.

Enter the deep dark world of wildlife trafficking, the third largest illicit trade in the world.

Be prepared for a vivid, detailed and dramatic trek of thrilling storytelling, drenched in the rain of sheer truth of his own experiences and fact findings.

SONU NIGAM Digitally signed by SONU NIGAM Date: 2025.05.21 15:39:00 +05'30'

SONU NIGAM
(Eminent Bollywood Singer)

I still remember the water hole count during a full moon night at Thumka Chowki when I first met Abhishek almost two decades back. Thumka chowki is a patrol camp located deep in the core zone of Ranthambhore Tiger Reserve. Prior to the advent of Camera traps and scientific estimation of wildlife, water hole count was the only accepted method of wildlife estimation. It was conducted on a selected full moon night of pinch summer months when the water holes are limited. Apart from the forest staff, wildlife volunteers were also involved in this exercise. Abhishek was one of the wildlife enthusiasts who opted to sit for the entire night near a water hole located in the premise of Thumka Chowki and to record and count whatever wild animals came to the water hole to drink water. Interestingly, Abhishek, a young lean and thin boy was introduced to me as a Bollywood singer and music composer whose solo album Udaas Paani with the legendary Gulzar, was already in news during beginning of millennium that he gifted me when we first met. I asked him what made a "Bollywood" artist deviate his path from concrete to the woods of Ranthambhore. Deep passion for wildlife and love for the nature was the simple reason that I was told.

Two decades had passed ever since and I had served in different capacities, managing forest and wildlife resources including environmental regulation and wildlife research while heading Project Tiger as Member Secretary, National Tiger Conservation Authority. Abhishek all of sudden again appeared and handed me his latest creation. This time it was not an album but a pen drive with some of the excerpts of his manuscript of newly written book, "Baagh Tiger-The Inside Story" that he just completed after a hard work of more than a decade. It was on a tiger. Actually, "Baagh" is a story of a poacher, his beloved and a tiger. This saga that revolves around Jaggu, Janhvi and a tiger is so delicately written, like a poetry that it touches your heart and reminds you that it is a meticulous work from an artist who not only composes music for your ears, but also creates a florid masterpiece on a rustic subject like wildlife conservation.

This novel is a contemporary jungle book based on true incidents, which throws light on wildlife trafficking. Jaggu's inward journey has a deep spiritual message for humanity. His inner transformation is reflective of our collective choice. Should we keep destroying nature in the name of development or become its protector. There isn't much time left.

Baagh is the real jungle book of today, an intriguing love story encompassing wildlife crime, action, adventure, contraband and a deep message for mandind.

I wish him all the best for the success of this riveting book. May this work ignite a spark for conservation in our coming generations.

Dr Gobind Sagar Bhardwaj
ADG Project Tiger and Member Secretary,
National Tiger Conservation Authority, New Delhi

Over the years I have worked with Abhishek on his compositions in the capacity of a singer.

I have always had great respect for him as an original and highly skilled and informed composer and music producer.

His integrity towards creating original unadulterated music content became more and more evident and I also began to realise this trait of his is not just limited to his music.

On delving deeper into his life and passions I realised how unique and unaffected he is with the insecurities of his profession.

On visiting **Sitabani Wildlife Reserve** near Jim Corbett, with my son, I got to witness his compelling passion for wildlife and environment preservation first hand.

Reading his book is another reminder to me of not just how multi faceted and creative Abhishek is, but also how committed he is to Wildlife conservation.

The story is gripping and inspiring with researched facts and truths.

The way he describes of pain and despair of a mother tigress is so real, so alive.

I am so proud of Abhishek for following his dreams and aspirations with such clarity and unwavered dedication. Kudos to him on this new adventure. And I can't wait to see what he does next.

SHAAN

(Illustrious Bollywood Singer)

An intriguing story from the tribal heartland of India which is reflective of the tiger's survival against all odds in today's human dominated landscape.

The author is a passionate wildlifer and conservationist. In his maiden attempt, he has woven the story in such a beautiful way that it strongly conveys importance of wildlife & forest conservation with community interface

The book traverses through the length and breadth of the subcontinent capturing the rich tapestry of human life intertwined with tribal wisdom, magnificent wildlife and untamed landscapes while tracking the dark world of tiger poaching.

A Bavaria tiger poacher, Jaggu avenges his past and becomes a true champion of the wild.

Jaggu's inward journey has a deep spiritual message for humanity.

His U - turn is reflective of our collective choice. Should we keep on destroying nature in the name of development - or become it's protector.

There isn't much time left.

S P YADAV
(Director General, IBCA, International Big Cat Alliance)

Abhishek's remarkable journey from a bollywood composer (that's how I met him years back) to a passionate conservationist is indeed very heartwarming.

He has channeled his love for nature by creating **Sitabani Wildlife Reserve** near Corbett National Park.

We recorded a **tiger anthem** for the Govt of India which meaningfully combines music and an activist purpose.

Knowing that he is such a multi talented person, I'm delighted to know that his passion for conservation has resulted in a book called '**BAAGH –Tiger- The Inside Story**.'

The protagonist of this book is Jaggu who belongs to a tribal clan of poachers called Bavaria. He ultimately succeeds in winning a battle against the evil forces of poaching, turning within himself and becoming a true champion of the wild.

Abhishek's cinematic approach to language, capturing the beauty and the drama of the environment , frame by frame, has left me quite speechless. One enters the dark world of wildlife poaching which is the third largest criminal activity in the world.

Jaggu's U-turn as a protector of wildlife resonates deeply within us invoking a sense of spiritual awakening within us all. Shouldn't we each do our part to safeguard our world, rather than destroy what little remains of its beauty and worth?

Kavita Krishnamurti

KAVITA KRISHNAMURTI
(Legendary Bollywood Vocalist)

A must read, real jungle book which traverses through an insightful deep dark world of wildlife poaching, trafficking and crime without frontiers. More interestingly it showcases a tribal tiger poacher turned true protector of the wild, whose inward journey has a deep spiritual message for humanity.

A powerful and captivating Tiger inside story encompassing crime, action, adventure and love reflecting on the very survival of the Tiger, against all odds in today's human controlled planet.

Indeed, a thought-provoking conservation narrative, reflective of our collective choice to choose on destroying nature or otherwise, as time seems to be running out.

Author Abhishek Ray is truly an ardent preservationist, apart from being a film composer and performing artist, par excellence. In recent times, he has associated with **National tiger Conservation Authority** bringing out the **Cheetah Anthem**, aptly written, composed, performed and filmed. He has also made the branding anthem and film of the **International Big Cat Alliance** on the seven big cats of the world for **UNDP and GOI**, which retells his passionate love for nature and Big-Cats. Having known Abhishek for sometime now,I would stand by his un-wavered commitment and passion for conservation, and wish him luck and best wishes.

Dr. *AmitMallick*
Fmr. Principal Chief Conservator Forest, Kerala, India
Fmr Inspector General, National Tiger Conservation Authority

It is with immense pleasure that I introduce you to Abhishek Ray's remarkable book, a testament to the transformative power of human spirit. I've had the privilege of knowing Abhishek since 2018, when his dedication to wildlife conservation was evident in his volunteer work during the **All-India Tiger Estimation** in **Pench Tiger Reserve**. Since then, I have had the pleasure of his company in many a nature reserve in Madhya Pradesh. In addition to his superlative work as a Bollywood composer and singer, his commitment and missionary zeal in matters related to the natural world comes through unceasingly.

Venture into the shadowy abyss of wildlife trafficking—the world's third largest illicit empire. This gripping saga echoes the tiger's desperate battle to survive in a landscape dominated by humans. This journey exposes the brutal, grim reality of tiger poaching from the highlands of the Deccan to the stately Sal forests of North India and on to the high passes of the Himalayas on the road to Tibet.

This book, detailing a journey from hunter to protector, is a powerful narrative of redemption and unwavering commitment. It's a story that transcends the personal, offering a profound message about our relationship with the natural world and the urgent need for its preservation. Abhishek's unique perspective, born from first-hand experience, provides a compelling insight into the complexities of wildlife protection and the importance of empathy in conservation efforts.

At the core of the protagonist's transformative journey, a spiritual awakening that speaks to the very soul of humanity. It raises the most important issue confronting mankind at present - will we continue to ravage nature in the name of development, or will we rise as its guardians? The time is running out—and the fate of the wild and ours hangs in the balance.

Prepare to be moved by Abhishek's story, and inspired by his unwavering dedication to everything wild!

Subharanjan Sen I.F.S

Principal Chief Conservator of Forest (Wildlife)

& Chief Wildlife Warden, Madhya Pradesh

Authors' Note

All characters in my book are fictitious but many of the incidents have been inspired by facts and real life occurences.

Most classic wildlife fictions have hinged on humanizing wild animals and creating interesting human dramatics out of animal characters.

While this may be commercially and cinematically engaging, but

today's jungle book is a very different ballgame.

Throw tigers, people and poverty in the mix, and you have India- a complex potpourri of **survival**-a magical country teeming with iconic mega-fauna coexisting with dense human populations.

Throughout my life as a **tiger-leopard tracker**, counting big-cats in various parts of the Indian sub-continent for the government, I have often felt the dire need for a detailed work of fiction — A novel that truly describes the complex dynamics of how a wild tiger survives and raises its cubs in an increasingly human dominated landscape constantly dodging highways, railway lines, factories, cultivation and deadly threats like **poachers**.

My protagonist **Jaggu**, the legendary tiger tracker of the deadly **Bavaria** poaching gang, turns against his own tribe, avengers his past and becomes a true sentinel of the wild. His gritty and fierce love story with Janhvi is set against the grim, murky world of **wildlife poaching** —a roller coaster ride encompassing wildlife, crime, action, adventure and contraband interlaced.

For me, the **tiger** epitomizes what is truly untamed and untameable. What is pure and raw. An enigmatic creature crafted by evolution and chiseled by time. It embodies the might and divine power of nature that protects virtue and destroys evil. In my story, the bond between Jaggu and the tiger is pure and sacred—like **kinred spirits**.

That explains how the most populous country in the world is still home to more than 70% of the global wild tiger population. Interestingly most of the mighty rivers of India also come out of tiger forests. Therefore the tiger is clearly an **indicator** and **guardian** of India's **freshwater** and natural life support systems.

My story aims to reveal an ancient **Vedic** value system, **tribal wisdom**, **tolerance** towards all lifeforms, worship of plants, animals, even rocks and powerful **conservation laws** which come together to create the deep seated preservation **ethos** of **India** surviving against all odds.

I have always felt that the term '**Wildlife**' is the greatest **conspiracy** hatched by civilised humans to label all free-ranging lifeforms that cannot be controlled by man — A good ploy for grabbing all resources of earth for human consumption only while the original inhabitants can be termed as 'wild' or untameable and dangerous and therefore locked up in **zoos** and tiny **islands** called animal parks.

For me 'wildlife' is nothing but **life itself** - life naturally endemic to planet earth.

I strongly feel that Jaggu's inward journey and **transformation** is reflective of the spiritual journey of humankind today.

We have one **mother**— the third planet from the Sun— the only one to harbor the miracle called life.

Just like Jaggu, we all have a choice…**Time is running out**..

PENCH TIGER RESERVE, MADHYA PRADESH

CERTIFICATE

This is to certify that

Mr. Abhishek Ray

has volunteered in

All India Tiger Estimation 2018

(K.K. Gurwani) IFS Joint Director Pench Tiger Reserve Seoni (M.P.)

(Subharanjan Sen) IFS Field Director Pench Tiger Reserve Seoni (M.P.)

BAAGH

Tiger - The Inside Srory

Abhishek Ray

This book is dedicated to my parents- Ma and Baba, who have stood by me and supported me in all the difficulties and uncertainities of my life's journey from a bollywood composer, playback singer, tiger-tracker, wildlife conservationist to the madness of creating Sitabani Wildlife Reserve.

This book is a tribute to my mentor Gulzar sahab, who introduced me to Bollywood with unique albums like Udaas Paani & Raat Chand aur Main.

This book is a tribute to my tiger guru, the late Dr.G.V.Reddy IFS (1960-2024) for introducing me to the fascinating world of tracking tigers on foot in Ranthambore in the early 2000's. He taught me to read the forest like an animal and face powerful wild predators on foot just by maintaining a calm demeanour.

This book is an ode to an unnamed wild tigress who reposed her trust in me and chose to give birth and rear her two cubs in and around my rewilded hill at Sitabani Wildlife Reserve setting a rare precedence in coexistence for the world.

This book is dedicated to all the secretive wild tigers and leopards who have met me on foot at different instances of my life, in various Indian jungles, looked me straight in the eye and decided to spare my life, thereby choosing me to write out their invaluable inside story for the world to witness. They have taught me valuable life-lessons in control over power, peace, freedom, detachment and minimalism.

Contents :

A storm brews over an ancient land...

The wind rises, pulling a vast, mournful murmur out of the dry leaves as dark nimbus clouds gather in the western horizon. The crimson sunset is obscured by the buildup of shades of gray and an untimely gale begins to howl, sweeping over the rolling hills and gouged ravines of this forgotten central Indian hinterland — a land of ghosts and grit, of legend and myth.

In the midst of this tempestuous twilight, a lone silhouette cuts across the storm-lit sky — a nomadic horseman, moving like a wraith borne of the howling wind. Cloaked in shadows and dust, he rides with an elemental grace, his form a fluid extension of the powerful black stallion beneath him. The sculpted muscles of rider and beast merge into one, thunderous and wild, as they carve a path through the serpentine ravines of stone and dust.

Jaggu.

The name hangs unspoken in the air, like the scent of rain before it falls.

The legendary tiger tracker of the infamous Bavaria tribesmen.

He rides like a spirit set free, his hair swept back by the gale, his eyes narrowed against the storm. As the ground drops into a narrow gorge, he spurs the stallion forward, and they charge across an ancient wooden bridge — aged, splintered, moaning under the weight of time and speed.

Below, the Dheel River churns, its waters muddied and restless. On its pale sandbanks, a cluster of muggers and gharials — freshwater crocodilians — lounge in silence. But the sudden tremor of hooves above jolts them from their slumber. One by one, with practiced ease, they slide into the choppy water, disappearing into the depths like living fossils, displaced by a thunderous legend galloping across forgotten bridges.

Not too far away, thunder murmurs deep in the belly of the sky as a dusky maiden gathers her laundry from a wicker fence — the frail boundary that encircles her humble home of stone and sunbaked mud.

The wind, now untamed, rushes down from the jagged cliffs like a mischievous spirit, showing little compassion towards the lonely maiden, lifting the drying clothes and scattering them into the wild. With a sigh of exasperation on her breath, she dashes after them, bare feet skimming the dust, her bangles clinking with each hurried step.

The wind, however, shows no mercy. It dances through her dark tresses, tossing them across her face like untamed thoughts. For a fleeting moment, as she wrestles with her stubborn dupatta and flying garments, the wind becomes a messenger of memory — and Janhvi feels the sharp tug of longing. The wild air reminds her of him — her storm-hearted lover — passionate, reckless, and as elusive as the monsoon in the dry ravines of central India.

The gathering storm resonates with the one that brews up inside Jaanvi's heart. As she snatches back her clothes from the clutches of the boisterous wind, she turns to look mournfully towards the long winding road that meanders through the rugged ravines and leads like a broken promise to her silent courtyard. Her gaze lingers there — where once hoofbeats echoed and laughter danced — but now, only a whirlwind of dust remains.

As the wind brushes against her with callous abandon, tracing her sensitive skin like a reckless memory, she is reminded of Jaggu's touch- fierce, passionate and unrelenting. The bleak emptiness of her vacant eyes carry the pain of seperation and now, as the sky darkens and her hair whips across her face, Janhvi feels the ache of being young and untended, the ache of growing wild in a world without his gaze. Alone, she must tame the wind, and her restless youth, without him.

The tempest rises in power and form and almost seems to blow away this flimsy mud house surrounded by crumbling cliffs, thorn-laced scrub, and skies heavy with unspoken words.

Yet Janhvi stands firm, her slender frame defying the chaos of the wind. Her loneliness, her longing — they rise with the gale, invisible but fierce. The storm outside may pass, but the one inside her has learned to stay.

The steppe eagles, soaring high on thermal currents, cast their unblinking gaze upon the tiny black speck weaving its way across the wind-swept badlands straddling the Rajasthan – Madhya Pradesh border. This raw, desolate land—etched with the memories of notorious dacoits—has long remained beyond the reach of law and order.

Jaggu spurs his panting black stallion onward, urging the beast to gallop faster against the gusts of the gathering storm. It has been months since that fateful day when his group poached a wild tigress deep in the forests of Assam, and ever since, he has lived the life of a fugitive—dodging forest officials, vanishing into shadows, staying away from his village, and most painfully, from her.

He rides now with a purpose, hoping the tempest cloaking the sky will serve as a veil, obscuring his return. He must see her. He has not laid eyes on Janhvi for three long months, and every sinew of his lean, weather-worn frame aches for her—to be held, to be forgiven, to be loved.

Janhvi, though deeply in love, has been irrational of late—her heart torn between desperation and denial. She yearns to be his bride, and yet, time and again, she turns him away because she detests his way of life. What can he do? He is a son of the infamous Bavaria tribe of central India— tied to the forests and their secrets by blood and tradition, tied to the ancient, illegal craft of big-cat hunting. He cannot simply walk away.

After his father's untimely death, it was Lakhan—his elder cousin—who took him in, who pulled him from the depths of despair and kept him fed and clothed when he had nothing. Jaggu owes him, owes the tribe.

Lakhan is the unchallenged leader of the poaching ring that operates like a phantom across the heart of India. Today, Jaggu is the chief tracker in Lakhan's infamous gang, a position earned not just by loyalty but by his uncanny ability to read the jungle like scripture.

Together, they have become a legend in the underworld—an elite unit of Bavaria poachers whose reputation stretches far beyond the

Vindhyas and the Aravallis, into the shadowy marketplaces of Nepal, Tibet, and even mainland China.

The subcontinent's enigmatic big cats have no greater enemy than the quiet efficiency of this gang.

And yet, tonight, Jaggu rides against the wind, against fate itself, propelled by a singular hope—that the storm might cleanse, or conceal, or deliver.

Kinred spirits...

Jaggu shifts course, pulling the reins lightly, steering the stallion towards a narrow shortcut known only to a few. It cuts across an ancient grassland that rolls like an ocean, its elephant grass now turned a burnished gold by the setting sun, dancing wildly to the rhythm of the storm.

It is here, in this vast sea of wind-tossed gold, that the black horse blazes ahead like a specter. The tall grasses part for them like waves, bowing to the oncoming tempest. But just as the narrow jungle trail takes an abrupt turn, the horse gives a sharp, shivering whimper and halts instinctively, rearing up on its hind legs.

Jaggu's heart leaps.

The winds pause—just for a moment—as though nature itself is holding its breath.

Jaggu steadies his breath, his sharp eyes narrowing as he tries to cut through the shimmering, fluid landscape before him. The storm-stirred grass moves like waves on a golden sea, and somewhere within it, danger slinks.

The stallion's pupils are wide with terror, its sinewy body taut as a bowstring. A low, anxious neigh escapes its throat, and Jaggu grips the horse's mane, not with fear, but with reverence—for he knows what dwells in such silences.

He scans the chaotic harmony of wind and grass until—there, just for a heartbeat—he catches a glimpse of something otherworldly. Black stripes—so seamless they appear to melt into the rippling grass—move with an ancient grace. A mirage at first. But then it takes form.

Man and beast freeze.

The sun, now a sliver at the edge of the world, casts a crimson hue over the expanse. The light softens, almost sacred in its beauty, as if nature itself is bowing its head in solemn awe.

Even the wild and boisterous gusts of breeze are lulled momentarily, as if the very wind holds its breath in deference to a higher force—the truly untamed and untameable, the guardian of these vast wildernesses.

And through the golden veil, the guardian emerges.

A sinewed form of fire and dusk.

The striped monk of ancient legends.

The vahan of Durga that protects virtue and destroys evil.

The regal and silent sentinel of the wild, fixes its amber gaze upon Jaggu.

The tiger's eyes, deep, primeval and unknowable, seem to peer into the very soul of his kindred spirit - the man before him. And Jaggu, seasoned though he may be, cannot help but meet that gaze—hypnotic, elemental—with a storm of emotions stirring within him.

Fear, yes. Awe, undoubtedly. But more than anything, a deep, primal reverence—one that has pulsed through his blood since childhood, since the first time he heard the call of the jungle in the dead of night.

The horse quivers beneath him, nostrils flaring, eyes wide with terror. It tries to rear, to throw him off and flee this sacred presence, but Jaggu grips its mane with quiet force, whispering low to calm the beast. All the while, his own breath comes shallow, his heart pounding in tandem with the earth.

The tiger, calm as the dusk, crosses the narrow trail in front of them with the unhurried grace of something born of both fire and silence. In the distance, the frenzied alarm calls of chital and sambar echo across the untamed grassland, a wild chorus heralding the passing of a king.

Then, just as suddenly as it appeared, the majestic predator vanishes—melting into the grassland once more like a spirit of the wind, a ghost of the wilderness.

All that remains is the hush, the heartbeat, and the memory of those burning amber eyes.

Caught between love and fate...

Not far away, under the same storm-laden sky, Janhvi whistles sharply to gather the herd of goats, ushering them quickly into the safety of the stone-walled courtyard. The wind whistles through the crags above, and already the hills seem to whisper of wolves and leopards—those hungry phantoms of night who descend silently to prey upon the unguarded. Her slender hands work swiftly and surely, barring the wooden gate, tucking in a kid that bleats nervously at her feet.

A single oil lamp flickers to life beside the tulsi plant in her courtyard, its pale flame swaying uncertainly in the breeze. The sacred basil's branches tremble gently, as if shivering in prayer. Dusk spreads it's dark veil across the rugged landscape, swallowing the stormy light, and softening the stone and dust with shadow.

Then, with a sudden gust, the wind makes one last, playful demand—it tugs at the clothes Janhvi is holding freeing her dupatta, lifting the sheer cloth into the air like a surrendering flag. It floats upward and then dances away, caught in the gale, carried toward the very path that winds down into her courtyard from the open wild beyond.

Janhvi rushes after the dupatta, her bare feet skimming over the earth, her breath caught between hope and despair. But midway through the chase, she halts—arrested by the faint, rhythmic drumming of hooves echoing through the canyons. Her chest rises with anticipation as she turns toward the sound. A glint—like a flicker of forgotten fire—returns to her otherwise vacant eyes.

Out of the gathering dusk, a dark silhouette gallops towards her, half-man, half-beast, borne out of storm and longing. The wind, as if conspiring with fate, carries the dupatta like a silken offering. It floats, arcs, and gently settles onto Jaggu's face just as his stallion comes to a halt—its flanks heaving, hooves stamping the dusty ground with the pride and weariness of the long ride.

Jaggu dismounts in one fluid motion, the fabric still clinging to his face like a veil. The horse gives a tired, satisfied neigh, nodding its head, while Janhvi, unable to restrain herself, runs forward—half in disbelief, half in yearning—and gently peels the dupatta from her beloved's face. Her fingers tremble as she does so, revealing the weather-beaten sharpness of his chiseled features, the familiar wildness in his eyes. They stand in silence for a heartbeat—storm, dusk, and dust suspended around them.

Janhvi, unable to contain the flood of emotions, runs into Jaggu's arms, her hands cupping his face, her voice trembling with pain and fury.

"Where were you all these days? Do you know how worried I was? I've been waiting, waiting, waiting endlessly—staring at that long winding road that snakes through the canyons. I cried so much... my tears have dried up. And you... you have no consideration whatsoever," she sobs, gripping his torso like a child begging for answers.

Jaggu doesn't speak. He just wraps his arms around her, pulling her close until her heaving bosom rests against his chest. The storm finally abates.

A single tear rolls down Janhvi's cheek, glistening like a drop of sorrow caught in the fading light—warm, silent, sacred—that begins to wash away the dust and distance between them. Suddenly, a sharp gust of wind sweeps through, sending her hair flying in wild disarray—nature itself seems to mirror the turbulence in her heart.

Coming back to her senses, Janhvi strikes Jaggu's chest with her fists, over and over again—small, trembling blows. Each strike was a question unanswered, each tear a memory relived.

Jaggu does't resist. He stands still, silent, bearing the storm of her emotions like a penitent soul. And then, without a word, he pulls her into his arms, tightly, as though trying to hold together all that had threatened to fall apart. In that fierce embrace, her weeping heart found a momentary refuge.

Janhvi weeps uncontrollably, her fists raining down upon Jaggu's chest as she cried, "What kind of work is this, Jaggu? What kind of life is this that you lead?"

Her voice trembles with pain, echoing the ache buried deep within her soul. Jaggu held her close and whispered softly, "Calm down, Janhvi… please, calm down. I'm here now. I've come back. Just calm down…"

Janhvi speaks through her tears, "You said you'd be gone for just a week—and then you disappeared." Her voice cracks, raw with months of longing. "It's been three months, Jaggu. Three ! To hell with such work!"

Jaggu's voice wavers, as though the weight of generations bore down upon his chest. "Janhvi, this... this is the only work we've known for centuries. It runs in our blood—our cursed inheritance. If I leave it behind, what will I become? A beggar with no land, no trade? We once had a patch of earth to call our own, but even that now lies under Lakhan's grip. Mortgaged. Marked. And he's circling like a vulture, waiting to devour it. What do I say? He's my cousin, yes—but more a debt collector than kin."

He pauses, his eyes clouded with helplessness. "Sometimes I wonder, Janhvi... am I running from the law or from fate itself?"

Janhvi says bitterly, dropping her voice low, "He's no cousin, he's a butcher. All your family—murderers, the lot of them."

The word murderer ignites something fierce in Jaggu. His eyes blaze with fury. In a sudden, uncontrollable moment, he grabs Janhvi by the throat.

"Tend to your own affairs, Janhvi, and pay heed to your own profession." he snarls, his voice trembling with rage. "What are you anyway? Just a singing doll—meant to entertain rich, corrupt, flirtatious men. That's all you are. Think about it?'"

Janhvi, with quiet defiance, says, "I burn my own soul to make a living, Jaggu—not that of voiceless creatures of God."

Jaggu stands frozen, his grip on her loosening as her words echo in the heavy silence.

Janhvi's tear-streaked face reflects the last remnants of the fading light, her eyes now resolute with the haunting reminder that sometimes, the fiercest battles are fought within the heart.

Without a word, Jaggu turns and walks away, his silhouette swallowed by the growing darkness, his heart torn between the life he knows and the love he can no longer claim.

The birdwatchers...

Three months ago…

On the outskirts of Kaziranga National Park, one serene morning, a group of enthusiastic children from Saint Paul's High School, Guwahati, gathered with their teachers with binoculars and notepads, ready for an exciting bird-watching adventure. The forest was alive with the melodious chirping of birds, the rustling of leaves, and the occasional call of distant wildlife. The children, guided by a local naturalist, eagerly scanned the treetops, bushes, and open skies, hoping to spot some of the park's famed avian inhabitants.

Kaziranga, renowned for its rich biodiversity, is home to numerous bird species, including the Great Hornbill, Bar-headed Geese, and the rare Bengal Florican. The children's eyes lit up as they identified colorful kingfishers darting across the silver streams and majestic raptors soaring high above the emerald canopy. Their whispers of excitement blended with the natural symphony of the morning.

As the sun climbed higher, casting a golden glow over the landscape, the children noted down their observations, sketching birds, trying to identify them from bird books and describing their behaviors. For many, this was not just a lesson in nature but an unforgettable experience that deepened their connection to the environment.

Suddenly a herd of graceful cheetal catches the attention of one of the excitable schoolgirl, Anya. The spotted deer (cheetal), moved fluidly through the undergrowth, their dappled coats blending seamlessly with the sunlight filtering through the trees. Enthralled by the sight, Anya and her closest friends Rajiv, and Aamir, followed with quiet excitement, venturing deeper into the dense forest.

Little did they know that their path would lead them away from the safety of the main group and into an unfamiliar part of the jungle. The cheerful chirping of birds faded, replaced by the rustling of leaves and creatures that moved in the shadows.

As they followed the deer, they stumbled upon a hidden stream, its clear waters reflecting the vibrant greens of the jungle. The trio paused, marveling at the serene beauty, but the realization of their isolation slowly dawned upon them. Their adventure was about to turn into a test of courage, quick thinking, and survival skills.

Unbeknownst to them, this shadowy realm that they entered, held not only beauty but also the untamed presence of Kaziranga's most iconic predator—the Royal Bengal Tiger along with Asiatic elephants and the iconic one-horned rhinoceros. The cheetal herd they are tracking, slips further into the tangled undergrowth.

And where prey goes, the predator is never far behind!

The children paused, sensing the stillness thickening around them, but their curiosity outweighed caution. They pressed on, eyes searching for signs, unaware of the silent menace that stalks nearby.

Suddenly, a gust of wind made the bush quiver.

A striped paw emerged—silent, deliberate.

The tigress advanced, her movements quantized, as she exactly placed her hind paws over the position of her front paws thereby ensuring that she does not step over a twig and make any sound accidentally. Her precision, chiseled over centuries of evolution, reflected in the manner she stalked, her amber gaze fixed, her body low, her breath controlled.

The forest deepened around the children, folding in like a green cathedral. Towering sal and red silk cotton trees cast long shadows, and the filtered sunlight, slanting through the leaves, turned golden in the hush of late afternoon. The children trod cautiously, tracking the chital herd that had vanished into the undergrowth. Their feet rustled the fallen leaves, cracked twigs underfoot, and left faint prints on the soft, damp earth.

Not far from them, the tigress moved like a shadow.

She was a creature of silence, her paws gliding over the forest floor without a sound. Muscles rippled beneath her striped coat as she skirted boulders and fallen logs, careful not to disturb the dry foliage that might betray her approach. Her whiskers twitched. Her ears flicked, maybe towards the faint rustling of hooves or the clumsy footsteps of the children. Her eyes, amber and unreadable, remained fixed ahead.

It seemed as if her line of movement was toward the children.

Aamir bent to examine a fresh hoofprint—shallow, delicate, still soft at the edges. Rajiv pointed to a faint scrape on the bark of a low-lying branch, whispering excitedly. They were consumed by their tracking, unaware that something else stirred in the forest with them.

A twig snapped beneath the girl's sandal.

The tigress paused. Her tail flicked once. Her nostrils flared, catching a mixture of scents—damp earth, prey, something unfamiliar.

Somewhere ahead, the chital raised their heads.

The tigress lowered her body further, every instinct of the hunt sharpened to a single moment.

Another step. Another crunch underfoot.

And then..

the forest exploded into sound.

Birds shrieked. Leaves shattered in the wake of powerful limbs.

The tigress leapt—muscles coiling, body arching through the air like a drawn arrow. She wasn't heading toward the children at all. She hadn't been.

She had been hunting.

Only now, as the deer scattered in panic emitting loud and sharp alarm calls, and the ground trembled with their retreat, did the illusion break.

The children stood rooted to the spot, hearts thudding in their chests. They watched in stunned silence as the tigress vanished into the thicket, chasing her true prey.

The silence that followed felt like the hush after a spell had been broken. The danger had not been meant for them. And yet, its presence had been all too real.

Then through the shafts of light slanting through the canopy, they caught a brief glimpse—an amber eye flashing through the undergrowth, the low ripple of muscle beneath striped skin, the turn of a head as the tigress withdrew. Her hunt had failed, probably because the chital were disturbed by the children's clumsy footsteps.

For a heartbeat, she seemed to look directly at them, holding them responsible for her missing her lunch. Then, as swiftly as she had come, she vanished into the shadows.

The children were still in stupor. They had accidentally witnessed one of the greatest and most ancient games of nature- the primitive dance of predator and prey.

They looked around cautiously catching their breath as their pulse gradually returned to normal.

"Did you know that only ten to twenty percent of tiger hunts succeed?", whispered Aamir.

Anya, still in awe of what just happened replied, "which means for every ten hunting attempts, the tiger goes hungry and exhausted eight or nine times."

"Hmmm. And we are forced to eat by our parents four times a day. What an irony?" chipped in Rajiv.

"So who is more rapacious and greedy, we or the tiger?" asked Aamir, his hands still trembling from the adrenaline rush.

The eyewitnesses...

All of a sudden, their hushed conversation was cut short by a bloodcurdling roar rising from the depths of the jungle. Not the kind born of dominance or territorial defiance, but something darker. Wrought from pain. Raw, shuddering pain.

It tore through the jungle like lightning.

The children stiffened.

Another roar followed, echoing off the tree trunks, followed by the sound of the tigress clawing furiously at the ground. It was no longer the sound of a hunt—it was agony. The children's eyes widen as they realize the tiger isn't moving toward them—but it's still too close for comfort.

Suddenly, the forest fell eerily silent, except for the labored breathing of the tigress. The children exchange nervous glances. "What's happening?" Rajiv asked, clutching Anya's arm.

"I think..." Anya remarked, "...she's hurt."

Terrified, the children hesitated. But curiosity and concern edged past their fear. One of them stepped forward. Then another. Quietly, they crept towards the sound, hearts hammering, breath shallow.

They pushed past a curtain of broad-leaved vines and ducked beneath a branch, finally reaching a dense clump of bushes. What they saw beyond it made their blood run cold.

The tigress had stepped into a trap. Her forepaw, powerful and graceful just moments ago, was now grotesquely caught in the merciless grip of a heavy-duty cast-iron snare—laid by unseen hands, ruthless and cunning.

She thrashed and struggled, but the metal held fast, digging deeper into her flesh, twisting cruelly by her efforts to free herself. Blood matted her fur and soaked the earth below.

Her eyes, wide and wild, burned with pain and terror.

Anya's heart sank. A poacher's snare. Her parents had often spoken about the cruel traps laid by hunters to catch animals in the park.

But what could they do? They were just kids, lost and powerless in the middle of a dangerous jungle.

Another roar tore through the green canopy—more desperate than the last, her strength visibly waned as blood continued to seep from the wound.

And the children, crouched behind the bushes, could do nothing but watch this terrible scene unravel—a queen of the jungle brought down not by fang or claw, but by human cruelty.

They held their breaths as they watched the horrific scene unfold from their hiding place. They saw a group of rough-looking men emerge from the bushes, carrying rifles, machetes, clubs, torches and ropes. They were dressed in paramilitary clothes, their faces hardened by years of extracting skin, flesh and bone from the unforgiving wilderness. Their eyes gleamed with a cruel mix of greed and cunning as they took in the sight of the trapped tigress.

Aamir raised a trembling finger to his lips, eyes wide with fear. "Poachers," he whispered, barely audible. "Not a sound."

The others stood frozen, a wave of dread sweeping over them, silencing even the chirping of the forest, as they stared beyond the leafy shadows—trembling in sheer terror.

The tigress emitted another guttural roar, her amber eyes blazing with defiance despite her agonizing pain. She thrashed violently, blood spraying onto the dry leaves and rocks around her. But the more she struggled, the deeper the cruel snare cut into her leg.

One of the men, Lakhan, who seemed to be the leader, stepped closer, a cruel smirk on his face. "She's a big one," he said, his voice low and gravelly. "Her skin alone will fetch a fortune."

Another dark, wiry man Chimpta, chuckled darkly. "And her bones? Precious. The Chinese buyers will pay handsomely for tiger bones. Horny, impotent men. Huh!"

The third man, lean and muscular, lagged a few paces behind, his expression dark, conflicted.

To the children's surprise, this man named Jaggu halted abruptly. His chest rose and fell heavily. He turned away, staring into the trees as if searching for something to hold onto.

"I can't watch this," he muttered under his breath. Then louder, to the others, his voice sharp, breaking with emotion—"Wait. Not in front of me."

The other poachers turned, momentarily confused.

Jaggu's jaw tightened. "I will not be able to see this horrific gore. I have done my job. Have got her on a platter for you. Do your dirty job after I leave."

The children's hearts race as they realize the men's intentions. Aamir clenches his fists, his face pale with fear and anger. "They're going to kill her," he whispers, his voice barely audible.

Meanwhile, the ringleader Lakhan stepped forward towards Jaggu, his frame bulky and swaggering, face twisted in disdain.

"Run away, you spineless bastard," he spat. "Always knew you had a woman's heart. Should've stayed back with that goat girl of yours, suckling pity from her lap. You're not one of us, Jaggu. Never were."

Jaggu froze mid-step. For a moment, the jungle was silent again, save for the desperate heaving of the tigress, her paw still clenched in the cruel iron trap.

Without turning around, Jaggu spoke, his voice low but edged with fury.

"Don't accuse me later that I didn't warn you," he said. "This tigress… she's a mother. Her teats are swollen. She has cubs hidden somewhere in this forest, waiting for her. I told you I would find the male for your cursed deals very soon, but you didn't listen."

He turned slowly now, facing Lakhan, his eyes burning.

"The Vandevi, the goddess of the forest, will never forgive us for killing a lactating mother. Her wrath will hunt you down to ends of the world. Her curse will ride the wind, and you will pay. Mind my words Lakhan."

Then, without waiting for a response, Jaggu turned his back to them all and disappeared into the shadows of the forest, leaving only a sense of looming retribution behind.

"We have to do something," Anya said, though her voice wavered with uncertainty. She looked around desperately, trying to think of a plan. But what could three children possibly do against a group of armed poachers?

"Sedate her first," Lakhan ordered. "We can't risk her fighting back when we get her out of the trap."One of the men, Bhola takes out a long syringe filled with a clear liquid and moved toward the tigress.

The tigress growled fiercely, her ears flattening against her head. Even in her weakened state, she exuded an aura of power and determination. Her rage made the man stop dead in his tracks. " Can't do it boss. She is too powerful. One swipe and she will rip my intestines out of my belly.", he replied to Lakhan.

Meanwhile Rajiv whispered urgently, "We need to distract them.

"How?" Aamir asked, his voice shaking.

Anya took a deep breath, her mind racing. "We'll throw stones... make noise from different directions. Let's try to confuse them."

The children exchanged nervous glances, knowing the risk they're about to take. But the sight of the tigress, majestic even in her suffering, steeled their resolve. Quietly, they gathered a few small rocks from the ground, their hands trembling.

"On my count," Anya whispers. "One... two... three."

They hurled the stones in different directions, the sharp clatter echoing through the forest.

The poachers whip around, startled. "What was that?" Beera, the shooter hissed, raising his rifle.

"Is someone out there?" Bhudev, the cunning Assamese informer of the gang asked, scanning the trees nervously.

Lakhan growled, his face darkening. "Spread out! Find whoever's making that noise. And hurry—we don't have much time."

As the men fanned out, the children crouched lower behind the bushes, their hearts pounding. The poachers fail to locate them as most of their attention was focused on harvesting their prized catch. The brave children seemed to have bought the tigress some time—but what could they do next?

They watched on helplessly as Lakhan, the mastermind of the group, commanded one of his men, Chimpta, who promptly came out of the bush with a spear-like object in hand. Another man, Bhola, shone a bright torch-like object into the tigress's eyes. The tigress charged, opening its mouth, and immediately, Chimpta, the wiry thug, pierced the tigress's mouth with that sharp spear-like object. The tigress was now moaning in agony, not being able to roar because it had the spear-like object thrust in its throat.

Now a fourth man, Beera, a large, dark skinned tribal with a tilak smeared on his forehead came out with a heavy baseball-like object, a club, in his hand. Lakhan deftly darted behind the tigress and grabbed her tail pulling it with all his might and then he yelled at Bhola to go for the kill.

The children watch in horror as on Lakhan's instructions, the hulk struck the tigress's skull .One could hear the bones cracking as the man kept on smashing the skull with the blunt object.

Lakhan warned him, "Do not damage the skin. Hit at an angle that the skin is preserved. "

The tigress moaned in pain—her final cry—anguished, rebellious — a cry guttural, primitive and heart wrenching imploring mankind to rise from its slumber.

Finally the battered queen emitted one last gravelly groan and collapsed on the forest floor with a dull thud. Fatigue, exertion, mortal injury and excruciating pain squeezed the last drop of life from her sculpted form.

The other poachers quickly start the heinous and cruel task of de-skinning the tigress to extract her precious remains.

The elephantine chase...

As the three children trembled in visceral terror at the brutal killing of the tigress, suddenly one of them, Anya, started vomiting because she was horrified watching the cruel scene unfold in front of her eyes. Soon the sounds of her uneasiness reached the poacher's ears. Lakhan, the cruel mastermind, sharply looked in the direction where the children were hidden, and instructed one of his men, Bhudev Barua to go and investigate what was happening.

As Bhudev started zeroing in on the location of the sound, the three children burst out of the bushes and started sprinting through the dense forest, their breathing ragged and desperate. Anya, pale and trembling, stumbled frequently, her legs buckling under the strain. Her two companions struggled to keep her upright, gripping her arms and pulling her along as best they could.

Branches whipped at their faces, and thorny vines snagged their clothes as they pushed through the undergrowth. The uneven forest floor, littered with roots and stones, made every step treacherous.

Behind them, Bhudev Barua charged forward with the precision of a predator, his footsteps, swift and sure, his lean frame navigating the terrain effortlessly. The gap between him and the children narrowed with each passing moment, his sharp gaze locked on his prey. "You can't escape, meddling critters!" he bellowed, his voice echoing through the trees.

The children, hearing his shout, pressed on with renewed urgency. Their hearts pounded like drums in their chests as they burst through grasslands and wove around clusters of thick bamboo. Nidhi stumbled again, falling hard to the ground, her knees scraping against sharp rocks. The other two stopped, their faces etched with terror and determination. They hauled her to her feet, whispering frantic reassurances while stealing fearful glances behind them.

Just as Bhudev closed in, the forest opened up to reveal a shimmering river. The children instinctively veered towards the bank, their feet kicking up sprays of mud as they ran alongside the water. The air was heavy with the scent of wet earth and the cool spray of the river.

Nearby, a herd of Asian elephants stood at the water's edge, their massive forms silhouetted against the glinting surface of the river. The elephants, about a dozen strong, included towering adults with long, curved tusks and smaller calves huddled close to their mothers. Their rough, gray skin glistened with water as they drank and bathed, their trunks dipping and curling gracefully.

The children's sudden arrival shattered the tranquility of the riverine meadow. Alarmed by the unexpected commotion, the elephants trumpeted loudly, their ears flaring and tails swishing. The calves panicked, darting to their mothers for protection. The adults quickly formed a protective circle, their trunks raised and tusks gleaming in the sunlight. The three children froze for a moment, paralyzed by the sight of the enormous creatures.

Meanwhile Bhudev Barua, oblivious to the danger, leapt forward, his focus solely on capturing the children. But as he neared the herd, the largest bull elephant, with tusks as thick as tree trunks, let out an earth-shaking roar and charged towards Barua.

Sensing a sliver of hope, the children darted ahead, leaving the charging elephants behind. The ground vibrated as the entire herd thundered towards Barua, their massive feet pounding the earth. Trapped and overwhelmed by the colossal animals, he was forced to dive behind a tree to avoid being trampled. allowing the children a narrow but miraculous escape.

As the children seized the moment and sprinted away, the air behind them was filled with the trumpeting of the elephants and the chaos of breaking branches and thudding hooves.

The elephants eventually calmed down, their defensive formation dissolving. The calves tentatively emerged, and the herd resumed its movements by the river, leaving the panicked Bhudev stranded and defeated.

The lost and exhausted children pushed forward into the forest, their legs heavy with fatigue but driven by sheer desperation. The sun dipped lower on the horizon, casting long shadows over the Kaziranga landscape. The golden light painted the grasslands, but instead of beauty, the children saw danger. They knew that once darkness fell, the forest would come alive with predators—and they would be vulnerable.

Rajiv, leading the way, glanced repeatedly at his phone, silently praying for a signal. Each step felt like a gamble, their survival hinging on reaching help before night consumed the forest. Suddenly, his phone buzzed to life. A faint signal bar appeared, and Rajiv's heart leapt. Relief washed over him as he realized that they are close to the main gate.

Fumbling with trembling hands, he quickly dialed their group teacher, Aparna. After a tense moment, the call connected.

"Hello? Ma'am!" Rajiv exclaimed, his voice trembling with relief.

"Rajiv!" Aparna's voice filled with a mix of relief and anger. "Where are the three of you? We've been looking for you since this morning! The whole day has gone by! Every teacher and staff member is worried sick. You just vanished!"

Rajiv, still panting, replied, "It's a long story, ma'am. I'll explain everything when we see you. For now, I'm sending you our live location on WhatsApp. Please send help—quickly!"

He hung up and immediately shared their location with Aparna. The children slumped onto the ground, their bodies aching but buoyed by the hope of rescue. The distant calls of birds and the rustling of leaves reminded them of the encroaching night, but they clung to the thought of safety.

Minutes later, the sound of approaching vehicles broke the silence. Flashlights swept through the trees, and the familiar voices of their teachers, nature guides and forest rangers called out to them. The children jumped to their feet, tears of relief streaming down their faces as they ran towards the rescuers.

Aparna rushed forward, her stern expression softening into one of concern as she pulled them into a hug. "You're safe now," she said, her voice breaking. "You have no idea how worried we were!"

The forest rangers, their rifles slung across their shoulders, scanned the area cautiously. "We need to move quickly," one of them said. "This part of the forest is not safe after dark."

The children were escorted back to the safety of the vehicles, their ordeal finally over. As they drove away, the sun disappeared completely, leaving the Kaziranga wilderness cloaked in darkness with a hint of blazing red in the western horizon.

A man of steel...

A Mahindra jeep sped along a dusty path skirting the edge of the Kaziranga forest, its engine growling as it navigated the uneven terrain. The vehicle kicked up a thick trail of dust that rose like smoke into the blue- grey twilight as the setting sun left a scar of fiery red in the western horizon. The jeep's headlights cast long shadows behind the dense sal forest that stretched endlessly toward the horizon. The air was thick with the earthy aroma of the forest, mingling with the faint scent of dew laced, wild grass crushed under the jeep's wheels.

Inside the jeep, the Divisional Forest Officer (DFO), Amit Verma, sat upright, his expression calm but face ruddy with urgency. Beside him, a ranger clutched a map, while three forest guards, armed and alert, sat in the back, their eyes scanning the forest boundary for any signs of trouble.

In his mid-forties, Verma had the steely resolve of a man who had spent decades battling the horrors of poaching and illegal wildlife trade. His sharp features and upright posture reflected the demeanor of an honest officer, someone deeply committed to protecting the wilderness under his care.

Amit Verma held a phone to his ear, speaking in a hurried and anxious tone. "What's the situation?" he asked sharply, his voice cutting through the hum of the jeep's engine.

From the other end, a voice crackled, the faint accent of a forest ranger coming through. "Sir, the three children encountered a ghastly tiger poaching. They're terrified—shaken and bruised. Even more scared than them is their teacher, Aparna. She's been frantic ever since they were found."

Amit's brow furrowed. His grip on the phone tightened. "I'm on my way," he said firmly. "I'll be at the office soon. Make sure the children are escorted there safely. Treat them with utmost care and reassure Aparna that everything is under control. I'll handle the rest when I arrive."

"Yes, sir," the voice on the other end replied.

Amit ended the call and turned to the ranger seated beside him. "Increase the speed," he instructed. "We can't waste a second. Those kids have been through hell, and we need to ensure their safety and well-being." The ranger nodded and relayed the order to the driver. The jeep surged forward, the roar of its engine echoing through the quiet wilderness. Amit leaned back momentarily. He was no stranger to the horrors of poaching, but the involvement of children made this case even more distressing.

Inside the old forest forest department compound, the DFO's room was spacious, with a large Victorian structure that exuded old-world charm. Its tall ceiling, wooden walls, and large windows gave it an air of authority and history. The faint smell of polished wood lingered in the air. Three children sat on a long wooden bench, their faces pale and drawn. Beside them, their teacher, Aparna, sat protectively, her arm draped around the youngest child Anya. She looked equally shaken, her worry etched deeply into her expression.

Two forest officers stood nearby, one holding a tray of biscuits. They offered the children some, speaking in low, gentle tones, trying to ease their tension. One of the officers, Ravi, leaned forward slightly and asked, "So, tell us, Rajiv, what exactly did you see in the forest?"

Before the boy could respond, the sound of screeching tires cut through the quiet room.

Outside, a Mahindra jeep came to a sharp halt in the compound. Dust swirled briefly in the air as the driver killed the engine. The steely frame of Divisional Forest Officer Amit Verma emerged from the vehicle. His brisk strides toward the DFO's cabin exuded authority and determination, his boots crunching on the gravel path. When Amit entered the room, his sharp eyes immediately took in the scene. He frowned slightly, displeased with how the children were being questioned.

His tone was firm but not harsh as he addressed Ravi. "This is no way to ask them," he said. "Let it be. Let me take over."

DFO Verma approached Aparna first. Her distress was evident, and she was clearly shielding the children, her voice trembling as she spoke. "Sir, please... the children have been through so much already. "

Amit's voice softened, but his resolve remained firm. "Ma'am, I understand your concern," he said, his calm tone radiating reassurance. "But this is a serious matter. We need to know exactly what happened. I guarantee that there will be absolutely no trouble for the kids. But a tigress has been poached, and the information these children have could be vital to the country."

Reluctantly, Aparna nodded, her worry still evident but tempered by Amit's calm demeanor.

Amit said gently. "It's okay.You're safe here. No one will harm you, I promise. But I need you to help us understand what you saw. Take your time. Speak when you're ready."

The children exchanged nervous glances but slowly began to open up. Their voices were quiet at first, halting as they recounted the horrors of the poaching incident.

Amit turned to the children, lowering his voice and kneeling slightly to meet their eyes. "I need your help to understand what happened. Can you tell me—how many men were there?"

Rajiv, the eldest of the three, hesitated for a moment before replying. "There were five of them, sir. One of them gave orders... the others followed."

"And how did they approach the tigress?" Amit asked, his tone patient but focused.

"They used a torch to blind her," Rajiv continued, his voice shaky but clear. "And one man had a spear... he stabbed her in the mouth when she opened it." chipped in Anya.

Amit's jaw tightened at the description, but he kept his tone even. "What kind of trap did they use? Did you see how they snared her?"

"They used a cast-iron snare," Aamir interjected. "It was tied to a tree. The tigress got caught in it, and she couldn't move."

"How did the tigress react?" Amit asked, his voice calm, though his knuckles tightened slightly.

"She tried to free herself," Anya sobbed. "She kept pulling at the snare, moaning in agony as there was blood dripping from her paw. They surrounded her. One of them stabbed her… and another, a big, burly man, kept hitting her on the head." Her throat felt swollen and she stuttered while speaking.

Amit listened intently, his face grave but patient. He asked no unnecessary questions, letting the children speak at their own pace.

The DFO took a deep breath, letting the weight of the children's words settle. Then, he asked gently, "Did you manage to take any photographs?"

At this, Rajiv hesitated before speaking. "Yes, Sir. I took a photograph with my mobile phone."

Verma's eyes lit up with interest. "Can I see it?"

Aparna watched silently, her tension rising. "I don't want them involved in any legal troubles. They've seen enough horror for one lifetime." she said with a worried frown.

Verma interjected with a firm and low voice, "Ma'am, with due respect to your concerns, please understand that this is India and we take our tigers very seriously. We have the world's finest conservation laws. While I am liable to provide the children the care and comfort they need, I am also duty bound to ensure justice for the tigress whose life had been cruelly taken. Please have some faith in us."

Aparna hesitated but nodded reluctantly, comforted by his steady demeanor.

Rajiv nodded and handed over his phone. Amit Verma examined the image carefully, his expression darkening as the brutal scene unfolded in vivid detail. He passed the phone to ranger Ravi. "Download this immediately and save it for evidence," he instructed.

Ravi nodded and set to work transferring the photograph.

Turning back to the children, Amit Verma smiled reassuringly. "You've done the right thing by sharing this with us. I promise, we'll take it from here. You have done a great service to your country.."

The children relaxed slightly, their trust in Amit growing. Aparna watched silently, her earlier tension easing as she realized the officer's genuine intent.

Finally, Amit spoke again, his tone firm but inviting. "Can you take us to the spot where this incident happened first thing in the morning?"

The children exchanged glances before Rajiv nodded. "Yes, sir," he said quietly.

By the time the children finished their story, the room was heavy with the weight of their words. Amit stood, his jaw set with determination. Turning to his team of rangers, foresters and forest guards, he said, "This isn't just a crime—it's an atrocity. We need to act fast."

Aparna hugged the children tightly, silently grateful for Amit's understanding.

Outside, the forest compound seemed to darken with the approaching night, the urgency of justice hanging in the air, but inside, Amit Verma's resolve shone brightly—a beacon of hope and justice for the tigress whose life had been taken so brutally. Her innocent cubs would be hiding somewhere in the dangerous dark forest, hungry and thirsty, desperately waiting for her to return. Little would the innocent bundles of fur know that she never will.

The scene of crime...

The first light of dawn painted the Kaziranga landscape in hues of crimson and gold. The misty wetlands shimmered under the soft glow of the rising sun, reflecting the beauty of the surrounding wilderness. Herds of eastern swamp deer or barasingha with unique splayed hooves looked golden in the morning light as they moved gracefully towards the riverbanks. Wild buffalo stood in stoic clusters, their silhouettes framed against the fiery sky and their breath visible in the crisp morning air as they drank from the tranquil waters. A hispid hare with its bristly coat and long brown tail peeped out of the grasses, it's black eyes, catching a glint of the early morning sun.

In the swamps, the unique and rare one-horned Indian rhinoceros trudged through the reeds, its robust frame cutting an imposing figure in the soft light of dawn. Not far away, a herd of wild elephants traversed the landscape in slow, deliberate movements, their calves playfully nudging one another as they followed the matriarch.

Overhead, the great hornbills soared, their striking black-and-white plumage and distinctive casques catching the morning sun. A symphony of bird calls filled the air, as a kaleidoscope of avian life added vibrant colors to the awakening forest canopy.

Down a winding dirt track, a convoy of forest jeeps rolled through the dew-dropped grasslands, leaving faint trails of dust in their wake. The hum of their engines grew faint as the jeeps came to a halt near the shimmering river. Divisional Forest Officer Amit Verma climbed out of the lead jeep, flanked by rangers and guards. His gaze swept across the landscape, his expression one of focused determination.

Behind him, Aparna helped her students—Aamir, Rajiv, and Anya—step down from the jeep. The children, still shaken but resolute, followed Amit as he led the group toward the crime scene along with rangers, rifle guards, members of the WCCB

(Wildlife Crime Control Bureau), Assam Police and forensic officials. Aparna stayed close to them, her protective instincts heightened.

They moved through the dew-drenched grass, the morning air cool and fresh, the landscape serene despite the dark purpose of their journey. The group navigated through the lush terrain, stepping over roots, puddles and elephant tracks reminding the children of their narrow escapade, the previous evening where the 'Haathis' had played a crucial role.

As they approached the designated spot, Aamir's footsteps slowed. He pointed toward a clearing near the tree line, his voice steady despite the weight of his words. "This is where it happened," he said quietly.

The group halted, their gazes fixed on the spot Aamir had indicated. The once serene landscape seemed to hold a heavy silence, as if mourning the tragedy that had unfolded there. Amit Verma crouched down, examining the area with a practiced eye. The forest officers spread out, scanning for clues, while the children and Aparna stood at a distance, their emotions a mix of sorrow, fear and unease.

Amit Verma, along with his team, moved cautiously through the clearing, scanning every inch of the ground. His sharp eyes fell upon a heavy, cast-duty metal snare lying amidst the grass. It was stained with blood and bore clumps of golden fur, undeniable testimony to the tigress's agonizing struggle. Amit crouched down, running his fingers just above the bloodstained metal, his expression darkening "They left in haste", he muttered, his voice cold with restrained fury....

The dusty ground surrounding the snare was a canvas of chaos, etched with the tragic story of the tigress's final moments. Deep scrape marks from her claws scored the earth, evidence of her desperate fight to free herself. Sprinkles of dried blood dotted the scene, now swarmed by buzzing flies, adding to the macabre atmosphere.

As Amit rose to his feet, he signaled his team to spread out and inspect the area further. Officers and forensic experts from the Wildlife Crime Control Bureau began meticulously combing the landscape and collecting fur, nail and tissue for DNA analysis.

Not far from the snare, one of the officers called out, "Sir, over here!" Amit quickly made his way to the spot, where they discovered a grotesque sight: the tigress's intestines, discarded carelessly amidst the undergrowth. The sight was both revolting and telling. Amit's face hardened as he studied the remains.

The serene beauty of Kaziranga was abruptly overshadowed by the grim evidence of brutality.

He gestured to the forensic team, who began photographing and collecting samples from the scene. Amit's gaze swept the area, noting the faint imprints of boot marks in the soft earth. The tracks suggested the poachers had worked quickly to remove her prized parts like her skin, claws, teeth and even her blood. Everything had all been taken with precision, undoubtedly destined for the illegal wildlife trade in Southeast Asia, where they would fetch a high price.

As the rising sun cast a golden hue over the dense Kaziranga landscape, the juxtaposition of natural beauty and human cruelty weighed heavily on everyone present.

The atmosphere was heavy with silence, broken only by the eerie calls of the Pallas's Fish Eagle echoing from the riverside.

Amit Verma rose and turned to his team with his resolve strengthened. "This is more than just poaching," he said. "This is a crime against mother nature, against the very spirit of India and we will ensure these men are brought to justice. Document everything. Every track, every mark, every piece of evidence. We owe it to this tigress and the planet."

The Bangladeshi connection...

The poachers were trembling with fear after the incident. Without wasting a moment, they bolted toward the park's border, desperate to escape. Under the cover of darkness, they found refuge in an illegal Bangladeshi immigrant settlement—an overcrowded basti hidden within the labyrinth of the slums.

The basti was a maze of crumbling shanties made from rusted tin sheets, bamboo, and tattered plastic sheets barely holding up against the wind. Open drains ran along the narrow, muddy lanes, their stench mixing with the aroma of fried fish and cheap liquor. Dim, flickering bulbs and smoky kerosene lamps cast eerie shadows, revealing the makeshift homes packed together like a hive. Children with hollow eyes and dirt-smeared faces played barefoot in the grime, while women in faded saris sat outside their shacks, cooking fish and rice over open fires. A few men stood at street corners, their eyes watchful, speaking in hushed voices. This was a place where the law barely reached—where survival dictated the rules.

Deep inside the maze of lanes, within a dimly lit shack, Jaggu and Lakhan sat cross-legged on a tattered rug, the strong scent of desi sharab (locally brewed alcohol) mixing with the dampness in the air. A flickering candle on a wooden crate provided the only source of light. The walls were lined with sacks of rice, a few rusting utensils, and a wooden plank serving as a bed.

A group of Bangladeshi immigrants sat with them, sipping from dented tin cups. Their faces were gaunt, their skin weathered from years of hardship.

The man who spoke first, Azam, had sharp, sunken eyes and a thick stubble. His dark complexion was further darkened by layers of grime, and his cheekbones jutted out like blades. He wore a loose, stained vest and a checkered lungi, his bony fingers tightly gripping his cup.

He leaned forward, lowering his voice. "Look, brother, this is dangerous—far more dangerous than you realize," he muttered, his voice hoarse, perhaps from years of smoking cheap beedis. He shifted uncomfortably, eyes darting toward the entrance of the shack as if expecting someone to barge in.

Another immigrant, a wiry Rohingya, with sharp eyes, set his drink down with a thud and muttered, "You people killed a tigress, and to top it all, those children saw everything. Do you know what that means?" His voice dropped to a whisper. "The entire legal machinery will come down like fire—police, forest department, maybe even the BSF."

Next to him, Mazhar, an older man with deep lines on his forehead took a slow sip from his cup. His eyes, clouded with age and experience, studied Jaggu and Lakhan intently. He wore a tattered kurta, its sleeves rolled up to reveal arms covered in scars—whether from fights or labor, no one could tell.

Jaggu shifted uneasily, but before he could speak, Mazhar interjected, his voice laced with anger. "And yet, in your foolishness, you've brought the tiger's remains here? Are you out of your minds? Keeping poached tiger parts in this settlement is suicide. We'll all go down with you."

The tension in the room was thick, the only sound the occasional clinking of metal cups and the distant hum of crickets.

Lakhan wiped his sweaty brow and took a long sip from his drink. Just then, his phone vibrated in his pocket. He pulled it out and frowned at the screen. Nepal.

He stepped away from the group, gripping his phone tightly. The flickering candlelight cast shadows on his tense face as he hesitated before answering.

"Haan, bolo." (Yes. Tell me.)

A harsh, clipped voice erupted from the other end which spoke rapidly. Whatever was being said made his face go pale.

"This is not done, Lakhan!" the voice barked. "We've been waiting for too long. You were supposed to deliver tigers, and yet, every time, you send us leopard parts. Do you take us for fools?"

Lakhan swallowed hard, his free hand clenching into a fist.

"Bhaiji pranam. Things have been difficult," he said carefully, his voice laced with unease. "Tigers are becoming rare in the subcontinent outside protected areas. We've been trying our best to meet your demands with leopard parts from fringe forests—"

"Enough with your excuses!" the voice snapped. "The entire ring—businessmen, traders, the bosses—they are all furious. You are constantly letting us down, Lakhan. If you don't deliver, there will be consequences. Now, tell me—when are we getting our RBT (code for wild Royal Bengal Tiger) consignment?"

Lakhan wiped the sweat beading on his forehead. "Bhai ji, we've finally had a stroke of luck," he said cautiously. "We recently poached a tigress. If all had gone as planned, we would have gotten the cubs too. They were right there. But..." He hesitated.

"But what?" the voice demanded.

Lakhan exhaled sharply. "Nothing much. The situation got messy. Will tell you later."

Silence. A dangerous silence.

Then, the voice on the other end spoke, low and threatening. "And what are you doing about it?"

Lakhan licked his dry lips. "We are handling it. But things are even more complicated now. Interpol has deployed a new officer at Kathmandu—Russel Hogg. He's ruthless. He's tightened Indo-Nepal and Indo-Myanmar border controls. Working closely with the Indian BSF (Border Security Force), he has conducted successful raids on the ivory and rhino horn mafia in the border areas..The Myanmaar border is very dicy right now. Moving our products across has become a nightmare. We are trying the Nepal route. We need a little time."

The voice sneered. "Time? Time is a luxury you don't have, Lakhan."

Before Lakhan could respond, a commotion erupted near the entrance of the shack. A young Bangladeshi lad, breathless and wide-eyed, burst in.

"Bhai! The roads—three of the border roads—naka bandi!" he gasped. "The BSF and police have sealed them off!"

Jaggu, who had been listening intently, bolted upright. His face drained of color. The other men in the shack exchanged uneasy glances.

Lakhan's grip on his phone tightened as the voice on the other end spoke again, this time dangerously soft. "Well, Lakhan… it seems your troubles are only beginning."

The call disconnected.

A heavy silence hung in the air, broken only by the distant crackle of a dying fire outside. The poachers exchanged uneasy glances, the weight of their predicament sinking in. Their escape routes were closing in.

Then, from the dimly lit corner of the shack, a raspy voice cut through the tension.

"There's only one solution to your problem."

Jaggu and Lakhan turned sharply toward the speaker, sitting in a dimly lit corner of the room— Ali, a scrawny Rohingya man with a peculiar Chinese-style beard, yellowed, crooked teeth, and a thin, scraggly mustache. He had only one eye, the other socket covered by a sunken patch of dark skin. His remaining eye gleamed in the candlelight as he took a slow sip from his tin cup.

Jaggu narrowed his eyes. "And what solution is that?"

Ali smirked, revealing even more of his rotting teeth. He leaned forward, his breath reeking of stale beedis and alcohol.

"Hasan Chacha."

A murmur rippled through the group. A few of the men stiffened. Someone whispered a curse under their breath.

Lakhan frowned. "Who?"

Ali chuckled, shaking his head as if amused by their ignorance. "Hasan Chacha runs this area. He's the real power here.."

Jaggu exchanged a wary glance with Lakhan. "And what's the catch?"

Ali's smile faded. "The catch? He doesn't work with strangers. He has his own tight circle—men who have been with him for years. He doesn't trust outsiders. And if he doesn't like you..." Ali dragged a finger across his throat, making a soft slicing sound.

Lakhan exhaled slowly. "Hmmm. Then how do we reach him?"

Ali leaned back, taking another swig of his drink. "We'll try to put you on to him. The rest..." He smirked. "Depends on your luck."

The candle flickered, casting long shadows on the shack's cracked walls. Outside, the night deepened, the streets of the basti restless with unseen dangers. And in that moment, Jaggu and Lakhan knew—they were stepping into something far more dangerous than they had ever imagined.

Hasan Chacha...

The old clock in the shack struck three, its muffled chime barely audible over the night's eerie silence. The settlement, usually alive with murmurs, stray dog barks, and the occasional drunken brawl, now lay in an uneasy stillness.

Suddenly, the shack's flimsy wooden door burst open. Ali, his single eye gleaming in the darkness, whispered harshly, "The time is right. Come along."

Jaggu and Lakhan, already on edge, rose to their feet. Without another word, they followed him out into the night.

The alleyways of the basti were a twisted, suffocating maze—narrow paths barely wide enough for two people to walk side by side. The walls of the makeshift houses leaned in dangerously, their tin sheets rattling with the occasional gust of wind.

They passed a group of shadowy figures huddled around a fire, their faces barely visible. Someone laughed—a deep, guttural sound that held no warmth. Further ahead, a pair of bloodshot eyes peered out from behind a tattered curtain, watching them suspiciously as they passed. This was not a place for hesitation.

At the edge of the slum, the alleyways opened into a dirt path leading to the fringes of the forest. Here, the huts were fewer, the darkness thicker. Trees loomed like silent sentinels, their branches whispering secrets to the wind. The ground was uneven, littered with broken glass, discarded liquor bottles, and cigarette butts.

A giant denizen of the night, the dusky eagle owl swooped overhead, its wings massive and ghostly against the black sky. It let out a deep, haunting hoot, sending an involuntary shiver down Lakhan's spine.

"Bad omen," Jaggu muttered under his breath.

Ali shot him a warning glance. "Keep walking."

Ali led them deeper, until they reached another hidden ghetto, one that felt even more sinister and forgotten. Unlike the previous basti, this one was colder, quieter, and filled with a suffocating sense of secrecy. The few structures here were more fortified, with barbed wire fences, wooden spikes, and reinforced doors—as if the inhabitants were expecting war.

A few malnourished dogs with matted fur prowled near the entrances, their yellow eyes gleaming hungrily in the darkness. Somewhere in the distance, a woman sobbed softly, but no one seemed to care.

Ali stopped before a large iron gate, rusted but solid. Two burly men stood guard, their faces half-hidden beneath scarves. Their eyes, cold and suspicious, studied the newcomers.

The guards were not just muscle—they were killers, their very presence radiating silent threat. One of them Hameed, a giant man of Afghani origin with a broken nose and deep scars running down his forearms, stepped forward and shoved Lakhan hard against the gate.

"Search them."

The second guard, Jamil, a lean Rohingya with sharp, rat-like features, patted them down roughly, his calloused hands checking for weapons. When he was satisfied, he nodded to Ali.

"They can go in. But if they try anything…" He flashed a knife from his belt, its blade glinting in the dim lantern light. "…we gut them like pigs."

Ali smirked. "No need for that. They're here for business."

The iron gate groaned open.

The trio stepped into a vast, dimly lit compound, hidden between the forest's edge and the shadowy ghetto. At the center of the compound stood a sprawling, decayed mansion, a dilapidated Victorian structure, its walls covered in moss, its windows blackened with grime. The structure was a relic from the British colonial time, long abandoned by its original owners and now the den of the most feared smuggler in the region.

Inside, lanterns flickered against the damp walls, casting long, shifting shadows. A group of armed men, all with dead eyes and trigger-ready fingers, stood along the walls, watching every movement.

At the very end of the room, sitting on an ornate wooden chair, was Hasan Chacha.

Hasan Chacha was old but not weak. His long, grizzled beard reached his chest, his skin was leathery from years of sun and crime, and his piercing black eyes seemed to drill into a man's soul, a testament to the countless wars he had fought in the underworld.

He wore a long Pathani kurta and a dangerously silent, predatory expression.

Close by, on a low wooden table, sat an ivory-handled revolver, a knife and a polished rhino horn, its surface smooth and gleaming.

Hasan Chacha exhaled a long, slow breath. He took his time before finally speaking, his voice a low, menacing growl.

"So... you are the ones who have brought trouble to my doorstep."

His eyes—black and bottomless—locked onto Ali.

And then, in a voice so soft it was almost a hiss, he said:

"Who gave you permission..." the words were slow, like drops of poison, "...to bring unknown strangers into my den?"

No one spoke.

"You bring them here..." Hasan continued, "...to show them my hideout?"

He got up from his chair, picked up the curved knife which glistened from the leather sheath. His right hand grip on the knife never loosened, his thumb running slow, deliberate circles along the blade's edge. He leaned forward ever so slightly.

"Should I carve you into little pieces for this?"

The words were calm—too calm. The kind of calm that sent a bolt of fear through Ali and Lakhan's spines.

And then, Ali mustered up just enough courage to speak a few words.

His voice, usually smooth and confident, cracked.

"Hasan Bhai…" Ali began, bowing his head slightly. "These men are new here. They're not from around this region—they come from Bundelkhand and Madhya Pradesh. They operate in Central India. They specialise in RBT and leopard. They are the infamous Bavaria's and their name carries weight all the way upto Kathmandu and Lhasa."

Hasan Chacha's black eyes, cold and unblinking, bored into Jaggu and Lakhan like twin daggers as he took a menacing circle before reclining back on his chair.

Ali continued, speaking faster now, as though every second without a bullet was a small victory.

"Just last week, they killed a tigress nearby," Ali said, his voice hushed but steady. "But things got complicated. A group of students witnessed the kill. Now the police and forest department are after them."

Jaggu and Lakhan shifted uncomfortably, feeling Hasan's gaze cut through them like a blade.

"They've brought the tiger parts here," Ali went on. "They want to smuggle them across the border. That's why they came to me… but I told them…"

He paused for effect, letting the silence build like a taut wire.

"I told them you are the only man who can make this happen."

Hasan's jaw tightened ever so slightly.

It was a deadly silence.

Then, Lakhan, despite the fear twisting his gut, gathered what little courage he had left.

"Bhaijaan…" his voice cracked, but he forced himself to speak. "We don't want any trouble. We just need help to move the stuff across the border… to Nepal. That's all."

Still nothing from Hasan.

"We are ready to meet your demands."

The air inside Hasan Chacha's lair grew even colder. The faint crackle of burning wood and the distant hoot of the horned owl outside were the only sounds breaking the suffocating silence.

The fingers of his left hand, rough and scarred from years of violence, slid slowly over the handle of the ivory-plated revolver resting on the table.

Then, without a word, Hasan gave a slight nod to his strongmen.

It was like a silent order.

The four strongmen moved instantly. They didn't just step forward—they closed in, forming a tight circle around Jaggu, Lakhan, and Ali. The walls seemed to press in with them.

One of the men, Nabeel—a beast of a figure with a thick black beard—shoved Jaggu hard, making him stumble back.

"Show us the stuff," the bearded man growled, his voice like gravel scraping stone.

The second strongman, Yunus—short, stocky, with a crooked nose and dead eyes—cracked his knuckles.

"Now."

Lakhan's fingers fumbled as he untied the brown sack slung over his shoulder. His hands shook—not from the weight of the bag, but from the weight of what was about to happen.

Slowly, piece by piece, he unfolded the tigress's remains onto the floor.

The skin came first—a beautiful, blood-stained pelt with bold black stripes running through golden fur. It shimmered faintly in the dim lantern light, a tragic symbol of both beauty and death.

Then the claws—yellowed and hooked, clicking softly as they hit the wooden floor.

The teeth—long, curved, and deadly, still stained with a trace of blood from the last kill the tigress ever made.

And finally, the bones—bundled together with rough string, the remains of a once-majestic creature now reduced to contraband.

A low murmur rippled through the strongmen.

One of them—a tall, gaunt man with a tattoo of a snake winding around his neck—squatted down, running his hand over the pelt, his fingers lingering on the blood-matted fur.

Another character picked up a tooth, rolling it between his fingers before glancing at Hasan.

The room felt even smaller now. The weight of the tigress's remains lay heavy between them—a silent, grotesque offering.

Finally, Hasan Chacha moved.

He didn't touch the parts—he simply stared at them. His eyes, cold as death, flicked from the tiger's skin to Lakhan, then to Jaggu.

Then, with a slow, deliberate pause, he spoke.

"This… isn't cheap."

The tall strongman—the one with the snake tattoo—grinned faintly.

"Two lakhs for a safe passage to Nepal?" Lakhan managed, his voice barely above a whisper.

Hasan's eyes snapped back to him—sharp, unforgiving.

"No."

The word hit like a gunshot.

"Three and half."

The air went deathly still.

"The faintest flicker of a smile ghosted across Hasan Chacha's lips — not of amusement, but of quiet, controlled menace.

"Or I leave your bodies in the forest for the jackals tonight." Hasan said, his voice like ice.

The strongmen circled like vultures, their fingers inched a little closer to their weapons.

Hasan's cold, unblinking stare shifted from the tigress's remains back to Ali, his face a mask of pure menace. His voice, when it finally broke the silence, was low and cutting—like the blade he still gripped in his hand.

"Get the cash from them. By seven tomorrow morning."

Ali gave a quick, jerking nod, his mouth too dry to respond.

Hasan's gaze didn't move, drilling into Ali's soul.

"Deposit it in my stronghouse."

The command wasn't a suggestion—it was an order sealed in blood. Without breaking eye contact, Hasan lifted two fingers.

One of his strongmen, Nabeel, immediately understood. He disappeared into a dark room at the back of the lair, the door creaking open and shut like the hinge of a coffin. Moments later, he returned, holding two large stickers of 'Noor Bhasmati Rice'—the kind used to mark vehicles for smuggling operations.

The rice brand wasn't important—it was a code. A silent signal at the border, known only to those in Hasan's network.

Hasan took the stickers and, without a word, stalked towards Lakhan.

Before Lakhan could react, Hasan grabbed him by the collar—yanking him forward so hard Lakhan's feet nearly left the ground. The knife in Hasan's hand hovered dangerously close to Lakhan's throat.

The sharp edge of the blade kissed his skin—not enough to cut, but enough to promise death.

"Do exactly as I say. I don't trust your kind.," Hasan growled, his voice a deadly whisper. "Any ambiguity… any variation…"

The knife pressed ever so slightly, a whisper of a cut.

"And I'll slit your throat right here."

Lakhan's heart pounded so loudly he was sure Hasan could hear it. His mouth trembled as he stammered:

"No… no… sir… I will do exactly as you say.I swear."

The room felt like a trap — the air thick, the shadows long and suffocating. Every breath felt like it could be their last.

Finally, Hasan let go—pushing Lakhan back roughly.

He held up the two rice stickers.

"These will be handed to you tomorrow." His voice was steady, cold. "After you give us the cash."

Lakhan nodded frantically.

"Paste them on both the front doors of your vehicle," Hasan continued. "Tomorrow. When we indicate, you drive straight to the border."

A pause.

Hasan's black eyes locked onto Lakhan's.

"What's the number of the vehicle?"

Lakhan's throat tightened. His mind, clouded with panic, struggled to grasp the question.

"It's… it's… a Maruti Van, sir…" he finally stammered. "Number… 4-4-4…"

A slap echoed in the room—Yunus, one of Hasan's strongmen struck Lakhan across the face.

"The number, you fool!"

Blood trickled from the corner of Lakhan's mouth as he coughed, gasping out:

"4-9-0-7, sir..."

Hasan's expression didn't change.

He stepped away, moving to a shadowed corner of the room. From the folds of his kurta, he produced an old, battered cellphone.

The room was so silent, they could hear the faint clicks as Hasan dialed a number.

The call connected.

Hasan's voice was soft, almost casual—yet laced with lethal intent.

"Bhaijaan, hamari ek gaadi aayegi." (Brother, one of our cars will come.)

A pause.

"4907."

Another pause—longer this time.

" Maruti Van 4907."

Hasan's gaze never left Lakhan.

"Tell the guards on duty."

The line went dead.

Hasan slid the phone back into his kurta pocket, the faintest smirk tugging at the corner of his lips.

"The border will be waiting."

Noor Basmati Rice ...

The sky burned with the last embers of the setting sun, a streak of fiery red cutting across the western horizon as the Himalayas loomed in silent majesty. The mountains — dark and foreboding — cast long shadows across the winding roads of the Indo-Nepal border. The air was cold, crisp, and still, broken only by the distant howl of the wind through the valleys.

Through this quiet, a lone Maruti van crept along the narrow mountain path, its tires crunching over loose gravel. The headlights cut weak beams through the dusk, flickering every time the van hit a bump — an old, battered vehicle that seemed as anxious as its passengers.

Inside, Jaggu and Lakhan sat in rigid silence. The tension was thick enough to choke on.

Lakhan's fingers drummed restlessly against his knee. His breathing was shallow, his throat dry. He kept stealing glances at the bundle hidden under a dirty cloth in the back — the tigress's remains — every bone, tooth, and claw a silent scream of the crime they had committed.

Jaggu, gripping the steering wheel so tight his knuckles had gone white, muttered under his breath:

"Just keep driving... act normal."

But it was hard to "act normal" when death seemed to be swooping down upon them from the rocky enscarpments like famished raptors.

Ahead, the road twisted once more — and then they saw it.

The Nakabandi.

A makeshift checkpoint where BSF guards stood like silent sentinels, their rifles slung across their chests. A long line of vehicles snaked along the road, every car being stopped, every driver questioned, every trunk checked.

The guards weren't rushing. They were thorough, methodical — opening glove compartments, slapping the sides of vehicles, poking into the hidden corners of every car.

The poachers' hearts pounded louder than the idling engine.

Up ahead, a man from another car leaned out of his window, his voice carrying through the cold air:

"Kya baat hai, saab? Kya chal raha hai? Aaj itni checking kyun?" (What's the matter, sir? Why so much checking today?)

One of the BSF guards — a stern-faced man with a thick mustache — didn't bother to answer. He simply waved the man off and moved to the next car.

Jaggu's palms were slick with sweat.

"They're checking everything," Lakhan whispered hoarsely, his voice barely audible over the rumble of the van's engine. "We're finished… we're done for…"

Jaggu didn't respond — his brain was scrambling for a way out.

And then — the guards were in front of their van.

Two BSF men approached, their boots crunching on the gravel. One tapped the hood of the van with his rifle butt.

"Papers."

Jaggu fumbled, his hands trembling as he passed over the documents of the ramshackled vehicle.

The taller guard — with sharp, eagle-like eyes — studied the papers while his companion, a younger man with a scar along his jawline, stepped toward the back of the van.

"We need to check the trunk," the scarred guard said, reaching for the handle of the dickey.

Lakhan's heart nearly stopped.

The lock clicked.

The guard's fingers gripped the edge of the trunk — about to lift the lid and reveal the damning evidence inside.

Jaggu's mind screamed for a way out. Anything.

And then — with a flash of inspiration — his hand subtly tilted the rear view mirror mounted on the right door of the car.

Just enough for the tall guard to spot the Noor Basmati Rice sticker plastered on the van's side.

The guard's sharp eyes flicked from the papers to the sticker — and then back again.

A silent message passed between him and his partner.

For a moment, the scarred guard's hand hovered on the edge of the trunk, his fingers lightly tapping the lid. It was half-open — one more inch and it would all be over.

The tall guard, still holding the papers, let out a small, almost imperceptible smile.

"Theek hai," he muttered softly. (It's fine.)

The scarred guard looked confused — his brow furrowed — but the tall one gave him a quick shake of the head.

And just like that, the younger guard's hand slammed the trunk shut.

Bang.

Jaggu and Lakhan flinched at the sound — but it wasn't the sound of their doom.

It was of their salvation.

The tall guard handed the papers back with a curt nod.

"Chalo. Nikal jao." (Go. Move along.)

Jaggu didn't need to be told twice. His foot pressed the accelerator, and the van lurched forward, wheels spitting gravel as they passed through the Nakabandi.

Varad Praja ...

The Himalayan valley was cloaked in silence, broken only by the distant gurgling of a mountain brook and the soft hum of an approaching engine. The setting sun had long vanished behind the jagged peaks, but a faint streak of crimson still bled across the western horizon — a final scar of dying light.

Through the creeping mist, a Maruti van crawled along the winding mountain road, its bleak headlights flickering weakly against the swirling fog. The road was narrow, flanked by dense forests on one side and a sheer drop into shadowed valleys on the other. The van's tires gripped the loose gravel, every twist and turn making Jaggu clench the steering wheel tighter.

The mist thickened, swallowing the trees and blanketing the road ahead in an eerie stillness. With every passing second, the van pushed deeper — further into the remote wilderness, further away from any trace of civilization.

Lakhan, sitting in the passenger seat, peered into the murky darkness, his nerves frayed from the Nakabandi escape. His fingers still twitched from the adrenaline, his mind replaying the moment the BSF guard had slammed the trunk shut — a hairsbreadth from exposing the tigress's remains hidden inside.

"How much further?" Lakhan muttered, his voice hoarse.

Jaggu didn't answer — his eyes were fixed on the road ahead, searching.

And then — through the mist, around a long, winding turn — they saw it.

A large black SUV.

It stood there, parked at the side of the desolate road, its taillights glowing red like two sinister eyes in the dark. The vehicle's polished surface reflected faint streaks of moonlight breaking through the mist — a beast lurking in the shadows, waiting.

Jaggu's foot eased off the accelerator, and the Maruti van rolled to a slow, almost reluctant stop a few feet behind the SUV. The engine groaned and fell silent.

For a long moment — there was only silence.

The mist coiled between the two vehicles, and the darkness pressed in closer. The faint outline of trees loomed in the background like ghostly sentinels.

Lakhan swallowed hard.

"Is this… them?" he whispered, though he already knew the answer.

Jaggu didn't respond. His hand hovered near the gear stick, ready — just in case.

The night clung to the mountains like a heavy cloak, and the mist curled tighter around the two vehicles — the battered Maruti van and the sleek, predatory black SUV. An uneasy silence thickened the air, a quiet tension crackling between them like static before a storm.

The seconds dragged on. No one moved. No one spoke.

Then — with a low, mechanical slide — the back door of the SUV opened.

From the shadows within, a figure emerged.

He was big — a towering, burly man with a thick neck and a shaved head, and shoulders broad enough to fill the doorframe. Dressed in a dark jacket, his heavy boots crunched against the gravel as he stepped out, the sound oddly loud in the mountain's hush. His face was a hard mask of scars and stubble, and the way he moved — slow, deliberate, like a predator — made the hair on Jaggu's neck stand on end.

The man didn't say a word. He simply started walking — straight towards the Maruti van.

Jaggu's grip tightened around the steering wheel. His heart thundered in his chest, and his mind raced. He didn't know if this man was here to negotiate or slit their throats.

He was just about to push the door open — ready to face whatever came next — when Lakhan's hand shot out and grabbed his shoulder.

"You stay inside," Lakhan hissed, his voice low but firm. "Let me handle this."

Jaggu swallowed, but didn't argue. He knew better than to question Lakhan right now.

With a deep breath, Lakhan slowly opened the van door and stepped out into the foggy night. His legs felt heavier than they should — like the very ground beneath him was warning him not to move forward.

The burly man stopped a few feet away.

His eyes, dark and unreadable, studied Lakhan for a moment — then, in a gravelly voice, he said:

"Boss is calling you."

Lakhan didn't dare glance back at Jaggu. He simply nodded.

"Let's go."

The man turned without another word and strode back to the SUV, his footsteps echoing in the silence.

Lakhan followed. Every step felt like he was walking deeper into a pit he might never crawl out of.

As they neared the SUV, Lakhan's gaze flicked to the open back door.

Two Nepalese men were sitting inside — one in the back seat and one in the driver's — both shrouded in shadow, their faces covered by scarves and woolen caps pulled low over their foreheads. Their eyes were the only visible feature — cold, sharp, and unblinking. Weapons glinted faintly beneath their coats — pistols tucked snugly into shoulder holsters.

Neither man spoke. They just watched.

And then, from the darkness inside the SUV, a voice rasped:

"Aao...baitho." (Come... sit.)

Lakhan's stomach twisted into a knot.

But he climbed in anyway.

The moment Lakhan's foot crossed the threshold of the SUV, the air seemed to shift — thickening with an unspoken threat. The scent of leather, stale tobacco, and something metallic hung in the cramped interior. Shadows clung to the corners, and the only sounds were the faint creak of the leather seats and Lakhan's own unsteady breathing.

But before he could even process what was happening —

A hand shot out from the back seat cloaked in darkness.

CRACK.

A hard fist collided with Lakhan's cheekbone — a brutal, bone-jarring punch that sent a white-hot flash of pain exploding through his skull.

His body jerked sideways from the sheer force of the blow. His head snapped back, and the world spun.

Before he could regain his balance —a second blow and he was airborne.

The impact had launched him clean out of the SUV. His body twisted midair, and with a sickening thud, he crashed onto the gravel road outside. Loose stones scraped his palms and knees, and the taste of blood filled his mouth.

Jaggu, still frozen in the Maruti van, gripped the steering wheel tightly. He wanted to rush to Lakhan's aid but better sense prevailed. He clenched his teeth, sitting in the van, watching the proceedings with an unflinching gaze.

The night seemed even darker now — the mist swirling thicker around him like a vulture circling a dying animal.

From the SUV, a figure leaned forward.

Then, with a slow, almost methodical movement, he stepped out onto the gravel road. The faint beam of the van's headlights caught the sharp angles of his face — gaunt, sunken cheeks, a cruel mouth hidden beneath the scarf, and a cold, empty stare that spoke of violence without hesitation.

As his boots crunched against the stones, his voice — calm yet venomous — sliced through the silence:

"Bloody wimp."

The words were spit out like poison.

This ominous character — tall, lean, and exuding a cruel, predatory aura was Varad Praja — the infamous Nepalese wildlife smuggler, a name whispered in fear across the Indo-Nepal border. A man whose reputation was carved in blood and bone — the kingpin of tiger and rhino horn trafficking.

He rotated his right shoulder slightly while watching Lakhan with a murderous glare. His face was half-hidden by the scarf wound tightly around his lower jaw.

Lakhan's head throbbed, his cheek already swelling from the brutal punch, but the pain was nothing compared to the icy dread creeping through his bones. He didn't dare move. His mind was a storm of fear and confusion.

Meanwhile Jaggu watched intently from the van. His heart pounded like a war drum, but his legs refused to move.

The burly man — the one who had fetched Lakhan, was none other than Bhanu Tamang — known for breaking bones as casually as snapping twigs. He now stood towering over him, a silent enforcer, Varad's chief bodyguard, his massive fists hanging like sledgehammers at his sides.

Varad shifted slightly, his fingers tapping an idle rhythm on the gun holstered beneath his coat. And then — his voice, a low, venomous growl, cut through the silence:

"You think you can cheat us?" he hissed, his voice deadly calm now.

Lakhan coughed, spitting a glob of blood onto the gravel.

Varad's cold, piercing eyes — dark as a moonless night — black, unblinking —fixed on Lakhan like a predator watching wounded prey

"Why don't you become a cobbler, Lakhan?" he hissed.

Lakhan blinked in confusion, his heart thudding louder.

Praja took a step closer.

"Yes… a cobbler." He sneered. "Make shoes out of animal skin if you don't have the fire left in you anymore to hunt tigers."

Another step.

"For six months — six long months — we've been asking for tiger parts." His voice darkened, each word landing like a lash. "And what have you given us? Leopard. Again and again."

The man in the driving seat shifted. Dhruva Tharu— another lethal strongman — pushed his door open and stepped out as well, his hand resting on the handle of a pistol peeking from his waist. His face was marked with an old burn scar running down his temple. He had an unsettling calmness in his eyes burning with cold fury. Silent, watchful, and quick with a blade, his mere presence made Lakhan's stomach churn.

Now, three figures — the lean Varad Praja, Bhanu the burly enforcer, and Dhruva the lethal driver— slowly closed in on Lakhan, their shadows stretching long and menacing under the pale headlights.

Lakhan, still on the ground, felt his chest tighten. His mind was screaming at him to run, but his body was frozen, locked in place by sheer terror.

Varad Praja crouched down, his face now inches from Lakhan's swollen cheek. His voice was a deadly whisper:

"You think this game can go on?"

Lakhan's throat was dry. He tried to speak — to explain, to beg — but no words came out.

The man didn't blink.

"All our bosses — every single one of them — is angry. Furious." His lips curled into something that might have been a smile — or a snarl. "And do you know what they told me to do?"

Silence.

Then —

"Eliminate you."

Lakhan's heart stopped.

Dhruva's hand tightened on his pistol. Bhanu cracked his knuckles, the sound echoing like distant gunfire.

Varad stood up slowly — as though savoring the moment — and looked down at Lakhan like a judge about to deliver a death sentence.

"They've decided you're a nuisance. Your clumsy ways will compromise our sophisticated trade."

Jaggu, still frozen in the Maruti van, watched the scene unfold — sweat trickling down his neck, his hand shaking against the gear stick.

Lakhan's voice quivered as he spoke, each word dragging out of his mouth like it was being pulled by force. His hands trembled, his cheek still throbbing from the brutal punch, but he managed to fold his palms together in a desperate gesture of respect.

"Bhaiji… Pranam."

The title hung in the air — a plea disguised as a greeting.

Varad didn't move, didn't blink — his black eyes locked onto Lakhan like a snake watching a rat.

Lakhan swallowed hard. His voice cracked as he pressed on:

"Times have been tough, Bhaiji. Things are not easy anymore."

No reaction.

"Tigers… they're getting harder and rarer to find in the subcontinent. Most of them — they're in protected areas now."

A muscle twitched in the Varad's jaw. The mention of "protected areas" was clearly a poor choice of words — it only underscored Lakhan's failure.

Lakhan stammered, pushing forward, his mind racing to stitch a story together:

"But… but we've been trying. We never stopped. We kept supplying you whatever we could. When we couldn't find tiger, we—" his voice dipped, "we tried to meet your demand with leopard."

The moment the word "leopard" left his lips, Varad's nostrils flared. His teeth clenched so tightly the muscles in his neck rippled.

Lakhan saw the flash of anger and hurried to explain:

"Bhaiji — listen — we had no choice. But finally, after so much struggle..." his voice rose, desperate to show progress, "we found a tigress. A big one. In her prime. We made a clean kill."

Varad's eyes narrowed ever so slightly. The silence was suffocating now — a thin thread ready to snap.

Lakhan pressed his palms tighter together, his words tumbling out in a frantic stream:

"We would have gotten the cubs too — they were nearby. We were so close."

A flicker of something — interest? — passed through the Varad's eyes, but it vanished as quickly as it came.

"But then... an untoward incident happened."

The words were weak — pathetic — but Lakhan had no better way to explain it.

He licked his dry lips, his heart pounding against his ribs.

"A group of school kids — they saw us. They saw the kill."

A pin-drop silence followed.

Varad's head tilted ever so slightly, like a wolf hearing a distant sound.

Lakhan's voice broke again:

"We handled it... we tried. But things got messy."

Bhanu Tamang shifted his weight, his jaw set like a block of stone.

The mountain air was cold — but the danger was burning hot.

And then...

Varad finally spoke.

"So..." his voice was soft, almost a whisper, "not only did you fail for six months... but now you've got witnesses?"

The red glow of the SUV's taillights flickered in the misty air, casting an ominous hue across the deserted mountain road.

Lakhan, still sprawled on the gravel from the brutal punch, wiped the blood from the corner of his mouth. His folded hands trembled, but he kept them raised in a gesture of respect.

"Just look at this stuff once," he said, his words a blend of pleading and persuasion. "It will make you really happy. It's fresh — straight from the source."

Varad didn't blink.

Silence.

Jaggu sat frozen in the Maruti van, barely breathing. His wide eyes darted between Lakhan, the three men, and the dark forest that loomed behind them.

Realizing the wary Varad Praja wasn't going to respond without proof, Lakhan shifted slightly and gave a quick nod towards Jaggu. It was subtle — but Jaggu caught it immediately.

Dhruva's hand lingered on his pistol.

Jaggu reached behind the driver's seat and pulled out a rough, weathered bundle wrapped in dark cloth. His heart pounded against his ribs as he stepped out of the van, the weight of the package sending a chill through his spine — as if the tigress's spirit was still alive inside.

He moved slowly, cautiously — aware that the bodyguard's hand was still dangerously close to his gun.

Jaggu placed the cloth-wrapped package on the ground between Lakhan and the three men, then quickly took a step back, his breath ragged.

Lakhan knelt down, his fingers fumbling as he unfolded the cloth, revealing the grim contents within:

• The tiger's skin — gleaming, golden, with bold black stripes.

• Claws — razor-sharp, cruelly curved.

• Teeth — yellowed with age, still bearing the stains of the tigress's final kill.

• And bones — bundled together, clean and ready for sale.

Bhanu quickly switched on his pencil torch and directed the beam towards the contraband.

For a brief moment, the lean man's eyes flicked downward examining the content — and for the first time, Lakhan saw something that resembled… satisfaction.

It was faint, fleeting — but it was there.

Lakhan seized the moment.

“Look, Bhai… we have everything.” His voice wobbled but carried a thin thread of confidence. "Skin, nails, teeth, bones — all exactly as per your demand."

He took a shallow breath — and gambled his next words.

“And about the kids… don’t worry.”

Varad’s gaze snapped back to Lakhan — hard and unblinking.

Lakhan kept his voice low, calm, but firm:

“It’s a small job. We’re handling it. It’s our mess — not yours.”

Jaggu stood frozen, staring at the tiger parts like they might spring to life.

Bhanu's jaw unclenched ever so slightly.

But Varad… he didn’t move.

The silence was unbearable.

Then, finally — a whisper:

“You better handle it, Lakhan.”

A sliver of a smile crept beneath his scarf — cold, predatory.

“Because if those kids speak…” Varad’s voice dropped even lower — a venomous hiss — “…you’ll be nothing but another bundle of bones in these unforgiving mountains.”

Varad didn't move. His stillness was more terrifying than violence.

Then, with the slightest tilt of his head, he signaled the SUV driver. Dhruva immediately obeyed, his boots crunching against the gravel, and disappeared behind the vehicle. Moments later, he returned with a black leather bag, worn and scuffed — a bag that seemed far too heavy for its size.

Without a word, Varad unzipped it, his fingers moving with calm precision, and opened the flap. Inside were neatly stacked wads of currency notes — thick bundles of Indian rupees and Nepalese rupees, their edges slightly crumpled but unmistakably real. The faint smell of ink and leather filled the air.

The only sound was the soft rustling of cash as Varad's fingers quickly counted the bundles.

Without warning, he threw the bag at Lakhan's chest.

The force of the toss sent Lakhan stumbling backward —blood from his split lip smeared against the bag's surface as he scrambled to grab it, his hands still unsteady.

Holding the bag close to his chest, he starts flicking through the notes with the practiced ease of a man who had done this a thousand times before until he is abruptly interrupted by Varad Praja's voice cutting through the silence:

"Sixteen lakhs. Not a single rupee more."

His voice was calm — too calm — and that made it even more terrifying.

Trying hard to keep a steady voice, Lakhan implored " Bhaiji you forgot about last times consignment — two leopard skins and one pangolin. That payment is also pending."

Dhruva Tharu cracked his knuckles. Bhanu Tamang fingered the blade at his waist.

Lakhan gathered what little courage he had left. His voice was hoarse but steady, a mix of desperation and defiance.

"Bhai ji," Lakhan began, his words careful but firm, "big cats are getting rarer and harder to find outside Tiger Reserves. The administration, the police department, the forest officers—everyone is after our lives. It's not just the hunt... it's the constant danger we face, the risk at every step."

Jaggu shuddered in terror watching wide-eyed, barely daring to breathe.. These were not just petty criminals. They were monsters in human skin.

Lakhan wiped a trickle of blood from his lip trying to muster up some courage. "You know what it costs us to bring you this material," he said, his voice rising just a little. "The price we pay — not just in money, but in blood, in fear, in sleepless nights."

The air between Varad Praja and Lakhan was razor-sharp with tension.

Lakhan swallowed hard but pressed on. "This amount…" he lifted the money bag slightly, "this is too low, Bhai ji. Please… give us the amount you promised."

For a long moment, there was nothing but silence. Dhruva Tharu shifted his weight slightly, his hand still resting on his holster. Varad didn't blink. His thin lips curled — not into a smile, but into something colder.

"Promised amount?" he repeated softly. His voice was calm — too calm. "You speak of promises… while you fed me leopard parts for six months."

Lakhan's heart pounded in his chest like a drum.

Varad took a slow step forward.

"The cost of this game isn't yours alone to bear, Lakhan." His voice was a whisper now, deadly and smooth. "I pay a price too — in loyalty, in silence, in blood."

He leaned in so close that Lakhan could smell the faint scent of tobacco on his breath.

"You want the promised amount?" Varad's whisper felt like a blade at Lakhan's throat. "Then prove you're worth it."

"Do you think you're the only supplier desperate to work with us?" he hissed, his words slicing through the night air. "There are at least two others — one from South India, another from Uttarakhand and Uttar Pradesh. Both deal in fresh tiger products — not leopards, not excuses — and they're begging for a chance to replace you."

Lakhan's throat went dry. He could feel the weight of Jaggu's terrified stare from the van, but he didn't dare turn his head.

Varad inched even closer, his voice a deadly calm. "We've kept you on because of old relations, Lakhan… but loyalty has limits."

He glanced at his bodyguards — Dhruva Tharu and Bhanu Tamang — and with just a flicker of a look, the men stepped forward.

Before Lakhan could react, Bhanu grabbed him by the collar, yanking him to his feet like a rag doll. His legs wobbled, his face still smeared with blood and dust, but the grip on his shirt was like a vice.

At that moment, Jaggu's instinct kicked in. His body lurched forward, his hand half-reaching for Lakhan — a desperate, reflexive attempt to protect his partner.

But before he could take another step, Dhruva moved like a flash. His hand shot out, grabbing Jaggu by the collar and yanking him back with such force that Jaggu nearly lost his balance.

"Stay where you are," Dhruva snarled, his voice a low, menacing growl.

Jaggu froze. His breath came in short, panicked bursts as he stared into the cold, unforgiving eyes of the bodyguard.

Meanwhile, Bhanu leaned in close to Lakhan, his grip still tight on his collar. "One more failure…" he muttered, his words a slow burn, "… and you know the consequences."

Lakhan's heart pounded against his ribs. He couldn't move. His mouth opened, but no words came.

Varad's voice rang out again, cold and final, cuting through the night like a knife:

"Money means nothing without loyalty."

Lakhan's breath hitched.

"I don't trust men who fail," Varad said bluntly.

"The rest of the payment…" he said, almost as an afterthought, "… will be adjusted against your next delivery. Provided you make it on time."

And just like that, Bhanu shoved Lakhan backward. His boots skidded on the gravel, and he hit the ground hard, a fresh wave of pain shooting through his ribs.

Dhruva released Jaggu's collar with a rough push, sending him stumbling back towards the van.

"Chalo re !" (C'mon.. let's go.) Varad commanded his strongmen. The bodyguards didn't spare them another glance. They turned sharply, striding back to the SUV.

Lakhan barely registered the sound of the car doors slamming shut — his head still spinning from the shove.

Then came the growl of the engine, and the black SUV roared to life. The red taillights flared like twin embers in the dark, casting an eerie glow on the road behind them.

In a matter of seconds, the vehicle sped off into the night, swallowed by the twisting mountain roads leaving the duo— heart pounding, mind racing.

The Underdog ...

Somewhere in the distant alpine forest — barely audible over the the faint rustling of leaves — a Mountain Scops Owl uttered it's plaintive cry.

Lakhan threw three wads of cash at Jaggu's face disrespectfully. Jaggu managed to catch one mid-air and the other two fall at his feet.

"Buy some bangles and good clothes for that goat-girl of yours."he adds grinning at Jaggu.

Jaggu stood frozen for a moment, after picking up the other two wads of cash now clutched tightly in his hand. The night air was sharp, but not as sharp as the bitterness now hanging between him and Lakhan. His chest heaved, and his jaw tightened as he shoved the money into his jacket pocket.

But something snapped.

“This is all you’re giving me?” Jaggu's voice cut through the silence like a whip. "A measly one and half lakhs for three projects?"

Lakhan, still standing by the open van door, shot him a cold look. “Take it and stop talking.”

Jaggu stepped closer, his fists balled at his sides. His face was a mixture of rage and hurt. “I’m the lead tracker! Who sets the jaw traps? Who roams the jungle for days, following paw prints, tracking their movements? It’s me! Without me, you wouldn’t find a single tiger or leopard!”

Lakhan’s eyes darkened. “So?”

Jaggu’s voice cracked with fury. “Without me, there’s no hunt, but you keep throwing crumbs at me. I’ve been with you for years, and every time you just toss me a bit of money like I’m nothing.”

Lakhan’s fingers twitched at his side, his temper bubbling to the surface. “Know your place, Jaggu.”

But Jaggu wasn’t done. His voice rose. “And what about my land? The land you grabbed? I’ve asked you for it time and again — that was my ancestral land, passed down from my father and his father! You took it, just like you take my share of the money."

Lakhan's face twisted into a snarl. He took a threatening step forward. "Watch your mouth."

Jaggu's breath came hard and fast. "I want more money. This is too little."

In a flash, Lakhan's hand shot out. A loud crack echoed through the night as his palm connected with Jaggu's cheek. The force of the slap made Jaggu stumble back, his face burning both from the hit and the humiliation.

Lakhan's voice was pure venom. "You? You're asking for more money? You're just a tracker — you only find the target!"

He advanced on Jaggu, jabbing a finger at his chest.

"We're the ones who kill it, pull out its teeth, skin it, and strip the bones. I'm the one who finds the buyers — in Nepal, in Tibet. You just point us to the tiger's trail."

Lakhan's voice grew louder, his words hitting Jaggu like blows.

"Without our muscle and network, you're nothing. You're just a tracker. A coward."

The insult hung in the air like poison.

Jaggu's eyes burned — not just with anger, but with unshed tears. His cheeks were wet, whether from the slap or the sting of betrayal, it was hard to tell.

For a moment, the two men just stared at each other — the silence of the mountains swallowing their rage.

Finally, Lakhan growled, his voice low and dangerous. "Now drive. We're getting late."

Jaggu's shoulders slumped. His pride was in pieces, but he said nothing. His hand, still shaking, picked up the cash and reached for the car door. He slid into the driver's seat without a word.

Lakhan climbed back into the van, still seething.

The engine coughed, sputtered, then roared back to life.

With a jolt, the Maruti van lurched forward, its bleak headlights once again slicing through the rising mist.

The road ahead was long and winding, disappearing into the unforgiving Himalayan night.

Barkhor Street ...

Barkhor Street, a vibrant yet ancient artery of Lhasa, coils around the sacred Jokhang Temple. The rhythmic shuffle of pilgrims walking clockwise, prayer wheels spinning in their hands, and the soft hum of mantras create an air of devotion.

Incense drifts from the temple steps, mingling with the scent of yak butter lamps flickering in the evening breeze. Shops lining the street burst with colors—prayer flags, turquoise jewelry, traditional thangka paintings—but behind this spiritual veneer lurks a dark undercurrent.

Down a narrow alley off Barkhor Street, where the light barely reaches and the noise from the main road dulls into a murmur, stands an unmarked, weathered shop. At first glance, it appears as just another old curio store, its faded silk curtains concealing what lies within.

But a closer look reveals the grim reality — wild animal skins hang like macabre trophies outside, swaying slightly in the cold mountain wind. The golden pelt of a tiger, its black stripes cutting sharply through the fur, is draped next to the rosetted hides of leopards and the ghostly, spotted coats of snow leopards. The coarse, brown and black bear skins, some still with the claws attached, hides of Eurasian Lynxes, shaggy grey coats of Himalayan wolves, Shahtoosh shawls made from the fur of the rare Chiru (Tibetan Antelope) hang ominously in the facade.

Yet the horror doesn't stop there. The shop is dimly lit, the air thick with the musty scent of fur and a faint metallic tang — perhaps from the dried blood of the animals whose parts now lie in glass jars and dusty containers lining the shelves — each holding something more sinister than the last. Pangolin skins and scales, carefully packed in clear plastic bags, sit next to jars labeled with handwritten Chinese characters, filled with dark powders:

LIMiS CURIO SHOP
BAPKHORD
SNOW LEAKHADR STREET

tiger blood powder, bone powder, and crushed rhino horn. Smaller containers display more grotesque items — the dried, shriveled penises of tigers and leopards, which superstitious buyers believe enhance virility, lie stacked like grim relics.

The Tibetan shopkeeper Dechen Limi's face is weathered by both age and secrecy. Sporting a Chinese beard and wearing a fake smile revealing yellow teeth, he moves behind the counter with quiet efficiency. His narrow eyes, sharp and calculating, flicker with a blend of caution and indifference. His graying hair is pulled back into a loose ponytail, partially hidden beneath a faded woolen cap.

The shop is far from empty. A few Black American tourists, some whispering to the shopkeeper about "rare" products, others silently running their hands over the folded animal pelts. They speak in hushed tones as they eye the powdered contraband — crushed rhino horn and cobra venom wine — calculating the price of these so-called elixirs, intoxicants and aphrodisiacs.

Then, the small bronze bell above the door jangles softly. A Chinese man enters, dressed in a stylish black jacket with a high collar, his shoes polished to a mirror shine. He moves with confidence, his eyes darting across the shelves as if searching for something specific. He barely acknowledges the other customers, his focus solely on the shopkeeper.

Approaching the counter, the Chinese man lowers his voice, though there's no need — everyone in the room knows why they're here. "Tiger penis powder," he says, his words clipped and direct.

The Tibetan shopkeeper's lips curl into a slight smile — a practiced expression, equal parts charm and calculation. His voice, calm and almost reassuring, answers softly, "Don't worry, sir. You will perform with the stamina of a tiger."

These customers aren't here by chance — they know what they want, and they know this shop's reputation.

The products here, sourced from smugglers and poachers, have traveled a long, bloody route.

From the forests of Nepal and Bhutan to the jungles of India, Myanmar and Sri Lanka, every pelt and bone has passed through a ruthless network of wildlife criminals, crossing borders, bribing officials, and slipping past authorities — all to end up here, in the dark alley of Barkhor Street.

And just outside, the faint silhouette of a Chinese soldier patrols the main street, his rifle casually slung over his shoulder. His gaze passes briefly over the alley, but he doesn't stop. Perhaps he knows, or perhaps he simply doesn't care.

Either way, the market of death thrives, untouched and unchallenged deep inside the 'City of Sunshine' at a staggering elevation of 3656 metres.

Megh Malhar ...

Set amongst the highlands of the dry, brown, and dusty Deccan Plateau, Janhvi's house stands quietly, a small, humble structure surrounded by towering cliffs that loom like ancient sentinels.

The house has a few simple rooms, each bearing the marks of time, the walls cracked but steadfast, holding the weight of generations past, the curtains washed but torn by the relentless wind howling down from the ridges.

One stormy evening, Janhvi sits cross-legged on the cool mud floor of one of the rooms, her back straight, eyes closed in focus. The air is still, save for the soft strains of music echoing through the modest home.

Her father, a learned musician with wise eyes and worn fingers, guides her through her riyaz — their daily practice. His voice, rich with experience, rises and falls like the wind outside, and Janhvi carefully mimics each note, her voice still young but filled with promise. His fingers caress a rustic tribal instrument, its strings humming softly with each touch.

Outside, the sky has turned a brooding shade of gray. Dark nimbus clouds swell in the heavens, heavy with rain, their edges flickering with occasional bursts of lightning..

Suddenly, a shadow moves beneath the old shisham tree standing just outside Janhvi's quaint wooden window. A faint rustling of leaves, then the shadow takes form...

Jaggu.

Jaggu's clothes cling to his lean frame, soaked through from the rain, his hair plastered to his forehead. He stands there, his body half-hidden by the tree and his face — weathered by days in the wild — carrying an edge of restlessness.

Though the storm has eased, the air is thick with its remnants — the scent of wet earth, the whisper of distant thunder.

He raps on the wooden window three times — a sharp, familiar rhythm — then waits. His breath is shallow, anticipation crackling in the silence.

Inside, Janhvi's voice falters mid-note. The old house is quiet but for the music, the rain a distant murmur now.

Another knock — more urgent.

Janhvi's head jerks toward the adjacent room. Her heart quickens. She swallows hard, forcing her voice steady as she speaks. "Baba, I need to check the stove... the wind might be blowing in."

Her father only nods, still lost in his world of melodies.

Janhvi moves swiftly, slipping into the next room. The moment she reaches the window, she stops — her breath catching.

'Jaggu.'

The storm may be on the horizon, but another, a far more dangerous one seems to have already arrived at Janhvi's doorstep. Their eyes lock. His, dark and hungry. Hers, wide with surprise and an unmistakable flicker of longing.

Janvi gasps."You look different. You've grown a moustache?"

"Yes for you..." Jaggu's voice is hoarse, roughened by the cold.

"I just finished a deal in Nepal and got a tiny respite from work. So I came from afar... just to see you."

For a heartbeat, they simply stare — the world around them blurring, the rain, the music, her father's presence in the next room — none of it mattered.

Without a word, Janhvi hurries to the door, her heart pounding against her ribs. She unlatches it carefully, easing it open just enough for Jaggu to slip in. The door creaks softly, but the music drowns the sound.

The moment it shuts behind him, Jaggu moves — his fingers curling around her waist, pulling her into a fierce embrace. His body is cold and damp, but his grip is burning. Janhvi's hands instinctively find his back, her fingers pressing into the soaked fabric of his shirt.

"Your clothes... you're drenched," she whispers, her voice breaking slightly, her lips brushing against his ear. "You'll catch a cold."

Jaggu's lips graze her jaw, a rough smile tugging at the corner of his mouth. "I don't care… I'm starving, Janhvi. I haven't eaten for days."

Her eyes soften, but before she can respond, her father's voice calls from the other room. "Janhvi?"

She stiffens. "Yes, Baba, the kitchen is in a mess. Give me some time. I'm coming!" she shouts, her voice too quick, too loud.

Jaggu doesn't move his hands. His fingers remain pressed against the small of her back, pulling her just a little closer.

"Wait here," she whispers, voice shaky, her body still pressed against his.

She darts into the small kitchen, heart thudding, grabbing a plate of bajre ki roti and dal. Then, careful not to make a sound, she leads him to the small room adjacent to the kitchen — a dimly lit, secluded corner of the old house.

As she moves to hand him the plate, Jaggu doesn't take it. Instead, his hand catches her wrist again, gently pushing the plate aside.

"Jaggu..." Janhvi starts, but her words are swallowed when his lips crash against hers.

It's fierce, desperate. His wet shirt clings to her as their bodies press together — her soft curves against his lean robust frame. Janhvi's breath quickens, her chest rising and falling, her bosom brushing against him with every beat of her heart.

She tilts her head back slightly, letting his lips claim hers more deeply. As his hand moves from her back to her waist, Janhvi lets

out a soft gasp, her fingers tangling in his hair — pulling him closer, as though the space between them is unbearable.

For a moment, the world melts away.

But then — her father's voice again.

"Janhvi!"

She breaks the kiss, breathless, her lips still parted. "Jaggu… we can't," she whispers, her voice trembling — but not with fear.

"I have to go," she whispers again.

As she turns to leave, she stops at the doorway, looking back, still catching her breath, her fingers trembling slightly as she adjusts the edge of her dupatta. Jaggu's touch still lingers on her skin.

"Baba is teaching me what to sing tonight," she whispers. "There's a function at the home of the local politician… Raju Bhaiya."

Jaggu's face darkens instantly. His jaw tightens, and a flash of anger ignites in his eyes. "You're performing for Raju Bhaiya? That corrupt politician?"

Janhvi blinks, caught off guard by the sudden shift in his tone. "Yes," she says softly, "Baba says it's important… for our survival."

Jaggu takes a step closer, his fists clenching and unclenching at his sides. "How can you do that, Janhvi?" he hisses. "That's a dishonor to music… prostitution of music."

Her eyes widen. "Jaggu!"

For a moment, silence swells between them — raw and unyielding.

In the adjacent room, the faint glow of an oil lamp casts flickering shadows on the cracked walls. The face of an elderly man comes into view — Janhvi's father — his eyes closed, his weathered face a portrait of both pain and peace. His frail frame sways slightly as he sings, his voice rising and falling with the haunting notes of Raag Megh Malhar, the raga of rain clouds.

The torn curtains flutter in the breeze from the storm brewing outside, and the distant growl of thunder seems to echo the depth of his melody.

Janhvi's father has spent his entire life in devotion to music, a constant battle between art and survival. The early death of his wife left an unhealed wound in his heart, but all his love, every ounce of it, has since poured into his only daughter. Janhvi is the thread holding him together — his last anchor in this unforgiving world.

From the dimly lit corner of the adjacent room, Jaggu and Janhvi stand frozen, the echo of her father's voice filling the silence between them.

Jaggu's eyes narrow as he watches the old man, his voice soft but laced with bitter anger. "Look at him, Janhvi," he says, his voice a quiet growl. "Your father... such a dedicated musician. A man who has given his entire life to music."

"And look at you," Jaggu continues, his words slicing through the delicate melody floating through the house. "You're going to perform at a gathering full of politicians, their sons, gundas, henchmen, corrupt miners, and builders? Is that a mehfil? Is that what music is meant for?"

Janhvi doesn't move, her gaze fixed on the ground.

"Music is meant to be pure, Janhvi," he says, his hand tightening around her wrist again. "Not something you put on display for a bunch of lecherous old men to gawk at you while they sip their whiskey."

Janhvi's breath quickens. Her eyes, once soft and loving, now burn with a fiery defiance.

Tears streak down her cheeks, but her voice is fierce, unwavering. "Do you have any consideration, Jaggu?" she snaps, her words

cutting through the air like a blade. "Do you even know how we survive? How we run this house? How we make ends meet?"

A heavy silence falls between them — broken only by the relentless rhythm of rain against the roof and the mournful strains of Raag Megh Malhar still echoing from the next room.

She steps closer to Jaggu, her chest heaving, her tears now mixing with the faint sheen of sweat on her face. The room seems smaller, the walls tighter, the air heavier with unspoken pain.

She lets out a short, bitter laugh, her eyes still blazing. "Look at yourself. Look at your profession. How long will you keep killing innocent wild animals to make a living? Till when will you trade blood for money?"

Jaggu's fists clench at his sides, but he doesn't dare interrupt her now.

"I've been telling you for so long," Janhvi says, her voice breaking now — a mixture of anger, sadness, and desperate hope. "Leave this profession, Jaggu. Leave this blood and gore behind."

She takes a step back, her hand brushing against the edge of the kitchen door, her fingers trembling. "Come with me," she pleads, her voice softer now. "Let's leave everything behind. Let's go to the city and live a life of honesty. Whatever little we earn, we'll make an honest living out of it."

Jaggu's gaze burns into Janhvi. For a moment, the room is deathly silent — only the faint patter of rain on the roof fills the space. Then, without a word, Jaggu's hand lashes out. The plate of bajre ki roti and dal crashes to the floor, shattering the quiet. The food spills across the cracked kitchen tiles — a violent smear of yellow and brown against the dull earth tones of the house.

"Bitiya ho kya raha hai ? Kya gira diya ?" (What's happening my child? What did you drop ?) her father asks from the adjacent room, his rendition brought to an abrupt halt by the sudden clanging of utensils.

Janhvi gasps, stepping back, her hand flying to her mouth.

Jaggu's body is rigid with rage. His face darkens like the storm outside, and before Janhvi can speak, he storms out of the kitchen, pushing the wooden door open so hard it bangs against the wall.

Janhvi stands frozen for a moment, the silence deafening now — except for the relentless storm. Then, as if snapped from a trance, she replies to her father, "I am coming. Just a moment."and runs to the window.

Through the gaps in the torn curtains, she sees Jaggu's silhouette fading into the storm, his form blurred by the rain and mist. His figure grows smaller and smaller until it's gone.

Her heart clenches, a storm inside her chest matching the fury outside. The wind howls through the cracks in the old walls, and the rain taps fiercely against the window, but the wetness on Janhvi's cheeks isn't from the storm.

The Mukhbir ...

The forest guard stepped out of the ranger station, his uniform now replaced by a simple shirt and faded trousers — the kind worn by countless villagers in the region. His boots, caked with mud from the park's trails, had been swapped for worn-out sandals. Nothing about him suggested he worked for Kaziranga National Park.

He walked briskly but carefully, taking a narrow path that wound through the tall elephant grass, leading to a small village hugging the park's boundary. Bamboo huts stood in uneven rows, their thatched roofs swaying gently in the late afternoon breeze. Children played barefoot in the dust, and the air buzzed with the distant hum of insects and a faint smell of woodsmoke.

Arriving at a modest house tucked away at the end of the village, he knocked twice — a quiet, deliberate rhythm. Moments later, a man in his forties opened the door just enough to peer out, his face lined with caution. He was a mukhbir, a secret informer for the forest department, someone who risked more than most by passing on whispers of poachers' movements and illegal trades.

The guard kept his voice low. "DFO sahab has called you," he said, referring to the Divisional Forest Officer. "He wants you to come to the office — it's important."

The informer's eyes flicked past the guard, scanning the street for any unwanted attention. After a brief pause, he gave a small nod. "Alright. I'll come," he murmured.

The guard stepped back into the fading light, blending once more into the village's quiet rhythm, while the informer shut his door softly behind him — both men aware that in this delicate game of shadows and silence, one wrong move could cost them everything.

Within the administrative headquarters of Kaziranga National Park, the evening light slants through venetian blinds in the cabin of DFO Amit Verma. Maps of the park's sectors line the walls, marked with red pins indicating recent patrol routes and wildlife sightings. A weathered wooden desk dominates the room, covered with stacks of reports and satellite imagery.

Verma's khaki uniform is crisp despite the humid heat. Five rangers in similar uniforms stand at attention before him, their faces grim.

"Three tigers in two months," Verma says, tapping a folder on his desk. "Not just any poaching—surgical. They're taking only what fetches the highest price across the border. Teeth, claws, select organs. They know exactly what they're doing."

The youngest ranger shifts uncomfortably. "Sir, they must have inside information about our patrol patterns."

Verma nods slowly, his expression darkening. "That's what concerns me most."

A knock interrupts them. Verma's assistant pokes his head in, speaking in a hushed tone. "Sir, he's here. Entered through the back gate as instructed."

Verma straightens, addressing his team. "We'll continue this later. I need the room."

The rangers exchange glances but file out silently, understanding the protocol for informant meetings. The last one closes the door behind him with a soft click.

Moments later, a man slips into the office from a back door—his face partially obscured by a cotton scarf wrapped around his head. Only his eyes are visible, darting nervously around the room before settling on Verma.

"Lock it," Verma instructs, gesturing to the door.

The informer turns the deadbolt and approaches the desk, his footsteps nearly silent on the worn floor. Verma motions to a chair positioned away from the windows.

The office falls into silence as the ceiling fan whirs overhead, creating a cocoon of white noise that ensures their conversation remains private.

Verma leans forward, his voice barely audible even in the quiet office. "I need to know who's behind the tiger killed in the eastern sector," he says, eyes locked on the informer. "My best tracker said it was professionals—clean work."

The informer, Ripan, removes his scarf just enough to speak clearly, revealing a face weathered by hard years. He glances at the door before responding.

"It's the Bavaria gang, sir." His words hang in the still air. "They've returned to Kaziranga."

Verma's expression hardens. "You're certain?"

"Three of them were spotted in Dhakuakhana village last week. They come from Central India—Madhya Pradesh. They are not ordinary poachers." Ripan's fingers tap nervously against his knee. "These men are specialists. They study the tigers for days, know their habits, their trails. They kill only high-value targets—breeding females, dominant males. They leave nothing to chance."

"And the tigress from last week?" Verma presses.

"Bavaria's work, without question. The precision of the cuts, the organs they selected—it carries their signature." Ripan shifts in his chair. "They have new buyers across the border willing to pay triple the usual rate. Word is they've promised five tigers from Kaziranga before the monsoon."

Verma's fist tightens against the desk. He reaches for his phone, unlocks it with his thumbprint, and scrolls through several images.

"There's something else you should know," he says, his tone grave. "Three kids who had gone bird watching inside Kaziranga National Park became eyewitnesses to this horrific crime. One of them, managed to capture this on his phone before they fled."

He turns the screen toward the informer. The image is taken from a good quality mobile phone. It is surprisingly sharp despite being taken from a distance. It shows the poachers hunched over the fallen tigress. One man's face is clearly visible as he is looking up, perhaps startled by a sound in the forest. His features are distinct—Assamese, a dark birthmark across his left cheek, dark slanted eyes set deep under thin brows.

Ripan studies the photograph intently. His eyebrows rise in recognition, and he draws in a sharp breath.

"This man," he says, tapping the screen with a trembling finger, his eyes ablaze with haunting memories.

Verma leaned in closer, his sharp eyes fixed on the photograph. “You recognize him?”

Ripan’s gaze hardens. “I do,” he said, his tone grave.

The leopard trap...

The mukhbir shifts in his seat, his voice lowering as though the walls might be listening. "In the summer of 2019, there was a leopard troubling the people of Dhakuakhana village — kept attacking their cattle, one after another. The villagers lost nearly a dozen animals. They were furious, on the edge. You could feel the anger simmering under their skin."

Verma's fingers drum softly against the wooden desk, a slow and thoughtful rhythm.

Ripan continues, his words picking up pace. "One day, about thirty of them marched to the range office — they didn't just come to talk; they came to surround the place, a full-blown protest. They shouted, demanding action, refusing to leave until something was done."

Verma gives a slight nod. "Let me guess — the ranger tried to calm them down."

"Yes," Ripan says, his jaw tight. "The ranger on duty kept repeating the same promise: 'We'll set up a trap cage and catch the leopard soon. We'll relocate it safely back into the forest. Trust us.' But the crowd wasn't having it. Their patience was long gone."

He pauses, then points at the face in the photograph again. "That's when I first saw this man — Bhudev Barua. He wasn't like the others. While most of the villagers were angry but willing to listen, Bhudev... he was different. More aggressive. More dangerous."

Verma's eyes narrow. "What did he do?"

Ripan's voice drops even lower. "He stepped right up to the ranger — almost chest to chest — and said, 'If this leopard isn't caught in two days, your leopard won't be found alive.'"

Silence settles in the room, heavy and unyielding.

Verma leans back slowly, his face unreadable. "And the leopard?" he asks — though there is a grim knowingness in his voice, as if he already suspected the answer.

Ripan narrates the incident in detail:

" The night lay draped in silver, the full moon casting a cold glow over the cliffs of Kaziranga.Then, slicing through the stillness, came a soft, desperate bleat.

In the neighbouring fields, a goat, tied inside the forest department's double-chambered trap cage, struggled against its tether. Fear clouded its wide eyes as it stood frozen, a helpless lure for the predator hidden in the shadows above.

And then, the leopard appeared — a ripple of muscle and rosette-spotted fur moving down the Karbi-Anglong hills slinking into the sugarcane fields.

It moved like liquid shadow, yellow-green eyes fixed on its prey. Each step was a masterclass in stealth, a silent promise of death.The goat bleated again.

The big cat entered the cage cautiously, sensing human scent all around with its quivering nostrils.

And then...

In a flash, he struck like lightning — powerful paws slamming into the bars, jaws snapping an inch from the goat's neck. The sudden impact triggered the trap. The metal door behind the leopard clanged shut.

The beast was caught.

From the shadows, I watched, my breath caught in my throat. But before I could exhale, another figure emerged from the darkness — Bhudev Barua.

A cruel smile crept across Bhudev's face as he stared at the trapped leopard. He didn't move closer — instead, he melted back into the night like a snake slipping into the grass.

My heart pounded knowing exactly what was about to happen.

Without wasting a second, I turned and ran — feet pounding the forest floor as I tore through the trees, heading straight for the forest department office. The branches whipped at my face, but I didn't slow down. I had to get the guards and stop this at any cost.

By the time I burst into the office, gasping for breath, the words tumbled out. 'The leopard—caught—mob—Bhudev—hurry!'

The forest guards grabbed their batons and torches, and without a moment's delay, followed me back into the night.

But when they arrived at the scene, it was already too late.

A crowd of villagers had gathered — a seething, angry mob, their faces twisted with rage. Torches burned high, and at the center of it all stood Bhudev Barua, his voice cutting through the chaos like a blade.

'There's your man-eater!' Bhudev bellowed. 'Let the forest department take it away, and next time it'll be your children it comes for!'

The crowd roared in agreement.

Beneath the metal trap cage, villagers were already piling twigs and dry branches, snapping them from trees, stacking them higher and higher. The leopard roared, hurling itself against the metal bars, its fury and fear intertwining into a single, bone-chilling sound.

'Stop this!' shouted one of the forest guards, stepping forward. 'This is an endangered animal — it's a crime to kill it!'

Another guard joined him, voice firm but desperate. 'We will relocate the leopard. Step aside and let us do our job!'

But the mob was in no mood to listen. Someone shoved a guard back. Another man pointed a finger in my face, accusing me of siding with the killers of their cattle.

Bhudev smirked, saying nothing, letting the mob's anger speak for him.

A spark.

A match flared, and then another. Flames leapt to life, curling hungrily around the dry branches.

The leopard thrashed inside the cage, its roars growing frantic as the fire spread — smoke seeping into the metal trap, flames licking at its fur.

The forest guards tried to drag the cage away, but the villagers blocked them, shoving, shouting — a wall of human rage against a handful of powerless officers.

I watched in horror, fists clenched at my sides, my voice lost in the madness.

The fire climbed higher. The metal bars of the cage glowed red-hot. The leopard's roars grew weaker, until at last, they stopped.

Silence.

The mob slowly dispersed, their anger burned out with the flames. Bhudev lingered at the edge of the clearing, a cruel satisfaction playing across his face.

I stood frozen, my heart heavy with the weight of what I had just witnessed. I desperately tried to stop it — I had run, brought help — but it wasn't enough.

I failed.

Sir ..

I failed."

Ripan breaks down sobbing, recounting the horrific incident.

A heavy silence hangs in the forest department office, broken only by the faint hum of a ceiling fan spinning overhead. DFO Amit Verma's brows furrow with anger— Ripan's words still echoing in his mind — the crackle of flames, the helpless roars of the leopard, the mob's fury.

The informer quickly regains control of his emotions and his sobbing voice breaks the silence, soft but firm. "Mr. Verma... Bhudev Barua is a very cruel and dangerous man. After that night, I realized something — he is the arch-enemy of wildlife. I've heard from secret sources... Bhudev doesn't just incite mobs — he works with professional poachers. He supplies them with information about tiger and leopard movements inside Kaziranga."

Verma's eyes darken, and then — a flash of realization. His fingers stilled mid-tap on the desk. "Oh," he muttered, almost to himself.

"That's why he was there at the crime scene when the tigress was killed."

Ripan nods solemnly.

Verma's fingers resume their rhythmic tapping against his desk — a quiet drum of thought. "Keep a close watch on Bhudev Barua," he instructs. "Observe who he meets, what he says, where he goes. Every detail matters..."

He pauses, his gaze hardening. "When the time is right, we'll strike — and nab him."

Ripan gives a firm nod. "I will, sir."

"And use the code-word Guldaar (Leopard in rural Indian dialect) for yourself from today." Amit suggested." It's a good idea to change code-words every few days."

The air in the room seems to thicken — a silent promise exchanged between a protector of the forest and his loyal informer.

The trophy room ...

The moon hung high in the night sky of Karauli, a small dusty town of central India. It cast a silver glow over the sprawling haveli of the former minister, Rajpal Singh — known to all as Raju Bhaiya. The mansion, a silent fortress of wealth and power, was a blend of old-world grandeur and modern opulence, its towering pillars adorned with intricate carvings that shimmered under the soft lights. A large swimming pool stretched along one side of the haveli, its still water reflecting the golden hues of the surrounding lamps.

The night seemed still, yet the air was heavy — with secrets, with whispers, with danger.

Armed guards stood atop every pillar, their sharp eyes scanning the gathering below. The driveway was lined with luxury cars — both Indian and foreign — parked like gleaming beasts, silent symbols of power and influence.

It wasn't just any meeting — powerful figures had assembled, both from within the country and abroad. Their hushed conversations rippled through the night air, accompanied by the clinking of glasses and the soft rustle of silk and suits. The atmosphere was thick with an unspoken intensity, a sense that this was more than just a social event.

Deep within this sprawling estate, tucked away in a secluded wing, lay a room — a world shaped by blood and steel — the domain of Raju Bhaiya's only son, Harpal Singh. A national-level shooter, Harpal's reputation extended far beyond the shooting ranges. His room was a chilling reflection of his passion — not just for marksmanship, but for hunting.

Rifles of every make and model lined the walls, polished to perfection, each one a symbol of his obsession.

The air smelled faintly of gun oil and polished wood. Rows of rifles — of every make and model — lined the shelves, each weapon gleaming under the dim lighting. From classic double-barrel shotguns to modern high-powered sniper rifles equipped with advanced telescopic sights, it was an arsenal fit for a man whose hunger for the hunt knew no bounds. Scopes, range finders, and night-vision binoculars sat neatly on a glass-topped table.

Mounted heads of wild animals, frozen in their final expressions of fear and fury, served as grim trophies — a silent testament to his cruel hobby. The decor spoke louder than words: Harpal Singh wasn't just a sportsman; he was a man who found a dark thrill in taking the lives of wild creatures.

That night, Harpal stood in the middle of this sinister display, his hulky frame catching the faint glow of a bedside lamp. A scar ran down his arm — a reminder of a past hunt gone wrong, a battle wound he wore with pride. His gaze roamed his collection, lingering on a new addition — a pair of blackbuck antlers — sharp and spiraled, the latest victim of his brutal hobby.

Two of his friends wearing Pagdis (Headgear) lounged in the leather chairs by the fireplace, glasses of whiskey in hand, their eyes flitting between the mounted trophies and the array of weapons. They spoke with an exaggerated awe, their words dripping with flattery.

"Harpal, your aim is something else," one of them said, his voice a smooth blend of admiration and calculated praise. "Not just on the shooting range... but in the wild too. Every time you pull that trigger, the beast doesn't stand a chance."

The other chimed in, a sly grin spreading across his face. "It's no surprise, really. With a collection like this" — he gestured at the rifles, the animal heads, the antlers — "you're more than just a shooter. You're a perfect predator, designed to kill."
Harpal's lips curled into a small, predatory smile. He didn't need to respond. The trophies on his walls spoke for him — louder than any words ever could.

Beyond the window, the faint murmur of voices from the poolside gathering floated into the room. Raju Bhaiya's high-profile meeting continued in the luxurious glow of lanterns and fine wine.

As the conversation unfolded, a sudden rhythmic beat echoed through the room — the distant sound of a tabla, sharp and insistent, breaking the stillness.

And then, a woman's voice—soft, melodic, and haunting—began to sing.

Harpal's entire demeanor shifted in an instant. His head snapped toward the window, his ears straining to catch every note. His friends exchanged a glance, sensing the change in him.

A slow smile crept across Harpal's face, his voice barely above a whisper. "Ah," he murmured, "that voice... I'm a slave to it."

The air in the room, once heavy with talk of guns and trophies, now seemed to hum with a strange tension—an unexpected moment of quiet desire in the midst of his world of violence.

The poolside party...

"Come on guys, time to enter the party.", Harpal grinned mischievously while wearing his royal silk shirt and gesturing to his friends. The three men come out of the room like predators and enter the poolside where the private party unfolded beneath the soft glow of ornate lanterns.

The air was thick with the scent of expensive liquor, imported cigars, and the faint trace of jasmine from the night-blooming flowers. Crystal glasses clinked, soft laughter rippled through the night, and the surface of the pool gleamed like liquid silver under the moonlight.

Raju Bhaiya presided over the gathering — a perfect host, his smile warm but his eyes calculating. Plates of lavish food were passed around and glasses refilled. It wasn't just a dinner party — it was a meeting of minds, of people with influence, wealth, and perhaps, dangerous intentions.

In one corner, by the shimmering poolside, a small but elegantly decorated stage stood — a delicate arrangement of silk drapes and golden lights. At its center was Janhvi, the striking dusky woman whose voice poured like honey into the night. Flanked by two musicians, one expertly teasing the strings of a 12 string guitar and the other coaxing a heady rhythm from the tabla, Janhvi's song was a blend of grace and longing. Each note seemed to weave a spell over the gathering, drawing lingering glances and hushed whispers.

Harpal and his friends passed by the stage - slow calculated, powerful steps - while they walked towards the table reserved for them at the other end of the poolside. All through, Harpal's predatory gaze was locked on target — locked on the woman whose voice seemed to have pierced through the armor of his violent world.

Raju Bhaiya leaned back in his chair seated at a prime table near the stage, a half-empty glass of whiskey resting in his hand. His companions — two Chinese associates, their sharp suits and quiet, calculated smiles hinting at a more sinister purpose beneath the guise of polite diplomacy. Alongside them, sat two or three wealthy Indian businessmen — their bellies full and their eyes wandering as they drank deeply, indulging in the heady mix of alcohol, women, and music.

And Mohammad Hanif..

Hanif was a name whispered in political circles with both fear and respect. A political fixer, a builder with deep pockets, and a ruthless player in the mining mafia world— Hanif was a man who thrived in the shadows. His gold watch gleamed as brightly as his slicked-back hair and his laughter was just a bit louder than the others at the table.

Hanif broke the silence, his voice insistent. "So, Bhaiya, what's the delay now? Our Chinese partners are ready — they have the technology, the resources. All it takes is a little push here and there, and the dam project will get approved."

The two Chinese men exchanged subtle glances, their polite smiles masking the sharpness in their eyes.

Raju Bhaiya swirled the whiskey in his glass, his expression calm but firm. "It's not that simple, Hanif," he said with a quiet authority. "The river's too small — barely enough for power generation. The land is forested, so there's a mountain of environmental clearances to deal with. And to top it all off, the damn government has changed. It's like adding bitter gourd to neem — an already tough situation just got worse."

He sighed, his words a blend of frustration and realism. "Getting those approvals won't be easy. We'll have to pull every string we've got — and push harder than ever."

The Chinese associates chuckled, as if they were familiar with the game of bending rules.

Hanif smirked. "Strings can be pulled, Bhaiya. It's all about how hard you're willing to tug."

Raju Bhaiya didn't respond immediately. His fingers traced the rim of his glass, his gaze fixed somewhere beyond the glowing pool, lost in thought.

Janhvi's voice floated through the night air — a song drenched in shringar rasa, the delicate essence of love and longing. Her melody was soft yet commanding, each note weaving its way into the hearts of those present.

Harpal Singh, Raju Bhaiya's only son, now sat poolside with two of his friends, dressed in an expensive, well-tailored shirt and a sleek blazer, a look both sophisticated and effortlessly chic.

His friends, ever eager to please, continued to flatter him, their voices a murmur compared to the music.

One of them reclined in his chair, a sly grin spreading across his face. "Bhaijaan," he said, his voice laced with admiration, "your aim today was something else. Dropped that huge male from such a distance—didn't even give it a chance — pure class."

Harpal smirked, his fingers idly tracing the curve of a wine glass. "This was barely any marksmanship. You haven't seen anything yet," he smirked, his voice calm but edged with pride. "Come on, let's have kebabs made from that very nilgai tonight. A well earned meal."

Harpal barely responded to complements from the excitable young women around him. His gaze was transfixed on the stage, on Janhvi. The way she swayed gently to her own music, her voice flowing like silk, seemed to pull him in, his expression shifting from casual confidence to something more entranced — almost possessive.

Standing nearby, blending seamlessly into the crowd, was Lakhan. To anyone else, he appeared to be just another of Harpal's loyal servants — a silent figure lurking at the edges of the party. But those who truly knew him were aware of the truth — Lakhan wasn't just a servant. He was the ringleader of a ruthless poaching group, a man who moved in the shadows, his loyalty to Harpal running deeper than mere servitude.

Harpal, his eyes still locked on Janhvi, gave a slight nod in Lakhan's direction. The man stepped forward swiftly, his movements practiced and precise.

Without a word, Harpal slid a few crisp five-hundred-rupee notes into Lakhan's hand. Then, grabbing a napkin from the table, he scrawled something across it — short, direct.

"Take this to Janhvi," Harpal said softly, his voice calm yet firm. "Tell her this song is my special request."

Lakhan's lips barely moved, but a slight smirk played at the corner of his mouth as he tucked the money into his pocket and folded the napkin with care.

"As you wish, sir," Lakhan replied, his tone respectful, though a glimmer of something darker flickered in his eyes.

He moved toward the stage, his steps light and deliberate, weaving through the crowd like a snake through grass.

Harpal leaned back in his chair, swirling the whiskey in his glass, his lips curving into a slight smile. His gaze never left Janhvi — as though, through that note, he had already staked his claim.

But for a moment, as Janhvi's voice soared into a delicate crescendo, even the most powerful men at the table fell silent, their heads tilting slightly — captivated by the song, or perhaps by the woman singing it.

Lakhan moved with quiet confidence, climbing up onto the stage. His boots made a dull thud against the wooden floor, but the sound was barely noticeable beneath the melody. He cut through the musicians effortlessly, his presence disrupting the delicate atmosphere, but he didn't care. His target was Janhvi.

She was mid-verse when he reached her, standing just close enough to make his presence known without interrupting her performance outright. With a smirk, he extended his closed fist, fingers wrapped tightly around the napkin. His expression carried an unspoken message—one of authority, of expectation.

Janhvi's eyes flickered to him for a brief second, but she didn't stop singing. She hesitated, but the interlude of the song was approaching. As soon as the instruments took over, she took the note from his hand, her fingers brushing against the crumpled paper.

Lakhan stepped back, the smirk still playing on his lips as he watched her unfold it.

Janhvi's eyes scanned the words quickly. Even before she looked down, she already knew who had sent it. And when she did glance toward the poolside, her forced smile barely hid the loathing in her gaze.

Harpal sat in his chair, lounging casually, his whiskey glass resting on the armrest. He met her eyes with a slow, knowing smile, as if he had already won.

Janhvi swallowed the resentment rising in her throat and masked it behind a delicate nod, her fingers tightening around the note. The show must go on.

The atmosphere at Raju Bhaiya's table had shifted. Mohammed Hanif, usually composed, leaned forward, his gaze turning to his assistant, Mohsin.

"There's a matter we need to resolve before the dam project can even begin," Hanif muttered, lowering his voice. "The river—it cuts right through the Tiger-Leopard Corridor."

Raju Bhaiya exhaled slowly. "And?"

Hanif's jaw tightened. "And there's a problem. A stubborn wildlife activist from an NGO is causing trouble." He turned to Mohsin. "What's his name?"

"Jayant Ghosh," Mohsin replied.

Hanif clicked his tongue in irritation. "That man is destined to die an early death, I think."

At the mention of this name, one of the Chinese men at the table—wearing an expensive suit and an expression of mild impatience—raised an eyebrow. His associate, a broader man with slicked-back hair, shifted slightly in his seat, clearly interested in the conversation.

Hanif continued, his voice edged with frustration. "This man—he's in his mid-thirties—focused, determined. He's not just another activist making noise. He's making a strong case to have the entire reserve forest converted into a tiger reserve. He's collecting evidence, gathering reports, and he knows how to build a case. If he succeeds, that dam will never get built."

Raju Bhaiya's fingers paused mid-swirl.

Mohsin leaned in. "Some say he's also sending data to the NGT—the National Green Tribunal. If that's true, he's not just making trouble locally. He could escalate this to Delhi, block the project entirely."

A tense silence followed.

Mohsin added, "I've also heard he's feeding sensitive wildlife data to the NTCA—the National Tiger Conservation Authority. He's setting up camera traps in the forest, monitoring tiger and leopard movements, and preparing to take legal action on environmental grounds."

One of the Chinese men sighed loudly, setting his glass down with a deliberate clink. "This is not good," he said in a heavy accent, looking straight at Raju Bhaiya. "We do not have time for such problems. We need clearance fast."

His companion nodded, frowning, his impatience growing, "We have already committed resources—Technology, manpower. We cannot afford delays. If there is an obstacle, remove it." His words were clipped, final.

Raju Bhaiya finally set his glass down, his fingers drumming lightly against the table. His expression was unreadable, but the men at the table knew—when Raju Bhaiya thought, decisions followed. And his decisions were rarely merciful.

Harpal smirked, swirling the drink in his hand, his eyes fixed intently on Janhvi. A crude chuckle escaped him as he gestured toward her, nudging his friends with an indecent signal. His companions snicker, indulging his arrogance, while Janhvi, mid-performance, kept her gaze averted, pretending not to notice. But there was a flicker of contempt in her eyes, betraying the disgust she felt.

Beneath the veil of indulgence—alcohol, music, and laughter—an undercurrent of tension flowed at Raju Bhaiya's table. "If the reserved forest gains the status of a tiger reserve, we're finished," Mohsin stated firmly. "According to the Supreme court judgement, the area will fall under strict environmental protection. Not only will deforestation become impossible, but within a one-kilometer radius of the boundary, all dam construction and river mining, will be completely banned."

The Chinese counterparts exchanged glances, their expressions growing tense. Raju Bhaiya exhaled deeply, rubbing his chin as he processes the weight of the conversation. The stakes were high, and the pressure was mounting.

Meanwhile at Harpal's table, a moment of seriousness emerged. Chuckling slightly, Harpal leaned in and said to his friends,

"Did you know? The land holders of Bihar have sent me an invitation. They're fed up with nilgai. These animals keep invading farmlands, destroying crops, and the farmers have had enough—they're staging protests. So, the estate owners wants us to step in and cull about 250 nilgai. Moving live targets. It's going to be quite a game."

He took a slow sip of his drink, eyes gleaming with excitement. "So… who's coming with me?" As Harpal continued his conversation, a servant approached with a bottle of beer, standing quietly beside him. Without even glancing at the servant, Harpal absentmindedly reached out and touched the bottle with his finger. A split second later, his expression darkened, his face flushing with sudden rage.

Without warning, he grabbed the bottle and smashed it over the servant's head. The sharp crack of shattering glass echoed through the air as the servant let out a pained cry.

"You worthless fool! I asked for a chilled beer! Does this feel cold to you?" Harpal bellowed, his voice dripping with fury.

For a moment, the entire gathering fell into stunned silence. Janhvi's song came to an abrupt halt as all eyes turned toward the scene, the tension in the air thick and unyielding.

Blasé to the incident, Harpal rose from his chair, nonchalant, still holding his glass, and swaggered toward the adjacent table where his father, Raju Bhaiya, was deep in discussion with Mohammed Hanif and the Chinese businessmen. As he walked, he broke into a playful jig, his expensive shoes tapping against the polished floor in an exaggerated rhythm. A few of his friends laughed, but most of the guests simply watched, unsure whether to be amused or uncomfortable.

Reaching the table, Harpal leaned in with a smug grin and raised his glass in a mock toast. His eyes flicked toward the Chinese guests.

"So, sir," he drawled, "I hear you gentlemen have an instinctive taste for wild meat. China is famous for its... exotic delicacies. Right?"

He let the words hang in the air before lowering his voice slightly, his smirk widening. "How about some Indian bush meat exotica? Fresh. Straight from the jungle."

The Chinese businessmen exchanged quick glances, and then their eyes gleamed with excitement, a mix of curiosity and greed flashing across their expressions. One of them chuckled, while another cheered, clearly interested.

Raju Bhaiya and Hanif remained quiet, observing the exchange. The air at the table shifted subtly, the earlier tension momentarily defused by the thrill of the hunt.

The barasingha hunt...

Harpal flicked his fingers in Lakhan's direction, a silent command that needed no words. "Take out my car." His voice was casual, but his tone carried authority.

Lakhan nodded and disappeared into the shadows. Moments later, the deep, guttural roar of an engine echoed through the estate. The massive black Hummer—Harpal's personal beast—emerged from the garage, its headlights slicing through the night.

As the Hummer rolled forward, Dhama, a towering figure with sharp, watchful eyes, stepped forward. Dhama was no ordinary man—he was one of Raju Bhaiya and Harpal Singh's most trusted personal bodyguards, a shadow that never left their side. Alongside him, two other Scorpios—dark, menacing, and packed with armed men—stood ready, their engines humming like restless predators.

The night air crackled with energy. Something was about to happen.

The massive black Hummer shot out of Raju Bhaiya's estate, its engine growling like a beast, followed closely by the two Scorpios. Their headlights cut through the darkness, illuminating the winding road that led towards the forest.

Inside the giant moving SUV, two Chinese guests exchanged excited glances. Their anticipation was palpable, their eyes gleaming under the dim interior lights. Seated beside them, Mohammed Hanif leaned back with a smug grin, his fingers lightly tapping the leather armrest.

"What all do we find here?" Hanif mused aloud, turning to Harpal, who lounged confidently in his VIP seat, twirling a cigar between his fingers. "What kind of game does this part of the forest hold?"

Harpal smirked and glanced toward the rear of the vehicle. "Where's our tracker boy?"

A calm but firm voice answered from the shadows. "I'm here, sir."

Jaggu emerged slightly from his corner rear seat, his sharp eyes scanning the dark road ahead through the windshield. He knew his job well—perhaps too well. Deep inside, he despised what he had to do, but in this world, choices were a luxury he didn't have.

Harpal exhaled a cloud of smoke and grinned. "Jaggu, what do we have here in this part of the jungle? Chital? Sambar? Chinkara? Nilgai? Or Barasingha? What can you find for us tonight?"

Before Jaggu could respond, one of the Chinese men leaned forward eagerly. "Lets try Barasingha. Never got a chance to taste that animal..Swamp deer..Right?" he said, his voice tinged with excitement. His companion nodded in agreement, an unmistakable glint of hunger in his eyes.

Harpal let out a short laugh and clapped his hands together. "Barasingha it is, then."

The Hummer picked up speed, the convoy heading deeper into the forest, toward the unsuspecting wildlife that lurked beyond the tree line.

"Whatever you order Hukm," Jaggu muttered under his breath.

He leaned forward and instructed the driver to take a couple of sharp turns, navigating the massive Hummer deeper into the forest. The headlights barely penetrated the thickening darkness as the convoy of three vehicles snaked through the dense wilderness. The towering trees soon gave way to a vast grassland stretching beside a slow-moving river, its surface glistening under the moonlight.

Jaggu raised a hand, signaling the vehicles to halt. "No noise," he whispered.

The three vehicles came to a silent stop at the edge of the riverine grassland. The armed men inside remained still, their breaths hushed in anticipation. Jaggu stepped out first, his movements

fluid, almost animalistic. He crouched low, scanning the ground with a trained eye. His fingers brushed against the grass, feeling for signs of recent movement. He picked up a few leaves of half eaten aquatic vegetation from the damp ground, crushing them between his fingers and bringing them to his nose, inhaling deeply. "A barasingha has been here earlier tonight. " he muttered softly. "They love going into the water and munching on aquatic vegetation."

Then, without a word, he scooped up a handful of dry earth and let it trickle from his fingers. The dust swirled in the moonlight, caught by the invisible hand of the night breeze. He noted the direction carefully.

He then strode straight to the Hummer, his head slightly bowed.

"Hukm," he said, his voice low but obedient. "Bring your gun."

Harpal, eager and grinning, stepped out of the vehicle, his prized rifle slung over his shoulder. As soon as he did, the two Chinese gentlemen exchanged excited glances and followed him, unable to contain their curiosity.

Jaggu led them a short distance away, weaving carefully through the tall grass, their footsteps barely making a sound.

At last, Jaggu stopped behind a thick clump of bushes. He gestured for Harpal to crouch.

"Wait here, Hukm," Jaggu instructed.

Harpal settled in behind the cover, gripping his rifle tightly, his breathing controlled. The two Chinese men stood slightly behind him, eyes gleaming with anticipation.

The night stretched ahead, silent and watchful.

The sudden cry of a river lapwing pierced the stillness of the night, a sharp, urgent alarm that sent ripples of unease through the air. Jaggu stiffened. He raised a finger to his lips, signaling absolute silence. Every muscle in his body was taut with focus. He had spent enough time in the wild to understand these signs—something was moving, something large.

Then, breaking the silvery shimmer of the river's surface, a pair of immense antlers emerged, glistening with water. A magnificent barasinga rose from the shallows, stepping onto the grassy bank. Droplets of water trickled from its soaked coat, pattering onto the grassland as it moved forward. The enormous stag, carried itself with slow, deliberate grace, each step disturbing the still water.

It strode forward with a regal confidence, oblivious to the eyes watching from the shadows. It had been feeding on water plants, and now, chewing its cud, it ventured further onto the open grassland.

Harpal raised his rifle, his breath steady, his finger tightening on the trigger.

Jaggu, still crouched beside him, whispered urgently, "Wait, Hukm. He will come closer."

Harpal exhaled through his nose, but obeyed. The stag advanced further, its powerful legs treading the grass lightly, its ears flicking occasionally. It was close now, dangerously close. The night air felt thick with the weight of the moment.

Then, without warning, Harpal squeezed the trigger.

The rifle cracked through the night like a thunderclap. The bullet tore through the Barasinga's skull, and the magnificent beast crumpled instantly, collapsing onto the ground with a resounding thud.

The rifle shot shattered the night.

The explosion sent ripples of chaos through the silent wilderness. A frenzy of wings erupted from the riverbank—ducks, geese, snipes, sandpipers, and egrets took to the air in a frantic burst of motion. Their pale forms shimmered in the moonlight, rising like spectral fairies, their cries echoing through the vast emptiness.

But as the echoes of the gunshot faded, another storm raged within Jaggu.

Visions of childhood...

The sharp crack of the rifle sent him spiraling—hurtling backward in time, back to a different time zone.

Another gunshot.

Another flock of birds erupting from the canopy, their frantic wings carving through the jungle sky.

And beneath them, a boy—barefoot, clad only in his underwear, wild as the forest itself, darted through the undergrowth with the grace of a wild animal, his heart pounding in sync with nature's own rhythm.

Twelve year old Jaggu was not an ordinary child. He was the jungle's own.

He ran, leaped, climbed, moved like a creature born of the wilderness.

Barefoot and agile, he streaked across the forest floor, his body moving with the same raw energy as the wild denizens he shared this world with.

His eyes gleamed with untamed curiosity as he crouched suddenly, pressing his palm against the damp earth. He inhaled deeply, his sharp nose picking up scents hidden from ordinary men. Then, with a practiced motion, he lifted a handful of dust, letting it slip through his fingers as he studied its weight and direction.

Nearby, four men stood watching him—his father, his father's elder brother and two Bavariya hunters, all gripping their rifles. They weren't here to admire the jungle's beauty. They were here for tiger.

But Jaggu wasn't thinking about the hunt. He moved like a whisper through the grass, his fingers tracing the outline of a massive pugmark left behind by the king of the forest. He

measured its length, brushing his fingertips over its edges, his mind racing through possibilities.

He moved from one sign to another—the broken grass, the scent of crushed herbs, the freshness of animal droppings. He sniffed the leaves, scanning the undergrowth with an intensity far beyond his years. Then, without a word, he sprinted forward, his small frame darting through the trees.

Like a leopard cub testing its limbs, he leaped, grasped the rough bark of a tree, and scrambled up, his muscles taut with energy. Perched high above, he scanned the distance, his eyes narrowing. He was looking for something, searching… tracking.

From below, the hunters watched in silence.

To them, he was just a boy—small, scrawny, half-naked.

But to the jungle, he was something else entirely.

And if the jungle had a soul, he would have paused to watch Jaggu in wonder.

And then Jaggu's breath hitched in his throat. His body tensed involuntarily. The memory was like a wound torn open afresh, dragging him into the past, to a time when he had first learned what a gunshot truly meant.

Back in the present, the scent of gunpowder still hung in the air.

Jaggu blinked.

The forest had changed.

The boy who once tracked animals with awe now tracked them for a different reason. The same instincts that once connected him to the wild were now used to betray it.

And as Harpal Singh lowered his smoking rifle, the Chinese guests let out a triumphant chuckle. Jaggu remained still, his jaw tightening.

Because deep inside, despite the years that had passed, one truth had never changed—

He was still listening to the jungle.

And the jungle was screaming.

Droplets of water slid from the fallen stag's coat, soaking into the earth. The scent of blood would soon spread, summoning scavengers from the shadows.......

Jaggu stood motionless, his eyes locked on the stag's lifeless body sprawled across the damp grass, but his mind was no longer in the present. The memories surged again, vivid and unstoppable.

The jungle of his childhood unfolded before his eyes.

Four men—lean, wiry, hardened by years of hunting—moved through the undergrowth with quiet precision. Their rifles slung over their shoulders, their eyes fixed ahead, they paid no attention to the wild, barefoot boy darting through the forest beside them.

But Jaggu was in his element.

He wasn't just running—he was reading. The forest spoke to him in whispers carried by the wind, in the crushed scent of disturbed leaves, in the faintest imprint of a paw against the earth. He climbed trees like a monkey, leaped down like a leopard, and sprinted ahead with unshaken certainty.

The men veered off in another direction, following their own instincts.

Jaggu stopped mid-run, his small chest heaving. He turned, his sharp eyes scanning the forest once more. Something wasn't right.

And then it hit him.

He whipped around and bolted back toward his father and Tauji. With a child's urgency, he skidded to a stop in front of them, arms outstretched, blocking their path.

"No! You're going the wrong way!"

His voice was firm, unquestioning. The certainty in his tone made even the seasoned hunters pause.

"The tiger isn't this way," he said, breathless but unwavering. "It's on the other side. Follow me."

The men almost laughed at Jaggu's audacity. One of them smirked and said, "Oh? So now this newly hatched chick will teach us how to track a tiger, huh?"

Tauji, his father's elder brother, turned sharply, his glare cutting through the amusement. "Listen, boy," he said, his voice laced with irritation. "Don't try to act like our grandfather. We've been doing this for decades. Just follow us."

Then, without another glance at Jaggu, he motioned to the others. "Chalo re. To the left."

But Jaggu wasn't done.

He lunged forward, grabbing the edge of Tauji's kurta, his small hands clutching the fabric with desperate insistence. "No, Tauji! You're wrong. Please, listen to me!"

Tauji shook him off with an impatient jerk. "Enough! We're wasting time." He turned away, leading the men deeper into the jungle.

As the men moved deeper into the forest, veering left, Jaggu stood frozen in place, his small hand still outstretched, pointing in the exact opposite direction. His eyes were wide with urgency, his lips parted as if to call out one last time—but no one was listening.

And then, just seconds later, the jungle proved him right.

From the dense undergrowth on the right side, exactly where Jaggu had been pointing, a massive male tiger emerged.

Silent, powerful. Its muscles rippled beneath its golden coat as it stepped out of the shadows, its amber eyes scanning the forest.

The great beast paused, locking eyes with the oblivious hunters who had gone the other way. For a fleeting moment, it watched them and then turned it's amber gaze at Jaggu, it's kindred spirit.

The group of Bavaria hunters were transfixed, not being able to believe their eyes, their years of experience crumbling in front of a young boy's forest instincts.

The tiger's tail flicked once. Then, unbothered, it continued on its path, vanishing into the depths of the jungle.

Jaggu remained still, watching the tiger disappear, his heart pounding—not in fear, but in the quiet, electric thrill of knowing the forest had spoken through him.

Training sessions...

The forest lay still, golden shafts of morning light slicing through the canopy, casting a golden-green haze over the damp earth. The jungle was alive—parakeets screeched in the distance, langurs leaped from tree to tree, and the occasional rustle in the undergrowth hinted at unseen creatures moving through the foliage.

But within this wilderness, another group of creatures moved through the undergrowth—silent, calculated, predatory—men, rehearsing the art of the kill. They did not stumble over roots or snap twigs underfoot. Every movement was deliberate, precise, trained for the kill.

Jaggu led them, darting through the trees with feline grace, his body weaving effortlessly through the dense foliage, his lean but muscular frame making him appear more like a stalking beast than a man. "Faster!" he hissed, urging the others forward. The men mimicked his every move, their bodies low to the ground, their steps soundless. They leaped over fallen logs, rolled under branches, and blended with the shadows. Jaggu turned, his sharp eyes scanning them. "A tiger doesn't just run. It vanishes. Do it again!"

He demonstrated how to run soundlessly on all fours, to crouch low like a tiger in ambush, to creep through the underbrush without disturbing a single leaf. The recruits followed, their bare feet pressing against the soft forest floor, their breath controlled, their bodies molded into weapons of stealth.

A little farther off, in a clearing, Lakhan stood by a wooden post where a dummy tiger had been crudely fashioned out of straw and animal hide. His arms, thick and scarred, flexed as he raised a heavy wooden club. With one swift motion, he brought it crashing down on the dummy's skull. "This is how you kill without damaging the skin," he barked. He struck again. And again. At a certain angle. "Ten times for a full-grown male. Eight for a tigress. No mistakes." He said.

The recruits watched, their faces set in grim concentration. Lakhan stepped back, gesturing to a young man. "Your turn." The man stepped forward, gripping the club tightly. His first strike was weak.

Lakhan's glare cut through him like a blade. "The skull is thick. You hesitate, you fail." The man nodded, raised the club again, and struck harder. The dummy shook under the impact.

Jaggu looked away, his jaw tightening.

Lakhan now picked up a long spear, its tip gleaming in the sunlight. He motioned toward the dummy. "If the animal is still moving, if the club isn't enough, you drive this straight into its mouth. Through the throat into the brain. Quick. Precise. The skin stays untouched." He demonstrated, thrusting the spear into the dummy's mouth with force. "No bullet marks. No visible wounds. Just a clean skin, ready for the market."

At another spot in the jungle, Jaggu crouched down, running his fingers over the damp earth, his sharp eyes scanning the patterns of tracks pressed into the soil. The recruits gathered around, waiting for instruction.
Jaggu pointed at a set of large, round impressions. "Tell me. What is this?"

One of the men hesitated. "Tiger?"

Jaggu shook his head. "Look again. The shape, the depth, the bodyweight on the paw—this is a leopard. A tiger's pug marks are bigger, rounder, with no visible claws and deeper imprints because of more body weight. See the size? The spacing? The toes are more compact. Only an expert can distinguish the pugmark of a juvenile tiger from an adult leopard." He moved a few steps ahead, pointing at another track—elongated and sharp-edged. "And this?"

"Chital?" one of the new recruits guessed.

"Wrong." Jaggu smirked. "Chital hoof prints are smaller and more delicate. This is a sambar. See the deep imprint? A heavy animal. Strong legs. Walks with purpose."

He moved on, running his fingers over another set of prints, long and widely spaced. "And this?"

"Nilgai," one of the older men said confidently.

Jaggu nodded in approval. "Yes. Largest among the antelopes."

The men absorbed the lesson, their eyes darting between the tracks, their minds working to memorize each pattern.

Lakhan, watching from a distance, gave a slow nod. "Enough learning. Time to put that knowledge to use." He motioned toward the forest. "Go. Track something. Bring me proof."

The recruits scattered, their eyes now sharper, their senses attuned to the silent stories etched into the earth.

Beyond the training grounds, the rhythmic clang of a hammer echoed from the blacksmith's shop, a brutal symphony of death being crafted with precision. In a corner, half-assembled traps lay in rows, their twisted, cruel forms waiting to be deployed into the forest.

Inside the dimly lit inner room, the real tools of their trade were being forged. Sparks flew as the hammer crashed down on searing-hot iron. The blacksmith, his face slick with sweat, worked methodically, his hands shaping the deadly jaws of the infamous Bavaria jaw trap. The metal glowed red-hot in the furnace, taking shape under the pounding strikes while the teeth of the snare gleamed menacingly. Soon, they would be buried deep in the forest beneath dry leaves, waiting to snap shut on the leg of an unsuspecting tiger.

Back in the clearing, Lakhan gets into a mock wrestling match with Jaggu to display his supremacy to the rest of the gang and teach them moves.

But Jaggu makes him bite the dust with his agility and superior combat manoeuvres. After out performing Lakhan in the mock contest, Jaggu stood by, watching as the recruits repeated their drills with spears, clubs and knives.

A short distance away, another group of men was working with quiet efficiency. Armed with spades, they were digging a deep pit, nearly ten feet across. Once it was ready, they stretched a thin muslin cloth across the opening, lining it with dry leaves and twigs., ensuring it looked like solid ground.

"This is how you catch the cubs," one of the older poachers murmured, wiping sweat off his brow. "They follow their mother, step right in, and fall through. No mess, no chase. Just make the edges steep so that they can't clamber out."

Jaggu glanced at the finished pit, its mouth gaping like a silent predator, waiting for an unsuspecting victim. He had seen cubs fall into these traps before—small, frightened things, their wide eyes darting around in confusion, their tiny paws scraping helplessly at the dirt walls.

They wouldn't be killed like the adults. They were too valuable alive especially for the private zoos, collectors and illegal pet markets.

A short distance away, Chimta, a wiry man with calloused hands, demonstrated another technique. He held up a thin but deadly wire—bike clutch wire, stripped from stolen motorcycles. With practiced ease, he fashioned it into a loop, twisting and securing it in place.

"This is how you catch deer," Chimta said. "A snare like this can instantly trap most kinds efficiently. You place it along a game trail, where the animal is bound to step. The moment it does—" He yanked the wire sharply. "—it tightens. No escape."

He handed the wire to a younger recruit, guiding his hands as he shaped another snare. "You learn this well, and you'll never go hungry in the jungle."

The training continued. The men moved through the jungle like shadows, their bodies honed for silence, their minds trained for the hunt.

No hesitation, no mistakes. By the time they were done, they would be ready—ready to become the deadliest predators of the wild.

The forest absorbed their movements, the wind carried their whispers, and the river beyond flowed as it always had—unaware that its lands were being turned into a battleground for man's greed and the wild's survival.

The wildlife researcher...

The sun cast long, golden fingers through the dense canopy of the deciduous forest, illuminating the riverine terrain along the Dheel River. A man in his mid-thirties moved with quiet precision through the undergrowth, his sharp eyes scanning the landscape. Jayant Ghosh, a wildlife researcher, adjusted the strap of his backpack, which was filled with camera traps, batteries, and notepads filled with meticulous observations.

He crouched near a game trail—one well-worn by the passage of predators and prey alike. With practiced ease, he secured a camera trap to a sturdy tree trunk, ensuring the lens faced an opening between rocks where signs of movement had been spotted earlier. His fingers worked quickly, checking the alignment and activating the sensor. Satisfied, he stepped back and surveyed his placement before moving to the next location.

Hours later, within the forewalls of his little office room, Jayant retrieved the memory cards from several traps and inserted them into his rugged laptop one by one.

A smile broke across his face as the screen filled with images—tigers slinking through the night, a sloth bear sniffing the air, wild boars foraging in the damp soil. Chinkaras and blackbucks grazing on the dry grass, while smaller and rarer feline species—rusty spotted cats and caracals —prowling in moonlight.

Jayant also managed to capture some co-predators of the region like the dens of the elusive Indian Gray Wolf and Striped Hyenas especially around the mudbanks and dry riverbeds.

It was a rich, thriving ecosystem with enormous biodiversity, and he had solid scientific evidence to justify his mission: pushing for the area's conversion into a protected tiger reserve.

Jayant's work, however, was not limited to data collection. He believed that conservation required the involvement of the local communities. The next day, he walked into a small village near the forest's edge, carrying laminated charts of different animals.

The morning sun bathed the Kela Devi forest in golden hues as Jayant Ghosh walked briskly toward the village school, his backpack slung over one shoulder. Inside, a group of eager children sat cross-legged on the floor, waiting for his lesson. Their teacher, an elderly man with kind eyes, gave Jayant a welcoming nod.

Jayant unrolled a large laminated chart and pinned it to the blackboard. "Today, we're going to talk about something very special—wild animals and their footprints."

The children leaned in with curiosity as he pointed to the first image. "This is a tiger's footprint. Notice how the toes look? Flatter, right?"

The kids nodded.

"Now, look at this one," he continued, pointing to another track. "This is a tigress's footprint. Can anyone spot the difference?"

A young boy at the front hesitated before raising his hand. "The toes… they look sharper?"

"Exactly!" Jayant smiled. "The tigress's footprint has more pointed fingers, while the male tiger's are broader and flatter. These little details help us track them in the wild."

The students murmured in amazement as he flipped to another section of the chart.

"But did you know that tigers and leopards are more than just kings of the jungle?" he asked, looking around. "They tell us how healthy our rivers are."

The children exchanged puzzled glances.

"Tigers need vast undisturbed forests to survive and these forests are like sponges which soak up extra rain water. These forests which are like huge underground lakes, later release the same water in trickles throughout the year. These trickles join to form streams and tributaries. This is the planet's natural way of conserving precious freshwater." Jayant explained. "In simple words, most of the mighty rivers of Bharat flow out of forests guarded by tigers and leopards."

The children nodded in unison, their young minds absorbing the connection between wildlife and their own lives.

After the lesson, Jayant walked outside to the fringe of the forest with a few of the older students, pointing to the dusty ground.

"See that track?" he asked. "That's from a chowsingha—a rare species called four-horned antelope. And over there, those crescent-shaped prints? Those belong to a wild boar."

The students crouched, studying the prints closely.

"Learning to read the forest is like learning a language," Jayant explained. "The more you observe, the better you can protect these animals."

The villagers listened intently as he spoke about the importance of the forest and its inhabitants.

"The tiger is an ancient warrior, the guardian of our freshwater, fertility and clean air. The vahana of goddess Durga which protects virtue and destroys evil." he said with conviction.

As he packed up his charts and waved goodbye, Jayant knew that the seeds of awareness had been planted. These children, growing up at the edge of the forest, would one day become its protectors.

Van Devi...

The ancient banyan tree stood tall and sprawling on the banks of the Dheel, its massive gnarled roots gripping the earth like fingers holding onto something sacred, it's branches like the veins of the forest itself, its thick, leafy foliage providing a canopy of shade. Beneath it stood the crumbling yet revered temple of Vandevi, the goddess of the forest. The Dheel river flowed gently nearby, its waters reflecting the golden hues of the setting sun. Today was the puja of Vandevi, a day when the villagers—her true devotees—gathered from far and wide to seek her blessings.

Men, women, and children filled the temple courtyard, their voices murmuring prayers as they placed offerings of fruits, rice, and marigold garlands before the deity. The women, clad in vibrant leheriya and bandhani sarees of Rajasthan and Madhya Pradesh, had their heads modestly covered with their odhni. Their silver jewelry glinted in the dappled sunlight filtering through the banyan leaves. The older men, dressed in dhoti-kurta, sat in small groups, their weathered faces marked with wisdom and concern.

Away from the main ceremonial gathering, under a shaded alcove near the temple, Jayant Ghosh sat cross-legged on a charpoy, deep in conversation with Gram Pradhan Ramdayal. The village elder, a man in his sixties with a thick white mustache and piercing eyes, listened intently as Jayant spoke.

"The builders and the mining mafia are closing in, Pradhanji," Jayant said, his voice low but urgent. "They want to rip this land apart. They have already made deals with corrupt politicians like Raju Bhaiya. If we don't resist, this entire forest—the home of Vandevi—will be gone."

"Raju Bhaiya," muttered one of the elders. "That man has never cared for this land. He only cares for money." By now, villagers

from far and wide had gathered, their expressions a mix of curiosity and concern. Jayant rose to address them. His eyes, sharp and determined, scanned the crowd. Unbeknownst to him, Hanif's assistant, Mohsin, a thin, sharp-featured bearded man with calculating eyes, stood among the villagers, blending in. He listened intently, his fists clenched, his eyes burning with concealed anger.

The air smelled of burning camphor, incense and marigold flowers, but the real fire was in the words of Jayant Ghosh.

"If a dam is built across this river," he said, pointing toward the gently flowing Dheel, "this land will drown. The forests, the fields, the villages—everything will disappear beneath the water."

A few older villagers exchanged worried glances. They had seen this pattern before, in other parts of the country.

"But that's not the only disaster," Jayant continued. "Once the dam is built, the river downstream will start drying up. And when that happens, the mining mafia will take over. They will strip the dried riverbed, mining stones, white sand, and minerals—filling their pockets while we are left with nothing. Our forests will be destroyed, and our lands will become barren."

A hush spread among the listeners who had gathered around them—elders, farmers, herders, and young boys who had stopped in their tracks, drawn by the serious discussion.

"These small rivers—rivers like the Dheel—they don't have enough water to generate real hydroelectric power," Jayant went on. "Yet, these corrupt politicians push these dam projects forward. Why? Because of big kickbacks from builders. Chinese kickbacks. They don't care about our forests. They don't care about our rivers. They only care about their own profits."

Some of the women, holding brass kalash filled with water for the rituals, exchanged worried glances. Hanif's assistant's face darkened. His jaw tightened. He had to inform Hanif about this interference—this Jayant Ghosh was stirring up trouble.

One of the younger men, his face dark with anger, clenched his fists. "And they call it development! What development? The moment the mining starts, our wells will dry up. Our fields will turn to dust."

The Gram Pradhan exhaled deeply, staring at the temple. "Vandevi has protected this forest for centuries," he murmured. "If the Gods abandon us, who will save our land?"

Jayant placed a firm hand on the old man's shoulder. "We will. But we have to act now. We must stand against them before it's too late."

The villagers listened with rapt attention, their hearts stirred. The puja bells rang in the distance, their chimes blending with the rustling of the banyan leaves—a silent prayer from the forest itself.

The bridge on the river Dheel...

The Dheel River shimmered under the scorching midday sun, its murky waters incandescent. The narrow British-era bridge stretched across the river, its old iron railings rusted by time, its wood and stones worn smooth by decades of monsoons.

Jayant Ghosh knew this bridge well. He crossed it every day, heading into the dense riverine forest beyond. But today, something was different.

A warm breeze carried the scent of wet earth and distant foliage, ruffling the surface of the river. Below, in the shimmering depths, a sudden splash—sharp and quick—disturbed the stillness. The unmistakable sound of a large fish being ambushed by a crocodile echoed against the stone of the bridge. Just above the gleaming waters, sinister eyes and snouts of crocodiles sometimes broke the surface, patrolling the slow-moving tributary, silent predators lurking beneath the current.

At the center of the bridge, Jaggu stood waiting. His posture was relaxed, his hands tucked behind his back, but there was an unnatural patience in his stance. His sharp eyes flickered with quiet intent as he watched the road ahead.

Lakhan and Chimta were also there—but unseen. They crouched in the thick brush near the entrance of the bridge, their figures merging with the shadows of the undergrowth. Jaggu was the bait. They were the ambush.

Then, in the distance, a low murmur—steady, growing louder.

The distinct purr of a motorcycle engine echoed across the riverbanks. Jayant Ghosh was approaching.

His dust-covered bike emerged from the forest road, kicking up gravel as it neared the bridge. The moment he entered the bridge and reached its middle, Jaggu stepped forward—his hand rising in a casual wave, signaling him to stop.

Jayant instinctively slowed down. The old bridge was narrow. There was nowhere to go but forward or back.

He looked ahead at Jaggu, standing with an unreadable expression, the faintest trace of urgency in his eyes.

Jaggu stepped forward, hands raised slightly—not in aggression, but in an appeal.

“Brother, whether you consider me your enemy or friend, I don’t care. But I have come in peace. I mean no harm.” His voice carried an unusual sincerity. "Meri baat sun lena (please listen to me). I don’t want anything bad to happen to you."

Jayant’s brows furrowed. He didn’t trust a man like Jaggu, a Bavaria tracker whose reputation was stained with blood and shadows.

Jaggu took a step closer. “Stop provoking the villagers—especially against the dam project. Your life is in danger. I’ve come here to warn you.”

Jayant’s temper flared. His hands tightened around the handlebars before he abruptly kicked the stand down and swung his leg off the bike. He walked straight up to Jaggu, closing the distance between them, his eyes blazing with defiance.

With one swift motion, he shoved Jaggu back.

“What?” Jayant’s voice was sharp, fearless. “Are you trying to intimidate me? You think you can scare me?”

Jaggu staggered slightly but did not retaliate. He had no intention of fighting Jayant.

Jayant took another step forward, his voice cold. "Do you even know who I am? I am not scared of anything. I walk these forests alone. I am not scared of the big cats that prowl these lands—do you think I will be scared of you? A small time poacher?

A coward who helps hunt voiceless animals ?"

He could see the faint hesitation in Jaggu’s posture, but he wasn’t going to let this moment pass without reminding him of his past.

“I think your blood is boiling too much, Jaggu.” Jayant’s voice was ice-cold, measured. “Do you have a short memory? Or should I remind you?”

Jaggu's jaw tightened, but he stayed silent.

Jayant took a step closer. "Have you forgotten when you got caught in my camera trap with a firearm? When I had you sent to prison?" His words were laced with quiet triumph. "Do you want to go back there?"

Jaggu still didn't answer. In the shadows, Lakhan and Chimta exchanged a glance.

They had been watching, waiting. And now, as Jayant pushed harder, they seized the moment.

Jayant threatens, " You want to go in ? Again ?"

From the dark edges of the bridge, Lakhan and Chimta emerged.

Before Jayant could react, rough hands grabbed him from both sides. His arms were twisted back with force, and a sudden wave of pain shot through his shoulders.

They mock him by repeating," We want to go in. Take us. Take us now strong man" They giggle maliciously.

Jayant struggled, but Lakhan's grip was like iron. Chimta's hold was unyielding.

They shoved him toward the edge of the bridge, pressing him against the old iron railing. Jayant gritted his teeth and tried to resist, but the two men were stronger than he had anticipated.

Lakhan leaned in close, his breath heavy with the scent of bidis and sweat. "You've been barking too much, Ghosh. It's time someone shut you up."

Jayant struggled, his muscles straining against Lakhan and Chimta's crushing grip, but it was futile. They were too strong. A dull ache burned in his shoulders as they lifted him off the ground.

The world tilted.

He barely had time to react before he felt the cold railing dig into his ribs. And then— his body lurched forward.

Half of him now dangled over the river.

Below, the Dheel River shimmered under the afternoon sun, deceptively serene. But the surface rippled unnaturally—dark, scaly figures shifted just beneath the water.

Jayant gasped, his hands clawing at the air, his legs kicking against the stone.

"Leave me! Let me go!" His voice broke into panic as he tried to wriggle free, but Lakhan and Chimta held him like a vice.

Lakhan chuckled darkly. "Look down, Ghosh. Your friends are waiting."

A couple of large muggers (freshwater crocodiles) surfaced, their armored snouts breaking the water. Their cold, unblinking eyes fixed on the struggling man above, as if they understood what was coming. One of them slowly opened its jaws— rows of yellowed, jagged teeth glistening in the sunlight.

Jayant's stomach churned. He could smell the rancid, damp stench of the reptile's breath.

Lakhan leaned in, his voice a low growl. "See those jaws? They're ready to swallow all your precious proofs. All your hard work—your camera traps, your photos, your reports—they will go down their bellies. No one will ever find a trace." He laughed cruelly. "Not even of you."

Jayant thrashed wildly. "You bastards—"

"Stop struggling." Lakhan's grip tightened as he shoved Jayant lower, closer to the gaping jaws. The crocodile let out a guttural hiss, shifting beneath the bridge, anticipating its meal.

Lakhan's voice turned to a whisper, dangerously calm. "Shall I let go? Should I throw you down?"

Jayant's breath came in ragged gasps. His heart pounded in his ears.

And then—

A voice. A scream.

"Jayant ji!"

The cry sliced through the tense air like a blade.

Lakhan and Chimta stiffened, their heads snapping toward the sound.

Down the winding road, running at full speed, was Janhvi.

Her hair flew wildly behind her, her sandals barely touching the ground as she sprinted towards them, her face etched with desperation.

Even from a distance, they could hear her frantic breath. "Stop! Let him go!"

For the first time, Lakhan hesitated.

Jayant twisted his head just enough to see her— her figure growing larger as she ran, unafraid.

Jaggu, who had been standing quietly, suddenly stepped forward. His instincts flared— he moved swiftly, catching Janhvi before she could throw herself at them.

The moment stretched, thick with tension.

The crocodiles floated below, the men stood frozen on the bridge, and Janhvi's voice echoed through the jungle.

"Jaggu, what are you doing? What are you all doing?" Janhvi cried out, her voice trembling between terror and determination as she reached Jaggu on the bridge.

Jaggu's eyes darted around, trying to shield her from the chaos unfolding. "Nothing, nothing," he replied curtly. "Just stay silent. Don't get involved in this."

"But what are you doing? What are you doing to Jayant ji?" Janhvi persisted, her words laced with desperation as she strained to see through the tense standoff.

Jaggu tried to deflect her questions, his tone strained. "It's nothing—just nothing. Please, Janhvi, don't—" He trailed off, attempting to control her involvement, his focus divided between her and the threatening presence of Lakhan and Chimta.

Before Jaggu could further dissuade her, Lakhan and Chimta, their grip still unyielding, finally hauled Jayant Ghosh back onto the bridge. Lakhan's voice dropped to a dangerous murmur as he glared down at Jayant. "Run..Get out quickly, before I change my mind," he threatened in rough, colloquial tones that echoed with menace.

Bruised and battered, Jayant staggered to his bike. His eyes burned with a mix of defiance and pain as he fumbled with the ignition. Finally, the engine roared to life. "You really think you can stop me?" he spat, his voice trembling with adrenaline. "I walk with tigers . I'm not scared of filthy rats."

The words hung in the heavy air as Jayant sped off, leaving behind a bridge still echoing with the tension of that confrontation, while Jaggu forces Janhvi to leave with him leaving the lecherous duo behind.

Face Off...

Later that night, as the moon hid behind the rugged cliffs surrounding Janhvi's house, a heated exchange unfolded in the quiet darkness. In the cool solitude of a small courtyard, the leaves of the tulsi plant quivered in the night breeze. Jaggu and Janhvi faced each other, voices low but laced with fierce emotion.

"What is your problem with Jayant Ghosh?" Janhvi demanded, her tone both angry and protective. "He's a good man." Jaggu repliied in a sympathetic tone, "I was only trying to explain—with all the love in my heart—that he should stay out of these dangerous affairs. He should not provoke the villagers about the dam project. But you know how it is—these educated, big people never listen to uneducated folks like us. They treat us like nothing more than flies and mosquitoes."

Janhvi's eyes blazed as she continued, "No, what you're saying is wrong. Jayant Ghosh is dedicated. He's working for a cause—for the villagers, for nature. Everything he does is for our own good, Jaggu."

Jaggu's face hardened in response. "These people do nothing but run an NGO in the name of saving the environment," he spat bitterly. "They scoop up international funds and live lives of splendor and opulence. We, simple villagers, are cheated time and again. The whole world pays them under the guise of tiger and leopard conservation, and what do they do? They fly club class in airplanes, attend highfalutin conferences, fool people like us with their fancy words and sell our misery to the world at a premium price."

Jaggu's voice softened with a mix of frustration and sorrow as he countered, "Don't be fooled by their tricks and their smart words." he paused. Jahnvi's fierce gaze suddenly drifted into the distance as if recalling a memory. "And tell me, what would have happened that night, two years ago, if Jayant hadn't appeared on the scene?"

The question hung in the air, heavy with unspoken implications and the dark night seemed to listen, bearing silent witness to their passionate debate.

Janhvi's voice trembled with a mix of rage and disbelief as she took a step closer to Jaggu, her eyes burning with hurt.

"Have you forgotten that night, Jaggu?" she demanded, her voice rising. "Two years ago, that fateful night when I was returning from a night program at someone's house? Don't you remember? I was surrounded by Lakhan and his drunken chamchas—his filthy, disgusting friends. They blocked my way on the road, teased me mercilessly, hurled the most vile words at me. They grabbed my hands, they pulled my dupatta away." Her voice broke for a second, but she swallowed hard and continued, her hands clenched into fists.

"It was by sheer chance that Jayant Ghosh happened to be passing by on his bike. He could have ignored it, ridden away like most men would. But he didn't. He stopped. He got off his bike and stood up to them—alone. He fought them, Jaggu. Yes, he got badly bruised, he bled, but he saved me." Her breath came in ragged bursts now, her anger overflowing.

"Do you understand what I'm saying, Jaggu? I would have been raped that night. Raped! If not for Jayant ji! And today, this is what you're doing to that man?"

Jaggu's face twitched, but he said nothing, looking away.

Janhvi's words sliced through the silence like a blade. The night air, thick with the scent of dust and distant river water, held its breath. A lone jackal yelped somewhere in the darkness, the only sound in the charged stillness between them.

Her voice softened as she stepped closer to Jaggu, her fingers trembling as she reached for him. She pulled him into her arms, pressing his head gently against her shoulder. "Jaggu, my Jaggu," she whispered, her breath warm against his ear. "Please listen."

Jaggu stiffened, then abruptly shrugged her away, his face dark with frustration. "Listen to me, Janhvi," he said, his voice low but firm. "If this man doesn't stop provoking the villagers and instigating them against the dam project, he's a dead man. I'm telling you very seriously—these are dangerous people. There's a lot at stake, a lot of money involved. Even if I try my hardest, I won't be able to save him."

Janhvi's heart pounded. She stepped forward again, refusing to let him turn away. Wrapping her arms around his neck, she pulled him close to her bosom, her fingers running through his hair. "Please, Jaggu," she murmured, her voice pleading. "Save him. You're my hero, Jaggu. You can do anything. He's a good man. For me—spare him." Her lips brushed against his cheek in a passionate kiss, lingering, warm, full of unspoken emotions.

Jaggu took a deep, shuddering breath, his hands resting on her waist. He exhaled slowly, his resolve wavering. "Oh," he muttered, shaking his head with a half-smile, "this is what you do. I know... You are the source of all my weaknesses."

He cupped Janhvi's face gently in his calloused hands and kissed her forehead, his lips lingering there, as if imprinting a silent promise.

Above them, the silent night stretched endlessly, the stars shimmering over the dark cliffs, bearing witness to their moment. The night breeze murmured in the distance, carrying secrets through the dark ravines of the untamed deccan, lost in the eternal flow of time.

Khabar...

The night was alive around the DFO's residential bungalow in the forest department compound, wrapped in the dense, breathing canopy of Kaziranga. The calls of nocturnal creatures filled the air—some near, some distant. The rhythmic, almost eerie song of the jungle nightjars echoed across the trees, joined intermittently by the melancholic notes of the brown boobook.

Amidst this wild orchestra, a shadow detached itself from the darkness and approached the gates of the DFO's bungalow. The dim light of a lantern by the gatepost barely revealed his features hidden by a gamcha (Indian towel). His steps were cautious but determined.

The forest guard on duty stepped forward, gripping his rifle. "Ruko Kaun ho?" (Stop, who are you?)

The man spoke in a hushed yet urgent voice. "I have special permissions to meet DFO Sahab. It's urgent. Right now."

The guard frowned. " Sir is having dinner. What could be so urgent at this hour?"

The man glanced over his shoulder, as if making sure no one had followed him. "Go and ask him. Tell him Guldaar is here." (Meaning leopard in Indian dialect. Code name used by the informer.)

Hearing the name, the guard hesiated for a moment, then turned and walked toward the bungalow.

Inside, Amit Verma sat at his wooden dining table, his meal of dal, rice, and sabzi untouched. His thoughts were elsewhere—his mind preoccupied with the growing threat of poaching in Kaziranga.

The orderly entered and spoke hesitantly. "Sir, Guldaar is here. He wants to meet you at this hour. I declined several times but he is hell bent .Says it's very important and he has some special permission."

Verma stiffened. Ripan coming at this hour? That could only mean trouble.

He wiped his hands with a napkin and got up. "Bring him in.. Immediately."

The guard signaled to Ripan, who quickly stepped into the verandah of the bungalow. The hanging lantern above them flickered in the breeze, casting shifting shadows on the wooden floor.

Amit Verma studied him closely. "What is it, Ripan? Why have you come so late?

Ripan swallowed hard. His face was lined with worry, his voice urgent.

"Sir, Bhudev Barua..."

He paused, glancing around nervously, before continuing in a whisper. What he was about to reveal could change everything.

Amit Verma eyed Ripan warily before glancing toward the bungalow's dimly lit interiors. He didn't want this conversation to take place inside. Too many ears. Too many risks.

Without a word, he stepped off the verandah, motioning for Ripan to follow him. They moved into the dark courtyard, away from the glow of the lantern, into the shadows where the jungle murmured in the night.

From a distance, their silhouettes are shrouded in mist—a quiet but intense conversation unfolding between the two figures in the dark. The DFO listened intently as Ripan spoke in hurried, hushed tones. His hands moved urgently, sometimes pointing into the distance. The jungle sounds swallowed their words, but the tension between them was clear.

Verma's face darkened as he processed the information, his jaw tightening. Without a word, he reached into his pocket, pulled out his mobile phone and made a couple of quick calls, his voice low but firm. Whatever was being set into motion, it needed to happen fast.

A few tense minutes later, the distant rumble of engines broke through the night's stillness.

From the far end of the dirt road, two forest jeeps roared into view, their headlights slicing through the dark. Behind them, a local police vehicle followed closely, its red beacon flashing in silence.

The convoy came to a halt outside Verma's gate. Armed forest guards jumped out first, rifles slung over their shoulders, followed by the local police personnel, their uniforms blending into the night. The air grew thick with urgency.

Without hesitation, Amit Verma placed his service revolver in its holster and strode toward his jeep. His rifle guard and driver were already in position. Ripan, keeping his face covered with his gamcha, quickly slipped into the vehicle beside him.

The jeep's engine revved, and in the next instant, it sped off into the night, kicking up a trail of dust behind it.

The police car followed, its headlights bouncing over the uneven terrain. The second forest department jeep, packed with more guards, brought up the rear.

The jungle had witnessed their departure. Now, only the dust swirled where they had stood moments ago.

Hunting down the hunter...

The convoy of jeeps rumbled through the dirt road, their headlights slicing through the dense forest. Suddenly, a herd of cheetal deer, startled by the roar of the approaching vehicles, leapt from the left side of the road, their sleek bodies illuminated for a fleeting moment before they disappeared into the dark foliage on the other side. The forest seemed to hold its breath for a moment before returning to its nocturnal rhythm.

In the first jeep, Amit Verma sat beside the driver, his phone pressed to his ear, his voice sharp and urgent. In the back seat, Ripan leaned forward, his face partially hidden in the shadows, his voice tense as he gave directions—"Right! Now left! Keep going straight! Take the next turn right!" He knew exactly where they needed to go, his words guiding them through the labyrinth of forest paths.

A forest guard, gripping his rifle, turned toward Verma and muttered, "The villagers always said this man never buys meat from the market. He only eats what he hunts. And at night, he sets up a naked electric fence around his fields. Any animal that comes near—gone. Electrocution is nothing new for him."

Amit Verma's eyes darkened. The night ahead promised no mercy.

On the informer's cue, the three jeeps rolled to a stop at the edge of a beautiful moonlit glade, where the dense forest opened up into a clearing. The night hung thick and heavy, the air alive with the soft flicker of fireflies drifting lazily above the grass. A distant alarm call of a sambar deer rang out—sharp, urgent.

Ripan, his face tense in the dim light, quickly raised a finger to his lips, signaling silence. Immediately DFO Verma commanded the men to kill the engines and switch off the headlights. One by one,

the jeeps went dark, their presence melting into the shadows. For about twenty minutes, the convoy waited in breathless stillness, the silence broken only by the rustle of leaves and the distant croaking of frogs.

Then—a sound.

A faint, scraping noise, followed by the unmistakable grunt of effort. In the darkness, figures dragging something heavy through the grass. A muffled curse. A twig snapping.

Amit Verma's hand shot up, signaling his men through walkie-talkies commands. In a single motion, the three jeeps roared back to life, their floodlights bursting into brilliance. The clearing exploded in harsh white light, tearing the shadows apart.

There, caught like cornered animals, stood two men—one heavily built, wearing a loose shirt, the other lean and wiry, both blinking furiously, their faces twisted in shock. They were dragging the body of a freshly killed sambar deer, its lifeless eyes glinting in the artificial light. The streaks of blood on the grass showed they had only just started hauling it away.

Amit Verma leaped out of the jeep, his voice booming through the glade.

"Stop! Don't move! Drop your weapons!"

The forest guards and police officers surged forward, their rifles aimed, fingers tight on the triggers.

For a fraction of a second, they were paralyzed—trapped like startled prey. Then, as if a switch had been flipped, their survival instinct kicked in. Bhudev Barua and his accomplice bolted.

They abandoned the sambar's body, its weight thudding onto the damp forest floor,

"Freeze! I will shoot! Don't take my words lightly—I never miss.", shouted Verma.

But the two poachers tore through the undergrowth, their feet pounding against the earth.

Leaves and twigs snapped beneath them as they plunged blindly into the trees, desperate to escape.

"Run!" Bhudev hissed. "Faster, you fool!"

But Amit Verma was already in pursuit, his pulse surging as he raced forward. Behind him, his men followed—rifles at the ready, voices shouting.

The chase was on.

Bhudev and his accomplice dodged between trees, their shoulders slamming into thick trunks, pushing through low-hanging branches that lashed at their skin. The sound of pursuit grew louder, closer—boots crunching, men yelling.

Up ahead, through the trees, the moonlight shimmered on water.

The river —they stumbled toward it, panting, eyes darting. If they could reach the river, they could wade across, disappear into the reeds.

But Amit Verma wasn't giving them that chance. "Stop now!" his voice rang out, echoing through the night. "This is your final warning!"

The poachers didn't listen.

Amit gritted his teeth, skidding to a halt. He raised his revolver, aimed—A shot cracked through the forest.

The bullet tore through Bhudev's right leg. He let out a guttural scream, his body crumpling as his injured leg buckled beneath him. His accomplice whirled in horror, hands raised in surrender, his chest heaving.

"Aaaah!" Bhudev howled, clutching his leg, writhing in agony on the damp earth. Blood seeped through his fingers, dark and sticky in the moonlight.Bhudev lay, gasping in pain, his face contorted in agony. Amit Verma loomed over Bhudev, his revolver still raised. His breath was steady, his eyes cold.

"The hunt is over," he said. "And this time, you're the prey."

Hospital...

The morning sun cast a pale glow over the hospital at Kohora, its whitewashed walls stained with time and humidity. Inside, the air smelled of disinfectant and damp cloth, mingling with the faint aroma of medicinal herbs brought in by visiting relatives. The corridor outside the patient ward was quiet, except for the occasional murmur of nurses and the rhythmic squeak of a stretcher wheel rolling past.

Behind a half-open door, Bhudev Barua lay on a rickety hospital bed, his face twisted in pain and rage. His right leg was suspended in the air, bound by white bandages, tied up with medical slings, and hoisted by a metal frame. His injury had swollen, the bullet wound cleaned but still throbbing with each beat of his pulse.

Outside his room, two uniformed police guards stood on duty, their rifles slung over their shoulders. They eyed every passerby with quiet suspicion.

From down the corridor, footsteps echoed—firm, purposeful.

DFO Amit Verma entered the hallway, his presence commanding. Walking beside him, three young figures moved hesitantly—Rajiv, Aamir, and Anya. Their eyes darted nervously toward the guarded room ahead.

"Is… is he inside?" Anya whispered, swallowing hard.

Mr. Verma nodded, his expression unreadable. He led them forward, his boots clicking against the cold floor. The three students followed, their fingers twitching with apprehension.

As they approached the door, the dull hum of a ceiling fan stirred the air, ruffling the loose strands of Anya's hair. Through the narrow, open gap in the door, they could see a figure lying motionless on the hospital bed.

The moment Rajiv's eyes fell on him, his breath hitched.

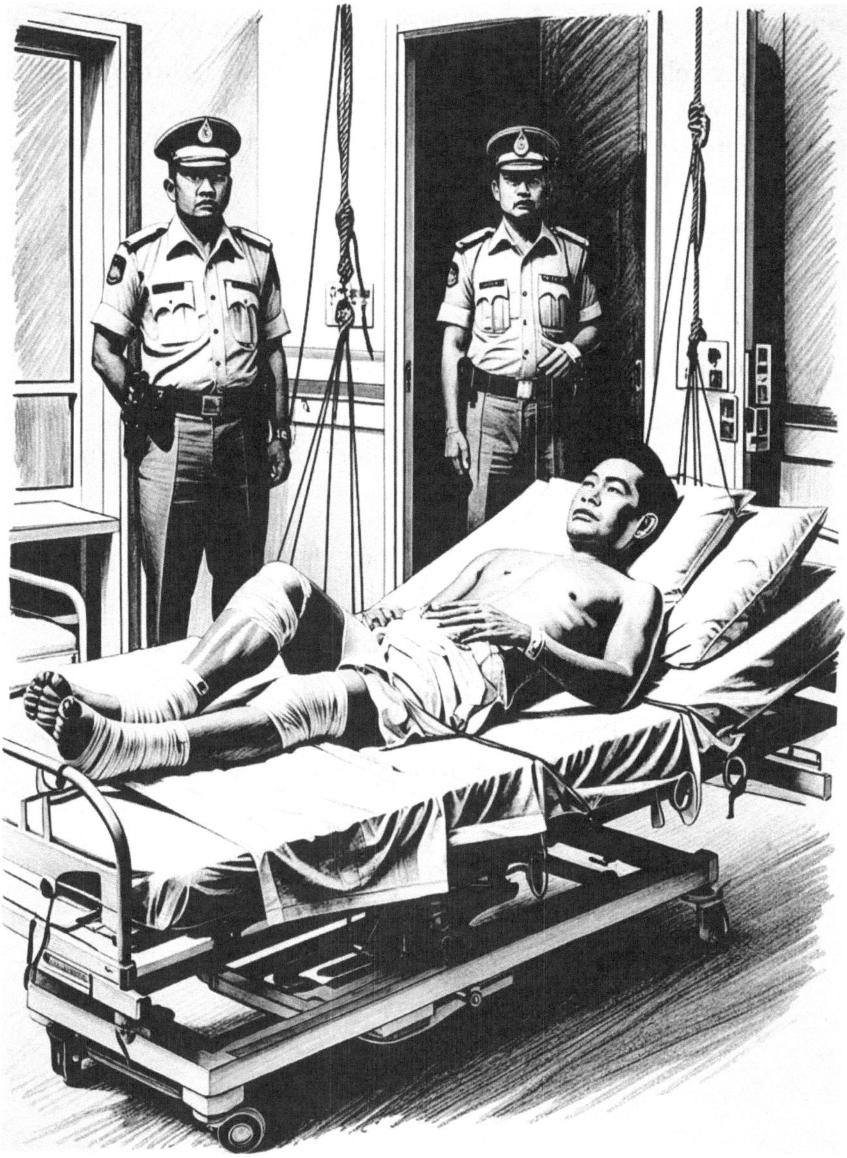

Aamir's hands curled into fists.

Nidhi grabbed Rajiv's arm, her voice barely a whisper. "Yes... yes, that's him," she said.

Rajiv nodded. "I'll never forget his face," he murmured.

Aamir's jaw clenched. "He was the one," he said through gritted teeth. "He was the one who chased us that evening... from the tiger poaching site. Luckily we got saved by the timely intervention of the elephant herd. Otherwise this man...."

Inside the room, a semi-conscious Bhudev stirred.

Perhaps it was the whispering voices, perhaps it was an eerie instinct, but his eyes fluttered open, glaring toward the doorway.

For a moment, his gaze locked onto the students.

Then, as recognition flickered in his expression, his eyes narrowed—sharp, dangerous, like a wounded predator backed into a corner.

A cold smirk ghosted his lips.

"So... you little brats think you've won?" he rasped, his voice hoarse but laced with venom.

The students stiffened, but Mr. Verma stepped forward, his presence like a wall between them and Bhudev.

"Your time is up, Bhudev Barua," he said, his voice calm, yet laced with quiet authority. "You're finished."

Shoot on sight...

The Bangladeshi basti was alive with the faint sounds of hushed conversations, the occasional clang of metal, and the distant barking of a stray dog. The air smelled of damp earth, burning wood, and the distinct tang of desi sharaab being passed around in chipped glasses. Inside a dimly lit shack made out of bamboo, Jaggu, Lakhan, Bhola, and Pratap were drinking with a few Bangladeshi poachers. Their faces were partially illuminated by a hanging bulb, some sitting on a wooden table and a few scattered around. A small canoe lay on one side, which was used by the rhino poachers to go from one island to another in pursuit of animals trapped in the flood waters of the Brahmaputra.

Ali glared at Lakhan, his voice low but sharp with insulted pride. “Where’s my commission, fellas? I’m the one who introduced you to Hasan Chacha and made it possible for your precious contraband to cross the damn border and reach your buyer in Nepal.”

He laughed bitterly, shaking his head. “Typical. Now your channel with Hasan Chacha is direct. You don’t need me anymore. When the job’s dirty, you need me. When the money flows, I vanish from your memories.”.”

Lakhan leaned back, stretching his legs, and let out a cynical laugh while deliberately changing the topic. "Now prepare to die, fellows. You and your rhino horn business. Huh! do you even understand what a shoot-on-sight order means?"

The men exchanged uneasy glances. One of them, a wiry Rohingya with a thick beard, sighed. "Brother, we’re not new to this trade. But now, entering the jungle is as good as walking into death."

An older Bangladeshi Azam, nursing his drink, grunted. "Whatever it is, the demand right now is at an all-time high. The price is skyrocketing across the border in Myanmar as some new buyers from Chinese mainland want rhino horns at any cost."A few of them nodded, but others shifted uncomfortably. One of the Bangladeshi men muttered, "The current Indian government is coming down hard on illegal immigrants. If we're caught, we won't get bail. We'll rot in the dungeons for years before being thrown back across the border. And now, they're tightening the noose on illegal voter IDs and Aadhaar cards. If they check our documents, we'll be easily identified."

The air grew heavy with their words. Jaggu, who had been silent until now, finally spoke, his voice low and deliberate. "Also, earlier the rangers weren't this alert. But now the Indian government has given a shoot-on-sight order in the jungle for rhino poachers. Farooq and Suleiman got shot at, didn't they?" His gaze flickered to motley group, as if challenging them.

Before they could reply, a loud commotion erupted outside. The hurried sound of footsteps grew closer. The next moment, Chimta burst into the shack, panting, his face slick with sweat.

"Oh God, he's been caught! He's been caught!"

The men straightened. Lakhan's eyes darkened. "What?"

"Bhudev! He's been shot in the leg! And at the hospital... the children have identified him!"

Jaggu clenched his jaw, exhaling sharply. His voice wavered slightly before he added in a low murmur, almost talking to himself. " We enraged the goddess of the forest. We went after a lactating mother.The curse of Vandevi is on us now. We are doomed. "

Lakhan's head snapped toward him, rage flashing in his eyes. He lunged forward, grabbing Jaggu by the collar and yanking him up.

"Shut up, you coward!" he spat. "Now I'll handle this myself."

Releasing Jaggu roughly, he turned to Chimta, his expression deadly serious.

“Chimta, listen,” Lakhan said in a tense whisper, eyes scanning the darkening tree line. “It's not safe here anymore. The kids—they've identified Barua. And if that idiot opens his mouth, the police will be sniffing around this hideout in no time."

He stepped closer, voice dropping further. "We need to move. Immediately. Tell the boys to pack up—no questions, no delays. And as for those pesky kids…"

Lakhan paused, his jaw clenched. "We'll have to deal with them first. Permanently. We can't risk them running around testifying against us, compromising everything we've built."

The kidnapping...

The night was alive with the crackling of the bonfire, casting flickering shadows on the towering trees that fringed the glade. The Brahmaputra flowed gently nearby, its waters glistening under the starlit sky. The students of St. Peter's School, on their nature camp, sat around the fire, enjoying a night of music, laughter, and storytelling. Someone strummed a guitar while a group of students hummed along, singing a song in reverence to the king of the Indian jungle—'Walk like a tiger, stalk like a tiger.'

Beyond the warm glow of the campfire, the forest loomed in darkness, silent yet watchful. The chuk-chuk-chuk-chuk call of jungle nightjars filled the air as two of them nimbly flitted past overhead, disappearing into the trees. Occasionally, the eerie, wavering scream of a mottled wood owl rang out from the surrounding forest, sending a brief hush over the smaller nocturnal sounds. The students, however, remained unaware of the lurking presence beyond their circle of light.

A shadow detached itself from the darkness, moving with practiced stealth. A pair of gleaming eyes surveyed the group, lingering on their faces before settling on one—Rajiv. The shadow melted back into the night, waiting for the right moment.

Rajiv finished his meal and, wiping his hands on a napkin, stood up. "I'll just wash up," he told no one in particular, stepping away from the group towards the small stream that trickled past the edge of the glade. The others, engrossed in their singing and conversation, paid no attention as he walked into the dimly lit wilderness. At the water's edge, he crouched to splash his face, the coolness refreshing against his skin. He cupped water in his hands, rinsed his mouth, and then straightened up — only to feel something rush at him from behind.

A strong arm wrapped around his chest, yanking him backward. Before he could cry out, a muslin cloth was pressed firmly over his nose and mouth. The sharp, sickly-sweet scent of chloroform filled his nostrils. He thrashed, his hands clawing at the attacker's grip, but his strength drained rapidly. His vision blurred. His body sagged. Two more shadows emerged from the trees. Without a word, they grabbed Rajiv's limp body, each holding an arm as the first attacker supported his legs. The three figures moved swiftly, dragging him into the dense forest, their movements drowned out by the sound of laughter and music from the bonfire.

Back at the camp, the students clapped and sang, their voices mingling with the jungle nightjar's calls. They had no idea that one of them had just vanished into the darkness. Ms. Aparna dusted off her hands after finishing her dinner and stood up, stretching slightly. The bonfire crackled gently, casting flickering patterns of light and shadow on the students gathered around. The guitar had quieted down, but murmurs of conversation and soft laughter still filled the air.

"Alright, everyone," she announced, her voice carrying over the glade. "Make sure you get to bed on time. Tomorrow morning at 5 a.m., we have yoga by the river, and I don't want anyone making excuses about being too tired. Understood?"

A few students groaned playfully, but most nodded, accustomed to her discipline. "Good night, everyone," she added and then glanced around the group. Her brow furrowed slightly. Something felt off. She scanned the students' faces, counting them instinctively. "Where is Rajiv?" she asked, her tone shifting from casual to mildly concerned. "I can't seem to find him."

The students exchanged glances, some shrugging. "He went to wash up by the stream," Aamir offered.

"That was a while ago," added Anya, looking towards the darkened forest beyond the campfire's reach. A chill crept into the air, not from the night breeze, but from the unspoken unease settling over them.

Highway to hell...

A long line of trucks stood still on National Highway No. 715, their engines rumbling in the darkness. The highway cut along the southern boundary of Kaziranga National Park, flanked by dense jungle on one side and open fields on the other. The night air was thick with humidity, laced with the distant calls of crickets and the occasional growl of an engine inching forward.

At a checkpoint up ahead, uniformed police officers moved methodically, inspecting each vehicle with torches, peering into the cabs, opening truck rears, and questioning drivers before waving them on. Flashlights flickered like fireflies in the night as trucks crept forward, one by one.

In the cabin of a truck with an MP number plate, Chimta sat beside the driver, his face impassive but his fingers nervously tapping his knee. The driver, a grizzled man with a beedi clamped between his teeth, stole a glance at him. "Relax," he muttered under his breath. "They won't find anything if you don't look guilty."

In the rear of the truck, hidden among sacks and crates, Bhola and Pratap lay flat on their backs, their faces covered with cloth to avoid unwanted attention. Between them, concealed beneath an old tarpaulin, was a large burlap sack. Inside it, Rajiv lay unconscious, bound and gagged, his breath shallow. The faint rustling of the sack was drowned out by the truck's idling engine and the hum of nearby vehicles. There were other sacks filled with grain and some potato crates thrown around randomly to confuse any onlooker.

As the truck edged closer to the checkpoint, tension thickened inside the cabin. Chimta wiped the sweat from his brow. "They're checking thoroughly," he muttered, watching the officers flash their torches into truck after truck.

"Let me handle it," the driver said, shifting gears as they finally rolled up to the checkpoint.

A cop raised his hand, signaling them to stop. "Where are you coming from?" the officer asked, stepping up to the cabin.

"From a rice mill in Nagaon," the driver replied smoothly. "Taking grain sacks to a godown in Jorhat."

The officer's flashlight moved over Chimta, lingering a second too long. "You don't look like a helper," he remarked, narrowing his eyes. "Step out, both of you."

Chimta's breath caught in his throat. But before the situation could escalate, Bhola, still hidden in the back, made a sudden move. He knocked over a small crate of potatoes, spilling them onto the road with a loud clatter.

"Hey! Watch it!" the driver yelled in exaggerated irritation, jumping down from the truck.

The officer turned, momentarily distracted by the rolling vegetables. "What the hell—"

"Sir, it's just food supplies," the driver interjected, pretending to scramble after the runaway potatoes. "We're already late on delivery!"

The officer hesitated, annoyed by the commotion. Another truck behind them honked impatiently. A second officer, growing tired of the delay, muttered, "Let them go, let's keep the line moving."

The first officer gave them a final glance, noted the number of the truck and finally waved them through. "Next time, keep your load secure." The driver quickly climbed back into the cabin, and the truck rumbled forward. Inside the cargo hold, Bhola and Pratap exchanged a look of relief as they repositioned the sack beneath the other baggage. The darkness swallowed them once more as the truck sped deeper into the night—taking Rajiv further away from any chance of rescue.

The interrogation...

The dimly lit chamber reeked of sweat and fear. A single, flickering bulb swayed slightly from the ceiling, casting eerie shadows on the damp concrete walls. Bhudev Barua hung from an iron hook, his wrists tied with thick ropes, his bare feet barely touching the ground. His body was bruised, his swollen face streaked with dried blood.

Divisional Forest Officer Amit Verma stood in the shadows, his sharp eyes fixed on the trembling man. Next to him, CID Inspector Hazarika adjusted his belt, his expression stone-cold. Two constables flanked the room, their hands resting on wooden batons, waiting for the next order.

Hazarika's voice was calm but razor-sharp. "You were at the tiger poaching site. You ran after the students. You know exactly where the Bavaria poachers—the tiger hunters from Central India—are hiding."

Bhudev's breath came in ragged gasps. His lips were cracked, his body trembling. "I don't know..." he croaked. "They keep moving... They don't stay in one place..."

A nod from the inspector. A constable stepped forward and delivered a brutal strike to Bhudev's ribs with a baton. A sickening crack filled the room. Bhudev howled in pain, his body jerking violently.

"Names!" Hazarika's voice rose, his patience thinning. "Who is giving them shelter? Who is helping them?"

Bhudev panted, his chest rising and falling in quick, shallow breaths.

"I don't know... I swear, I don't know—"

Another nod. Another strike. This time, across his thighs. The pain sent Bhudev into a fit of coughing. He gasped for air, his body trembling.

Amit Verma stepped forward, his voice eerily calm. "According to our information, you provided local knowledge about the movements of tigers and leopards of this area to the Bavaria poachers and helped facilitate that gruesome hunt of our tigress. You know exactly where these men are hiding."

Bhudev squeezed his eyes shut, shaking his head weakly.

"You want me to believe," Verma continued, "that you don't know who's sheltering them? Who's feeding them? Who is supplying them with weapons?"

Hazarika tilted his head. "Or should we assume that you're protecting them? That you are their handler?"

"She was a lactating mother of three healthy cubs, you imbecile.."Verma screamed.

"We lost four healthy tigers because of you...You slimy bloodthirsty parasite."

Bhudev's eyes snapped open in panic. "No, no, I swear! I am not their handler! They— they keep moving— they don't stay in one place!"

Verma's voice remained unwavering. "Who is helping them?"

Bhudev gulped, his breathing ragged. The pain, the exhaustion—it was too much. His resolve cracked.

"The Bangladeshi immigrants… They help them… They stay near the basti… But sometimes, they move to the river islands—"

"The Char islands?" Verma interjected.

"Yes… Yes… The Chars. The river islands in the Brahmaputra. They move there when things get risky… Hide in abandoned huts… But I don't know exactly where!"

Verma exchanged a glance with Hazarika. The chars—small shifting islands in the Brahmaputra—were notorious for harboring criminals. Difficult to patrol, constantly changing with the river's flow.

Hazarika's face hardened. "And who gives them food? Who supplies them with weapons?"

Bhudev swallowed hard. "A man named Majid… He's a Rohingya… He works with Hasan Chacha… He arranges everything. Food, weapons, fake IDs—"

Hazarika turned to one of the constables. "Write that down. We'll pick up Majid next."

Bhudev's head drooped. His body sagged in exhaustion, but the officers weren't done with him yet.

Amit Verma took a slow step forward, lowering his voice. "One last thing, Bhudev. What are they planning next? Another tiger? A rhino? Or something bigger?"

Bhudev hesitated. A sharp slap cracked across his face. Blood trickled from his split lip.

He gasped. "Rhino… Rhino horn… There's demand from Myanmar… They were talking about a hunt soon…The Brahmaputra flood plains."

Verma's eyes darkened. He turned to the inspector. "We need to move fast. When the floodwaters enter Kaziranga, many animals are forced to move out of the forest. That's when they become easy targets. I know some riverine islands where rhinos come out when the floodwaters rise. There aren't many forest guards there."

Bhudev whimpered. "Please… I told you everything… Let me go…" The inspector smirked. "We'll see about that." He gestured to the constables. "Call the doctors in. Take good care of him. We will have more questions later."

As they dragged Bhudev away, Amit Verma exhaled. The pieces were finally falling into place...

The Char islands...

The Brahmaputra stretched wide under the pale moonlight, its dark waters swirling around the scattered char islands—isolated, ever-shifting hideouts that had long shielded those who thrived in the shadows. Illegal immigrants, poachers, and traffickers had often made these islands their temporary hideout, operating fearlessly on the fringes of Kaziranga. But tonight was different. The law was coming for them.

A convoy of Assam Police jeeps, forest department jeeps, and immigration officers in SUVs moved in eerie silence along the dirt tracks leading to the settlement at the forest fringe. Their headlights were switched off, weapons primed. Inside the lead vehicle, Divisional Forest Officer Amit Verma sat stiffly, his face unreadable. Beside him, Inspector Hazarika checked his rifle.

"No mistakes tonight," the inspector muttered. "We take them all."

Verma gave a curt nod. Thanks to Bhudev Barua's brutal interrogation, they had every detail—the hideouts, supply routes, and key names.

A single red flare exploded in the night sky, painting the basti in a fiery glow.

"RAID!"

The night erupted into chaos as Assam Police, Forest Department officers, and immigration officials stormed into the illegal settlement. Officers kicked down doors, dragged out men, and tore apart the makeshift homes that had housed criminals for years.

"ID cards! Show your ID cards!" an immigration officer barked.

Fake Aadhaar cards, forged voter IDs, and counterfeit ration books were discovered hidden inside mattresses, buried in clay pots, or tucked inside walls.

FORST
FOREST
POLICE

Hundreds of illegal immigrants—many involved in poaching, smuggling, and other shadowy activities—were rounded up. Some screamed, some begged, but the officers were sharp and focussed.

A little further, deep in the chars, in the dimly lit interior of a rickety bamboo shack, Hasan Chacha—the lethal, old but sharp-witted poacher—sat on a rustic chair, counting crisp wads of currency under a flickering kerosene lamp surrounded by his strongmen Nabeel, Hameed, Jamil and Yunus .

Suddenly, Ali burst through the doorway, breathless, his one eye wide with terror. Hasan's loyal informer, the scrawny Rohingya man yelled, revealing his yellow rotten teeth.

"Chacha! Raid shuru ho gaya hai! Police main basti tak pahunch gayi hai!" (Chacha! The raid in on! The police have reached the main basti!)

For a second, everything froze. The men exchanged panicked glances.

"Move!" Hasan Chacha hissed, kicking over a wooden crate.

"Those bloody Bavarias have ruined us. We should have never helped them with their confounded tiger skin. Its all your fault Ali.", Hameed the burly Afghan shouted.

In seconds, some essentials and illegal weapons were thrown into sacks. Hasan Chacha grabbed a small metal box—likely stuffed with cash and fake identity documents—and shoved it into his satchel. The rest of their loot was left behind in haste.

"The back route!" Hasan snapped. "Across the swamp—into the river!"

The men sprinted into the darkness, ducking through a hidden exit behind the hut. They could hear the muffled bark of police orders echoing through the trees, drawing closer with each passing moment—boots crunching twigs, flashlights flickering between the undergrowth. The chase was no longer a possibility; it was right on their heels.

With the agility of men who had spent their lives evading the law, they plunged into the marshy undergrowth, moving swiftly through the reeds, heading toward the river's edge. In the distance, the first gunshot rang out, followed by screams.

They didn't look back.

Meanwhile as officials burst into Hasan's temporary dingy refuge near the forest's edge, a young constable let out a sharp cry.

"Sir! Rhino horns!"

In a dark corner, hidden under layers of burlap sacks, they uncovered four freshly cut rhino horns, their bases dark with dried blood.

In another shack, a horrific stash was uncovered—

Leopard skins stacked in piles, their once-majestic coats now stripped and lifeless, Sambar antlers, wild buffalo hooves, and Barasingha horns, bundled together for transport.

They also found endangered wild birds stuffed inside cages, their panicked fluttering echoing in the night.

Inside a wooden crate, the gruesome tools of poaching were found—Rusty wire snares, still holding tufts of animal fur and iron jaw traps, their spiked teeth coated in dried blood.

Additionally, the seizure of high-powered rifles, silencers, and night-vision scopes from the spot proved that these weren't mere hunters, but professional smugglers dealing in wildlife contraband as well as illegal weapons.

"These bastards weren't just poaching—they were running an entire illegal wildlife trade mafia operation!" an officer spat.

By dawn, over 200 illegal immigrants were arrested. Many would be deported—but the poachers, the traffickers—those would rot in prison.

The settlement lay in ruins.

Hasan Chacha and his key members had slipped away, but their hideouts, their weapons, and their entire network had been crushed. And one of his main operators - Majid had been arrested.

Amit Verma stood at the edge of the site, watching as the confiscated rhino horns and leopard skins were loaded into evidence trucks.

Despite the success of the raid, his face remained grim.

He turned to inspector Hazarika, his jaw tight. “We failed.”

The inspector looked at him, confused. “What do you mean? We shut down their entire operation. Hundreds of arrests. We found everything—horns, skins, weapons.”

Amit shook his head. “But not the Bavariya poachers. Not the smuggler Hasan chacha. Not the parts of the tigress. That tigress was from Kaziranga, and I needed that skin as raw evidence to build a watertight case in court.” His fists clenched. “Without it, they’ll just vanish and keep killing.”

Beside him, Inspector Hazarika lit a cigarette, exhaling slowly. “They ran this time.” He flicked the lighter shut. “But we have enough evidence in hand. And we have caught one of Hasan’s men, Majid.”

"Let's make this bird sing till he divulges everything."Amit chipped in, his gaze fixed on the distant treeline."I want to know where my tigress is headed for."

Breaking Majid...

The heavy iron door of the interrogation room swings open with a loud clang, and Majid is thrown inside like a ragdoll. He stumbles, barely catching his balance, his breath ragged. The stench of blood, sweat, and stale fear hangs thick in the dimly lit room. Next to him, Bhudev Barua lies groaning on a stretcher, his face swollen, his body a map of bruises and cuts.

A rough voice cuts through the silence. "Majid, last month, you killed a rhino and escaped with the horn. We have hard evidence." CID Inspector Hazarika, the tough man with a thick mustache, stepped forward. His hand gripped a sturdy wooden baton, and his eyes gleamed with a sadistic glint. "Now, will you talk, or should I turn you into a crumpled mess like your friend here?"

Majid's lips tremble, his head shaking frantically. "I... I don't know anything!" he stammers.

The inspector exhales impatiently before stepping toward Bhudev. With a deliberate motion, he presses the tip of his wooden baton into the bullet wound of Bhudev's leg.

Bhudev's entire body jerks as a scream erupts from his throat. "Aaaahhhh! Stop! Please!" Bhudev arched his back, his face contorted in unbearable agony. His body trembled violently, and his hands clutched the stretcher as if trying to escape his own pain.

Majid flinches, his breath coming in short gasps. His legs wobble.

From the shadows, Amit Verma steps into the dim light, his piercing gaze locking onto Majid's trembling form. He walks closer, his slow, deliberate steps echoing in the silence, his voice calm but razor-sharp. "Majid," he says smoothly, "I don't think you understand your position. If you want to leave this room in one piece, you will tell me where the rhino horns and tiger skins are going."

Majid looks around wildly, his body shaking. "I... I swear on my mother, I don't know!"

A sharp CRACK! splits the air. The inspector delivers a brutal slap to Majid's face, sending him staggering sideways. Blood trickles from his ear.

Majid wails. "Aaaah! " He clutches his ear, whimpering like a wounded animal.

Hazarika crouches before him and tosses a set of photographs on the cold floor—rhino horns, leopard skins, ungulate hooves, all seized from the raid. "This is your trade."

Then, a second set of photographs is dropped—AK-47 rifles, stacks of cartridges, and thick bundles of foreign currency. "But what about these?"

Majid's face drains of colour.

"You think we don't know?" the inspector growls, stepping closer. "This isn't just about poaching. This is funding terror groups. Who is your handler?"

Majid shivers violently. His lips quiver, but no words come out.

The inspector clenches his jaw and swings the baton—this time striking Majid's shin. "Aaaahhh!" Majid collapses to the floor, writhing in pain.

"If I talk, Hasan Chacha will kill me," he gasps, his forehead damp with sweat.

The inspector smirks coldly. "And if you don't, we will."

Majid opened his mouth to speak, but before a word could escape, a loud, resounding slap landed on his left ear.

THWACK! The impact is brutal. A sharp ringing fills Majid's skull, and his ear starts bleeding.

"Bol!" (Speak!)

Majid clutches his ear, his body shuddering from pain and terror. Tears stream down his dust-caked face.

He gulps and, finally, a broken whisper escapes his lips.

"They... they send the rhino horns west... to the border... into Nepal."

Amit Verma's eyes narrow. "Which crossing?"

Majid hesitates, his pulse hammering in his throat. "Birgunj. That's where the handoff happens."

"What about the eastern passage?" the inspector thunders.

Majid's breath hitches. His terrified eyes dart between the men in the room.

"Yes Sir, some stuff is sent to Moreh in Manipur and then onwards across the border to Tamu in Myanmar. Our Rohingya team handles the eastern operations whereas Hasan Chacha specialises in the Nepal route.", Majid stammers while divulging this.

Verma folds his arms, his stare boring into Majid's soul. Then, he shifts his gaze to Bhudev.

"And what about the Bavarias? The tiger hunters from Central India. Where have they gone?"

Bhudev groans, his body convulsing. "I... I don't know..."

The inspector growls and presses the baton deeper into his wound.

"Aaahhh! Please, Please, Stop!" Bhudev wails. His back arches off the stretcher, his fists clenching in agony.

Then as the inspector steps towards Majid, He suddenly blurts out in panic, his voice high-pitched, almost hysterical. "Yes! The Bavarias left in haste a few days back! They are trying to move the tiger skin and parts through the road routes to Kathmandu first with the help of Hasan Chacha, and eventually China! That's where the main buyers are!"

Amit Verma's voice remains eerily calm. "Who is the contact in Nepal?"

Majid's lips tremble. His eyes fill with dread. He knows what saying this name will mean for him. Seconds go by and he doesn't utter a word.

Suddenly Hazarika takes out his service pistol and places the muzzle on Majid's right knee. "A little squeeze on the trigger and your knee will be blown to smithereens." he laughed menacingly." Ask your dear friend Bhudev how it feels."

Majid looks momentarily at Bhudev Barua who lay next to him on a bloodstained stretcher, groaning in pain, his body wracked with fresh wounds. His half-open eyes flickered in terror. His leg, the one with the bullet wound, twitches involuntarily, fresh blood seeping through the bandages.

Majid's eyes go wide in sheer horror. His legs shake uncontrollably, and then, a dark patch spreads across his trousers—he wets himself in fear.

The stench of urine fills the room, but no one reacts. The officers had seen many men break in this room.

"A trader... Varad Praja. He owns a pet shop in Thamel Street, Kathmandu." he blurts out in panic. "O Allah please save me from the wrath of Hasan Chacha." he then mutters silently to himself.

Amit Verma's expression darkens. Varad Praja. The name had surfaced before—an elusive ghost in the wildlife trade, hidden in the chaotic backstreets of Kathmandu.

Verma turns to the inspector. "We have our lead. Now we have to activate interpol immediately. If that tiger skin leaves Kathmandu, it'll vanish into thin air."

The inspector nods grimly. The truth had been extracted. The secrets were out.

But the real hunt had just begun.

The kidnapper's lair..

Deep in the dusty, arid plains near the Madhya Pradesh-Rajasthan border, the poachers kept Rajiv confined in a dark, suffocating room—a makeshift kalkothri with walls of crumbling brick and a damp, earthy smell. The single bulb flickered dimly, casting long, shifting shadows that made the place even more unsettling.

Rajiv lay in a corner, groggy from exhaustion and dehydration. His hands were tied behind his back, his body sore from the rough journey in the truck. His mind reeled from the fear of the unknown—where was he, and what did these men want from him?

The burly ruffian of the gang with a thick mustache, Beera, squatted next to him, holding a dented steel plate with rice and some watery dal. "Eat," he grunted, shoving the plate toward Rajiv.

Rajiv turned his face away, his stomach churning with nausea rather than hunger. His lips were cracked, his throat dry, but he refused to touch the food.

"I said eat!" Beera growled, this time pushing the plate against Rajiv's chest.

Rajiv shook his head stubbornly.

Beera's patience snapped. With a swift motion, he swung his rough hand across Rajiv's face. The slap landed hard, making Rajiv's head jerk to the side. A sharp sting spread across his cheek, and his eyes welled up involuntarily. He let out a pained gasp but still refused to utter a word.

Suddenly, Chimta, the leaner man standing near the door, let out a chuckle. "Look at him, Beera." His eyes gleamed with mockery as he pointed toward Rajiv's pants.

Rajiv shifted uncomfortably, realizing the dark stain spreading down his trousers. His body had betrayed him in his helpless state. His face flushed red with humiliation, but his voice trembled with frustration. "I... I needed to use the loo. You didn't even let me!"

Beera's expression darkened. "Ab sharam bhi karni hai tujhe?" (so you are ashamed of yourself now?) he sneered before raising his hand again. This time, his palm struck Rajiv's other cheek, sending another jolt of pain through him.

"Ziddi ladka,"(stubborn boy) Beera muttered under his breath, shaking his head in frustration. He stood up, cursing, and looked toward Chimta. "If he doesn't eat, let him rot."

Chimta smirked. "He'll break soon enough."

The door creaked shut, and the room was plunged into darkness once more, leaving Rajiv alone with his fear, his burning cheeks, the dampness of his soiled pants, and the sinking realization that he was far from home—and far from rescue.

The Uprising..

The air crackled with tension outside the towering iron gates of Hanif's warehouse, a grim, dust-laden fortress of industry standing in defiance of the land it sought to consume. Beyond the gates, bulldozers and JCB machines stood idle like metallic beasts, their rust-tinged claws poised to rip into the earth. Lined up in the distance were rows of heavy trucks, their monstrous presence signaling the relentless march of development—a march that threatened to drown an entire way of life.

Before this monument to greed, the people of the land had gathered. Farmers, fishermen, cattle herders, and village women stood shoulder to shoulder, their voices rising like an unrelenting tide against the sky. They held crude banners scrawled with desperate pleas—Save Our Forests, Save Our Homes! No Dam on the Dheel! Hanif, Stop the Loot! The words, written in uneven strokes, bore the tremble of hands that had tilled the soil, drawn water from the river, and lived in harmony with the wilderness long before men like Hanif arrived with their contracts and machines.

At the front of the crowd, Jayant Ghosh stood tall, his face resolute, his eyes burning with conviction. This was not just a protest against a dam—it was a battle for the soul of a place, for the whispering trees and the beasts that roamed their shade, for the unseen footprints of generations who had called this land home. His voice, clear and unwavering, rose above the cacophony.

"This river is older than your laws, older than your blueprints! The forests that you call 'wasteland' are the homes of tigers, leopards, and bears. The same tiger that is the Vahan of Vandevi, the goddess of the forest—the one you claim to revere—but when it comes to his real home, you drown it for profit!"

HANIIF'S
WAREHOUSE
SAVE OUR FORESTS.
SAVE OUR FORESTS.
SAVE OUR HOMES.!
SAVE OUR HOMES!

A roar of agreement erupted from the villagers. A woman with a child on her hip raised her fist. "If the river dies, we die! This land feeds us!"

Inside the site office, shielded by thick walls and tinted glass, Mohammad Hanif sat in a leather chair, frowning as he watched the spectacle outside. The muffled chants seeped through the walls, carrying with them the scent of rebellion. Around him, Mohsin his assistant and a few local toughs—men who didn't shy away from breaking a few bones for a price—waited for his orders.

Hanif tapped his fingers against the polished wood of his desk, his frustration mounting. He had promised the Chinese investors smooth progress. The contracts were ready, the bribed officials had signed off. The only obstacle was this wretched 'environmentalist' and his ragtag army of villagers.

"We can't let this nonsense go on," he muttered. His men leaned in, waiting. "This nuisance—Jayant Ghosh—he's the one stirring the pot. As long as he stands, these people will keep screaming."

One of the henchmen smirked. "Should we rough him up a little? Teach him to keep his mouth shut?"

Hanif exhaled slowly, a sinister gleam in his eyes. "No. That won't be enough." He glanced out at the protesters again, at the man standing defiantly in front of the crowd, rallying them against the weight of machines and money. A slow smile curled his lips.

"Jayant Ghosh has to disappear."

The decision hung in the air like an axe waiting to fall.

Hukum...

The night air was thick with the scent of damp earth and cigar smoke as Mohammad Hanif's SUV rolled into the colossal farmhouse of Raju Bhaiya. The mansion, a symbol of unchecked power, loomed in the dim glow of strategically placed floodlights, its massive courtyard flanked by luxury cars and armed guards who barely acknowledged Hanif's arrival.

Inside, in a grand, chandelier-lit hall, Raju Bhaiya reclined on a silk-covered couch, sipping a glass of whiskey, his fingers lazily drumming on the armrest. Around him, a few trusted aides lingered, including his old, bespectacled munshi, who was poring over ledgers with meticulous precision. The air buzzed with the soft murmur of calculations, numbers of trucks, weight of sand, volume of illegally mined boulders—all being cross-checked against the money that was to change hands tonight.

Hanif stood silently, waiting. The miner knew the rules of this game—patience, respect, and always remembering who the real king was. When the munshi finally closed his register and nodded, Raju Bhaiya stretched, letting out a satisfied sigh.

"So, Hanif bhai," he said, his voice slow, deliberate. "How much do I earn from my land today?"

Hanif took out an envelope, placing it on the table with a slight bow. "Your share, sir. As always, a percentage of every truck that crossed the river."

Raju Bhaiya glanced at the envelope but didn't touch it. He never counted. He didn't have to. Instead, he picked up his cigar and took a long drag before exhaling leisurely.

Hanif, sensing his moment, leaned in slightly. "Sir, a word in private?"

Raju Bhaiya raised an eyebrow but gestured towards the open courtyard. They stepped outside, where the night sky stretched over a garden of neatly trimmed hedges and an artificial waterfall that gurgled softly in the background. The guards stayed back, giving them space.

Hanif spoke first. "That man, Jayant."

Raju Bhaiya turned to him, unimpressed. "Who Jayant?"

Hanif's voice was edged with frustration. "Jayant Ghosh. That environmentalist working in the forests around Sheopur."

Raju Bhaiya took another puff from his cigar. "Yes? What about him?"

Hanif's face darkened. "If that nuisance is around, we will not be able to build the dam. Take my word for it, sir. The villagers look up to him. They trust him. He has been constantly poisoning their minds against the dam, provoking them. If he keeps this up, we will be stuck in legal battles for years. He needs to be handled."

Raju Bhaiya studied Hanif for a long moment, then reached into his pocket and pulled out his phone. The screen's glow reflected briefly in his calculating eyes as he scrolled through his contacts. Finally, he stopped, pressed a number, and brought the phone to his ear.

The call connected.

From the other end, a deep, familiar voice answered. "Yes, Malik (Boss)?"

"Lakhan," Raju Bhaiya said smoothly. "There's some work for you."

A short chuckle crackled through the speaker. "Yes hukum (order)?"

Raju Bhaiya flicked the ash off his cigar, his voice unwavering. "Jayant Ghosh. I want that man erased."

There was a pause, then Lakhan's voice, laced with amusement. "Consider it done."

Raju Bhaiya's tone remained cold. "Listen carefully. The guy is connected. He has links in Delhi. This has to be a clean job—no loose ends, no proof. And use the Dheel River. It has many hungry crocs. Feed them. Your Vandevi will be pleased with you with this sacrifice. " A subtle yet sinister smile slid accross his reptilian lips as from the other end, Lakhan let out a small laugh. "Understood Hukum."

The call ended.

Hanif bowed down to Raju Bhaiya and then stepped back towards his waiting SUV. As he drove off into the night, the weight of the conspiracy settled over the farmhouse, lingering like the smoke from Raju Bhaiya's cigar, curling and disappearing into the darkness.

Tiny office— Big dreams...

Inside a small, dimly lit room, the hum of an old ceiling fan mixed with the faint beeping of a modem struggling to maintain its connection. The NGO's field office was modest—just a plain wooden table, a plastic chair, and a single cupboard stacked with research papers, books on wildlife, and files filled with data. Against one wall, a dusty map of the Sheopur forests and the Dheel riverine landscape was pinned, marked with red and green dots indicating camera trap locations and known animal movement corridors.

Jayant Ghosh sat at the desk, eyes fixed on his laptop screen, his fingers deftly inserting a memory card into the slot. The card contained weeks of painstakingly collected data from camera traps he had strategically placed deep inside the forest. As the files loaded, the screen flickered with images—silent, grainy moments of the untamed world, frozen in time.

His heartbeat quickened when the first image appeared—a magnificent tiger, its muscular frame moving stealthily through the undergrowth, its striped coat blending with the dappled shadows of the jungle. The next image—a leopard, crouched low near a dry riverbed, its piercing eyes glowing in the night vision mode of the camera. Jayant leaned forward. These were the apex predators of the land, the rulers of this wilderness.

As he scrolled further, more inhabitants of this thriving ecosystem emerged. A sloth bear, its shaggy black fur standing out against the brown earth, was captured sniffing the bark of a tree, searching for termites. A pair of striped hyenas, their ears pricked, cautiously moving in the moonlight. A lone wolf, its silhouette striking against the open grassland. A pair of golden jackals playing near a stream. And finally, the Bengal fox, smaller than the jackal, moving elegantly with its bushy tail ending in a black spot.

Jayant couldn't help but smile. The sheer diversity of predators in this landscape was staggering. Here, in this relatively unexplored terrain, nature had created a rare balance where multiple carnivores coexisted, each playing its unique role in the ecosystem.

He clicked open another folder—Ungulates (Hoofed animals). The prey base. The foundation that sustained these carnivores.

A herd of cheetal (spotted deer), their delicate bodies frozen mid-leap as they dashed through the glades. The sturdy chocolate coloured sambar deer, their antlers grand like forest royalty, grazing by a watering hole. The agile chinkara (Indian gazelle), captured in motion, its slender legs carrying it over rocky terrain. The striking blackbuck, its spiraled horns rising like a warrior's weapon. and the rare chausingha (four-horned antelope), its presence in the images making Jayant's eyes widen—it was an indicator of pristine forest conditions.

Every photograph was more than just an image. It was proof. Proof of a thriving, interconnected ecosystem. A balance that nature had taken thousands of years to build. Proof that this land deserved urgent protection.

Jayant carefully recorded each observation. Next to each image, he entered the longitude, latitude, date, time, and camera ID. He added notes—was the animal alone or in a group? Any signs of mating, injury, or unusual behavior?

This wasn't just documentation. This was his battle plan.

He was building a file. His goal was clear: To upgrade the status of this wilderness from a Reserve Forest to a Tiger Reserve.

A reserve meant higher protection, stricter laws, and dedicated funding for anti-poaching measures. It meant fencing of critical areas, better patrols, and most importantly—keeping miners and land grabbers at bay.

Besides the Government was also very serious about Cheetah reintroduction to its erstwhile domains— various areas of central and western India like Nauradehi and Gandhi Sagar. Jayant saw promise in the forests of Sheopur with its typical mosaic habitat (grassland and woodland mix).

The dedicated researcher had been relentlessly sending data to his head office and to officials of the National Tiger Conservation Authority (NTCA).

He knew that NTCA was serious about adding tiger reserves by protecting key habitats. That's how India currently had fifty eight tiger reserves compared to its modest beginning of nine.

So every report, every photograph mattered.

He paused for a moment, stretching his stiff shoulders.

The modem blinked erratically, struggling with the weak connection. But Jayant was patient. He had learned patience from the forests he worked in.

As the first batch of files uploaded, he leaned back, rubbing his eyes. His fight was far from over.

The dam builders, the poachers, the miners—they were coming for this land.

But Jayant Ghosh had made up his mind.

They would have to go through him first.

The daylight abduction ...

The sun hung low over the bustling streets, casting long shadows on the dusty roads. The small town, with its chaotic blend of honking vehicles, roadside vendors, and chattering pedestrians, seemed oblivious to the storm that was about to unfold.

Jayant Ghosh stepped out of his NGO office, securing the lock on the faded wooden door with a familiar twist of his wrist. His laptop bag hung from his shoulder, a companion to his relentless pursuit of wildlife conservation. He adjusted the strap, took a deep breath of the warm, dry air, and walked towards his bike—a rugged old model, scratched and weathered by years of travel through the wilderness.

Swinging his leg over, he took the bike off its stand and kick-started the engine. The familiar rumble vibrated beneath him as he accelerated into the dusty, crowded roadside, weaving through bullock carts, auto-rickshaws, and small-town traffic with ease. His mind was elsewhere—on the tiger images he had uploaded, on the fight against Hanif's dam, on the next steps to push for the tiger reserve status.

He didn't notice them at first.

Two motorcycles, each carrying two men, blended seamlessly into the afternoon chaos. They trailed him with calculated precision, never too close to arouse suspicion, never too far to lose sight.

As Jayant approached a crossroad, he instinctively slowed down to take a turn.

And that's when they struck.

One bike surged ahead, blocking his path. The second bike closed in from behind. In a fraction of a second, he was trapped.

Before he could react, a man leaped off from the rear bike, landing onto Jayant's bike with practiced ease. A cold, metallic sensation pressed against his waist—a katta, a crude but deadly local country pistol, hidden beneath a gamcha, (a thin cotton towel) draped casually around the man's hand. The cloth concealed the weapon from prying eyes, making the entire act seem like nothing more than a casual ride.

"Chup chap chal," a gruff voice ordered, his breath hot against Jayant's ear. "Ek awaaz nikali toh yahin daag denge." (Drive quietly. One sound, and you're dead.)

Jayant's fingers tightened on the handlebars. He felt his heartbeat hammering against his ribcage. He wasn't new to danger—he had faced aggressive villagers, angry miners, even armed poachers. But this? This was something else.

The man with the katta slid behind him, keeping the weapon firmly against his side, the gamcha still covering it from view. Meanwhile, the second rider from the lead bike jumped onto Jayant's bike and took control, forcing him into the middle—sandwiched between his kidnappers.

The two motorcycles now flanked them, moving like a well-oiled machine. To any casual observer, it looked like a group of friends riding three bikes together—nothing out of the ordinary.

But Jayant knew better.

They were taking him. Their style, comical but lethal.

A typical central Indian mafia styled kidnapping was unfolding in broad daylight, As Jayant disappeared into the labyrinth of roads, swallowed by the dust and speed of his captors, no one seemed to notice.

Except for one person.

A young woman stood at a bus stop, waiting for her ride. She had been watching Jayant's bike just moments earlier—perhaps out of boredom, perhaps out of curiosity

Her breath hitched as she processed what she was witnessing.

Something was wrong.

Within seconds, she pulled out her phone and frantically dialed Janhvi's number.

"Janhvi! Listen—Jayant ji—he's being taken! Right now! Two bikes—four men—they forced him to stop! They've got a gun on him!"

Janhvi's voice crackled through the line, sharp and urgent. "Where? Where are you?"

"Near the Atta crossroad! They're heading toward the highway! Do something—FAST!"

Kaal-Kothri...

The dim glow of a flickering oil lamp barely pierced the suffocating darkness of the Kal-kothri—a damp, dingy room with cracked walls and the acrid stench of sweat, blood, and fear. The air inside was thick, heavy with the weight of dread.

A large, burly figure stood in the half-light, his shadow stretching grotesquely against the walls. His breath was slow and steady, a stark contrast to the sharp, merciless sound of flesh meeting flesh.

SLAP!

A muffled cry rang out.

SLAP!

A choked sob followed.

The man's back was visible, a broad, imposing silhouette. His hands were relentless, striking again and again with calculated cruelty. Rajiv's small, trembling form shuddered with each brutal impact. His cheeks burned like fire, his eyes welled up, but he bit his lip, struggling to hold back his sobs.

"Huh? You have a lot of arrogance, little child," the man growled, his voice deep, laced with venom. He grabbed Rajiv's face roughly, forcing the boy to look up at him. "Let's see what you're made of. Let's see how long you last."

SLAP!

Rajiv gasped, his head snapping sideways. The pain was unbearable. His entire face felt like it was being set ablaze.

Then, from the shadows near the door, came a stern voice, edged with quiet authority.

"That's it, Lakhan. That's more than enough."

The figure at the door stepped forward, his lean frame emerging from the darkness. It was Jaggu. His sharp, watchful eyes flickered with restrained anger as he took in the scene.

"He's only a little kid. Enough is enough!"

But Lakhan didn't stop. He ignored Jaggu, his fingers flexing as he raised his hand for another strike.

Jaggu's jaw clenched. He strode forward and placed a firm hand on Lakhan's shoulder, his grip tightening just enough to send a message.

"Lakhan, stop. Now!"

A tense silence hung in the air.

Lakhan froze for a second, then slowly lowered his hand. His body was still rigid, his breath sharp and uneven. With an irritated grunt, he pulled out his mobile phone from his pocket and thrust it at Rajiv.

"Connect the phone," he commanded.

Rajiv, gasping, his face flushed red with indignation, pain, and humiliation, hesitated. His fingers trembled as he took the phone. He could barely see through the haze of tears, but he still managed to press the numbers.

The ringing tone echoed in the silence.

Then—a voice from the other end.

"Hello?"

Before Rajiv could respond, Lakhan snatched the phone away with brutal force, nearly knocking it from the boy's grip.

He lifted the phone to his ear, his lips curling into a vicious smirk.

"Your boy. Your dear boy is with us," he taunted, his voice deliberately slow, dripping with malice.

"Who is this?" The voice on the other end was sharp, alarmed.

Lakhan chuckled darkly. "If that teacher, your over-smart teacher and those other two meddling kids open their mouths in court, you know what will happen to your precious son?" He let the words hang in the air for a moment, letting the fear seep in.

Then, in a chillingly casual voice, he added—"We'll make pieces of him. And we'll feed him to the wild animals of Kaziranga. They're always hungry..Ha..Ha.. Very, very hungry."

A silence, thick with horror.

Lakhan, satisfied, thrust the phone at Rajiv's face.

"Go on. Speak to your papa," he sneered.

The phone connection crackled as Rajiv's father, his voice visibly shaken, spoke into the receiver.

"Hello, beta... I hope you're fine."

On the other end, Rajiv squeezed his eyes shut, forcing back the tears that threatened to spill. His heart pounded against his ribs, but he knew he couldn't let his father hear his agony.

He had to be brave.

Mustering all his strength, he steadied his voice, trying to sound normal—trying to sound strong.

"Papa, I'm fine. Don't worry."

The words were barely out of his mouth when Lakhan yanked the phone away, his rough fingers digging into the boy's wrist as he snatched it.

"He will be fine," Lakhan said, his tone dripping with menace. "As long as you don't get over-smart. Understand?"

A tense pause.

Behind Lakhan, a dull thud echoed in the dimly lit room.

Three men, their faces hardened and impassive, had just heaved a heavy sack onto the ground. The fabric was stained, the shape inside unmistakably human. With practiced ease, one of them untied the rough knot at the mouth of the sack.

The crumpled, bruised face of Jayant Ghosh emerged from the shadows.

His eyes were barely open, swollen from relentless beatings. His breath was shallow. Blood crusted his split lips, and his cheeks bore the dark imprint of merciless fists.

Jaggu's stomach twisted slightly.

Even for a man who had seen plenty of brutality, this felt different.

Lakhan, however, grinned. He placed a firm pat on the backs of the kidnappers, his approval evident.

"Neat job."

The men nodded, their expressions void of emotion.

Meanwhile, on the phone, Rajiv's father's desperate voice crackled back to life.

"Hello? Hello? Hello? Where have you gone? I want to speak to my son!"

Lakhan's voice dropped to an eerie calm. He said, "One word to the police or the forest department, and you know what will happen...Your boy is in good hands as long as you stay obedient."

Lakhan exchanged a glance with Jaggu.

Then, without hesitation, he pressed the button and cut the call.

The dim light of the flickering lamp cast eerie shadows across the cold, damp walls of the kalkotri. The air inside was thick—a blend of sweat, dust, and something more sinister.

Lakhan crouched down beside the sack, his rough fingers caressing the hair of the wildlife researcher . A slow, deliberate motion—he wasn't in a hurry.

A man who had once moved through the wild with purpose, now lay crumpled, lifeless as a discarded doll.

Lakhan studied his prey for a moment, tilting his head, his lips curling into a smirk.

"Still out cold," he muttered. "Good."

Jaggu exhaled sharply, his jaw tightening.

The jungle's fiercest defender—now bound, helpless, and at their mercy.

The altercation...

The room crackled with tension, the flickering lamp throwing long shadows against the mud walls. Janhvi's breath was heavy with fury as she turned her fiery gaze toward Lakhan.

"It's you," she spat. "Your influence. Your shadow is dark—like the shadow of death. You are poisoning Jaggu's soul, making him do all these horrible things!"

Lakhan's jaw tightened. His eyes darkened, glinting like a predator's in the low light. His fists curled, the veins in his arms twitching with restraint.

He turned to Jaggu, his lips curling in contempt.

“Your little partridge has been talking too much these days,” he sneered.

Jaggu's head snapped up, his muscles tensing.

“You don't come between me and Janhvi,” he shot back, his voice sharp as a blade. “I will take care of her.”

Lakhan gave a harsh laugh, shaking his head.

“Enough nonsense,” he said, his patience thinning. “We've wasted too much time already. The order is from above. Tonight, the job has to be done. Are you coming or not?”

Before Jaggu could respond, Janhvi pressed both her palms hard against his chest, looking straight into his eyes.

“Jaggu, swear on me—you will not harm Jayant ji.”

Lakhan's face twisted with rage. His nostrils flared, his fists trembling with the sheer force of his anger.

"Now look at you!" he barked. "You're good for only one thing—hiding under Janhvi's ghagra (Ethnic Indian skirt).That's all you're capable of now. You've become a napunsak! (Impotent)"

The words hit Jaggu like a whiplash. His teeth clenched. His breath quickened. A slow, dangerous rage built up inside him.

Lakhan turned, about to leave.

But Jaggu exploded.

In a blur, he lunged forward, grabbing Lakhan's collar with both hands and yanking him back with brute force.

His face mere inches from Lakhan's, his voice was a low, guttural snarl.

"Be in your limits, Lakhan."

Lakhan smirked—then, without warning, he threw a brutal punch.

The impact cracked through the air.

Jaggu's head snapped back, and he staggered, falling hard against the ground.

Blood trickled from his nose.

Lakhan stood over him, eyes filled with disgust.

"Get lost, coward."

He dusted off his hands and sneered.

"I don't need you. That weak, diminutive Bengali boy? I'll take care of him myself. You be loyal as you want—to this scum woman of your choice till she turns you into a full fledged hijra (cuss word for transgender or third gender)."

Without another word, Lakhan turned on his heel, marched out, and slammed the door shut with a thunderous bang.

The silence that followed was heavy, suffocating.

Jaggu sat on the ground, his fists clenched, nails digging into his palms. His chest heaved as he wiped the blood off with the back of his hand and dusted his shirt. His eyes burned—not just with rage, but with something deeper, something torn.

Then, he shouted, his voice ringing through the night—

"Lakhan! Stop! I'm coming!"

He stumbled forward, determined to chase after Lakhan.

But before he could take another step, Janhvi grabbed his collar with both hands and yanked him back with force.

Her grip was iron.

Her eyes, wild with fury and desperation, pierced through him.

"Come back to your senses, Jaggu!" she cried, shaking him, her voice raw with emotion. "Where are you going? Have you lost your mind?"

Jaggu struggled against her hold, his breathing uneven.

Janhvi's voice rose, shaking with anguish and disbelief.

"After killing voiceless animals, now you are an accomplice to killing innocent humans too? Is that your new profession?

Her fingers tightened around his collar, her nails digging into the fabric of his shirt.

"That man is like God! He sacrifices his life for our future, our land, for the creatures that have no voice, for the forests that are disappearing! And this man—this dark soul, Lakhan—is corrupting you! Destroying you! And me! And everything we could ever have!"

Her voice broke. Tears welled in her eyes, but she refused to let them fall.

Jaggu stood frozen, his breath shallow, his body rigid. Something flickered in his eyes—a storm of emotions raging inside him.

For a brief moment, he wavered.

But then—in a flash, something hardened inside him.

Without a word, he shoved Janhvi away. The force sent her stumbling back, her hands clutching the empty air where his collar had been.

Janhvi gasped, her eyes widening in shock.

Before she could react, Jaggu spun on his heel, threw the door open, and disappeared into the dark night like a ghost.

Janhvi stood there, her chest rising and falling, staring at the empty doorway. "Jaggu"she cried out one last time weeping in agony.

The wind howled through the cliffs outside, carrying his name into the vast, merciless darkness.

Dark waters....

Dark and silent lay the waters of the River Dheel, curling like a black ribbon beneath the bridge. The current moved slow, deceptively calm, but the river had its own sentinels—reptilian eyes glowed in the moonlight, breaking the surface with an eerie stillness. Silent watchers, ancient killers, patient, opportunistic.
Only the snouts and eyes emerged; the rest of their massive, armored bodies remained submerged in the depths. Waiting. Watching.

Above the old bridge, a black SUV screeched to a halt, it's tyres skidding slightly on the gravel. The doors swung open and a couple of men emerged - silent, grim and purposeful. Between them, they dragged the limp body of Jayant Ghosh, his arms hanging lifelessly, head lolling with each step. The stillness of the river below seemed to mirror the chill in the air. The scene was set for death.

Two figures tightened their grip on the limp body of Jayant Ghosh. Bhola and Chimta.

One by the shoulders, the other by the feet.

With a grunt, they lifted him while another strongman, Beera helped.

They moved toward the edge of the bridge, their breath misting in the cool night air.

A final moment before the plunge.

But then—suddenly—another shadow moved.

It detached itself from the darkness at the eastern end of the bridge, blending at first with the murk of the night.

Then—it sprang forward.

A blur. A streak. A shadow that ran like a leopard.

The shadow dashed toward the car first, then pivoted—charging straight for the men at the bridge's edge.

Bhola and Chimta hoisted Jayant higher, ready to let go—

And that's when the shadow leapt.

A savage blur against the moonlit night.

And then—impact.

With razor sharp kicks and punches, Jaggu lashed out at the two men. Taken aback by this sudden attack, they released Jayant's body which fell on the asphalt with a dull thud.

"No! Stop!" Jaggu's voice was raw, desperate. He stepped forward towards his cousin, the big, burly ringleader Lakhan, hands raised.

"We cannot kill this man," he pleaded. "We are not murderers, Lakhan. Remember that. We are poachers."

Before Jaggu could move, Lakhan grabbed him from behind and shoved him backward.

He let out a bitter laugh, his grip tightening around Jaggu's torso "Shut up, coward. Tonight, we execute orders. No time for this nonsense"

Jaggu stumbled, his boots scraping against the rough surface of the bridge. His breath hitched.

Lakhan's voice was sharp, merciless. "Chimta! Bhola! Pratap! Get him up! Get him to the edge!"

The three men obeyed. Jayant's limp body was hauled closer to the railings.

Lakhan released Jaggu and turned to face him, his eyes cold, dark. A warning. A death sentence.

"Jaggu, don't interfere," Lakhan growled. "Stay out of this, or I swear—I'll forget that you are family ."

Jaggu clenched his fists. His chest rose and fell heavily.

He had always followed orders. Always bowed to Lakhan's dominance.

But not tonight.

Tonight, he made a choice.

A deep breath.

A heartbeat.

Then he ran.

Jaggu charged forward, his body coiled like a spring, his muscles tense with fury.

And then—he leapt.

CRACK!

Jaggu's foot collided with Lakhan's chest, sending him stumbling back.

Lakhan roared, barely catching himself before he hit the ground.

Jaggu landed lightly, his breath ragged, his fists clenched.

The air crackled with tension.

Lakhan straightened, his face contorted with rage. He lunged at Jaggu.

And then—all hell broke loose.

Lakhan swung a heavy punch. Jaggu ducked.

Jaggu countered with a swift uppercut to Lakhan's jaw.

Lakhan staggered, then recovered—fury in his eyes.

Chimta and Bhola rushed forward, trying to break them apart.

Jaggu kicked out—his boot slamming into Bhola's ribs, sending him flying.

Pratap grabbed Jaggu from behind, locking his arms.

Jaggu twisted violently and smashed his head backward—cracking into Pratap's nose.

Pratap yelled, stumbling back, blood spurting from his nostrils.

Jaggu turned just in time to see Lakhan's fist coming for his face.

THWACK!

Jaggu's head snapped sideways. Pain exploded in his skull.

Jaggu collapsed onto one knee, blood and saliva dripping from his mouth.

But he refused to fall.

This was his stand. His moment.

He was not going to let Jayant Ghosh die.

With a feral growl, Jaggu surged up, slamming his fist straight into Lakhan's throat.

Lakhan choked, stumbling back, gasping for breath.

Jaggu spun, kicking Chimta in the gut, sending him reeling.

But there were too many of them.

Lakhan recovered. And now, they all came for him.

Four against one.

Blows rained down. Fists, knees, boots.

Jaggu fought like a tiger surrounded by a pack of dholes (Indian wild dogs), every hit he took fueling him more.

His body was breaking.

But he didn't stop.

Because behind him—Jayant Ghosh still had a chance to live.

Then upon Lakhan's sharp signal, three other poachers led by Beera — burly, nameless shadows from the gang — lunge toward Jaggu like trained hounds. Jaggu barely has time to react.

They grab him violently — one locks his arms behind his back, another twists his wrist, and the third shoves a shoulder into his chest, pinning him hard. Jaggu writhes, grits his teeth, but he's locked in. His muscles strain in vain.

Lakhan storms up, eyes burning with fury.

He slams two brutal punches into Jaggu's stomach. THUD. THUD.

Jaggu buckles forward, coughing hard, winded, but still staring defiantly.

Then a lethal uppercut. A knee to the ribs.

Jaggu collapses, spitting blood onto the asphalt.

Lakhan steps back, straightens his collar, and points a trembling finger at him. "Don't you dare interfere again, Jaggu," he snarls. "This is your last warning. Or the crocodiles below will feast on your flesh like it's festival night."

He turns toward the edge of the bridge where Jayant Ghosh lies slumped like a broken doll — gagged, drenched in alcohol, hands tied, half-conscious and trembling from the cold wind.

Lakhan barks, "Chimta! Lift him up!"

Immediately, Chimta, Bhola, and Pratap spring into action, moving swiftly toward Jayant, ready to finish the job. The waters below wait in silence, rippling with moonlit menace.

The evil trio lift Jayant Ghosh's limp, soaked body into the air — one holds his legs, another grips his torso, the third braces his shoulders. They heave him up like a sandbag, dragging him over the cold iron railing of the bridge.

Jayant's head lolls to the side, his eyes fluttering — still semi-conscious, but too weak to resist. The wind catches his shirt, fluttering it like a tattered flag of surrender.

Below, the black waters of the Dheel ripple ominously, and several crocodilian eyes glimmer — patient, silent, waiting.

Lakhan grins. A cold, sinister grin.

He walks up, mockingly strokes Jayant's bruised cheek and says, "This one's still got some life in him."

He uncaps another bottle of alcohol, glugs it generously over Jayant's body, soaking his clothes, his hair — to make it look like a drunk man's fall into death.The stench of spirits and fear now clings to Jayant like a second skin.

Lakhan steps back and smirks. "Alright, boys. Haul him over."

The trio readies for the final shove.

Jayant dangles over the railing, the weight of his body teetering on the edge of death. Below, the river's gaping black mouth waits, crocodiles shifting lazily under the moon's reflection, jaws just beneath the surface.

And then —

BOOM!

Suddenly — floodlights explode to life from both ends of the bridge. The darkness vanishes in a blinding white blaze.

Harsh halogen beams slice through the night, illuminating the men, their faces stunned, caught mid-crime like statues. Shadows scatter. The silence is shattered.

A deep voice from a megaphone echoes across the bridge, "Release Jayant! Hands up! You are surrounded!"

The poachers freeze.

Jayant Ghosh, barely conscious, dangles in the air — his life hanging by a thread, but now, perhaps, hope has returned to the night.

The police had been there all along — hidden in the darkness, crouched behind boulders and vehicles, waiting.

It was Janhvi who had tipped them off, and they had laid the trap perfectly, watching the bridge in complete silence. Now, at the perfect moment, they revealed themselves in a blaze of light and noise.

From loudspeakers mounted on the police jeeps, a commanding voice boomed across the river:

"Release the man! Keep him safe! If you resist, we will open fire!"

Sirens wailed, splitting the night, echoing off the granite cliffs and the dark surface of the Dheel below. Police jeeps surged forward from both ends of the bridge, headlights blazing, tyres screeching on the stone.

The poachers panicked.

Chimta, Bhola, and Pratap hurriedly dropped Jayant's body back onto the bridge, where he collapsed in a heap, limbs twitching, breath shallow.

Lakhan spun around, face twisted in rage and disbelief. "Get in the car! Move, now!"

All seven ruffians rushed to the jeep. The vehicle roared to life, its engine snarling like a cornered beast. The headlights flared, and the jeep tore down the bridge, speeding toward the western end.

But it was already too late.

Police vehicles had sealed off the exit. Armed officers stood their ground, rifles raised.

The poachers didn't stop.

The jeep swerved violently, tires screeching, and with a shuddering crash, it rammed into one of the police jeeps, throwing it off the road into the ditch. Sparks flew. Metal twisted.

In the chaos, the poachers' jeep veered off and disappeared into the narrow dirt track that wound into the forest — vanishing into the night.

Silence returned. Just the whir of police radios, the hum of sirens fading.

On the bridge, under the cruel white light of the halogens, Jayant Ghosh lay barely conscious, drenched in sweat and alcohol, his body trembling.

Nearby, Jaggu, face bloodied and shirt torn, lay slumped against the railing — dazed, beaten, breathing heavily, but still on his feet. His eyes searched for Jayant, and seeing him alive, Jaggu allowed himself one broken smile of relief... before collapsing, exhausted and battered.

The night had not claimed them.

Not yet.

Stunned by the crash, two of the police jeeps immediately spin around and race after the poachers' vehicle, engines growling, red and blue lights slicing through the forested darkness.

Tyres screech, searchlights sweep wildly, and within seconds, the chase disappears into the shadows beyond the bridge.

The remaining two police vehicles halt near the middle of the bridge. Doors fling open and officers leap out, weapons drawn, storming toward the figures sprawled on the stone.

Jaggu lies collapsed, his lean frame broken by the fight, barely able to lift his head.

Jayant Ghosh is slumped against the bridge railing, body soaked in sweat, alcohol, and bruises — caught between consciousness and delirium.

A medical team rushes forward with a stretcher, lifting Jayant gently. An officer calls out, "He's alive! Get him into the ambulance!" Jayant is wheeled away, an oxygen mask pressed to his face, his fingers twitching faintly.

But before Jaggu can even speak, a group of policemen descend on him, guns raised, eyes blazing with suspicion.

Rough hands seize his arms, twist them behind his back.

Jaggu cries out, "Wait—wait! I'm not one of them! I came to save him! I fought them, I tried to stop them!"

But the officers are not convinced.

Jaggu struggles weakly. "Please! Jayant sir… Jayant sir, tell them! Tell them I saved you!"

Jayant, now strapped in the stretcher, can barely move. His eyes roll, mouth opening slightly, trying to form words — but he's too far gone. His head lolls to the side. He doesn't respond.

A cruel silence descends.

The commanding officer signals grimly. "Take him. We'll question him later."

Jaggu's pleas vanish into the night. His wrists are tied with plastic cuffs, and a cloth is gagged into his mouth. Two constables drag his limp, bruised form toward the van.

Jaggu looks back one last time, his eyes filled with despair — not because of the pain, but because he had tried to do the right thing, and no one saw it. After all he was a poacher. No one reposed any trust or respect in his words.

The van's door slams shut.

And the bridge falls silent again — lit by harsh white floodlights, stained with blood, and echoing with the ghosts of a fight that had almost taken two lives.

Kathmandu calling...

From the bloodstained stone of the Dark River Bridge in central India, the story lifted—up, away—rising into the skies above.... then slowly emerged into a breathtaking bird's-eye view.

A lone Himalayan griffon vulture glided silently on the rising thermals, its massive wings outstretched like ancient sails against the wind. Below it was the picturesque sprawl of Kathmandu — Nepal's magnificent hill town, steeped in history, mystery, and shadows.

Surrounded by the towering, snow-clad Himalayas, the city hummed quietly beneath the crisp blue sky.

The griffon's shadow glided silently over centuries-old stupas, ornate courtyards, golden spires and the tangled veins of alleyways, where tradition and modernity collide.

It veered—across rooftops of red clay tiles lined with prayer flags, past the Swayambhunath Stupa to the age-old bustle of Thamel and the stately calm of Durbar Square.

But then, it descended further..narrowing in... deeper into the city, towards the hidden corners where something darker awaited to unfold— where a singular structure rose, distinct yet cloaked in tradition.

The Interpol Liaison Office – Kathmandu Division.

From the outside, the building appeared to be just another part of the heritage skyline—red brick walls, delicately carved wooden balconies, latticed windows, and a tiered pagoda-style roof bearing strings of fluttering flags. It was silent, watchful—like a monk in meditation.

But within, the stillness faded.

The interior hummed with quiet urgency. Monitors glowed, keyboards clicked, and soft-spoken conversations in multiple languages filled the air. Interpol officers—dressed in everything from suits to tactical fatigues—moved with intent.

Some were focused on surveillance screens tracking satellite feeds, others marked up global maps detailing illegal wildlife trade, arms movement and narco routes.

A few spoke rapidly into encrypted phones, while others huddled around laptops displaying drone footage and thermal imaging from high-risk zones.

Near the back wing of the office, a large wooden door bore a polished brass plate that read:

RUSSEL HOGG – AGENT (SOUTH ASIA DESK)

Inside the room, the atmosphere was denser, the air tinged with espresso and intensity. Russel Hogg sat at his desk, surrounded by wall-mounted boards cluttered with photographs of trafficked goods—rhino horn stashes, bags of pangolin scales, tiger pelts. Lines of thread connected faces from across borders: poachers, middlemen, political fixers, and foreign buyers—a growing network of criminal convergence.

In his early forties, he was a broad-shouldered, athletic man, wearing a dark olive shirt with sleeves rolled up to the elbows.

There was a grit to Hogg, a kind of energy that simmered just below the surface. He possessed the instinct of a hunter and the intellect of a strategist—a man shaped by fieldwork, losses, victories, and long nights piecing together fragments of truth.

Two agents sat across from him, studying a dossier Hogg had just dropped on the table.

"...I don't care if the consignment changed hands at the Bhutan border," Hogg says, voice quiet but edged with steel. "That only means the route's more active than we thought. Arms, wildlife contraband, and now narcotics—they're not operating separately anymore. Someone is tying the threads."

He tapped the folder, where a blurry photo showed a clouded-leopard skin stuffed into a duffel bag, intercepted two days ago in a remote checkpoint.

"This is organized. This is layered. And if we don't cut through fast, we'll lose the trail forever. And maybe worse."

He paused, eyes drifting momentarily to the map behind him—Indian reserve forests with tiger-leopard presence, Myanmar, Lhasa, and now Kathmandu—linked not just by geography, but by the growing architecture of a shadow network.

Two agents sat across from Russel Hogg, leaning in as he spread open a fresh dossier on the table. Inside were marked satellite maps, photographs of intercepted consignments, and field reports.

Hogg's eyes burned with intensity as he began, his voice low but deliberate.

"There are two primary arteries they're using to funnel tiger skins and rhino horn out of India," he says, tapping the first map. "One, right here—through the forests of Bihar and eastern Uttar Pradesh, across the open Indo-Nepal border. From there, the goods are passed through Kathmandu or Birgunj, and then—via age-old high mountain passes or the Rasuwagadhi-Kerung border—into Tibet and mainland China. That route's old but still alive, especially with insiders greasing palms along the way."

He slid over a second map, this one highlighting northeastern India.

"The second route is more dangerous but cleaner for them—through Manipur and Mizoram into Myanmar. From there, the contraband flows along rebel-controlled corridors towards Yunnan province in China. We're seeing increased rhino horn traffic on that trail—smaller shipments, but more frequent."

One of the agents interjected, "The Myanmar route is often linked to arms smuggling networks too, right?"

Hogg nodded grimly. "Exactly. Arms in, wildlife out. It's a barter system now. Skins, bones, ivory, horn—all traded for Kalashnikovs and ammonium nitrate. This isn't just about poaching anymore. It's financing violence."

He paused, then leant forward.

"These routes are not separate—they're converging. Intelligence from Kaziranga and Panna matched chatter we picked up in Mandalay. Someone is tying them together. Someone big."

He closed the file with finality, eyes never leaving the agents.

"We have to stop them before another tiger disappears—and another gun shows up in a rebel camp."

Russel Hogg had just dismissed his agents when the mobile phone on his desk began to buzz again. He picked it up, eyes narrowing at the name flashing across the screen.

"Hello, speaking."

A familiar voice crackled from the other end.

"Oh, Mr. Verma."

DFO Amit Verma's voice was calm but carried a distinct urgency. "Hope you're doing fine, Russel. I can never forget how efficiently you dealt with the Chinese ivory mafia last year, acting swiftly on the tip we sent about the elephant poaching ring. This time, it's tiger… and I'm afraid things are moving even faster."

Russel leaned forward, his tone sharpening. "Go on."

"We've arrested a few Assamese, Rohingya and Bangladeshi immigrant poachers from the forest fringes near Kaziranga,"

Verma continued. "After intense interrogation—let's say persuasive methods—we extracted the name of a man who's not only dangerous but deeply embedded in your city. He's operating out of Kathmandu, and he's not just another trafficker, Russel. He's well-connected, ruthless, and he's hiding in plain sight."

Russel's pen paused above his notepad.

"Name?"

"Varad Praja," Verma said. "He owns a place called Praja Pet Shop, 36 Thamel Street. But don't be misled by the name—he's not selling parakeets and puppies. Under that pet shop façade, he's dealing in all kinds of prohibited wildlife contraband—leopard bones, pangolin scales, bear bile, and now… tiger parts."

Russel's eyes darkened. "Are you saying he has parts of the tigress killed in Kaziranga that you talked about the other day?"

"Yes. The Bavaria group poached her. They moved fast, and from what we've gathered, the parts have already reached Praja. We suspect they're being processed for sale or shipment to Tibet."

Russel Hogg leaned forward, still gripping the receiver tightly. "Understood. I'll have a team on Thamel Street before the sun rises."

But Amit Verma's voice instantly cut through, sharp and resolute. "No, Russel. You cannot send a team there. Not yet."

Russel paused, caught off guard. "Why not?"

"These men... they have informers everywhere—especially in Thamel Street," Verma said, his voice low but firm. "One wrong move, one unfamiliar face, and they'll know. They'll vanish. And worse, they'll move the tiger parts. Everything will be gone before your men even reach the shop. Besides the tiger parts need not be stashed at the pet shop."

Russel Hogg exhaled, the weight of Verma's warning settling in.

"So what do you suggest?"

"You'll have to trap him, Russel," Verma said. "Find a way to lure him out—make him feel safe, unsuspecting. Catch him outside his den. The rest... I trust you to know best."

There was a beat of silence. Hogg's sharp mind was already ticking, calculating. He knew Verma was right. This had to be done with precision. No uniforms. No sirens. Just a quiet, invisible snare closing in.

"Alright," Russel Hogg finally said, his voice quiet and resolved. "We'll bait the trap."

"Good luck, Russel. This one's important."

"Aren't they all?" Hogg said as he stood and turned to the city map pinned to the wall behind his desk.

His eyes locked on the tangled grid of Kathmandu—and then narrowed on Thamel Street.

Russel Hogg's gaze remained fixed on the map as he spoke into the receiver, his voice low and deliberate. "Varad Praja. Got that. Don't worry, Mr. Verma..." — his eyes narrowed — "The hunter will be extracted out of his lair and hunted down with precision. I give you my word."

On the other end, Amit Verma's voice was crisp, the urgency unmistakable. "I'm expecting rapid action on this, Russel—especially before the tiger parts are moved across Nepal into Tibet."

Russel gave a slight nod to himself. "Don't worry."

With that, the line clicked off. The room fell into silence again—except for the distant sounds of Kathmandu outside the window, and the faint creak of Hogg's leather chair as he stood up, ready to go to war with shadows.

Meanwhile the majestic griffon vulture wheeled above the ancient city, majestic and watchful, as if scanning the city's secrets.

The exquisite trap...

Two large-billed crows sliced through the morning air, darting and shrieking as they chased and mobbed the Himalayan griffon vulture over the tightly packed roofs of Kathmandu. Below them, the city pulsed with its usual mix of color, commerce, and shadowed secrets.

Inside the otherwise unassuming Interpol office, a different sort of transformation was underway. Behind a thick wooden door marked "Authorized Personnel Only," a sterile, brightly lit chamber had been temporarily converted into a clandestine prep room.

There, seated beneath a powerful ring of light, Russel Hogg sat motionless as a professional makeup artist hovered over him with focused precision. The artist's tools danced like a sculptor's chisel—layering contour, age lines, false blemishes, even altering the arch of his brows. Inch by inch, the hard-lined, clean-cut Interpol officer was disappearing. In his place emerged a man of illicit refinement—one who might be seen sipping expensive whiskey in black-market dens, negotiating for horn, bone, or skin with poise and detachment.

Russel's once-intense eyes were now hidden behind lightly tinted lenses; his salt-and-pepper hair had been dyed and styled into something rakish. His clothes had been handpicked to suggest old money: a silk Nehru jacket with understated embroidery, Italian leather shoes, and a cufflink bearing a Chinese insignia. The final touch—a subtle tiger's tooth pendant hanging from a gold chain—rested just beneath his collar.

He examined himself in the mirror. Gone was the razor-sharp Interpol agent with the investigator's mind. In the reflection stared back a collector of the forbidden—precisely the kind of man Varad Praja would welcome into his circle.

And the trap was just beginning to close.

Thamel Street was a throbbing artery of Kathmandu life—narrow, coiled like a serpent, and crammed with the scents and sounds of a city forever on the edge of motion. The air pulsed with the clang of cycle bells, the honk of rickshaws, and the rhythmic cries of street vendors hawking everything from hand-woven shawls to pungent Nepali spices.

Ethnic Nepali faces—Thakalis, Newars, Tamangs—merged into the throng, creating a mosaic of weathered expressions, wide-eyed tourists, and locals with the swiftness of mountain goats. Shopfronts spilled onto the footpath, displaying glinting silver jewelry, brass figurines, beaded malas, and wooden masks with eyes that seemed to follow passersby.

Into this chaos slid a vehicle that clearly did not belong—a long black limousine that moved through the crowded gully like a shark slicing through a coral reef. It advanced slowly, its polished exterior reflecting prayer flags and grimy shop awnings alike. Bicycles clattered aside, pedestrians flattened against chipped walls, and rickshaw drivers cursed as the vehicle edged forward, parting the street's natural rhythm with quiet menace.

Finally, the limousine came to a halt outside an aging shopfront marked in faded lettering: Praja Pet Shop.

Behind the smeared glass, a flicker of feathers and motion caught the eye. Inside, cages were stacked from floor to ceiling, each one containing a twitching creature—green parrots with curved beaks, sleepy owls, bright-yellow finches, and even a pair of rose finches glaring at the world through wire bars. The sound of fluttering wings and sharp squawks mixed with the oily scent of seed, mildew, and something far more elusive—secrecy.

Behind the pet shop's innocent façade, darker things stirred.

Bhanu Tamang moved toward the Englishman with the swagger of a man who'd handled trouble before. His bulk was intimidating, but his voice was smooth and calculated.

"What are you looking for, sir?" he asked, eyeing Russel Hogg from head to toe.

Russel gave him a pleasant nod, his voice rich with an upper-crust accent. "Ah, just admiring your little zoo here. You have quite a rare collection... Himalayan robins, Alexandrine parakeets, even a Khalij pheasant or two. Impressive."

Bhanu grunted in cautious approval, but said nothing more.

Russel wandered slowly from cage to cage, hands clasped behind his back like a gentleman appraising antiques. He offered quiet comments—some observations about diet, others about the rarity of species in the trade—while keeping one eye on the door. He moved with the unhurried ease of a man who'd done this before.

As they passed a pair of squabbling lorikeets, he casually asked, "You get much interest from collectors abroad?"

Bhanu nodded vaguely. "Some."

They continued to chat, but it was clear that Russel was buying time, waiting. A mother and her child sounded exited after purchasing a pair of parakeets. Then a local man who had been haggling over a mongoose, left with a small covered basket. Finally, when the last customer stepped out into the bustle of Thamel Street and the door's chime jingled shut, Russel's expression changed.

The easy smile gave way to something sharper. He stepped closer to the burly Bhanu, dropped his voice low, and said with a smirk:

"Tell me, apart from these chirping birds... do you also deal in roaring birds?"

Varad's loyal strongman stiffened, his eyes narrowing. "What did you say?"

Russel didn't blink. "Roaring birds. The striped variety ?."

There was a pause. Dhruva's first instinct was alarm, but then something clicked.

He looked around quickly, then gave a nod and jerked his head.

"Come with me."

They moved through a narrow corridor into the rear of the shop. The cages changed—no longer songbirds but strange and twitchy things: green vine snakes, twitching mongooses, lethargic iguanas, rare Himalayan Monals under red lamps, even a honey badger in a reinforced crate.

Bhanu didn't say a word as he led the Englishman through two more inner rooms, deeper into the hidden belly of the pet shop.

At the threshold of the last door stood another wall of muscle—Dhruva Tharu, Varad Praja's second bodyguard. He stepped in front of them, eyes fixed on Russel.

"Who's this?" he asked, flatly.

Bhanu responded, "He's here for business."

Dhruva didn't move. He stepped closer and looked the Englishman up and down with suspicion. "Arms out."

Russel raised his hands slowly. Dhruva began a thorough frisk—first the torso, then the arms, then the sides and legs. He checked the cuffs, the belt, even tapped the shoes for hidden compartments. His hands were swift but practiced, and his face didn't betray any emotion.

When satisfied, he stepped back and gave a nod.

"Alright. Go."

The final door opened.

The room was dimly lit by a single tungsten lamp swinging faintly from the ceiling. A thick, herbal smoke hung in the air. Strange jars lined the shelves. Animal bones, powders, dried herbs, and framed photographs of exotic hunts dotted the dark wooden walls.

At the far end of the dim, smoky room, lounging like a fat spider in the heart of his web, sat Varad Praja.

He looked up slowly, his thick fingers drumming the arm of his chair as his small eyes studied the Englishman stepping into his lair.

Then he leaned back in his dark teak chair, half-buried in shadows. Behind him, two Chinese porcelain dragons sat on a dusty shelf, their chipped fangs catching the flickering light. A brass fan rotated slowly above, groaning on each turn.

He didn't speak at first. His eyes moved like a crocodile's—slow, unblinking—studying the white man before him with the stillness of a predator. Russel Hogg stood calm, poised, his sharp European features softened under the skilled disguise of bronzer and shadow. His beard was expertly shaped, his hair slicked back, and a faint trace of an aftershave meant to evoke old-world money clung to him. He looked every bit the eccentric collector—part aristocrat, part predator.

"You're far from home, Mr…" Varad let his voice trail off, inviting a name.

Russel gave a brief, polished smile. "Call me Mr. Daxton."

Varad smirked and nodded toward a velvet-covered stool. "Sit."

Russel settled in, unhurried, crossing his legs with grace. His eyes scanned the walls lined with tribal masks, framed hunting knives, a bear paw mounted in a dusty glass case. He leaned forward slightly, his tone smooth, with just a hint of curiosity.

"I must say, your birds are... charming. But I'm looking for something with a bit more... roar."

Varad raised an eyebrow, his fingers steepling. "Roar?"

Russel gave a slow smile. "Yes. Something regal. Striped, perhaps. Skin, bones, claws, the full composition. Blood—dried if possible. And well... specialty parts. Everything the connoisseurs demand."

The room went still. Dhruva and Bhanu, standing near the door, exchanged a glance.

Varad chuckled low and dry. "Ah... now I understand. You're not just an ordinary bird lover."

Russel met his eyes with calm. "I have collectors across the Gulf. They want only the finest. I'm not here for leftovers."

Varad leaned forward, tapping the table softly. "You want RBT. (Royal Bengal Tiger). Potent..Wild. Not from farms. Not from stock. But from the deep forests of India, right?"

Russel nodded once. "From the heartland, yes. Must be fresh. Quality must be beyond question."

Varad smiled. "Yes, yes. Everything you ask—All body parts including penis! I have it. But..." He held up a thick finger. "For a price. Nothing comes cheap, Mr. Daxton. You pay well, I deliver well."

Russel's eyes didn't blink. "Money is not the issue here. I pay for perfection."

He slowly reached into his coat, producing a sleek leather wallet. He pulled out a stack of crisp foreign currency and pushed it forward across the table with a gloved hand.

"A handsome advance," he said, "for your assurance."

The currency sat like a silent promise. Varad's eyes glittered.

Just then, something caught his attention—a glint of gold and onyx from Russel's coat pocket. A pen.

"Ah," Varad said, leaning in slightly. "That's an interesting pen. May I?"

Russel tensed for a fraction of a second. Then, smiling as if it were nothing, he unpinned it from his pocket and handed it over.

Varad took it in his broad, scarred hands and examined the fine craftsmanship. He held it up, turning it slowly. His brows furrowed as he squinted near the clip.

The room thickened with tension. Russel's heartbeat slowed. His face remained unreadable.

"Where did you get this?" Varad asked.

"Egypt," said Russel with a faint smile. "A gift from an Emir. Long time ago."

Varad nodded slowly. "Hmm. Fancy things... you rich men carry."

Then, without suspicion, he handed it back.

Russel clipped it back into his coat, letting out a breath that never showed on his face.

"Now," he said, with the calm of a man who just survived a brush with death, "about the delivery. By when should I expect the consignment?"

Varad tapped his ringed finger on the table. "You don't worry, sir. We shall call you when it's time. Quietly. Discreetly."

"And where should I wait?" Russel asked.

Varad's eyes narrowed with businesslike efficiency. "Your hotel?"

"The Yak & Yeti," Russel answered. "Suite 701."

Varad smirked, gave a nod, a final one. "Good. You made the right choice by checking in there. Stay there. Stay low. You will hear from us."

Russel stood, gave a shallow bow, and turned slowly toward the exit. The pen in his pocket had captured it all—faces, voices, every word.

Outside, Thamel Street continued to roar with its chaos, but inside Russel Hogg's head, the trap had begun to close.

The hunter had stepped into the snare.

Prison bars...

A pair of black drongos erupted into a spirited aerial duel in the branches of a sprawling peepal tree outside the high sandstone walls of Karauli Central Jail. Their sharp, whistling calls sliced through the dry air, echoing like a cryptic code only they could understand. The lazy afternoon breeze stirred the tree's broad, heart-shaped leaves, sending waves of shimmer across its sun-dappled canopy.

The excitable and raucous birds flew around the peepal's swaying silhouette, over the imposing grey structure of the jail — its rusted grills, guard towers, and sprawling stone courtyards locked in time. Beyond the weather-beaten gate, one chased the other in reckless, acrobatic swoops over the boundary wall, the afternoon sun glinting off their forked tails. They darted past the grilled sentry post, across the barrack-lined yards and over the tangled barbed wire, eventually disappearing near the main building of the jail.

Inside, beyond thick iron doors and scanning eyes, in the visitor's room, the atmosphere was hushed — broken only by the muffled sound of a fan rotating overhead, clicking slightly on every swing.

Janhvi sat opposite the thick glass divider, her fingers gently curled around the edge of the table. Her face bore the quiet determination of someone who had walked through fire and come out stronger. Beside her sat Jayant Ghosh, dressed simply, his face still wearing red and blue bruise marks, his forest-stained notebook peeking from his satchel. His eyes with dark circles were fixed on the corridor behind the glass — waiting.

A creak.

The bolt slid.

And through the small steel door, led by a constable, Jaggu entered.

His eyes scanned the room quickly, adjusting to the light. His gait was slower, less defiant than before. The rough prison kurta hung on his lean frame, but his sharp eyes still held that flicker — the glint of a man who remembered the forest under his feet.

He sat. No words at first.

Only their eyes spoke.

Then Janhvi leaned forward, voice low and firm, breaking the silence.

"Jaggu... we need to talk. And this time, no more running. No more lying."

Jaggu looked at her, then at Jayant.

The air inside the visitor's room grew heavy, as if even the walls were holding their breath.

The drongos outside had fallen silent.

Jaggu's eyes flared as he looked hard at Janhvi — the muscles on his jaw clenched, his cuffed hands tightening into fists on the table. There was a rawness in his voice, unfiltered, as if the weeks of confinement had been building toward this one moment.

"Why have you come here?" he demanded, voice low but burning. "You're the one who called the police, weren't you? You didn't trust me, did you?" He leaned forward, eyes narrowing like a predator cornered. "I could've handled it, Janhvi. I was enough. Alone."

Janhvi didn't flinch. She met his stare with a fire of her own — pain and purpose laced into every word.

"I had no other alternative, Jaggu!" she shot back. "Lakhan— that Rakshas (demon) — had murder in his eyes. Jayant ji's life was hanging by a thread. And you were walking into a death trap!"

Jayant, who had been silent, finally spoke. His voice was calm, but carried the weight of bitter truth.

"Jaggu… listen to me." "Because you tried to save me, you've now declared yourself an enemy of your own world. Your giroh, your own pack, now sees you as a traitor."

Jaggu's face tightened.

Jayant's eyes didn't waver.

"And Raju Bhaiya…" Jayant continued, his voice almost a whisper now. "That haivan (monster) will not rest until your body is dumped in a ditch. The moment you're out of this prison, Jaggu… he'll come for you."

The ceiling fan above continued its slow, hypnotic rotation. Outside, the afternoon sun burned across the walls of Karauli Jail — but inside, the room had gone cold.

Jaggu's jaw stiffened as he leaned forward, his eyes ablaze, voice steady but brimming with fire.

"I am not scared of death," he said, each word deliberate. "I've been raised in forests where tigers snarl and leopards stalk in the dark. I know the scent of danger. I've looked into the eyes of death too many times to flinch now."

His fists clenched slowly on the table. "It's not about dying… not for me. But before I do, I want to end this bloody conspiracy — this empire of violence, of betrayal and greed." His voice dropped into a low growl. "And above all, the land — my ancestral land — the same soil my father had tilled with his bare hands, planting life into every inch… I want it back. From Lakhan's filthy clutches."

At the very mention of that name, Janhvi snapped.

"Don't take his name!" she spat, voice sharp and pained. "That butcher… that beast…"

Jaggu turned to her, puzzled. "Why? What happened?" A hint of concern softened his tone.

Janhvi looked away for a moment, her hands shaking slightly.

"What happened?" she echoed bitterly. "Jaggu, I'm alone. Do you even realize that?" Her voice cracked. "Have you ever thought about what I go through? How vulnerable I am?"

Jaggu's brow furrowed, his voice low now. "What did he do? Did Lakhan… do anything to you?"

Jayant spoke before she could answer, his eyes steady, words sharp.

"Once, she was coming back late— and some ruffians were molesting her. I happened to be there. I fought hard to stop them. But you think that kind of luck will repeat itself forever?" He shook his head slowly. "No, Jaggu. It won't."

Janhvi's voice trembled with a mix of rage and helplessness. "If something happens to me, Jaggu… you will be responsible."

Jayant nodded grimly. "You'll be rotting in this jail, and in a few months, I'll be transferred — project complete, file closed. And

Janhvi?" He glanced at her, then back at Jaggu. "She'll be left alone. Alone in a world filled with wolves and vultures ready to pounce. Who will protect her then?"

A bitter smile touched Jayant's lips. "Sometimes, learn to think with your mind Jaggu, not just your muscles. You're in a cage now. Powerless. And these men you're up against… they're not street thugs. They're kings in a jungle where you've been declawed."

Jaggu leaned back slightly, the fire in his eyes now shadowed by a storm of thought. For the first time, doubt crept into his hardened face. He looked not at his enemies, but at the two people who had stood by him when it mattered most.

Janhvi leaned in, her eyes glistening with urgency. Her hands slowly came together, trembling slightly, until her fingers pressed into a folded plea.

"I'm folding my hands, Jaggu…" she whispered. "Please. For once — for us — for yourself — tell them the truth."

Jayant interjected , "Tell the police and the forest department everything. The people behind this grisly business… the real monsters… bring them to light. Then the courts will certainly reduce your punishment."

Jaggu's jaw tightened. He looked away, the muscles in his neck tensing.

"They will never do that," he muttered. "I'm just a name on a list of criminals to them. A poacher. A number."

Jayant shook his head. His voice was calm but certain.

"No. They will. I've spoken to Mr. Verma — the DFO. At length. He has recently been posted as the Additional Director of WCCB (Wildlufe Crime Control Bureau). He's not like the rest. He's clean. He's honest. And now he has the power to fight this rot from the inside and go after the entire chain. And he understands your predicament, Jaggu."

He stepped closer, lowering his voice.

"He knows you're not just a criminal. He knows you're a man cornered by the system. He knows there's more to you than your past."

Janhvi nodded, her voice growing firmer now.

"Jaggu, you know everything — everything they're doing to these animals. From where the tigers and leopards are snatched, how they are killed, how the parts are stored and moved... the routes, the contacts, the buyers, the middlemen, the corrupted netas. You know every thread of this evil web. You have the power to tear it down."

She leaned forward, tears threatening to fall. "You're not beyond redemption, Jaggu. You never were. You just forgot who you really are."

Jayant added softly, "Step over. Cross the line. Come to our side — to the side of truth, of honesty, of courage. "

Janhvi's voice broke now, her hands still folded before him.

"Killing innocent creatures all your life... do you really think that will bring you peace? Is that the legacy you want? Come with us. Fight with us. Your life can change, Jaggu. So can mine."

Jayant's eyes narrowed as he looked at Jaggu — long and hard — searching for a flicker of emotion, a sign of change. But Jaggu sat there like a stone, his face unreadable, unmoved by pleading or persuasion.

Jayant's voice dropped, now stripped of warmth. "Whatever decision you take, Jaggu," he said gravely, "you better take it fast.You don't have the leverage of time. And you damn well know that."

He stepped closer, placing his palms on the table between them, his voice lowering but turning more intense.

"Do you remember that child ? The one who was kidnapped?"

Jaggu's eyes flickered, just for a second.

Jayant didn't miss it.

"He was kept in the same holding cell as me for a night. He told me everything. About what he saw. And he remembered you, Jaggu. Your face. He said you were there... at the scene... when the tigers were butchered in Kaziranga."

The words landed heavy — sharp and final.

"Don't forget, Jaggu. Now you're not just carrying the blood of tigers on your hands. You're tangled in a child kidnapping case too. Double crimes. Double burden. And you think time is on your side?"

He straightened up, his tone now like flint.

"This is your last window, Jaggu. To speak. To switch sides. Before the system shuts its doors forever."

Janhvi's eyes welled up again, but she didn't speak. Her silence was a quiet echo of Jayant's thunder — a final plea from someone still hoping.

Jayant abruptly pushed his chair back, the metal legs scraping sharply against the concrete floor. Without another word, he turned and walked toward the heavy iron door. But just as his hand touched the latch, he paused, turned halfway around, and shot a look at Janhvi — half-pity, half-command.

"Gift a little bit of grey matter to this madman," he said dryly, jerking his chin toward Jaggu, "or else..." Jayant took a deep breath.

Then he was gone — boots echoing down the corridor.

At that very moment, two female constables in khaki saris appeared at the door, their expressions flat and official. One of them tapped the doorframe and said firmly, "Samay poora ho gaya hai. Let's go. The meeting time is over."

Janhvi whipped her head around, eyes desperate, and pleaded, "Just one minute… please, just one last minute!"

The constables stepped forward, their posture unyielding.

She turned back to Jaggu, voice breaking as she cried out, "Jaggu, please agree! Please, Jaggu… whatever has happened, let it go. Let the past bury itself! We'll live honestly — maybe poor — but we'll have peace. We'll walk with our heads high. I'll be with you. Always. Together, we can make a difference…"

Her voice was trembling, rising, full of longing, agony and fear — but the constables didn't wait. They gently but firmly pulled her away. "Bas, chaliye madam."(Enough Madam, let's go.)

Janhvi twisted her neck, still trying to hold his gaze, but her feet were dragged backward.

Jaggu didn't say a word. Didn't move.

He just sat there — frozen — staring at her, as if trying to burn her image into memory. As she disappeared behind the metal door, his eyes remained locked on the empty space she had occupied.

Staring.

Nightmares of change...

Later that night, deep within the stone belly of Karauli Jail, in the damp, stinking dungeon, Jaggu lay on the hard, narrow bed. His eyes were wide open, staring at the cracks in the ceiling above, but seeing none of it. Sleep evaded him like a hunted animal. He turned to the left. Then to the right. Again and again. But the image wouldn't leave him — the sight of Janhvi being dragged away by the police constables, her face turned toward him, her voice trembling, pleading, fading into the corridor.

The heavy, inescapable echo of Janhvi's final plea kept ringing in his ears. Her imploring voice—"We'll have peace… we'll hold our heads high… together we can make a difference…"—echoes again and again in his mind.

"Jaggu, please agree…"

The whisper circled him like a noose.

Eventually, exhaustion overtook him. His breathing steadied. His muscles relaxed. He slipped into a shallow, tormented slumber — Sleep came — but it came like a storm.

He found himself behind the rusty bars of his cell, but what he saw outside was not the jail courtyard. It was a stage. A gaudy, bright-lit stage with cheap velvet curtains and loud music. Janhvi stood on a brightly lit stage, performing. The spotlight on her was harsh and cruel, unlike the gentle glow of moonlight she deserved. Her saree shimmered under the lights, and her voice quivered with emotion, but the crowd before her was a sea of shadows with eyes that gleamed with lust and greed. They leered. They whispered. They laughed.

And there, seated in a leather chair near the front, his legs casually crossed, a glass of whiskey in his hand, was Harpal Singh, the son of Raju Bhaiya — dressed in a velvet coat, his eyes cold and cruel, locked on Janhvi like a predator sizing up his prey. His fingers drum the armrest, eyes fixated with predatory intent.

He smiled — a slow, vile smile — as he leaned over to one of his friends and said something, pointing at her. The men around him laughed.

From behind the bars, Jaggu screamed.

"Janhvi! Get off that stage!"

But no sound came out of his throat. Nothing. He screamed harder. His hands shook the prison bars, he banged them, but no one heard.

Janhvi was on stage. He watched helplessly as Janhvi's eyes met his in the crowd—but she could't see him.

She was singing, just to make a living, her voice trembling. She had no other income, no one to protect her. The crowd in the rich man's farmhouse was filled with half-drunk, corrupt men, with gold chains on their necks, unbuttoned shirts, greasy smiles. One of them catcalled. Another blew a whistle. One man threw a bundle of notes on the stage. Another blew a kiss.

Janhvi continued to sing, but her eyes searched the crowd — for someone to save her. For Jaggu. But he was not there.

But there, seated at a richly adorned table, was Harpal Singh . He raised a glass and stared, his eyes burning through her like poison through silk.

Jaggu's fists bled from banging the metal.

And Harpal simply raised his glass, smiling directly at him, as if to say:

"She's mine now."

Jaggu jerked in his sleep, drenched in sweat, his breath coming out in gasps.

The dungeon was silent. Only the sound of dripping water in the corner echoed faintly. But Jaggu's eyeballs were quivering beneath closed eyelids, haunted. His face pale and distorted as the scene morphed and the horror changed form.

Jaggu found himself wandering through the emerald wilderness of Kaziranga. He was barefoot, a ghost among trees, his clothes tattered and wet with dew. The forest had once whispered to him like his mother. Jaggu had always been able to read it like a book — its calls, its silences, the rustle of leaves, the warning in the air.

As a boy, he'd known which tree the hornbill nested in, where the deer grazed, where the mighty tiger left its trail. He was freespirited, wild, intuitive, deeply connected to Mother Nature. That was his true gift.

But somewhere along the way, poverty hijacked that gift. Others used his instinct — not to protect, but to destroy.

And now, in the heart of his nightmare, he saw the cost.

He walked aimlessly, near the very patch where the magnificent tigress had once roamed—now reduced to skin and bones by his gang.

The air was heavy with the stink of rot.

And then he saw them..

Three small tiger cubs, lying lifeless in the grass, their ribcages still. The cubs had waited — eyes wide, hearts full of blind faith — for the mother who never returned. Milk never came. Warmth never came. Then they called out to her repeatedly till their voices weakened with thirst and hunger. She never came. Only the long night. And then death. Flies swarmed over their tiny, emaciated bodies.

Jaggu sank to his knees beside them. The weight of his guilt pressed against his chest like stone. Unable to stop his trembling hands, he touches their fur. His breath catches. His heart breaks. Flies circle his face, but he does not brush them away. His guilt weighs heavier than the humid air around him. Cold. Still. He let out a choked breath and hung his head low. Around him, the buzzing of flies grew louder, like the chanting of unseen ghosts. The jungle watched, silent and eternal.

And as the dream spiraled into a fog of remorse, Jaggu curled into himself beneath the harsh light of the prison cell, twitching, whispering in sleep.

And the flies kept buzzing but the dream shifts.

Then the most painful images rise—sharp and vivid.

He watched, as though in a trance, the crime unfold again.

He saw the entire killing of the tigress unfold before his eyes—vivid, bloody, brutal. Lakhan gripped the tigress's tail, yanking her back. Her paw was caught in the thick Bavarian cast-iron jaw snare, and blood dripped steadily into the soil. She roared in anguish, but the forest had no mercy.

Bhola's flashlight blinded her. Chimta, calm and mechanical, stepped forward and drove a long, sharp iron spear inro her open mouth right upto her brain—careful not to damage the prized skin. She thrashed, but she was trapped.

Then, the massive Beera with a baseball bat-like club approached. Without hesitation, he began striking the tigress's skull. Once. Twice. Thrice. Bones cracked. Her eyes flickered and rolled back.

The tigress groaned in agony—her final cry—a haunting, shuddering cry echoing through the forest canopy —desperate, defiant—a cry emanating from the belly of mother Earth asking humans to stop this carnage, one last time.

Then silence.

Her majestic body collapsed to the forest floor with a dull, final thud that echoed across time.

Back in his cell, Jaggu jerked awake, breathless. His shirt clung to his body, drenched in cold sweat. His face was tight with anguish, and his eyes stared blankly at the darkness. His breath came fast, shallow. His fingers trembled.

The dream was over, but its ghosts remained. The room was silent except for the distant clang of a guard's boots and the occasional cry of a spotted owlet beyond the barred window.

Slowly, he stood. Walked to the iron bars. Wrapped his fingers around them.

He spoke, quietly at first, then with rising clarity:

"Gareebi ne mujhe laachaar banake… mujhe gunaahon mein dhakela…" ("Poverty crippled me… and pushed me into sin …")

"Bas ab aur nahin… yahin tak… bas yahin tak." ("But no more… this far and no further.")

And then, with a sudden burst of emotion, Jaggu hit his forehead against the iron bars.

Hard.

His voice cracked — part sob, part vow:

"Janhvi… main aa raha hoon." ("Janhvi… I'm coming.")

"Main aa raha hoon tere paas. Tu hamesha sahi thi." ("I'm coming to you. You were always right.")

Outside, the prison remained silent.

But inside — something profound had changed forever.

The sweat on his body began to cool. His mind cleared like a storm passing over a quiet field.

A stillness filled the prison cell, but it was the stillness before the storm. A hero had risen from the ashes of a criminal. And he would not sleep again — not until the darkness was named, challenged, and defeated.

The man the world had written off as a beast… had finally remembered who he really was.

Yak and Yeti...

Kathmandu bustled beneath the majestic gaze of the Himalayas, its ancient soul humming under the clamor of honking scooters, temple bells, and the calls of street vendors. At the heart of this mosaic stod the elegant facade of Hotel Yak and Yeti, its polished brass doors revolving with a steady stream of foreign tourists, diplomats, and well-dressed locals.

Inside the opulent Presidential Suite, the air was still, tense — thick with anticipation. Interpol officer Russel Hogg, a man with raw determination and nerves of steel sat silently under warm vanity lights, as a makeup artist applied the final touches to his transformation. A hint of grey was added to his sideburns. His skin tone subtly altered. The kind of face hardened by money and stained by illicit deals.

He looked into the mirror as the artist drew the final touch — a scar, faint but menacing, just beneath his eye.

In the background, plain clothes officers from Interpol, WCCB and the Nepal Police CID stood ready — some posing as waiters, others as bellboys. Their eyes flickered with silent codes.

Russel adjusted his cufflinks, where a tiny listening device was embedded. He put the expensive onyx pen with the hidden camera in his coat pocket, adjusted it meticulously and nodded at the makeup artist.

The air conditioning hummed softly, but tension hung louder.

Elsewhere in the Hotel

Interpol sleuths and Kathmandu police officers were positioned all over the hotel — disguised as tourists, waiters, maintenance staff. A few were stationed discreetly in hallways, staircases, and even near the elevators. Weapons were hidden under jackets, behind belts. Walkie-talkies were off. Only coded vibrations and subtle gestures now guided the network. The trap was set.

YAK AND YETI
HOTEL
YAK & YETI

Suddenly, the second phone in Russel's pocket — the one used exclusively for this operation — started buzzing.

He held it up. The officers fell completely silent.

Russel answered in a deep, indifferent voice: "Hello?"

On the other end, the voice was crisp, thick with local grit — unmistakably that of Varad Praja, the infamous poacher and trafficker. The very man the task force has been after for months.

Varad (on phone): "I'll be reaching in a few minutes. Hope you're ready."

Russel: "You've got everything?"

Varad (almost insulted): "Whenever I come, I come with the full goods. My name is Varad, remember that. I carry everything... even the penis if it's a male. Unfortunately yours is a tigress..", ha ha , he laughs brazenly and chips in ,"All fresh. All real. I hope the entire amount is ready."

Russel (coolly): "As promised. Cash. Untraceable. I'll be waiting in the suite."

He hung up.

The entire suite jolted into controlled action.

Russel stood and adjusted the cuffs of his designer coat. One officer whispered into a hidden mic, "Target ETA 3 to 5 minutes. All units, prepare for interception. Repeat — prepare for interception."

A storm was about to hit.

Outside the hotel, a jet-black Toyota Land Cruiser pushed through the crowd. Behind the wheel, Varad Praja, a wiry man with hawk eyes and an old baseball cap, glanced in the rearview mirror. He was carrying more than just secrets today — inside the hidden compartment of the vehicle was a consignment of contraband wrapped in tarpaulin and straw to mask the stench.

Varad wiped a bead of sweat from his brow. He had done this before, but today felt different. Eyes seemed to follow him.

He pulled into the private service entrance at the back of Yak and Yeti. Two hotel staff — men bribed earlier by Varad's fat tips — nodded and opened the gate.

Inside the luxurious suite interior Russel looked at his watch.

Russel (into comms): "Everyone, positions. The fox is at the door."

Varad Praja, known on the streets as Varad Taja — the ghost of the Himalayan trafficking network entered the hotel quietly. Curiosly, the driver Rana, kept the engine humming instead of switching it off. These badass men were trained to trust no one.

Varad was dressed immaculately: a tailored charcoal-grey suit, patent leather shoes, and wore an expression of cold detachment. On either side of him are his trusted lieutenants:

• Bhanu Tamang – Burly, strong, beefed up with a steely gaze that scans the surroundings in milliseconds.

• Dhruva Tharu – Lean, mean, muscular with sharp eyes and a dark black overcoat hanging a little too heavy over his right shoulder.

From a distance, they looked like high-end businessmen.

But hidden beneath Dhruva Tharu's coat, carefully slung around his shoulder, was a sack —the kind that reeks of rot, blood, and extinction. Inside lay the broken remains of a tigress, a mother — its skin, bones, parts no man should trade.

Hotel Lobby – Seconds Later

They walked in with practiced nonchalance. The security guard at the door offered a slight nod, not even a pat-down. The receptionist looked up — and then quickly backed down. They all knew Varad Taja. He was a "regular." The kind of regular nobody wanted to question.

The three men walked past the elevator and pressed for the private lift — the one that went straight up to the top floor suites. The atmosphere was unnaturally calm. An elderly couple sipped coffee nearby. A boy ran past dragging a toy airplane.

What no one saw: A man reading a newspaper lowered his glasses — he was Interpol. A guest scrolling on her phone glanced up — she was CID Nepal. The front desk manager blinked twice — the silent signal.

In Suite 701, Russel checked his watch. "They're in," he muttered.

The countdown had begun.

The ambient jazz tune in the lobby played softly. The golden elevator numbers blinked downward: 6… 5… 4…

Varad Praja, Bhanu Tamang, and Dhruva Tharu stood in silence before the elevator doors. Dhruva adjusted his coat subtly, steadying the hidden sack beneath. Bhanu scanned the glass walls for any sign of threat.

Then — Praja's phone buzzed. A call. Unknown number, but the country code was India.

His brow furrowed. He answered, his voice low.

"Hello?"

The voice on the other end was curt.

"You're walking into a trap, Varad. They're all around you. Interpol. Nepal police. Plainclothes. You've been sold out."

For a moment, Praja said nothing. His pupils narrowed. He looked to the side, like a jungle cat sensing a rustle in the grass.

Then he snapped the phone shut, turned slightly toward Dhruva, and muttered under his breath:

"Trap. Call Rana immediately."

Bhanu's jaw tightened.

The elevator pinged.

But Praja didn't enter. He spun, pushing back towards the lobby entrance — a calculated exit.

Russel Hogg, watching from the suite monitor, saw Praja's sudden movement.

"Code Red. They're alert. Lock the exits. Now!" he said into his mic.

Immediately, hotel security disguised as bellboys moved. Plainclothes police in the lobby switched positions. The rooftop snipers realigned scopes.

Russel's voice crackled in everyone's earpiece:

"Don't let them reach that door. Move!"

As the word “trap” left Varad Praja’s lips, Bhanu Tamang and Dhruva Tharu move like clockwork. They flanked Praja, covering him like a human shield.

"Move!" Praja barked.

The three broke into a synchronized sprint, bolting across the lobby with the speed and precision of a well-trained escape unit — like a cheetah charging through the bush.

Russel shouted into his walkie-talkie:

"They’re fleeing. Seal the doors! Don't let them escape!"

But it was too late.

Before hotel security could even raise a hand, the trio fool everybody by pretending to move towards the main entrance and then suddenly changing course and dashing towards the private back entrance. The Toyota pickup skidded into the driveway, tires screeching. The driver barely slowed.

Varad Praja leapt in, body first, dragging the sack in with him. Dhruva and Bhanu piled in after him.

BANG! The car slammed shut just as a group of plainclothes officers broke through the lobby doors, weapons drawn.

Engines roared.

The black SUV accelerated with violent speed — smashing through a row of parked motorbikes. Metal crashed. Rubber burnt. Sparks flew.

Hotel guests screamt and dove for cover.

Russel, still in makeup, raced down the stairs with two Interpol men at his side, shouting:

"After them! Do not let them vanish!"

Catch me if you can...

Outside, the chase was on. Police jeeps and unmarked cars screeched into the lane, sirens wailing.

The majestic Griffon vulture looked down at the sudden activity with its binocular vision as Kathmandu's streets awakened to the howl of engines, screeching tires, and one of the biggest wildlife trafficking busts ever attempted.

The black SUV tore through the narrow streets, its engine roaring like a beast. Behind it, a convoy of Interpol and Nepalese police vehicles followed, sirens wailing, their lights flashing.

Dhruva Tharu gripped the steering wheel with white-knuckled tension, his eyes darting to the rearview mirror. Varad Praja, seated in the back with his bodyguard Bhanu Tamang, watched the growing line of police cars closing in. Varad's hand was poised over his revolver, fingers twitching.

Suddenly, Dhruva slammed the pedal down, the limousine surging forward. Tires squealed as it took the next sharp turn at breakneck speed, narrowly missing a pedestrian who jumped out of the way. The police cars struggled to keep up, their sirens blaring louder.

The serpentine streets of Kathmandu burnt with fury as the Interpol and police vehicles were in hot pursuit. At the intersection ahead, a police car attempted to box in the SUV, cutting it off from the left. But Dhruva wasn't fazed. He jerked the wheel hard to the right, sending the limousine fishtailing, narrowly avoiding the roadblock.

Behind him, an Interpol car sped up to take the lead, but Varad Praja and Bhanu Tamang weren't just passengers — they were ready to fight their way out. Without hesitation, Varad Praja pushed down the window, and with expert precision, he and

POICE
POLICE
POLICE
Katmanduu

Bhanu started firing their handguns at the police vehicles. Varad fired two shots, hitting the side mirror of an Interpol car, shattering it. Bhanu opened fire, hitting the tires of a pursuing police car, sending it spinning out of control.

Suddenly, Praja's phone rang. It was the same Indian number from earlier. He picked up the phone, gruffly, " Yes?"

Mysterious Indian Voice blurted out," Nepal has been compromised. The goods must not be seized. You have to get the shipment out. Lhasa is the only place it can go. They have cracked the tigress DNA in India."

Narrowing his eyes, Varad replied," Understood. No time to talk now."

Without a second thought, he slammed the phone down, his pulse quickening. He turned to Dhruva.

"Dhruva!" he barked. "We're running out of time. Get us to Swayambhunath. That's where we'll make the escape."

Dhruva didn't hesitate. With a tight nod, he turned the wheel hard, steering the limousine towards the Swayambhunath area, an old part of the city known for its labyrinthine alleys and thick crowds. The streets ahead grew narrower and more congested, a maze of bustling market stalls and temples. It was their best shot at losing the police.

Behind them, two police motorcycles tried to flank the limousine, but Bhanu leaned out of the window again, firing a shot that sent one of the riders tumbling to the ground.

Suddenly, Dhruva Tharu noticed a police blockade up ahead, a large roadblock set up to catch the criminals. It was a perfect trap.

Dhruva panicked,'" They're setting up a roadblock. Hold on!"

Varad replied coldly,"We're not stopping."

With a wild shout, Dhruva veered the limousine onto the dirt shoulder, accelerating past the blockade, just inches from colliding with a police car that was waiting to intercept them. The car swerved but barely avoided the crash.

The SUV barreled down a steep incline, narrowly avoiding falling rocks and tight hairpin turns. The police cars struggled to keep up on the twisting roads, their tires screeching as they tried to match the limousine's pace. "We can't let them catch us here," Varad muttered, his fingers tapping nervously on the door. "Get us to those narrow alleys near the temple."

Finally the chase entered Swayambhunath—a labyrinth of narrow alleys and crowded lanes. The road was full of pedestrians, monks, and tourists, all unaware of the violent chase unfolding just behind them. "Push harder!" Varad shouted.

But Dhruva shook his head. "It's too tight in here. We need an opening."

Just as the pressure was mounting, Dhruva spotted a gap ahead—a series of alleys twisting off to the right, leading to even more congested streets. It was their best chance. He turned the wheel sharply, sending the limousine down a narrower lane, almost scraping the walls on both sides. "We're almost there," he muttered, more to himself than anyone else.

From the top of one of the police SUVs, a sniper took aim, steadying himself against the roof. His rifle gleamed in the sunlight, the barrel fixed on the limousine's tires. The shot rang out, the high-pitched crack of the rifle cutting through the noise of the chase.

In an instant, the right rear tire of the limousine exploded, sending a violent shudder through the car. The vehicle swerved out of control, its momentum carrying it into a violent spin. The tires screeched, the vehicle rumbled and jerked violently, careening across the road, narrowly avoiding a collision with oncoming traffic. The police cars tried to take advantage, closing in on the now-crippled SUV. The vehicle finally came to a grinding halt, striking a divider with a deafening crash. The car's front end crumpled, the body jolting to a stop, the engine stuttering to silence.

Lanes of Swayambhunath...

Before the sound of the collision had even faded, Varad Praja and his bodyguards were already out of the car, moving with lethal speed. They leapt from the wreckage, their hands reaching for weapons and the sack containing the tiger parts.

The chase tore through the sunlit bylanes of Kathmandu like a thunderclap. The alleyways of the Swayambhunath temple area loomed ahead—a confusing labyrinth of tight lanes and hidden corners. Perfect for a quick escape.

The three men didn't look back as they bolted into the maze of bylanes. Bhanu took the lead, his revolver drawn, scanning every corner for danger.

Varad Praja, his charcoal-grey suit flapping behind him, ran like never before , his chest heaving, adrenaline coursing through his veins.

Dhruva Tharu held the sack firmly under his black overcoat, his eyes darting around as he flanked Varad from behind, watchful and alert, scanning for exits and ambushes.

The notorious dealer's mind raced with panic and calculation—They couldn't get caught here. Not now. Not when the tiger parts were so close to being out of Nepal.

Their rugged SUV, now crippled and smoldering by a road divider, was far behind them.

Ahead lay the congested warren of the old lanes near Swayambhunath, narrow as snake paths and teeming with life.

Behind them, the wail of sirens screamed through the heat-hazed afternoon, and the shouts of cops and Interpol agents grew louder with every second. But the criminals knew these lanes.

They darted into a narrow alleyway, flanked by towering brick buildings crowned with sloped wooden roofs and etched window lattices—the quintessential Newar architecture of old Kathmandu. The upper stories nearly touched overhead, casting deep shadows across the sunlit dust below.

The trio's boots pounded against worn flagstones, skidding slightly as they turned a corner. A cart laden with bangles and handwoven scarves stood in their path—no time to evade it. Bhanu rammed through it shoulder-first, sending an explosion of colored glass and fabric into the air. A cascade of beads flew like shrapnel, catching the sun in midair.

A clutch of hens burst from a bamboo cage just ahead, feathers exploding into the air as they flapped into the sky, squawking madly. Dhruva nearly tripped on one as it darted beneath his foot, but recovered and kept running, the sack of tiger parts slung tight under his arm like a rugby ball.

From behind, the police surged into view. The sharp crack of boots echoed through the lanes. "They're heading toward Swayambhu! Cut them off!" Russel Hogg barked into his walkie-talkie, his voice ice over chaos.

Spices were the next casualties. A stack of open sacks—turmeric, red chilli, fenugreek—lined the walls of a tiny shop. A stray elbow from Bhanu sent them tumbling. The air filled instantly with color—yellow, red, brown—forming a swirling cloud of fire and earth, blinding the men and painting them with dust.

They kept running. More vendors dove aside. A man selling Nepalese wood masks dropped his merchandise and ducked behind a column. His colorful masks, representing gods and demons, clattered to the ground—watching, impassive, as the chase trampled over them.

Ahead, the golden spire of the Swayambhunath stupa gleamed briefly between rooftops—a beacon, a destination.

Varad Praja saw it and shouted, breath ragged: "Head for the temple!"

A final twist in the path—an open square appeared.

The massive stone lions of the Temple gate stood like guardians at the edge of chaos.

The trio sprinted toward them, now filthy, streaked in sweat and spices, and still clutching the sack.

A group of pilgrims and tourists had gathered around the gate, snapping pictures, spinning prayer wheels, lighting incense.

Dhruva fired a shot in the air and roared at them—"Move!"—and plowed through the crowd. People screamed, scattered, stumbled.

In one last desperate push, the trio crossed the sacred threshold into the temple complex, where prayer flags danced overhead and ancient stone sculptures watched silently.

Monks and criminals...

Inside the ancient sanctuary of the Swayambhunath Temple, the air was hushed and perfumed with the sweet, smoky scent of incense. The stone walls, worn by centuries of prayer, glowed softly under shafts of sunlight that streamed in from latticed windows above. Rows of butter lamps flickered, casting long, trembling shadows across the floor.

The solemn hum of chanting monks echoed like the breath of the temple itself—low, rhythmic, and hypnotic as they sat in perfect symmetry across the temple floor, dressed in flowing saffron robes, their shaved heads bowed in devotion. The sound of metallic prayer bells and wooden drums rolled gently through the space like waves. The trio stumbled in, breathless, frantic, but aware that they had just seconds before the police would swarm the courtyard.

Dhruva, still holding the sack—now partially hidden in the folds of his jacket—spotted a row of folded robes resting on a carved wooden bench near the entrance, perhaps left for initiates or temple helpers. Without a word, the three men snatched the garments and slipped behind a tall, gilded pillar that supported an enormous prayer wheel.

In one swift, almost sacred choreography of desperation, they removed their black jackets and dusty street clothes. Moments later, all three emerged swathed in the flowing orange-saffron cloth of the monks, their rough movements quickly subdued into mimicked serenity. Dhruva concealed the sack beneath the loose folds of his robe, his face now calm, lips moving soundlessly as though in silent prayer. Bhanu clasped his hands together, his eyes closed. Varad lowered his gaze and folded his legs, seamlessly joining a row of monks chanting with their eyes shut.

Then came the clatter of police boots.

The lanes had slowed them. The crowd had broken their pace. And now, the prey had vanished into the maze of courtyards, shrines, and echoing stone halls of the sacred sanctuary.

Russel Hogg burst into the hall first, a pistol drawn and eyes sweeping. His officers followed close behind, surrounding the interior walls, their eyes scanning the seated congregation. But what they found was only serenity.

The monks did not flinch. The chanting did not stop. Some looked up, startled, but not alarmed. The orange sea of robes was undisturbed—uniform, anonymous, sacred.

Russel's breath was heavy. His eyes narrowed as he moved slowly along the perimeter, scanning faces, looking for a break in rhythm, a flicker of fear. He whispered into his walkie-talkie, "They're here… they're in here… I know it."

But he could not see them. The robes had done their work. The criminals had melted into the very soul of the temple.

A few of the officers moved among the congregation, hesitant, careful not to cause offense. One stepped on a corner of a robe, prompting a sharp look from an old monk who had clearly spent decades in the temple's embrace.

Russel cursed under his breath. "They couldn't have disappeared."

But they had. Or so it seemed.

On the rear side of the temple, hidden behind a large statue of Manjushri, was a narrow corridor that led to a small, weathered wooden door—half concealed by prayer flags and a leaning broom. The criminals had seen it before the police entered. They had waited for the moment when all attention was turned forward. One by one, silent as their new disguise required, the three slipped out through that door into the bright Kathmandu afternoon. A narrow alley welcomed them—a crumbling stairwell leading downward, out of sight.

By the time Russel discovered the back exit, the alley was empty. Alas, they were gone.

Good news and bad news...

High above the terracotta rooftops and temple spires of Kathmandu, the Himalayan Griffon Vulture circled, its massive wingspan catching the late afternoon sun. With feathers like weathered parchment and eyes like burnished onyx, it glided effortlessly, casting its vast shadow over the golden dome of Swayambhunath Temple below.

Beneath it, chaos was slowly giving way to silence.

The police force, weapons lowered, boots dusty, and eyes defeated, had begun to withdraw. Some scanned the city's crisscrossed lanes one last time, others merely shook their heads. The target had slipped through their fingers—vanished like smoke in a place heavy with history and faith.

The vulture tilted its wings lazily, circling once more, as if mocking the ground-dwellers' confusion. Then, with one slow beat, it turned—soaring past the prayer-flagged stupas, over the rustling bougainvillea, across ancient rooftops where stray dogs dozed in the sun, until it reached the district where the Interpol Nepal Bureau stood like a stone guardian. The griffon made a wide arc above the building, a silent witness to what humans below struggled to see—strategy, betrayal, and fate, all turning in the same invisible currents.

Inside the Interpol office, the low hum of machines, faint chatter of agents, and the periodic buzz of incoming data feeds created a tense atmosphere. The blinking lights of the tracking monitors still pulsed like dying stars. The air was heavy, thick with the lingering failure of a near-capture.

Russel Hogg sat alone in his glass-walled cabin, staring at the map spread before him—routes, red pins, CCTV grabs, and a single name circled in red ink: Varad Praja. A half-drunk cup of tea sat untouched beside a thick case file, the seal of Interpol embossed in red.

The official secure phone on his teakwood desk rang. Sharp. Urgent.

Russel picked it up.

"Hogg here."

A warm but serious voice came through the line. “Russel. This is Amit Verma.”

Russel exhaled, leaning back in his chair. “Mr. Verma… good to hear from you.”

Verma’s voice carried a calm steadiness. “I’ve got some good news.”

Russel let out a dry chuckle. “And I have som bad news.”

There was a pause as he ran a hand down his tired face.

Verma broke the silence,” Ok let’s hear the bad news first.”

Russel exhaled slowly. “We had them, Verma. They were inside the temple. We missed them by seconds. They blended with the monks and slipped through a side exit. We were outflanked… by instinct.”

There was a soft rustle on the other end. Papers, perhaps. Or just Verma thinking.

“Have we traced their escape route?” he asked.

“We’re working on it,” Russel replied. “They moved into the alleyways behind the Sanguna Temple. From there, it’s unclear. We’re scanning drone footage and traffic cams.”

There was silence. Then Amit Verma spoke again.

“Russel please keep the media out of this. No leaks. No fingerprints. And this time, don’t just follow them. Think like them. You’ve seen his face. You know how he moves. Anticipate it.”

A soft static hiss from the other side. Then Russel continued, “We’ve issued a Red Corner Notice through Interpol HQ. Every border, every airport, every outpost is on alert. Our informants say he didn’t wait in Kathmandu. He’s moving.”

“Where to?” Verma asked quietly.

Russel’s voice dropped. “Intel says he’s headed north. On foot. Through the mountains. Possibly being escorted. He’s carrying the goods. Our worst fear confirmed—tiger parts. Likely fresh. Possibly from Kaziranga. If he crosses into Tibet, the law will become politics, we may lose jurisdiction. And worse—face diplomatic stonewalls.”

There was silence on the line for a long second. Then Verma spoke.“I can’t believe he’s slipping through so many nets.”

"Classic deep-ops smuggler behavior." Russel said. "Had escape routes mapped. Safe houses, disguises, exit protocols."

Verma's voice was low, measured. "And now for the good news."

Russel raised an eyebrow. "Go on."

"The local police, along with our special wildlife cell, managed to capture someone crucial. The lead tracker of the Bavaria poaching gang. The man who led them to the tigers." Verma said.

Russel's fingers tightened around his pen. "You mean the infamous Jaggu Bavaria?"

"Yes," Verma replied. "Ace tiger tracker Jaggu. Silent, fast, efficient and until now, absolutely loyal to his tribe.

We didn't break him. We cracked him—emotionally. The man's rough, but something changed. His poaching clan tried to ambush the wildlife researcher Jayant Ghosh. Things went wrong. Jayant would have died. But Jaggu turned."

Russel's brow furrowed. "Turned?"

"Yes," Verma said. "Jayant told us later that Jaggu fought his own clan violently and got badly injured to save him from certain death." A long silence followed.

Russel let out a long, measured breath. "That's very good news."

"And there's more," Verma continued. "In one of our late-night sessions, Jaggu revealed something we didn't expect. He's been to Lhasa via Nepal. Not recently—about three years ago. For a deal involving a clouded leopard consignment. High risk. That's when he first met your man—Varad Praja."

Russel's eyes narrowed.

Verma said, "He remembers him clearly. Spoke of him with a mix of fear and awe. Said Varad's one of the only Nepalese men who could operate so freely in Tibet having access to the real players—hidden in the folds of the Himalayas, deep inside the old Buddhist alleys of Barkhor Street."

"Did he name anyone?" Russel asked quickly.

"Yes," Verma said. "An old Tibetan man. Runs a secret wildlife contraband shop beneath the gaze of the Chinese army. Jaggu called him Dechen Limi. Apparently a legend among the Tibetan underworld. He's the final distributor with links across the world. Specializes in tiger bone, skin, pangolins, bear gallbladders—anything that sells on the black market."

Russel closed his eyes and muttered under his breath, "That's the real destination. Not Kathmandu. The pipeline ends in Lhasa before it disperses to various buyers across the world."

Russel slowly stood up, eyes on the soaring vulture above the rooftops beyond the glass window. "It's time we tighten the net, Mr. Verma."

Verma replied, "I already have men tracking the backtrails of the gang in India. Jaggu knows the Indian kingpin who operates through Varad but we cannot prove anything in the court of law until we find the tiger parts and map the DNA back to India. You focus on the northern end and Russel, I have a special request."

Russel Hogg leaned in, sensing the shift. "Go ahead."

"Jaggu is an asset in bringing down the entire chain. Get papers ready for him. I am keen to bring him to Kathmandu with me to track our lost tigress. He's walked the ancient high mountain trade routes and passes they use to smuggle tiger, leopard, snow leopard, bear and pangolin parts through the Himalayan folds. And he's seen Varad Praja face-to-face. He can identify him even if he tries to change his appearance."

Russel hesitated, then said, "But TAR (Tibet Autonomous Region) is Chinese Territory. We'll need a whole raft of permissions. Travel clearance, local cooperation, maybe even a backdoor channel to slip in unnoticed."

"I know," Verma said. "But we can't afford to wait. Jaggu isn't just some informant. He's lived that world. He knows the symbols they use on the packaging. The code names. Even the passwords."

Russel exhaled slowly, the gears in his mind already turning. "And you trust him?"

Verma paused. "He betrayed his tribe to save a man he barely knew."

Russel nodded. "Alright. I'll try. I'll speak to the Chinese desk at Interpol, move some old favors. But this will take finesse. I'll also need a detailed case brief from your end—background, reasons for field deployment, and his importance to the investigation."

Verma said immediately, "You'll have it within the hour. Mail, encrypted line. I'll also send his record, his profile, a list of places he visited in Nepal and TAR."

Russel jotted something down in his notebook and said, "Let me try to make the mountain move."

And as the call ended, outside his window, the golden silhouette of the Himalayan Griffon Vulture wheeled one last time over the Interpol office and vanished beyond the hills—like a spirit from the old stories, carrying secrets on its wings.

The Limis...

High in the bosom of the Himalayas, where the air thins and the silence settles like snow, an ancient trade route carved by centuries of commerce wound its way across the jagged spine between Nepal and Tibet.

This was a road that remembered salt and silk, gold and grain. The high mountain winds whispered secrets of traders and monks who once carried incense and knowledge across the clouds. It was along this serpentine trail, framed by icy ridges and brooding cliffs, that the caravan moved—silent, deliberate and eternal in its rhythm.

A string of yaks trudged through the deep alpine snow, their breath steaming in the cold morning air. They were sturdy, shaggy creatures—beasts of burden shaped by altitude and hardship—each laden with heavy bundles wrapped in coarse, weathered cloth. The faint jingling of their bells echoed through the valley like a ghostly melody, the only sound in a world smothered by whiteness and stone.

The caravan belonged to the old Limi tribe, ancient custodians of the Himalayan passes. Draped in woollen robes dyed in ochre and maroon, with long braids, copper amulets, and deeply lined faces, they guided their yaks with quiet reverence. They walked with a grace born of generations of mountain living, their steps sure even on the knife-thin ledges that hugged the cliffs.

But today, among the seasoned traders, there were three who did not belong.

Clad in identical Limi robes, their faces shaded by sheepskin hats and weather-worn scarves, Varad Praja and his two bodyguards, Dhruva Tharu and Bhanu Tamang, moved without a word. Hidden in plain sight, they became part of the fabric of the caravan. Their eyes, however, betrayed their tension—darting across the ridges, scanning the horizon, watching for any sign of pursuit.

One of the yaks, larger than the rest, carried a carefully tied bundle beneath layers of dried meat, barley sacks, and wool. Inside, sealed in goatskin and cloth, were the bones, claws, and pelts—blood-stained remnants of a slaughtered tigress, a mother, now reduced to merchandise.

As they climbed a steep curve on the trail, a sudden disturbance rippled across the alpine meadow to their left. A herd of Bharal—Himalayan blue sheep—startled by an unseen sound, kicked up tufts of moss and powdery snow as they scattered. Agile and sure-footed, the wild sheep bounded effortlessly over boulders and crags, their curved horns glinting in the sunlight, disappearing into the rocky upper slopes with ghostlike swiftness.

Below, the caravan pressed on, weaving through gorges and ridgelines, where prayer flags flapped like whispers of forgotten prayers. Snow-covered mani stones stood like milestones of eternity, watching this fleeting passage of humans and secrets.

Varad walked silently behind his yak, head down, shoulders tense beneath his robes. The cold bit at his fingers, but he did not flinch. The caravan pushed on, climbing into thinner air and brighter sun, the snow reflecting their passage as if bearing silent witness.

Far behind them, invisible in the distance, the world they had fled was still searching—but here, amidst the eternal snows, they were ghosts among pilgrims.

A brand new avatar...

The thick iron gates of Karoli Central Jail groaned as they opened under the weight of years and authority. A muffled clang echoed across the compound, and a pair of uniformed guards stepped aside. Jaggu stepped out slowly, his head held high, eyes narrowed beneath the midmorning sun. He was lean as ever, but something about him had shifted—like a taut wire that had finally snapped free of its bindings.

Clutched in his calloused hand were a few worn clothes and his temporary release papers—official, stamped, and signed. Jaggu, the infamous tracker of the Bavaria poaching gang, had decided to turn and walk the path of truth.

Outside the jail gates, waiting under the shade of a dusty pipal tree, stood Amit Verma and Janhvi. Above them, the same drongos that had made the pipal tree their home for months now had chicks in their neat little nest—chirping, tiny beaks poking up, hungry for life. The parents took turns darting out and returning with food, their forked tails slicing the air with elegance. Life had gone on, quietly, purposefully.

Mr.Verma wore a khadi kurta, rolled up at the sleeves, his smile wide, though edged with disbelief. He stepped forward, grabbed Jaggu's hand firmly, and shook it with honest warmth. "This is the beginning of your new life, my friend," he said, gripping his shoulder. "You've made the right choice. There's still time to do the right things—for the forests, for the animals, for yourself."

Jaggu nodded, his voice quiet but resolute. "I've done enough harm, Sir. Time to fix what I can."

Janhvi stepped closer, her eyes filled with both pride and mischief. She carried a rugged canvas bag, which she handed to Jaggu. "I packed everything myself," she said. "Woolens, socks, some dried fruits, compass, torch... even your old black beanie." She winked. "Just don't lose it this time."

She reached out, stood on her toes, and gently kissed him—once on each cheek, and finally on his forehead. "For the first time," she whispered, her voice barely audible above the rustling leaves, "I'm truly proud of my man."

Jaggu looked down, momentarily speechless. He wasn't used to this—this kindness, this acceptance. His eyes flicked up to the drongo chicks calling softly from the branches. Fragile, defenseless, but with a future ahead. For a moment, he allowed himself to feel hope.

They turned toward the waiting jeep. Ahead lay treacherous terrain—mountains, frozen borders, and an enemy that moved like smoke. But Jaggu had made his choice.

And with Amit Verma at his side, and Janhvi watching with fierce, quiet strength, he was ready to begin afresh, to embark upon a new journey.

The falcon and the artist...

The Interpol office in Kathmandu sat regal in the crisp morning light—its traditional Nepali pagoda architecture rising with grace against the sky. Outside its red-brick façade, in the courtyard, hundreds of pigeons had gathered at dawn, pecking at scattered grains glinting in the sun.

A hush seemed to hold over the city, a brief silence before the machinery of the day roared to life. And then—sudden, ruthless motion.

A ghost streaked across the sky.

From far above, a peregrine falcon dove with terrifying speed—its wings slicing the air, its eyes locked on its target. With flawless timing, the world's fastest bird slammed into one of the pigeons mid-flight, decapitating it with surgical precision. A flurry of grey feathers exploded in the air. The pigeon crumpled, its body limp before it ever crashed to the ground. The falcon landed moments later with cruel grace, dug its talons into its catch, yellow eyes flicking once to the side—as if aware of the witness beyond the glass.

Inside the Interpol office, behind a large bay window with filigreed edges, stood Jaggu.

He didn't flinch. If anything, his eyes lingered on the falcon for a moment longer, before he turned back to the task at hand.

A charcoal-scented silence filled the room. The walls were decorated with black-and-white photos from decades of police operations. Files, maps, surveillance boards, and satellite prints cluttered the central table. But in the middle of it all was a fresh white canvas pinned to a drawing board.

Sitting beside it was a skilled Nepali artist—an old man with steady hands, grey hair tied in a knot behind his head, and the practiced calm of someone used to extracting faces from words.

A charcoal pencil danced between his fingers, already stained from earlier strokes.

Jaggu stood close, his brow furrowed in concentration. "No... his jawline is sharper. Yes, just like that. There's a scar—small, just under his right ear, half hidden by his hair. He usually keeps stubble, maybe three days' worth. Thick eyebrows… a cut on his upper lip—maybe from a knife fight, long ago."

The artist nodded wordlessly, adjusting the cheekbone with a flick of his eraser, darkening the shadows beneath the nose with a careful thumb smudge. The face was emerging from nothing, sharp and deliberate, like a criminal surfacing through fog.

Jaggu kept pacing slowly, watching each feature come to life. "His eyes—hawk eyes, small but intense. Like a jackal that knows too much. And there's a tattoo behind his neck. A blue dragon."

The artist paused. "You want me to draw the tattoo?"

Jaggu shook his head. "No need. The face is enough. You're doing it right."

Outside, the falcon was now tearing into its kill, pigeons scattering away in panic. But Jaggu's eyes were now on another predator.

On the paper, Varad Praja's likeness stared back. Cold. Sharp. Alive.

The hunter had been sketched. And now, the hunt could truly begin.

The roof of the world...

A caravan of horses wound its way through the ancient trails that twisted like serpents along the snow-clad slopes between Nepal and Tibet. The sky above was a flawless sheet of cobalt blue, and the mountains—those eternal sentinels of ice and stone—rose like white giants, their peaks shimmering beneath the Himalayan sun.

Jaggu Bavaria rode in silence.

He sat straight on his mountain horse, his sharp eyes scanning the landscape with the ease of a man who had lived more years in the jungle than in villages. Beside him rode Amit Verma, now Additional Director WCCB, clad in cold-weather gear, his eyes narrowed against the glare of sun on snow. Interpol's Russel Hogg followed, his foreign features flushed red from the chill, flanked by two Nepali Sherpas guiding the team with their quiet competence.

It was Jaggu who spoke first, his voice low, but filled with a strange reverence.

"These are not roads, saheb... they are memories carved by wind and hooves for centuries. Traders, pilgrims, smugglers, and shadows have passed through this same gorge."

The horses trudged slowly, their hooves crunching through layers of packed ice. The air was sharp with the scent of pine and old stone.

Suddenly the keen eyes of the professional big-cat tracker spotted a movement from afar.

"See that ridge?" Jaggu pointed with a gloved hand.

High above them, camouflaged almost perfectly against the lichen-streaked granite cliffs and snow, the grey ghost of the Himalayas watched.

A snow leopard mother lay crouched, regal and still, her thick tail curled protectively around two rambunctious cubs who tumbled over each other in the snow, swatting and wrestling in innocent play.

The wind played with the ruff of fur around its neck. It neither stirred nor hunted—it simply observed, a phantom witness to the trespass of men and beasts through its ancient realm.

"She watches," Jaggu whispered, half to himself. "Like the mountain watches. Silently, but never blind."

They passed beneath her, unaware that their every movement was marked by those pale silver eyes.

"We are on his trail and our horses are much faster and lighter than his yak caravan," Jaggu said. "The yak dung is fresh. He passed through here—maybe two days ago. He's dressed as a Limi tribesman. His eyes won't meet anyone's. That's how you know it's him."

Russel looked over at him. "And what will you do when you find him?"

Jaggu didn't respond immediately. He looked ahead, where the gorge opened into a wide, frozen meadow rimmed with prayer flags fluttering from a half-collapsed stupa.

"I'll do what the mountain taught me," he said softly. "Track what must be found. And silence what should never have lived."

The horses pushed forward, disappearing slowly into the white world of wind and legend—beneath the gaze of a mother snow leopard and the spirits of a thousand forgotten trails.

Jaggu Bavaria was no longer a prisoner. He was a seeker of justice now, riding into the Himalayas to confront the ghosts of his past.

Chiru...

A few miles ahead of the trackers, the Limi yak caravan trudged steadily onward, its hooves crunching softly over packed snow and thin layers of glacial ice. The sun had climbed higher, casting a silvery sheen over the high-altitude world. The wind carried with it a silence that was ancient and powerful.

At last, the caravan emerged from the narrow gorge into an awe-inspiring expanse—a vast, wind-swept plateau ringed by towering snow-capped peaks. It was like stepping into another realm—where the sky felt closer than the earth, and every breath tasted like the breath of gods.

The yaks snorted and grunted as they lumbered forward under their heavy loads. Varad Praja, cloaked in Limi wool and goggles over his eyes, rode near the center, flanked by his two bodyguards. He gazed over the open plateau with a calculating calm.

Bhanu Tamang, slightly behind him, pulled down his scarf and looked around, squinting through the crystalline air. The harsh landscape triggered a flicker of memory.

"Varad Dai," he said, his voice low but audible in the stillness, "I remember this area..."

Varad turned his head slightly.

"This is where we hunted the chiru once," Bhanu continued, scanning the frozen plains with a glimmer in his eyes. "You remember? The Tibetan antelope... the one with the softest underfur in the world.

We got a few. You had one of the hides turned into a exquisite chaitu shawl. Later we sold it in Milan for twenty thousand euros."

Varad's lips curled slightly, almost imperceptibly.

"The Italians paid like fools for that shawl," he said.

Bhanu grinned. "This region still has them, doesn't it? The chiru? We're passing right through their range. Maybe Dai, we get lucky again. Should we stay one extra night? Set up camp. We've got the rifle. The glacier edge is a good spot. I could take the shot."

Varad was quiet. Only the sound of the wind sweeping across the plateau filled the moment. He looked out over the emptiness, over the glinting plains where the shadows of regal Saker Falcons circled far overhead.

His eyes narrowed.

"One chiru hide," he murmured. "Is equal to a diplomat's monthly bribe."

He looked back at the caravan, the weary yaks, the fading sun.

"Alright," he said slowly. "One night. No more. We camp by the moraine ridge."

He turned his horse toward the gentle slope that led to the glacier's edge, where jagged blue ice met a field of yellowed alpine grass and moss.

Bhanu smiled to himself, already visualizing the antelope—elegant, rare, doomed.

High above, unnoticed, a Lammergeier, the majestic bearded vulture rode the thermals looking out for bones to crack.

And beyond the horizon, getting ever closer, Jaggu Bavaria and his team rode on.

Pashmina...

After navigating the treacherous ridges of the Nyalam Tongla Pass—locally whispered as the Kuti Pass—the horse caravan finally crossed over the spine of the Himalayas. The air was thin and sharp, every breath drawn with effort. From this vantage point, the world below looked folded and ancient, like a crumpled silk map of glacial blue and slate-gray valleys.

The group descended slowly into the vast water divide between the roaring Arun and the glistening Sankosi rivers. Jagged icefields melted into braided rivers that ran clear as crystal, tumbling down from distant snowfields.

Russel Hogg shaded his eyes as he gazed at the horizon—towering peaks watched like silent sentinels. Jaggu, ever alert, rode ahead, his gaze flicking across tracks, ridgelines, and clouds. Something primal stirred in him—he was back in the vast outdoors that his instincts were primed for. Mr. Verma sat astride his horse in quiet contemplation, while the two Sherpas led steadily, reading the wind and the sky.

As they descended further, the landscape transformed again.

The caravan came to a gentle halt in the heart of the alpine meadow—a vast green sea nestled like a secret between snow-draped ridgelines. The place felt untouched, sacred, a quiet gift of the high Himalayas. The air here was crisp and clear, thinner, yet filled with the scent of glacial springs, wild thyme, and damp earth.

Tiny streams carved through the grass, fed by melting glaciers above, their waters glassy blue against the lush moss-green. The thirsty mountain horses bent their necks and drank deeply, their nostrils flaring, water dripping from their whiskers.

Jaggu stepped away from the group, silent, purposeful.

He kneeled and scooped a handful of damp alpine soil, rubbing it between his fingers. Then, rising slowly, he tilted his face to the wind, closed his eyes, and let it speak to him. The air told a story—cold, bearing hints of campfire smoke, yak sweat, and something else—human presence. He released a pinch of earth into the breeze.

The soil danced in the air and scattered northward like brown snowflakes.

Jaggu opened his eyes. "He's close," he murmured, more to the wind than to anyone else.

Russel watched this in fascination. Even the Sherpas stood still, one of them muttering under his breath in awe, "Bavariya tracker…"

Then, from behind a ridge, emerged a slow-moving, serene flock of Pashmina goats—wooly, elegant, and glowing like pearls against the green.

A group of Pashmina herders surrounded the path—sun-browned men and women wrapped in yak-wool shawls, their cheeks leathery and red from the cold. One of them raised a hand in greeting. The caravan slowed. Jaggu watched the herders with a tracker's eyes—friendly, but measuring. These highland people, though remote, saw everything. The herders murmured in Tibetan dialects, some exchanging glances at the sight of the strangers.

Just then, from the far side of the meadow, came a boy—barefoot, lean, sun-baked. No older than twelve. A string of tiny Pashmina goats followed him, bells around their necks chimed in rhythm, soft and melancholic. He moved with ease over the grass, occasionally whistling to nudge a stray goat back in line.

Russel dismounted and gently approached him, offering dried figs as a gesture. The herder boy smiled, accepting them with a nod.

Verma nodded.

He crouched to the child's level, then slowly unrolled a carefully folded piece of paper. The paper held the charcoal sketch—sharp cheekbones, narrow eyes, a trimmed goatee, and the unmistakable lines of Varad Praja's face.

The child's dark eyes scanned the portrait.

He stared.

And then… he pointed.

With his thin arm stretched, he aimed straight towards the north—toward the looming, craggy spine of mountains where the wind howled like wolves and the valleys grew narrow and deep.

Russel glanced toward Jaggu, his eyes lighting up.

Thumbs up.

Jaggu nodded slightly, the corner of his mouth curling with satisfaction.

They mounted up again.

The horses plodded through the cold stream, splashing over mossy rocks. The goats scattered gently aside. The wind, now stronger, carried whispers of the road ahead.

The sun had already begun its slow descent behind the western snowcaps, spilling golden light that glazed the peaks and turned the glacial streams into molten silver. The horses were tired, their flanks rising and falling heavily.

Russel turned to Jaggu. "Should we camp here for the night?" he asked, his voice calm but edged with concern. "The horses are tired. The men too."

Jaggu didn't answer immediately. He was standing still, looking north, as if his eyes could part the mountains. Then he turned, face half-shadowed by the dying light. "No," he said firmly. "He's got one day on us. Maybe more. Every hour we waste, he climbs higher into the wind."

Russel studied him for a moment—then nodded.

The horses snorted, hooves heavy on the wet turf. The breeze grew sharper, more impatient. As they rode, the meadow thinned out, replaced by grey stone trails etched into the mountainsides like old scars. The green gave way to gravel. The air grew colder to their west, the sun dipped behind the ridgeline in a slow farewell, streaking the sky with ochre and ash.

Jaggu urged his horse forward, gaze locked on the rising dusk. Behind him, Russel followed—no longer questioning, only trusting.

The ridges ahead looked grey and bleak now, like sleeping giants carved out of sorrow. Wind picked up, whistling through the rocks, carrying faint howls and the rustle of unseen wings.

The group approached a narrow, windswept ledge that opened into a natural basin — a place once used by traders, now forgotten by time.

The remains of an old camp lay strewn across the clearing. Tattered blankets, half-burnt firewood, and a broken flask lay in the snow.

Nearby, the half-chewed rib bones of a mountain goat glistened under the moonlight — picked clean by Himalayan Griffons amd Golden Eagles and the marrow polished off by Lammergeirs.

Russel knelt beside a cluster of footprints leading away from the camp. He ran his fingers across one. "This wasn't long ago."

Jaggu nodded grimly. "About a night back. They were here."

The group moved forward cautiously. The trail now slithered along a knife-edge ridge, barely wide enough for the horses. One slip and they'd tumble into the icy gorge below.

The wind howled louder here, carrying with it the mournful sighs of the peaks and the fluttering of prayer flags long shredded by storms.

Finally, after an hour of navigating the ridge in bone-deep fatigue, the caravan came to a halt. The horses refused to go further. Their flanks trembled, and even Jaggu's sharp instincts were dulled by exhaustion. The moon now hung high — a cold white eye in a velvet sky scattered with stars.

And then they saw it.

Far across the dark stretch of the valley, near the curve of a distant mountain shoulder, a faint plume of smoke spiraled gently upward — a ghostly trail of grey ink against the moonlit horizon.

Russel narrowed his eyes. "A campfire," he murmured.

Jaggu didn't respond. His eyes had already locked onto the rising smoke, jaw tight. "We rest here," he said quietly, "but only till the first light. That smoke… that should be them."

The group dismounted, quickly setting up a barebones camp on the edge of the ridge. The wind blew hard, but no one spoke.

High above, like a silver ghost in the moonlight, a snow leopard mother watched from her ledge, her pale eyes scanning the activity below. Her two cubs bounded and rolled playfully in the snow beside her, sharpening their reflexes, unaware of the men and their quiet mission winding through the chiseled backbone of the world.

Silver wolves in moonlight...

The fire crackled low. Thin tendrils of smoke curled upward, mimicking the distant column on the horizon. One by one, the men drifted into uneasy sleep, wrapped in their cloaks, the horses tethered close, their breath misting under the frigid moon.

Jaggu lay wrapped in his sleeping bag, the fire a faint orange glow behind him. Above, the moon sailed silently through a velvet sky. His breath rose in little wisps and disappeared into the cold.

Sleep came quietly — but the dream thundered in.

He was on horseback — a tall, black beast, muscled and fierce, galloping across a dangerous, craggy trail, flanked by cliffs and loose gravel.

But he was not alone.

Janhvi rode with him, her dark hair flying in the wind like a wild banner, her eyes fierce, alive, her arms around his waist, her body pressed close to his back. He could feel her breath against his neck, the rhythm of her heartbeat in sync with his.

Above them, the sky opened like a velvet scroll — a million stars strewn across the heavens. The moon followed them, cold and luminous, casting long shadows on the rock and snow.

Sweat mingled where their bodies touched — not from fear or fatigue, but the raw intensity of closeness, of being together against the night.

The horse surged forward, hooves pounding over loose stone and brittle alpine grass, cutting through a vast, cold wilderness of jagged cliffs and shadowed ridges. Then — a sound.

A distant howl, low and tremulous, floated over the wind.

Another answered. Then another. Until the entire range echoed with the haunting song of the mysterious, the mythical—animals of Tibetan legend—silver spirits of the night—Himalayan wolves.

Janhvi stiffened. Her fingers dug into his shoulders. "Jaggu..." she whispered.

"Don't worry," he said, not looking back, his voice steady. "They'll try. But they won't catch us."

But the wolves did try. A pack emerged from behind a rise, their lean bodies loping over the stone and snow, eyes glowing like embers in the dark. They were swift. Coordinated. Alive with hunger.

The black horse pushed faster, its nostrils flaring. Jaggu leaned low, shielding Janhvi with his body, feeling her grip tighten as the howls swirled around them like wind.

Then — just ahead — a shape emerged on the trail.

The alpha male.

Massive. Silver-furred. Its eyes fixed on Jaggu. It stood still, head raised, and let out a long, primal howl that split the silence.

The sound was piercing.

And then—

Jaggu woke up.

Eyes wide open. Chest rising.

He was in his sleeping bag, beside the now-dead campfire. Ash drifted lazily in the air. The mountains around were still cloaked in moonlight.

But the howling? It hadn't ended.

In the distance, from across the ravines and ridgelines, the real wolves sang to the night — these wolves were as ancient as the mountains— not dreams, but flesh and fang.

Jaggu lay there quietly, watching the sky, remembering the warmth of Janhvi against him. And the chase that had followed.

His eyes scanned the ridgelines, and only then did he realize… they had unknowingly camped in sacred ground.

The territory of the Himalayan wolves.

These high mountain wolves were unlike any others in the world. Their fur was thicker, their eyes — golden or ice blue — gleamed with an intelligence that felt almost human, or older than human. The locals called them bhootya bhediya — ghost wolves —

believing their howls carried the voices of lost ancestors or forgotten gods.

More than half a dozen howls rose from different directions . They were encircled, not hunted — not yet. The wolves weren't attacking. Not stalking. Merely watching.

Curious.

Jaggu stood up slowly, careful not to wake the others just yet. He walked a few steps from the camp, letting the wind touch his face, and knelt down. He pressed his palm to the earth, listening to its stillness.

For a second, he thought of the dream. Janhvi's breath, the gallop of the black horse, the burning chase — and the alpha on the trail.

He looked up again at the moonlit cliffs.

Somewhere out there, the alpha was real.

Watching.

Some wolves ran in dreams.

Others waited in the dark.

Divine Guidance ...

The wolves had gone silent now — the way mountains fall silent before an avalanche. The campfire had died down to embers, faint warmth flickering in the chilly dawn breeze.

Jaggu rose slowly, careful not to disturb the others. The world around him was still bathed in a cold moonlight, but to the east, a faint crimson hue had begun to bleed into the dark — the very first breath of morning.

And then he saw it.

Framed against the low-hanging moon and the blushing eastern sky, a lone Himalayan wolf stood like a spirit carved in stone. It was the alpha — broad-shouldered, with a thick ruff of fur haloed by the dawn glow. Its pale, ancient eyes locked with Jaggu's.

It didn't move.

Until it did — with silent grace, slipping sideways along a narrow ridge, not fleeing, but leading.

Jaggu's heart beat a little faster. This wasn't chance.

He stood up and quietly nudged Russel and Mr. Verma awake. "Don't speak. Just follow me," he whispered. "We've got guidance."

Russel rubbed his eyes. "Guidance?"

Jaggu only gave a half-smile. "The mountain wolves," Jaggu said, voice low, reverent. "They're guiding us. We've entered their land. And they want us to see something."

Within minutes, the group was silently mounted, following Jaggu as he guided them along the wolf's path — up the cold, winding trail hugging the cliffs, hooves muffled by dew-drenched moss and loose shale. The horses were uneasy at first, sensing the presence of predators, but Jaggu whispered to them softly in his tribal

tongue. The mountains listened.

The silhouette of the wolf kept appearing ahead — vanishing, then reappearing on a ledge, as though tethered to some invisible path only Jaggu could sense.

Just as the sun's first light kissed the white tips of the peaks, a sudden crack tore the silence.

A gunshot.

Like a thunderclap tearing the sky, it rang from the north-northeast, echoing through the stillness.

Jaggu felt something stir deep within, an old instinct passed down through generations of hunters — something no compass or map could teach.

He turned his head slightly, scanning the lilac-drenched cliffs and valleys. The wind carried a faint but distinct scent — musky, powdery, wild — not wolf… antelope.

Chiru.

Jaggu turned slightly in the saddle. "That's them," he said quietly. "Dechen Limi. They're hunting Chiru. And they're close."

The wolves vanished into the dawn mist. But their work was done. They had brought the team exactly whereit needed to be.

Jaggu looked over his shoulder at Russel and Verma. "We're half a day behind them now. If we move fast, we may catch them before they leave the valley. "They're hunting on sacred land — the Gods may not forgive, but we'll make sure they pay." the two Sherpas said angrily.

And with that, the horse caravan plunged ahead through the pass, guided not just by man, but by legend.

Across the snow-kissed northern ridgeline contoured by the first golden rays of morning , a sharp wind swept across the Tibetan plateau. Perched high on a craggy outcrop, Varad Praja lay belly-down beside a rock, his gloved hands steadying the long-barreled rifle against a stone ledge. On either side of him, his two bodyguards — Bhanu, Dhruva and Gyaltsen, a Limi hunter — crouched low, eyes fixed on the vast openness below.

Far across the plateau, dusted in morning light, the Chiru had begun to emerge — spectral shapes at first, ghosting through the haze, their horns slender and curved, their coats glinting pale against the golden alpine grass. There must have been thirty or forty of them, slowly grazing, unaware of the hunters watching from above.

"This is it," Gyaltsen murmured. "This time, don't fire until they are in range. Be still. Let them come closer. Let them settle."

Varad adjusted the scope, held his breath. The faint click of the rifle's safety going off seemed to echo unnaturally in the stillness.

But then — chaos.

Without warning, the peaceful rhythm of the herd was shattered. Heads snapped up. Ears twitched. In the next heartbeat, the Chiru bolted, kicking up a storm of dust. Graceful limbs blurred as they surged across the plain in full flight, galloping away from the ridge, away from the hunters, vanishing fast.

"What the hell—?" Bhanu hissed. "What happened?"

Praja swore under his breath, scanning the plateau with his scope. And then he saw them.

A sleek, relentless pack of Himalayan wolves — seven in number — streaking across the expanse in perfect formation. They moved like spirits, each pelt distinct: silver-grey, black as basalt, coffee-colored, dusty brown, moving with chilling grace. At their helm ran the alpha — regal, powerful, its pale eyes locked onto the fleeing antelope. They weren't hunting to feed. Not yet. They were driving.

"Wolves," Praja growled. "Those bloody wolves. They've ruined everything."

"They drove the Chiru," Gyaltsen muttered. "On purpose?"

"No accident," Varad said bitterly, rising to his knees, slinging the rifle behind him. "They smelled us… or something else. Either way, the Chiru are gone. And so is today's hunt."

He spat in the dust, watching the wolves chase the herd into the distance, their silhouettes shrinking against the morning light.

"More than a full day wasted," Varad muttered. "And now we start again."

A little southwards, back in the wind-raked silence of the high Himalayas, Jaggu crouched low beside a stretch of snow-patched ground, his fingers brushing lightly over the hard-frozen crust. His eyes narrowed. A set of indentations — deep, sharp-edged — crisscrossed a vein of blue ice. Yak hooves. Heavy. Precise.

Russel and the Sherpas looked down.

"The edges of the hooves—" Jaggu explained, "—they're still sharp. The wind hasn't softened them, and there's no snow drift over the trail. These people... they're not more than half a day ahead of us."

He glanced up at the jagged trail that wound across the glacier.

For hours after that, the group moved in near silence, each hoof-fall and footstep a soft crunch against the snow. Time blurred. Breath misted. And still, Jaggu pressed on like a man chasing shadows.

Meanwhile a few valleys across, as the sun was sinking over the western rim of the Himalayas, casting long shadows over the jagged peaks, the Limi yak caravan showed no signs of stopping.

The yaks trudged on, their heavy breaths steaming in the cold air, their woolly coats dusted with fine frost. Their heads hung low, legs stiff with fatigue. A few stumbled over uneven stones, their bells clanging dully. The caravan, normally slow but rhythmic, now moved with forced urgency.

Varad Praja rode near the front, his jaw clenched, eyes fixed ahead. He hadn't spoken in a while, but his fury was palpable. Losing more than a day to a botched hunt had pushed him to the edge. He wanted ground covered. Fast.

A few of the Limis — thin, sunburnt men wrapped in patched wool and felt — paused to adjust the baggage on one of the staggering yaks. They muttered in Tibetan, exchanging worried glances. But before they could say anything further, Bhanu Tamang snapped, "No breaks. Push on!"

The bodyguards echoed the command. The caravan heaved forward into the deepening twilight, silhouettes stretched thin across the falling light. Eventually, the sun dropped behind the ridgeline and darkness poured into the valleys.

At last, grudgingly, the caravan slowed. Torches were lit. A few rough tents were hastily pitched on a narrow clearing beside a slope.

Cook fires sputtered to life. The yaks collapsed on their knees, groaning with exhaustion.

Miles away, nestled near a sparse Bhojpatra tree (Himalayan birch) grove on a ledge overlooking the high valley, Jaggu, Russel, Mr. Verma, and the Sherpas had set up camp. Their horses were tethered and feeding on crushed grains. A fire crackled in the center, casting flickering light on their wind-chapped faces. Steam curled from their mugs of yak- butter tea.

Russel raised his night binoculars and trained them across the far distance, over ridges shrouded in silver mist. The moon had risen now, casting a ghostly glow across the snow.

He focused. Adjusted. Then stilled.

"I see them," he murmured. "Far slope. They've camped."

Jaggu looked up.

Russel lowered the binoculars, his voice cool and certain: "We're closer than you think."

"Put the fire out immediately," he said sharply, "I don't want any of them to spot the smoke from a distance."

The Sherpas moved quickly, scooping snow and soil onto the flames. The fire hissed, flickered once, and went out, plunging the ledge into cold shadow. A faint wisp of smoke curled up and vanished into the black air.

They all huddled close. Supper was modest — a steaming broth of lentils and roots, with chunks of hard yak cheese softened by the heat.

Somewhere behind them, a Himalayan owl hooted once.

And pristine silences swallowed the mountain again.

Snowstorm...

The wind began to change. A steady hum grew louder, sharper, keening down from the north like a warning. Jaggu, still chewing, turned his face to the wind and frowned.

From beyond the northern mountains, the sky had begun to churn — grey clouds with jagged underbellies tore across the peaks. The moon blinked in and out of sight, cloaked by sudden gusts of cloud. A snowstorm was rising. A bad one.

"That looks like trouble," Russel muttered, scanning the sky with a veteran's calm.

Jaggu nodded grimly. "If it snows... by morning all the hoof marks of the yaks — they'll vanish. It'll be like they were never here."

Verma, still sipping his broth, chuckled and looked up at Jaggu through the steam. "A real tiger," he said, "makes use of an approaching storm to his advantage."

Jaggu cracked a small smile while his eyes remained on the dark sky, calculating.

Without another word, the group moved swiftly. The Sherpas led the way, guiding the horses and supplies behind a series of jagged boulders nearby. The rocks formed a natural windbreak, giving them some cover.

They hunkered down, tying down the tarps, tightening their cloaks, and securing the horses. The wind howled louder now — an ancient cry that echoed off the cliffs, as if the mountains themselves were warning them.

The first flakes began to fall — slow, silent, and cold.

As the first wave of the storm lashed against their rocky shelter, Russel unzipped a side pocket in his weatherproof backpack and pulled out a tiny object wrapped in silver foil. He unfolded it with precision — revealing a slender electronic chip, no larger than a thumbnail, blinking faintly with a green pulse.

He held it up against the storm-lit sky and turned to Jaggu.

"This is your ace," Russel said, his voice low but firm above the howling wind. "It's a satellite transmitter — military grade. Just attach it to the fur of the yak that's carrying the tiger parts. Don't worry, it'll stick through rain, snow, storm... even bullets."

He placed the chip in Jaggu's open palm.

Russel continued, "Once it's in place, I'll get the coordinates in real time on my laptop. We'll track the movement of that yak from Kathmandu HQ and relay it to Lhasa. After this, it won't matter even if an avalanche hits. We won't lose them again."

Mr. Verma, now standing beside them with a scarf around his face and frost in his mustache, gave Jaggu a look of half-teasing challenge and half-fatherly pride.

"Alright, Jaggu," he said, his voice gravelly. "This stormy night is your agnipariksha (trial by fire)... your test. Let's see how fearless a tiger you really are. How powerful you are in the wild."

Jaggu closed his fingers around the chip and nodded silently, eyes glinting in the storm-light.

Then, without a word, he adjusted the leather straps on his chest, pulled his cloak tighter, and moved into the dark mouth of the storm — just another shadow slipping into the blizzard, swallowed by the swirling wall of snow.

Wind howled like a wild spirit through the mountains, each gust lashing at him like a whip. Snowflakes, sharp as needles, stung his eyes. But Jaggu pushed on.

Through craggy ridges and across slippery mountain ledges, he moved like a nocturnal creature of the wilderness — crawling when needed, gripping ice-packed rocks, slipping into gorges and emerging with snow on his back and sweat on his brow. His breath fogged the freezing air, but he never paused. His eyes locked on the faint flicker ahead: the soft amber glow of a distant fire — the only sign of the Limis.

It took hours.

By the time Jaggu reached the outer ridge overlooking their camp, the snow had thinned, the storm had diminished in fury, and the moon had returned, casting an eerie glow through ghostly clouds. Down below, the Limis were asleep in their tightly pitched tents, their breath barely visible, their rifles stacked by the entrance.

The yaks stood tied in a cluster near a rocky slope, weary and quiet, their shaggy fur encrusted with snow, chewing the last remnants of fodder. He crouched low and like his childhood days in the jungle, he started moving on all fours — a beast among beasts.

His eyes scanned every yak, until he found it — the one with the unusually heavy saddlebag slung over its side. He remembered the bulge. The subtle shape that hinted at something stiff, not wool or gear, but bone… skin… death.

Keeping his weight low, Jaggu crawled closer, inch by inch. The yak turned its head and snorted. Jaggu froze. Not a sound. Then slowly, with a trembling hand, he reached under the long fur below the animal's neck.

The yak flinched but didn't cry out.

Jaggu pressed the chip deep into the fur, sticking it against the warm hide. He smoothed the fur over it, letting the long strands fall naturally to hide the device.The green light on the chip blinked once… then vanished beneath the fur.

But the moment his fingers withdrew, the yak jolted. It snorted, shook its head violently, and let out a low, unsettled grunt. The other yaks stirred in response, pulling at their tethers, hooves scraping the rocky ground, their guttural sounds piercing the stillness of the night.

Jaggu's eyes widened. He froze.

From one of the tents, a flap suddenly burst open. A silhouette emerged — one of the Limis, clutching a rifle tightly, eyes scanning the dim, snow-lit night. He clicked his tongue, a sharp tsak tsak sound meant to hush the herd, but the disturbance had already triggered his instincts.

He moved towards the yaks.

Jaggu didn't hesitate. Like an animal, he dropped on all fours, lowering his body into the shadows behind the animals, his childhood jungle instincts kicking in.

The rifles in the camp weren't just for show — one wrong move, and they'd shoot first, ask later.

He crawled fast, weaving through the tangle of yak legs, dung, and ice patches. The disturbed yak let out another snort, making the Limi quicken his steps.

The Limi cursed softly under his breath, thinking: Farah (Tibetan Wild Dog)? Wolf? Lynx?

Then he saw something—movement. A blur of form, fast and low to the ground, darting through the tail end of the caravan. The creature — whatever it was — bounded like a beast, not upright like a man.

Jaggu didn't stop. He galloped on all fours past the last of the yaks, heart thudding, lungs burning, but mind razor-sharp. He felt the cold bite of the storm again as he cleared the perimeter of the camp.

The Limi raised his rifle, squinted into the dark — but whatever it was had disappeared into the storm-shrouded ridge. Only the swaying yak lines remained.

The haunting howl of a Himalayan wolf came drifting from afar in the chilly storm breeze.

He stood silent for a moment. Listening. Watching. Then exhaled.

"Bloody wolf," he muttered to himself and turned back to the tent, zipping it shut behind him.

Far from the camp, Jaggu didn't stop until the sounds of yaks and the faint glow of the fire had completely vanished behind the rocks and ridges. He stood up slowly, panting, letting the wind and snow lick the sweat off his face.

The chip was in place.

Bingo...

Next morning, the storm had passed.

A crisp, surreal stillness blanketed the Himalayan expanse. The dawn sky blushed with a soft, majestic crimson, bathing the snow-covered peaks in a heavenly glow. The wind had settled into gentle whispers, and ragged, ghostlike wisps of storm cloud drifted lazily across the sky, dissolving into the light.

Russel Hogg stepped out from behind the rock shelter, stretching his arms stiff from the cold. He rubbed his hands together, breath visible in the chill, and unzipped the pouch on his weatherproof bag. Inside, snug between foam padding, was the device that could change everything.

He flipped open the rugged laptop and pressed the power button.

The screen blinked to life.

A moment passed, then another. The team gathered around — Mr. Verma adjusting his shawl, the Sherpas sipping steaming tea, and Jaggu standing silently, eyes fixed on the screen.

And then, with a soft digital beep — a small blinking dot appeared on the topographic map.

It was moving.

Russel's eyes gleamed. "He did it," he said, looking up at Jaggu.

Mr. Verma clapped Jaggu on the back. "The tiger has struck."

Jaggu gave a small nod, watching the dot advance slowly across the terrain. The beacon had been activated. The yak was on the move — and now, so were they.

Russel's fingers flew across the keys as he connected the satellite radio to his laptop. The cold wind whistled faintly over the ridge, but the camp was silent with attention.

He picked up the rugged radio handset, adjusted the frequency, and spoke with precision. "This is Russel Hogg, field unit northeast Himalayas. Beacon activated. I repeat — the beacon is moving. Coordinates are being transmitted live."

He paused, listening to the crackle and response.

Then continued, switching channels.

"Interpol Kathmandu — coordinate with Lhasa team immediately. I want the ground asset to intercept the beacon after rendezvous."

A beat.

"Also — inform the Lhasa team to prep the checkpoint with the sniffer dog unit. The beacon's direction suggests Varad Praja's team will attempt breaching the outer perimeter near the city. The tiger contraband is on the move."

He turned briefly to Jaggu and Mr. Verma, then back to the radio.

"A red-corner notice has already been issued on Varad Praja. He is armed, dangerous, and desperate. Reinforce the outer surveillance ring. If he slips through this net, we may never get another chance."

The reply came: affirmative clicks, confirmation codes, and voices of urgency crackling back. Russel lowered the handset and turned to the team.

"Come on, everyone," he said, lifting his eyes to the ridgeline beyond. "The beacon is moving towards Lhasa. We need to stay right on their heels. No delays now."

Wisps of pink clouds drifted above, aglow with the fire of morning. Russel stood quietly for a moment, taking in the sheer grandeur of the high mountains. Then, with a warm look, he turned to Jaggu and clapped him on the back.

"Well done," he said, voice low and firm. "You truly are a tiger."

The elite team...

Meanwhile, deep in the labyrinthine alleys of Lhasa's old quarter—where crimson-robed monks brushed shoulders with traders and pilgrims—an unmarked, inconspicuous safe house nestled between a thangka shop and a Tibetan eatery served as the temporary base for the Interpol team. The rising sun painted the ancient city in hues of gold and amber. Prayer wheels turned slowly in the breeze, and yak butter smoke curled from temple roofs into the pale morning sky.

Inside the inconspicuous, modest room, the Interpol team worked in silence. Their laptops were powered by portable battery packs. Surveillance feeds, satellite links, and the blinking red beacon from Russel's chip were projected onto a makeshift cloth screen pinned to the wall. All eyes were on it.

"It's moving..." whispered an agent with close-cropped hair and Tibetan features, pointing at the signal's slow crawl across the map. "All signs indicate it will enter through the northern pass. Their likely destination? Dechen Limi's curio shop."

The shop in question was infamous among wildlife investigators: tucked behind rows of antique stores and fake thangka stalls, it sold tiger skins, snow leopard pelts, pangolin scales, and bear bile—openly, brazenly, in glass display cases. Local officials turned a blind eye. Chinese soldiers often patrolled the neighborhood, not to stop the trade, but to monitor foreigners and dissent.

The team knew the risks.

"This is sensitive territory," murmured Tenzin Dorjee, their field lead—his voice low, his Mandarin-accented Tibetan precise. "We're not just dealing with criminals here. The Chinese army could intervene if they catch a foreign-led operation. No open comms."

At his feet, a lean, muscled German Shepherd sat alert, ears twitching, eyes fixed on his handler. The dog had been specially trained to sniff out wildlife contraband—bones, skins, horns, and blood.

"Dawa," Tenzin said softly looking at the dog and then, addressing the handler. "Your boy ready?"

The handler gave a short nod. "Dawa's nose is sharper than a customs knife. If the tiger parts are there, he'll find them."

The interpol team stood poised and focused. The air was taut with purpose as they moved into formation, each member prepared for the mission that lay ahead, comms tucked discreetly under collars, sidearms holstered. Each agent had been assigned a specific entry route into the marketplace to avoid spooking the suspects.

"Dechen Limi will have guards. Cameras. And probably locals paid to keep watch," Tenzin said, looking around at his team. "We go in soft, quiet. No alarms. No noise. No weapons unless absolutely necessary. If the chip leads us to the shop, Dawa goes in with the handler under the guise of a curious buyer. Once we confirm the parts are in, we coordinate the takedown silently."

The German Shepherd let out a low, soft whine, as if it could already sense the tension in the air.

Tenzin stepped to the window and carefully peered outside. A Chinese army truck rumbled past the far end of the alley.

"We're not just chasing smugglers," he said quietly. "We're hunting ghosts in a city built on secrets."

The red beacon...

The alleys around Barkhor Street throbbed with life — pilgrims spinning prayer wheels, monks murmuring sutras, and tourists inspecting souvenirs. Yet in one shadowed corner, three figures remained utterly still.

Russel Hogg, Amit Verma, and Jaggu had positioned themselves barely ten feet from Dechen Limi's shop.Their hair was dusted with dry storm grit. The stains of snows of the high passes still clung to their coats. They crouched low behind a stack of empty crates and prayer flag-draped debris beside an old wall. From this vantage point, they could see both the side alley and the narrow back entrance to the shop.

The front of the shop looked no different than usual — an aged wooden sign with faded Tibetan calligraphy, pelts draped casually inside, the faint scent of incense masking the odor of death. But behind that facade was a sophisticated smuggling operation woven into the fabric of Lhasa's underworld.

Russel held up his tablet; the beacon had stopped. "It's here," he murmured.

Moments later, the rhythmic clatter of hooves echoed down the alley.

The yak emerged, slow and lumbering, its burden covered under a thick, stained tarp. Beside it walked three men, faces covered with hoods.

Jaggu's keen eyes immediately identified Varad Praja when he rotated his shoulder out of his old compulsive habit — his dark eyes darting in every direction, flanked by his two hulking bodyguards. Their faces were weathered, scarred by the high passes, but their eyes betrayed intent.

The soft clatter of the yak's hooves had barely faded when the door to the animal pelt shop creaked open.

A narrow shaft of amber light spilled out, briefly cutting through the shadows of the alleyway.

Then he appeared.

Dechen Limi.

An old Tibetan man, stooped slightly with age but carrying an aura of sly alertness. His sun-leathered face was deeply wrinkled, each crease like a scar from years of dealing in forbidden things. His narrow eyes flicked around the alley with caution. The glint in his pupils was like ice — calculating, cold, and watchful.

A long, thin Chinese-style ponytail fell down the back of his thick maroon cloak, tied loosely just above the nape of his neck. Thin strands of grey-black hair, wiry and uneven, framed his gaunt face. A silver ring gleamed on his left index finger, worn and scratched. There was something reptilian in the way he blinked and moved — too quiet, too smooth.

He stepped out only for a moment, eyes darting along the rooftops and shadows as if sensing the presence of unseen eyes. Then, with a faint signal — no more than a twitch of his fingers — he beckoned the three men and the sack toward him.

No words were exchanged.

Jaggu's eyes narrowed. He tensed like a coiled spring, ready to pounce. But before he could move, Russel Hogg caught his arm.

"Wait," Russel whispered, voice calm but firm. "We don't make a move until Interpol arrives. One wrong step, and we lose everything."

Verma nodded beside him. "Too risky. We need to catch all of them. Not just the carrier."

Jaggu gritted his teeth but stayed put.

Without a word, Varad's loyal bodyguards untied the tarp-covered bundle, hoisted the sack off the yak's back, and carried it through the narrow door into the dim-lit shop.

Then, just as suddenly as he had appeared, Dechen vanished inside with them, the door shutting behind like the snapping of a trap. This was no ordinary shop. This was Dechen Limi's den — a temple of death for Himalayan wildlife, operating in plain sight.

In the shadows across the alley, Russel, Jaggu, and Verma remained motionless.

Jaggu's fingers twitched with urgency but Russel's voice was barely audible: "Now we wait for Interpol. The rats are in the hole."

Hanging from the beams above the entrance were an astonishing — and horrifying — array of furs: thick black pelts of Asiatic black bears, hides of Tibetan gazelle, the coarse brown fur of Himalayan brown bears, and the silvery, ghostly coat of the elusive Eurasian lynx. Across a wooden rail were draped the spiraling horns of ibex and markhor — grotesque trophies turned into macabre décor.

Many tense minutes crawled by like hours. The shadows lengthened on the cobbled alleyway as Russel Hogg, Amit Verma, and Jaggu remained huddled near the side of Dechen Limi's shop, hidden behind a row of stacked crates and worn prayer wheels. Inside, the muffled thuds of movement suggested negotiations or possibly packaging of the illegal goods. Russel checked his satellite communicator again. Still no signal from the Interpol team.

Meanwhile, across the city, the Interpol team was caught in a confrontation. At a small military checkpoint near the old Tibetan quarter, Chinese soldiers — expressionless and cold — scrutinized their documents with exaggerated slowness. The German Shepherd at their side barked and tugged at its leash, sensing urgency. But the soldiers paid no mind. One officer, with a stiff jaw and suspicious eyes, muttered something into his radio, then turned back with a faint smile.

"Routine verification," he said in Mandarin-accented English. "Just wait."

But it was no routine. It was a deliberate obstruction — a silent signal from the powerful underbelly of the Chinese state. The People's Army had long tolerated Dechen Limi's trade — in fact, many within its ranks were quiet beneficiaries of the smuggling network. This was no accident. It was an invisible shield being extended to Dechen — and a warning to those who dared intervene.

Back in Barkhor Street, the tension mounted to breaking point.

"Damn it," Russel muttered, eyes locked on the door. "They should've been here by now."

They shifted silently, moving closer to the shop's entrance — shadows among shadows — just off to the side, hidden behind a stack of yak-wool bundles and discarded wooden crates. From there, they could hear the murmur of voices inside. Any moment now, Varad Praja and his two bodyguards might step out — free men, slipping through their fingers.

Russel Hogg knelt beside a large crate, his face tense. With one hand he reached inside his coat and pulled out his compact SIG Sauer pistol. He checked the chamber, flicked the safety off, and held it low beside his thigh. Next to him, Amit Verma did the same with his service revolver — a heavy Indian-manufactured piece, solid and dependable. The two men exchanged a quick nod.

Jaggu crouched slightly ahead, his sharp eyes fixed on the door. From within the folds of his coat, he drew a long, curved knife — the blade hand-forged, with a rough wooden grip and a wicked gleam that caught the alley's dim light. It was not a modern weapon, but it fit him perfectly — wild, silent, dangerous.

Russel whispered, "If they come out of the shop…"

A beat passed. Jaggu's knuckles whitened around the handle.

"…we nab them," Russel finished.

Amit added quietly, "No warning shots."

Jaggu gave a faint, grim smile — a predator's smile — and nodded once, never taking his eyes off the door.

Inside, a loud thud echoed — a door closing, or a crate being dropped. Footsteps moved toward the entrance. The door latch rattled.

Time slowed. Breath held. Muscles tensed.

They were seconds from action.

Mayhem in Lhasa...

The heavy door of the shop creaked open.

The smell wafting from the shop was a pungent mix of old leather, animal musk, and medicinal herbs — a scent that clung to your clothes like guilt. Inside, it was dimly lit, its shelves cluttered with strange jars, old rifles, knives, and curious relics of a dark trade that had flourished in silence for decades.

Three men stepped out, hunched and hooded against the Himalayan cold, faces wrapped tightly in scarves. Their movements were casual, almost routine. But Jaggu, watching from the shadows, was still — eyes sharp, breath low. His gaze locked onto one of the men.

A subtle wrench of the shoulder.

That twitch.

That's him. Varad Praja.

Without hesitation, Jaggu pounced.

He exploded out of the shadows like a panther in the dark — feet slamming into the earth, arms lunging. Before the men could react, he collided with the middle one, tackling him to the ground. In a flash, his curved Nepali khukri was drawn, the blade pressed tight across the man's throat.

Jaggu snarled, "One move and I'll open his neck like a melon."

The body went rigid. It was Varad Praja. No mistake.

The two bodyguards shouted, turning to attack — fists clenched, faces wild under their scarves.

"STOP!" Jaggu roared. "Try me — I'll slit his throat right here!"

But the bodyguards didn't freeze — they flinched forward.

Two sharp clicks cut through the tension.

From behind, Russel Hogg and Amit Verma emerged with deadly calm, weapons raised, barrels pressed against the spines of the bodyguards. "Drop it," Russel said coldly. "You're done."

Now all three poachers were neutralized, locked in a triangle of threat.

But the market had already erupted.

Varad's muffled shouting had drawn attention. People had seen the gleam of steel, the flash of firearms. A woman screamed. Another dropped her shopping basket. Within seconds, the chaos was viral — children cried, stalls slammed shut, metal shutters clanged down one after another, merchants fled into alleys, and the narrow corridor of Barkhor Street became a hive of shrieks and panic.

And then — another twist.

The shop door opened again.

Dechen Limi's wrinkled, suspicious face peered out. The moment he saw Varad Praja being held at knifepoint, he ducked back in with uncanny speed and locked the front door from within.

"Damn it!" Russel cursed, turning toward the shop.

CRASH!

A backdoor burst open — Dechen Limi darted out with a heavy sack slung over his shoulder. The fabric bulged with raw, unmistakable shape — tiger parts. He bolted into the alley.

Russel spun to Verma. "Amit — go!"

Verma peeled away in pursuit, sprinting around the side, just in time to catch sight of Dechen Limi darting through a maze of vendors and alleyways, his long Chinese-style ponytail flapping behind him.

That movement changed everything.

Dhruva Tharu, one of the bodyguards, saw his chance. With Verma gone, only Russel stood behind them. In a flash, Dhruva spun, ducked under the gun, and drove his shoulder into Russel's chest.

Russel staggered back — a blow to the ribs.

The other bodyguard followed. Together, they swarmed Russel, fists flying. The gun clattered to the ground.

Jaggu shouted, pressing the blade tighter on Varad's neck, trying to keep his leverage, but the momentum had shifted. Russel struggled under the weight of two men, pinned against the stone wall.

Meanwhile Dechen Limi dashed through the rear alley, sack slung over his shoulder, boots thudding over ancient cobblestones slick with ice and dirt. The dense maze of Lhasa's old quarter unfurled before him — narrow, winding alleys flanked by thick-walled Tibetan homes. Prayer flags fluttered above, and the snowy peaks of the Himalayas loomed in the sky like silent gods watching over the chaos.

Amit Verma followed, sprinting hard, breath misting in the cold Himalayan air, boots pounding the stone.

As Dechen darted through an arched gateway, strange faces emerged — fierce, expressionless men from open windows and stone terraces. Their skin was wind-burnt, eyes sharp with suspicion. Tibetan mafia. Silent sentinels. Watching.

Verma felt the alley closing in — too many corners, too many turns. Dechen knew this terrain like a rat knows a tunnel. Verma was losing ground.

He raised his service pistol.

CRACK! — a warning shot shattered the silence.

The bullet struck a steel streetlight ahead of Dechen with a loud metallic clang, throwing sparks.

"Dechen! Stop or I'll shoot again!" Verma shouted, voice echoing off stone.

The old man slowed — his spine stiffened. He could feel the gun's aim drilling into his back. Then, without a word, he turned around.

Face-to-face.

Dechen stood beneath a crumbling prayer flag tied between two houses. The sack of contraband animal parts was still slung across one shoulder. His expression had changed. Calm. Ominous. He dropped into a low martial stance — one leg coiled beneath him, arms wide, fingers spread like talons. His wrinkled face twitched with a dark smirk.

Amit Verma slowed, pistol raised, confused. What the hell is he doing?

And then — Dechen moved.

He launched off the ground with a wild, sudden leap — more beast than man — and cracked a spinning reverse kick straight into Verma's shoulder.

Verma grunted, staggered, and fell — the pistol flew from his hand and skidded across the cobblestones.

The sack thudded to the ground beside Dechen. Without breaking stride, he grabbed it, slung it up again, and — like smoke — vanished into the maze of alleyways.

By the time Verma got to his knees, Dechen was gone.

As Verma pushed himself off the ground, clutching his bruised shoulder, he blinked hard, trying to steady his breath and vision. The sharp cold of Lhasa's thin air cut through his lungs like a blade. He staggered up, eyes scanning the alley where Dechen had vanished.

Determined, he began moving again, limping slightly but forcing himself forward into the twisting alleyway. Just as he turned a corner — he stopped dead in his tracks.

From the shadows ahead, three men stepped into the narrow lane. Muscular, broad-shouldered, clad in thick woollen jackets and heavy boots. Their faces were rough, hardened by the mountains and a life of lawlessness. Cruel, unreadable eyes glinted under weathered brows. Tibetan mafia.

They didn't speak.

They didn't need to.

Their presence was a warning — and a trap.

Verma's heart kicked hard in his chest. He took a slow step back. One of the men tilted his head ever so slightly, another flexed his knuckles with a faint pop. They were closing in.

Shit.

Verma spun on his heel and bolted.

The narrow alley twisted behind him, cobblestones slipping underfoot as he raced back the way he'd come. Adrenaline surged through him. He couldn't outfight those men — not now, not in this condition. His only option was to retreat, regroup.

He darted past shuttered windows and cracked walls, his breath loud in his ears.

Back toward Dechen Limi's shop.

Back to the storm he had momentarily escaped — only to run headlong into another.

Back to Russel and Jaggu.

Meanwhile, outside Limi's ominous shop — the situation had spiraled into a deadly stalemate.

Russel Hogg, the seasoned Interpol officer, was on his knees now, his face bloodied and bruised, his crisp jacket torn at the shoulder. Bhanu Tamang had twisted his arm viciously behind his back, locking it up in a painful hold, while Dhruva Tharu, stood beside him with a rusty, locally made Tibetan pistol pressed tightly against Russel's temple.

Dhruva's eyes were blazing — a dangerous cocktail of rage and cold calculation. One false move and he'd pull the trigger. His finger twitched.

On the other side of the narrow street, Jaggu stood like a wildcat, back to the stone wall, his chest heaving. His powerful arm was wrapped around Varad Praja's throat, holding him in a tight lock, the razor-sharp curve of his Nepalese khukuri pressed close to Varad's neck .

Varad, though terrified, was trying not to breathe too hard. The steel against his throat promised death.

Nobody moved.

One side held a hostage, a blade whispering death.

The other side held a gun to an Interpol officer's skull.

It was a frozen moment — where the wrong breath could tip the balance into blood and ruin.

Dhruva Tharu's boots crunched against the cold, gritty stone as he took slow, heavy steps toward Jaggu — his pistol never wavering from Russel Hogg's temple. His face was expressionless, carved from stone, but his eyes held fury.

Jaggu's grip on Varad tightened. The blade kissed deeper into the poacher's throat, drawing another thread of red.

"I said don't move," Jaggu growled, eyes locked on Dhruva.

But Dhruva didn't stop.

Another step.

Another.

The weight of imminent death hung in the air like smoke.

Then—

"FREEZE!"

The voice cracked through the Himalayan chill like a thunderclap.

Suddenly, shadows appeared from every corner of Barkhor Street — plain dressed operatives of the Interpol Special Task Force surged forward with swift precision, their weapons raised and locked.

"Drop your weapons. Hands in the air!"

Laser sights flickered red dots across Dhruva's chest. Bhanu's back was now a lattice of glowing points.

In a second, the hunters became the hunted.

At Russel Hogg's sharp nod, four Interpol operatives in tactical gear moved swiftly. With practiced precision, they seized Varad Praja, Dhruva Tharu, and Bhanu Tamang — cuffing their wrists behind their backs and yanking them to their feet. The three men, now stripped of any menace, were marched briskly through the narrow, panic-stricken alleyway and loaded into a waiting blue SUV parked discreetly at the end of the street. Its engine hummed low, like a beast waiting to move.

Russel exhaled, chest heaving, then turned to the remaining team. "Go. Breach it."

Two agents rushed forward with a battering ram, while others covered them, guns at the ready.

"Three, two, one—"

CRASH!

The heavy wooden door to Dechen Limi's shop splintered and burst open, echoing through the now-deserted Barkhor Street like a crack of thunder. The team stormed in — weapons raised, eyes scanning every corner.

The shop was a dark and chilling museum of death.

The walls were festooned with hanging pelts — ghostly remnants of critically endangered wildlife.

In glass jars and little wooden dabbas, they found powder and liquids — labeled in Chinese and Tibetan script.

Dried tiger penis. Bone fragments. Scales — pangolin, turtle, even snake. Rolled skins of Marbled and Pallas's cat, twisted dried lizards, owl feathers, and claws from the endangered clouded leopard.

Rolled parchments tied with silk cords hinted at dried tiger blood, while a heavy jar with a cracked lid bore what looked like fragments of rhino horn — dark, fibrous, and unmistakable.

A grotesque showcase of extinction.

"Christ," muttered one agent. "He's been butchering half the Himalayas in here."

Meanwhile, the crowd of Interpol agents and onlookers parted as Amit Verma emerged from the shadows of the alleyway — limping, blood streaked across his forehead, his left arm held tightly against his side. His shirt was torn, his eyes blazing with frustration.

Russel Hogg turned the moment he saw him.

Verma, catching his breath, said in a hoarse voice, "Limi escaped... despite my best efforts." He wiped the blood from the corner of his mouth, wincing. "He's taken the tigress's parts with him."

Everyone went silent.

"The forensic department at the Wildlife Institute Of India," Verma continued urgently, "has already secured the DNA samples from the poaching site in Kaziranga — blood, fur fragments, claw scrapings... everything. But unless we recover the tigress's parts here and match it with those samples, we'll never have a watertight case against these bastards."

He looked at Russel.

"We need that skin. That's the final nail. Without it, they'll walk."

Topdog...

Inside the ransacked and chaotic interior of Dechen Limi's shop, one of the Interpol agents — the seasoned dog handler — stepped forward, clutching the leash of a muscular German Shepherd. The dog was tense, alert, quivering with anticipation.

The bruised and panting Amit Verma pointed towards Dechen's chair and said "let the dog get his scent." The handler walked the Shepherd to a rickety wooden chair in the corner of the shop, where Dechen had been seated just minutes earlier. Draped across the backrest was a tattered but striking coat — Snow Leopard fur, unmistakable, still warm, still pungent with the oily scent of its fugitive owner.

The dog's nostrils flared. He sniffed intently, nose brushing the coat, then lifted his snout and let out a low, eager whine. The trainer gave him a soft pat on the side and unclipped the leash.

"Find!" he commanded sharply. "Search!"

In a blur of muscle and motion, the Shepherd bolted through the back door, claws scraping on stone. He yelped once — short and sharp — then took off into the maze of dark Tibetan alleys behind the shop, his nose low to the ground, tracking the fugitive scent of Dechen Limi with deadly precision.

The dog handler called into his radio: "Subject scent acquired. Tracking in progress. All teams be ready to intercept."

The narrow, ancient alleys of Lhasa were cloaked in silence, broken only by the soft thud of boots against stone and the faint jangling of the dog's long leash. The German Shepherd, muscles taut, snout low, moved with deadly intent — nose flicking from side to side. His handler, face cold and focused, kept pace a step behind, his eyes scanning every shadow.

On either side of him, Interpol agents moved in tactical formation with weapons held high and eyes cutting through the midday haze.

Close behind came Jaggu, crouched slightly, his khurki held flat against his chest. Verma limped but kept pace, blood drying on his brow, his breath short but steady. Russel Hogg, bruised and grim, his coat torn at the sleeve, was silent, pistol raised, eyes darting.

They were deep in the dark underbelly of Lhasa now — a part tourists never saw. From behind the carved wooden screens, behind half-drawn curtains and narrow terraces, fierce, weather-beaten Tibetan faces stared down at the group. Eyes heavy with suspicion. Lips sealed in silence.

The scent of smoke and old incense hung in the air. The alleys twisted like a serpent, and the deeper they went, the more the hush thickened.

Something was building.

A whisper of danger threaded the cold air in the labyrinthine stronghold of the Tibetan underworld. Somewhere ahead — not far — Dechen Limi was on the move, carrying the sack that could bring down a criminal empire.

Russel glanced up at a window where an old woman with tattooed cheeks held a parrot that didn't blink.

He murmured, "We're not welcome here. Be ready for anything."

The German Shepherd suddenly halted, growling low as he reached the massive wooden gates of an ancient Tibetan stronghouse — two-storied, its perimeter walled in thick, timeworn stone that stood like a fortress. The building loomed ominously under the grey Lhasa sky, its red window frames closed tight, its tiled rooftop gleaming with an eerie calm. The gate itself was carved with faded symbols and flanked by two brass lion heads — snarling, majestic, and mute sentinels of secrets.

The dog pawed at the gate and whimpered, snout pressed to the wood, tail stiff. The scent trail ended here.

The Interpol snipers arrived first, weapons drawn, scanning the height of the building. "He's inside," they muttered.

Russel moved in beside him, pistol raised. "Let's breach."

But the moment Verma's hand touched the brass lion head, all hell broke loose.

A thunderclap of gunfire erupted.

From narrow slits in the upper floor, from hidden corners on the sloped rooftops — Kalashnikov rifles roared.

Bullets rained down, biting into stone, ricocheting off prayer bells and chipping centuries-old bricks.

Dust and wood splinters filled the air as the Interpol team dove for cover — some flattening against the walls, others crouching behind carved stone troughs that once held water for passing pilgrims.

The dog let out a terrified bark and bolted behind his handler, who rolled with him, shielding him with his body.

Jaggu threw himself to the side, barely missing a round that cracked into the lion-headed door. "It's an ambush!" he shouted.

Verma ducked low, pain shooting up his already-bruised body.

Bullets still cracked through the air from the stronghouse — short, disciplined bursts of Kalashnikov fire. The old stones groaned under the assault, dust hanging like a ghostly veil.

Crouched low, Russel Hogg peered through a crack in the stone. "They've got height, visibility, and cover," he muttered. "We're pinned." He fired back once, a single shot into the rooftop where a shadow moved — and then took cover again.

But Jaggu didn't respond. He'd fallen slightly to the side, eyes narrowed, scanning the ancient neighborhood like a wildcat scenting danger.

The wooden gate remained shut — a cold, mocking wall between them and Dechen Limi. But now, beyond it, they knew for certain: this was his fortress.

Leaping panther...

Jaggu slipped away.

Like a shadow.

His instincts twitched — something primal, honed in the forests and badlands where ambush was always a breath away.

Backtracking silently through the winding lanes, he passed five, six houses. Every sense sharpened. He could feel the vibrations of gunfire through the cobblestones. Then he saw it — a squat, weathered house with a flat, low-hanging terrace. Cracked prayer flags fluttered above it, half-torn by wind and age.

Without hesitation, Jaggu stripped bare to lighten any load and then lunged.

One jump. Two.

He launched himself up the wall like a panther leaping for prey. His fingers gripped the edge of the terrace, legs swung up, and within seconds, he was belly-flat on the roof, eyes peering over the rim.

From this height, he had a clear flank view of the stronghouse.

He scanned the rooftops ahead.

The rooftops stretched in uneven rows — flat, mud-coated terraces, some with prayer wheels, some with sagging tarps. The gaps between them were narrow enough for a panther's leap. For his leap.

He began to move. One rooftop, then another.

A quick run — and he jumped. Landed in a controlled crouch. Rolled once. Stayed low.

Like in the jungles of Madhya Pradesh, where he tracked deer barefoot or climbed banyan trees as a child, his body moved with memory. This was his forest now. These rooftops were branches. And he was the panther.

Leap. Crouch. Breathe. Crawl.

He crouched low, scanning. The gunners on the Tibetan stronghouse still hadn't seen him. Their focus was on the alleyway. Their rifles continued to thunder.

Another leap.

This one longer — a three-meter gap. His muscles bunched like a spring.

He launched.

His boots kissed the next terrace without a sound.

He glided under laundry lines, skirted around satellite dishes, moved behind stacked yak dung bricks used for fuel. No one saw him.

He jumped again across a narrow alley.

Midair, for a second, he felt the wind howl beneath him, as if the Himalayas themselves were watching.

He landed in a crouch.

His silhouette melted into the rooftop shadows like he was made of smoke.

Jaggu slowed. .

Straight ahead now — the stronghouse's outer wall rose like a fortress, and the final rooftop before it was just ten feet away. The two gunners were now below him, one partially exposed. Armed with Kalashnikovs, were focused entirely on the alley below, unaware of the danger approaching from above.

Jaggu's hand slid to his belt.

He slid the khukuri from his belt, the blade catching the light. His eyes were cold. Focused.

He crawled forward, right up to the edge of the rooftop, crouching behind a rusted railing, peering down at the gunmen.

They still didn't know death was above them.

He rose into a crouch.

Muscles coiled. Shadow merged with sunlight.

And like a jungle cat, he pounced.

One sweep — the first gunman fell, a sharp cry escaping his lips before he slumped. The second turned, too late. Jaggu pounced, disarmed him with a twist, and brought his elbow hard into the man's face.

He went down like a sack of bricks.

Jaggu stood on the rooftop of the Tibetan stronghouse, breathing hard but steady, his khukuri still wet.

He turned, gave a sharp whistle — the signal.

The rooftop was now clear.

The sharp whistle from Jaggu cut through the air like a command.

It was time.

From behind the crumbling wall across the alley, the Interpol team sprang into action. In a synchronized move, they rushed to the front gate, rifles raised, boots pounding against the cobblestone street.

One of the agents hurled a small breaching charge at the aged wooden and iron-bound doors. The gate shuddered and splintered with a boom. With a loud crack, the two lion-heads carved into the doors split apart and the heavy gates swung inward.

The dog handler yelled, "Go!"

The German Shepherd darted in, nose low, tail straight, leading the team into the guts of the stronghouse — a place whispered about in Kathmandu and feared in Lhasa.

Meanwhile, on the rooftop…

Jaggu didn't wait.

He had neutralized the rooftop snipers — but his instincts told him the fight wasn't over.

He stepped over the fallen men, scanned the rooftop for any more threats, then located the trapdoor leading down into the second storey.

With a soft creak, he lifted the heavy wooden hatch and slipped inside.

A narrow ladder descended into a dusty corridor, thick with shadows and the musty scent of damp wood and old fur.

Jaggu moved quickly, his khukuri in hand, his body alert. The corridor led to a locked wooden door. From beyond it, he could hear muffled sounds — movement, voices, something being dragged.

Jaggu kicked open the storeroom door — and froze.

There, in the middle of the room lit dimly by thin beams of sunlight slanting through a carved wooden window, stood Dechen Limi, clutching the bloodied sack of the tigress' parts.

On either side of him were two fierce, barrel-chested Tibetan bodyguards, stripped down to their undershirts, sweat glistening on their skin. All three had adopted ancient martial arts stances — grounded, poised, deadly.

Dechen's eyes narrowed. "You shouldn't have come here alone – foolish jungle boy," he said coldly.

Jaggu didn't respond. He just exhaled — slow, sharp — and let his khukuri slide back into its sheath.

He didn't need a blade.

He dropped into a crouch, muscles coiled, hands open — the stance of a jungle-born predator, honed not in dojos, but in the raw wilderness of India. His feet shifted with the grace of a panther stalking prey, eyes locked, body balanced on the balls of his feet.

Then, the room exploded into violence.

The first bodyguard lunged — a spinning kick aimed at Jaggu's ribs. Jaggu ducked low, caught the man's leg mid-air, twisted, and slammed him to the ground, cracking the wooden planks.

The second charged, fists flying with furious speed. Jaggu took a hit to the shoulder but responded with a rapid barrage of punches, his fists a blur. He pivoted, elbowed the man in the temple, and swept his legs from under him.

Now it was just Jaggu and Dechen.

The Tibetan smuggler threw off his coat, revealing a coiled, muscular frame. He moved like a serpent, lightning fast, attacking with knife-hand chops and reverse kicks.

Jaggu matched him beat for beat.

Their fight was raw and primal, leaping over trunks of bones and hides, crashing into shelves stacked with illicit wildlife products. Dechen struck like a trained killer. Jaggu fought like a man defending every tiger and leopard he had ever seen butchered.

At one point, Dechen grabbed a bronze ritual bell and swung it at Jaggu's head.

Jaggu ducked, countered with a palm strike to the chin, and sent Dechen flying backward, crashing into the wall. The sack of tiger parts spilled open next to him.

Jaggu stood over him, breathing hard, knuckles bloodied but fists still clenched.

"I don't need a gun to end you," Jaggu growled.

Just as Jaggu twisted Dechen's arm behind his back and drove him against the cold stone wall, a sudden click — cold, metallic — pressed into his waist.

He froze.

Two Tibetan strongmen, bloodied but not broken, had risen behind him. One had a pistol jammed into Jaggu's ribs; the other raised a second gun, leveled at Jaggu's temple.

"One more move and you're a dead man," the taller one snarled, breath heavy and eyes blazing.

Dechen sneered, rubbing his bruised jaw, and turned around slowly, triumphant.

"You're not in the jungle anymore, tracker," he hissed as he lifted the sack putting the tiger parts back into it.

But then—

BOOM!

The storeroom door exploded open, splinters flying. Interpol boots thundered in, the room suddenly filled with the cold, hard glint of assault rifles.

"Drop your weapons. Interpol. Hands in the air!"

In the chaos, the German Shepherd lunged, fangs flashing. It leapt at Dechen's arm — the one clutching the sack.

CHOMP!

Dechen howled as the dog bit down, forcing him to release his grip. The sack tumbled to the floor. Without hesitation, the dog clamped its jaws around the canvas and trotted back, tail stiff, delivering it directly to his loyal handler.

The two gunmen hesitated. Too long.

Jaggu exploded into motion — smashing an elbow into one's throat, twisting the other's wrist until the weapon clattered down. The man screamed as Jaggu flung him into a pile of crates.

In seconds, the Interpol agents had the room locked down. Dechen stood cornered, bleeding and breathless.

The sack — the priceless evidence — now lay safely at the feet of the dog handler.

Jaggu stood tall, panting, blood trickling down his cheek — but victorious.

The three defeated men — Dechen and his two loyal bodyguards — were handcuffed, disarmed, and marched out by Interpol agents. The storm had passed, the room now silent except for the shuffling boots and the soft panting of the German Shepherd, tail flicking proudly.

Russel Hogg took the sack from the dog handler with care. He placed it on a wooden crate, unfastened the rough twine, and slowly peeled it open.

Inside lay a grim treasure trove — a full tiger skin, claws, powdered blood, bones, and glinting yellow nails. His face hardened. This was everything they needed.

At that moment, Amit Verma limped up the stairs, one hand braced on the wall, blood crusted at his temple, but his eyes sharp and alive.

Russel turned, smiled, and handed over the sack.

"There you are."

Verma took it with trembling hands, stared into the bag, and his exhausted face lit up with grim satisfaction.

He said, voice like steel. "WII (Wildlife Institute of India) will run the DNA. It will be a perfect match."

The political climate in Lhasa was volatile, and the team knew all too well that the Chinese authorities could intervene at any moment. A sudden clampdown could prevent them from transporting the seized contraband and prisoners out of TAR.

Every second counted. They mobilized without delay, determined to reach Kathmandu before any diplomatic hurdles could be thrown in their path — where they could safely build a watertight case against the powerful syndicate.

As Russel Hogg helped the limping Amit Verma down the creaky stairs of the old Tibetan stronghouse, he looked up, breathing heavy.

"The tigress didn't die for nothing. Now I'll nail the entire chain of crooks, every last one of them — poachers, hitmen, corrupt politicians, smugglers — they'll all go behind bars."

Nilgai...

Deep inside Kathmandu's wildlife crime control bureau's cell, a burly interrogating officer had Varad Praja's hair gripped tightly, plunging his face again and again into a grimy tub of ice-cold water. His wrists and ankles were bound, his shirt was torn in several places, bruises and welts marking his flesh like ink on parchment. He thrashed helplessly, gasping each time his face was yanked back up.

Surrounding him were members of Nepal Police, SAWEN (South Asia Wildlife Enforcement Network) and grim-faced Interpol agents — and at their center stood Russel Hogg, expression carved in stone.

At that moment, the door creaked open, and Russel's assistant entered, escorting a limping but resolute Amit Verma inside.

Verma approached the Nepalese kingpin slowly, wordless. He leaned in, his voice like a blade drawn in the dark:

"Tumhare Indian aaqa… jisse tum roz baat karte ho… jiska chehra kabhi nahi dekha kisi ne — ab usi ko milao. Abhi. Yahin. Milao." (Your Indian handler, whom you have apparently never met, whom you speak to daily. Dial his number. Now !)

Varad's body stiffened. The interrogation room fell into a suffocating silence, save for the faint dripping of water and Varad's own trembling breath.

"Both your bodyguards whom we have been interrogating separately have already divulged enough. Now it's best for your health and longevity that you do exactly as told." Said Russel with a voice of steel.

Again, Varad's face was abruptly plunged into the tub of icy water.

After what seemed like an eternity of torment, the officer hauled his head out of the water. Varad coughed violently, chest heaving, eyes wild with fear and rage. He barely had a moment's respite before the officer stepped forward, lifted Varad's left hand, and placed a steel scalpel right on the tip of his index finger.

"I promise you," he said coldly, pressing down just enough for a thin stream of blood to trail down the finger, "you won't need ten fingers where you're going. But I'll make sure you feel the loss of each one."

Praja let out a guttural scream, twisting under his restraints.

Under the cold stare of Russel Hogg and Amit Verma, Varad's trembling hands were untied just enough to operate his mobile phone. He dialed a specific number from memory, one he's used many times before.

The phone rang.

And rang.

But no one picked up.

A pause of tension filled the room, thick as smoke.

Meanwhile in another part of the subcontinent, two jeeps tore through the dust with reckless swagger in the golden blaze of an early afternoon sun. The jeeps were splattered with mud and fitted with crude reinforcements, but they roared like beasts—untamed and arrogant.

In one of them, two men—faces unseen—stood upright, bracing themselves on the metal rails as they unleashed shot after shot with their mounted telescopic rifles. The air cracked with each echoing blast.

The marksmen laughed, voices thick with local dialect.

"Bhaiya, lag gaya! Arre dekh na, ghoom ke gira woh… woh bhi gaya!"

"Wah bhai, kya kamaal ka nishana hai, ekdum chakachak!"

(Brother you got him..There he falls.. Wow..And the other, spinning before she falls..Wah brother, what a crackshot you are..Fantastic!)

Their comments spilled out between shots like a celebration of violence. They were't just shooters—they were trained, perhaps even bored by the ease of their brutality.

Between bursts of gunfire, a mobile phone rang incessantly, its shrill tone out of place amidst the chaos. It lay discarded in the corner of the jeep, half-buried under a cloth sack.

Unheard.

Russel Hogg stood before Varad, arms folded, watching every flicker of expression. The first attempt went unanswered. Russel growled, “Try again.”

Varad dialed the number once more, hands shaking. One ring. Two.

Then—click.

A voice answered from the other end. Gruff. Relaxed. Confident. “Hello?”

Immediately, one of the Interpol cyber-intelligence officers, seated at a portable laptop station nearby, began working his magic. His fingers flew across the keyboard as he accessed the signal trace through Interpol's secure call tracking software.

Varad stiffened. “Hello sir.”

From the other end, the voice responded casually, “Jaldi bolo, Varad.”(Speak up Varad, be quick.)

Varad licked his cracked lips, then said, with practiced urgency, “There is an immediate demand for three full RBT (Royal Bengal Tigers). Customers are building pressure on my dealer from Lhasa. Big industrialists from mainland China.”

A beat of silence. Then, CRACK! — a shot rang out on the other side of the call, echoing with metallic clarity.

The same voice chuckled darkly, “ Okay but I am a little preoccupied right now, am in the middle of live target practice at the behest of some farmers and landowners who have specially invited me to get rid of vermins from their fields.”

The line went silent, except for the distant roar of an engine and another burst of gunfire.

In the torture room, the Interpol techie lifted his head, gave Russel Hogg a tight nod and a thumbs up.

“We’re triangulating the call origin and bounce paths,” the officer mutters.

A few seconds passed.

“We’ve got something.”

On the screen, a digital map bloomed — a call route appeared, bouncing between proxy networks and relay towers — but then narrowed.

"India… eastern sector," he said.

Another few keystrokes, a zoom-in.

"Bihar," he confirmed.

Back in the vast crop fields of central Bihar, the tranquil countryside was shattered by the thunder of two racing jeeps, kicking up dust along a narrow dirt road between rows of swaying sugarcane. The sunlight glinted off the metal frames of the vehicles, but the real drama was unfolding just beyond the road.

A herd of magnificent nilgai—Asia's largest antelope species—exploded from the foliage, running for their lives. The blue-grey males led the charge, flanked by brown-coated females and wide-eyed calves. Their robust bodies moved with speed and fear, hooves pounding the soft earth. Among them, a mother ran hard, her young calf pressed close behind her, nearly tripping to keep pace.

From the back of the trailing jeep, a sharp-eyed marksman steadied his rifle. A sudden gust of wind tore the muffler from his face, letting it flutter away like a dark ribbon.

In that fleeting moment, the concealed identity was laid bare — sharp features, a cold, calculating gaze. It was none other than the shooter, Harpal Singh, sitting among his cohort of bootlickers. He squinted, exhaled, and pulled the trigger.

CRACK!

The bullet punched through the back of the mother's skull. She collapsed mid-stride, crumpling to the ground in a heap of motionless flesh. The calf, galloping right behind her, skidded to a halt and stared at her lifeless body. Confused, terrified, it nudged her with its head, let out a faint bleat, and circled her fallen form, refusing to move on.

In the jeep, the shooter spoke coolly into the phone pressed against his ear. "Varad, the situation is bad. Some of our key men—ones working with the Bangladeshis in Assam—have been arrested. A large stash of weapons and product has been seized."

On the other end of the line, Varad's voice trembled with pressure. "Sir, this is urgent. These are high-profile clients—they are not willing to wait."

The shooter raised his rifle again, took aim at another figure in the stampeding herd. "I understand. I'll get to base and handle it from there. I'm a little busy right now."

Another sharp CRACK! echoed across the field.

The call ended. The phone, dimmed to black.

With that final, merciless shot, another magnificent nilgai bull collapsed to the ground, its powerful frame crashing into the dust. His entire herd—five graceful females and all their young—had already been wiped out in the last fifteen to twenty minutes.

Meanwhile, at Kathmandu the Interpol IT cell agents closed in around the screen tracking the call.

"It's not a city... this looks like rural... wait... crop fields."

The blinking red dot rested on a faint network tower surrounded by agricultural land.

Russel turns to Verma. "Does that mean anything to you?"

Verma's eyes narrow. "Yes. Jaggu was always right. We just never had any concrete evidence. A national level shooter and this is how he does his live target practice. Huh !"

He gripped the revolver tighter. "This influencial ex-politician's son has been controlling the shadowy supply chain from central India all this while. And the Bavarias are just one of his assets."

"But this will be his endgame. Now we have his voice recorded negotiating with a Nepalese dealer. We have all the ammunition of evidence now to bring the entire chain down." chipped in Russel with a smile of satisfaction.

Meanwhile the fields, moments ago full of life, now lay bloodstained and broken. The once-lively family that moved through the sugarcane fields in harmony now lay scattered and still, victims of senseless cruelty. The air was heavy with gunpowder and the echo of violence.

The wind rustled the tall stalks of sugarcane, whispering accusations no one would dare speak aloud.

Whose land is this, after all? Who has stolen it from whom? Who are the real vermins? Who gives humans the right to cull other living beings as if they don't matter? Aren't humans the only invasive species today, which urgently needs population control?

These questions echoed in the vast silence left behind by the massacre. Somewhere, amidst the wreckage of the blue-blooded fallen giants, an orphaned calf cried softly for its mother, its voice lost in the heavy stillness that follows death.

Chameleon...

Inside the CID office of Sheopur, Madhya Pradesh, a transformation was underway. Jaggu sat still as skilled makeup artists worked swiftly, turning him into a turbaned catering staff member. A neatly tied saffron-colored safa was wrapped around his head, and his rugged features were softened with makeup and disguise.

Inspector Bhadoriya from the CID special force crouched beside him, discreetly slipping thin electronic chips into the lining of Jaggu's belt. "Tracking chips," he said in a low voice. "If you get close to the goods, activate them discreetly. Our tech team will monitor the signal."

Around the room stood a mixed group—officials from the Wildlife Crime Control Bureau, razor sharp DRI (Department of Revenue Intelligence) officers, a few serious-looking forest department officers, and among them, DFO Amit Verma, his injured leg resting slightly on a footstool.

One of the forest officials, a senior man with a stern face, spoke: "Remember what you said, Jaggu—that you can sniff out tiger skin, bones. Trust your instincts. Once you're in and you spot the goods, plant the chip. Don't mess it up."

Jaggu nodded silently, his eyes already sharpening with focus.

As he turned to leave, Jayant Ghosh intercepted him with a quiet word: "And Jaggu... don't get too emotional about Janhvi. Keep your head clear. Don't let things fall apart because of personal attachments."

Jaggu gave a faint, unreadable smile. "Yes, sir," he said, and walked out, his gait now transformed into that of an obedient, unassuming waiter.

The grand party...

Night has descended upon the opulent estate of Raju Bhaiya, and the bungalow shimmers like a jewel under a canopy of multi-colored lights. The air hums with celebration — it is a night of indulgence and power.

Outside the sprawling mansion, a fleet of luxurious vehicles, both Indian and foreign, line the driveway. From each car step out men of influence, draped in sharp suits and traditional finery, their faces marked by authority and ambition.

The estate is fortified on all sides by high walls, with towering columns at regular intervals. On each of these columns, sentries stand alert, and trained snipers, barely visible in the shadows, scan the periphery with cold precision. The security is airtight — this is not merely a party; it is a fortress dressed in silk.

Within the compound, the bungalow glows with grandiosity. The façade is bathed in hues of blue, gold, and red, each light casting intricate reflections across the marble floors. The area around the swimming pool is adorned with festoon lights that twinkle like stars, draped over trees and canopies, forming a celestial veil. The water in the pool sparkles under their glow, catching the rhythm of music that pulses from the speakers.

The night is young, and the stage is set — a night of secrets, power, and spectacle.

At one end of the grand swimming pool, a beautifully crafted stage gleams under focused spotlights. Draped in shimmering fabric and adorned with fresh flowers, the stage seems to float like a dream over the glowing water. And tonight, at the center of that dream, is Janhvi.

Wearing a dazzling outfit that sparkles with every move, Janhvi is in her element — her voice electric, her presence magnetic. She belts out a sensual love ballad, her tone full of lilt, charm and bold confidence. The performance is a spectacle of synchronized chaos — hips sway, lights flash, hair whips in the air. The dancers, dressed in vibrant costumes, move like fire around Janhvi, enhancing her charisma as she commands the stage with a mix of sultry grace and raw energy. Applause rises from the crowd lounging poolside with drinks in hand, many of them captivated not just by the performance, but by Janhvi herself — the queen of the night.

In the stylishly lit lounging area beside the pool, guests move about with glasses of fine liquor and plates of gourmet snacks. Some recline on cushioned daybeds, puffing on cigars or hookahs, while others sip cocktails and murmur in conspiratorial tones, laughter punctuating their hushed conversations.

At one of the more private tables sits Harpal Singh, surrounded by a small group of his young, well-dressed friends — a mix of men and women equally intoxicated by the luxury of the moment. Their conversation drifts from high-end rifles to past hunting expeditions in distant forests, peppered with boisterous boasts and occasional bursts of laughter. The tone is light, indulgent, but always returning to one theme — the thrill of the hunt.

Harpal leans back in his chair, a crystal tumbler swirling in his hand. Yet despite the laughter around him, his focus is clearly elsewhere. His gaze keeps straying toward the stage, toward Janhvi. With each turn of her hips and every flick of her hair, his eyes follow her like a predator tracking its prey — admiring, calculating, hungry.

Wait for the waiter...

A tray glides toward Harpal, balanced perfectly in the hands of a liveried attendant. On it, chilled beer bottles rest against clinking cubes of ice. One bottle catches the soft glow of the pool lights as it's presented to him.

Harpal, in his signature nonchalant style, extends a single finger and presses it against the condensation on the bottle's neck. The coolness satisfies him. Without shifting his gaze from the stage — where Janhvi continues her vibrant, intoxicating performance — he gestures with his other hand, a small flick of the wrist.

"Alright. Pour it," he says casually.

The attendant nods and leans in, expertly uncapping the bottle and tilting it into Harpal's waiting glass. The waiter's gloved hand seems graceful and deliberate as it tilts the chilled beer bottle over the rim of Harpal's glass.

But beneath this polished surface, something else unfolds.

The waiter's other hand, slow and practiced, slides into Harpal's pocket with the silence of a pickpocket trained by years of necessity. The movement is masked by the angle of his body and the distraction of the moment. A quiet intrusion, executed with precision.

The glass fills gradually. The golden liquid rises, froths gently, and settles — just as Harpal takes a slow sip, his eyes still fixed on Janhvi like a man possessed. In the same moment, the waiter's fingers emerge from the pocket, now holding a small bunch of keys, which he quickly tucks away. He straightens, adjusting the edge of his waistcoat, saying softly, "A little more?" Harpal nods absentmindedly, eyes still on the stage.

"I'll pour again," the waiter adds in a low voice, almost as if he's referring to more than just the drink. And just like that, he blends back into the ambient luxury — as if nothing had happened.

It was then, in the soft poolside light, that his face comes into view — beneath the crisp turban, the thick moustache and a layer of latex used for special effects makeup, it is Jaggu, disguised flawlessly.

Near the swimming pool, at the most opulent table in the center, Raju Bhaiya sits with Mohammad Hanif, two heavyset foreign guests, and the Chinese men involved in the dam construction deal. Their laughter rises above the soft music, the table crowded with expensive drinks, half-eaten platters of delicacies, and the unmistakable scent of power and privilege.

These are the political fixers, the dealmakers who move millions with a phone call and alter landscapes with a signature. Raju Bhaiya, dressed in a fine white kurta with a shawl draped casually over one shoulder, sips slowly from his glass.

Every now and then, his eyes drift toward Harpal's table. His son sits among a group of young women and their stylish friends but it isn't the laughter of his guests that holds Harpal's attention — it is Janhvi. She is still performing on the stage, her energy electric, her beauty irresistible. Harpal's gaze follows her with an intensity that doesn't go unnoticed by his father.

Jaggu, still in his perfect disguise as a turbaned waiter, moves silently through the grand halls of the bungalow. He carries himself with the casual air of a servant who belonged—head slightly lowered, steps measured, attention fixed on his imaginary duties. But beneath that calm exterior, his senses are razor sharp.

Avoiding the gaze of the patrolling guards and slipping past the sentries stationed near the rear corridor, he climbs the side staircase with practiced ease. The music and laughter from the poolside grows fainter as he reaches the private quarters.

At the far end of the hallway, behind a pair of carved wooden doors, is Harpal's room—the infamous den lined with trophies, rifles, and hunting memorabilia. Jaggu pauses for a breath, makes sure no one is around, and then he steps forward and quietly approaches the door.

Jaggu slips his hand into his pocket, draws out the bunch of keys and brings the keyring close to the lock, testing one key after another with careful, deliberate movements. Each turn of a wrong key sends a small metallic scrape echoing into the silence, sharp enough to make his breath catch.

His eyes flick over his shoulder again and again, scanning the corridor, alert to every creak, every whisper of motion. A guard's footsteps echoing from a distance makes his pulse spike—but the sound fades, moving away. Jaggu returns to his task, calmer but tense.

Finally, with a soft click, one of the keys finds its match. The door gives way just slightly. He pauses, listening. No one had seen him. The corridor remained empty.

He pushes the door open just enough to slip through—and vanishes inside Harpal's secret chamber like a shadow.

At that moment, outside by the shimmering poolside stage, Janhvi's sultry, melodic song draws to a close. The final orgasmic note lingering in the air before dissolving into an eruption of applause. Loud, enthusiastic claps echo through the lavish estate, mingling with whistles and cheers. The crowd, now fully intoxicated by the glamour and rhythm of the evening, begin shouting for more.

"Janhvi! One more! This time - an item number please!" voices called out, their hunger for spectacle unabated.

Now, inside Harpal's secret room—stuffed with weapons, hunting trophies, and dark secrets—Jaggu stands alone, focused and ready. The party roars on, unaware that danger had already entered the lion's den.

Jaggu moves like an animal bred for the shadows—silent, alert, and precise. He doesn't switch on the lights; any sudden glow might draw suspicion. Instead, he pulls out a small torch, covering half its beam with his fingers to dull the brightness.

The narrow cone of light sweeps across the room, revealing what Jaggu already suspected. Rows of rifles mounted on the wall, boxes of cartridges stacked with obsessive order, and in the far corner—an iron trunk, large and heavy. He kneels beside it, gently lifts the lid, and his eyes narrow.

Inside lie animal skins, claws, and teeth—trophies of a cruel obsession. Each piece is catalogued, preserved, and stored like treasure. Jaggu doesn't waste time. He pulls a small electronic chip from his pocket and, with practiced fingers, tucks it beneath a fold of the tiger skin inside the trunk. Then he closes the lid softly, careful to leave everything just as it was.

Outside on stage, Janhvi commands the spotlight as she begins belting out an electrifying item number. Her voice rides over the frenzy, sultry and full of fire. Her gaze—calculated, seductive—sweeps over the crowd like a queen surveying her court. Every step, every note, is deliberate, pulling the strings of the evening like a seasoned performer who knows exactly how far to go, and just when to hold back.

Jaggu turns his attention to the right wall. Mounted across the room like grotesque decorations are the severed heads of creatures once wild and free.

A Markhor with its spiraling horns stares blankly into the void. Next to it, the snarling face of a Sambar, its powerful antlers still proud in death, hangs beside the unmistakable twelve-tined antlers of a Barasingha. And draped like an expensive rug of horror—lies the spotted pelt of a leopard, stretched wide across a wooden panel. One by one, he plants discreet tracking chips behind the mounts—tucked behind ears, slipped into folds of fur, lodged beneath plaques. His work is fast, silent, surgical.

The other wall is lined with framed certificates—each bearing seals, signatures, and accolades. Below them, an array of shining trophies rests on a polished wooden shelf, their brass and silver catching the faint beam of Jaggu's torch. They speak volumes.

"National Level Shooting Championship – Gold Medalist."

"All India Rifle Accuracy Competition – First Place."

"Junior State Champion – Precision Shooting."

Jaggu scans the names and dates, his jaw tightening. This wasn't just a hunter—this was a man trained to kill with clinical precision. The trophies and certificates form a silent chorus, echoing Harpal's pride and obsession. To him, this wasn't cruelty. It was sport. It was legacy. It was art.

And in the middle of it all, the party climbs toward a crescendo—opulent, intoxicating, and utterly unaware of what's unfolding in the shadows just beyond its glittering edge.The dancers' movements become bolder, their steps sharper, as the music pounds louder through the night air. Several guests, glasses sloshing with expensive liquor, rise from their seats and drift toward the stage, swaying with the rhythm, intoxicated by the glamour and heat of the moment.

Janhvi, lost in her performance, moves like fire—graceful, untamed, her sultry voice dancing with the rhythm, she casts a subtle, sweeping glance across the room. It's not the gaze of a performer seeking applause—it's sharper, more deliberate. Beneath the dazzle of her smile and the swing of her hips, her eyes move with quiet urgency. Her gaze drifts past the drunk laughter, past the clinking glasses and the hypnotized faces—searching, trying to locate Jaggu.

And then, quite suddenly, her searching gaze collides with Harpal's eyes.He's been watching her intently, waiting for just such a moment. Sensing the chance, Harpal leans back with casual arrogance and throws her a lewd, suggestive smile—one that carries the weight of entitlement, not charm. But Janhvi doesn't flinch. Her expression remains untouched, her performance seamless. With practiced ease, she looks right through him, as though he's invisible—an insect not worth noticing. Her voice never falters, her movements stay in rhythm, but her eyes move on.

Party fever...

A few miles away, sirens pierce the stillness of night. Police jeeps tear down the highway, their red-and-blue beacons slicing through the darkness. The convoy grows — right behind them follow the Forest Department and Wildlife Crime Control Bureau vehicles, their presence, grim and determined, marking the seriousness of the operation.

At the lavish party, Mohammad Hanif — flushed with drink and arrogance — sways in a drunken stupor, his arms draped over two scantily clad dancers. The Chinese guests are no different — laughing loudly, spilling liquor, and grinding awkwardly to the booming music as they cling to the voluptuous item girls, completely immersed in their indulgence.

Janhvi stands at the center of it all — radiant and magnetic. Singing with unrelenting energy, every flick of her wrist, every tilt of her head is laced with performance — a mix of charm, seduction, and carefully honed art.

Slipping past the rest of the patrolling staff with practiced ease, Jaggu slips into the bungalow's large kitchen. The air is thick with the smell of spices, smoke, and something darker — the lingering scent of raw flesh.

He moves swiftly to the walk-in freezer at the back. The heavy metal door creaks slightly as he pulls it open. A blast of cold air escapes. The stench of raw meat fills the air, mingling with the sharp, metallic scent of the freezer. Inside, the shelves are stacked high with carcasses of various animals — some recognizable, others barely identifiable beneath layers of frozen blood and flesh.

Hanging from hooks in the farthest corner are the limp, lifeless bodies of chinkaras — their delicate, slender legs draped awkwardly. Next to them, slabs of blackbuck meat are neatly stacked, their dark, marbled flesh reflecting the dim light.

Piles of frozen meat from sambar, their thick, muscled limbs still intact, are stacked next to neatly wrapped portions of nilgai, their lean bodies frozen in mid-motion as if they were still running through the fields.

Each cut of meat tells a grim story of poaching and illegal hunting. The deep red and brown hues of the flesh glisten under the harsh fluorescent light, a stark contrast to the chill in the room. Amidst this grisly collection, he finds the hoof of a spotted deer, carelessly left among the other cuttings. Without hesitation, he places the chip, tucking it beneath the hoof before moving away swiftly, making sure not to leave a trace of his presence.

The police jeep cruises down the road, its siren wailing through the night air. Inside, Inspector Bhadoriya's eyes are fixed on the screen of his laptop. His face is lit by the screen's glow. Suddenly, three to four red markers begin flashing on the digital map.

He exhales sharply. "Jaggu has planted the chips."

Each blinking dot tells a story — a location where proof hides in plain sight. Some mark the mansion's perimeters, others flag deeper within. One blinks steadily right from inside Harpal's room.

Without a moment's hesitation, Bhadoriya reaches for the walkie-talkie beside him, his hand steady but urgent.

"All units, prepare for action," he commands into the device, his voice cutting through the static. "Target location is in range. Stay sharp, we move in immediately."

The team responds in unison, their voices crackling over the walkie-talkies. As the convoy barrels forward, the faint headlights gleam through the darkness, creating streaks of light that seem to merge with the night itself.

Suddenly, from a side road, two more jeeps join the fray — this time, from the DRI (Directorate of Revenue Intelligence). The added force increases the momentum of the convoy, and now the fleet is a formidable presence, a blend of law enforcement determined to close in on their target.

The operation is about to unfold in the darkness, the tension is palpable, and Amit Verma sitting in the forest department jeep, knows this is the moment they've been waiting for.

Meanwhile Janhvi's song reaches its peak, the music vibrant and full of energy. Raju Bhaiya and all his guests are completely immersed in the intoxication of the evening, their senses dulled by the alcohol. They are caught up in the revelry, clinging to the lady dancers as they sway and gyrate, lost in the pleasure of the moment. Their movements are uninhibited, and the atmosphere is thick with desire and excitement.

Finally the song reaches its orgasmic crescendo, the music swelling to its peak before gradually fading away, bringing the dance to a halt. The energy in the room lingers as Janhvi steps down from the stage. Her presence still commanding attention as she gracefully walks toward the washroom. From a distance, Jaggu's eyes fixate on her, observing her every move. His gaze is sharp, following her with quiet intensity, his mind working, as he remains hidden in the shadows, unseen by the revelers.

In the luxurious washroom, Janhvi's reflection appears in the mirror as she splashes water on her face. After a brief moment, she opens her eyes, and as her gaze meets the mirror, the shadow of Harpal materializes behind her. Startled, Janhvi turns, her voice betraying her surprise.

"You?" she says, her eyes wide with a mix of confusion and unease.

Harpal smirks slightly, his gaze lingering on Janhvi as he says, "Your lover boy is in jail for good now and I doubt that he will see the light of day any time soon." His eyes move slowly from top to bottom burning through her skin. Janhvi stiffens, her body instinctively tensing. Harpal's voice, laced with an unsettling calm, continues, "You're in your prime, Janhvi. And your youth, turbulent. You need a man to protect you."

Janhvi tries to step away in anger, but Harpal grabs her wrist firmly. His voice is low, almost mocking as he says, "Arrey? Why are you so worried? I am not dead yet." His grip tightens slightly, the smirk never leaving his face.

Janhvi's face turns red with fury. She tries to slap Harpal with her other hand, but he quickly grabs that wrist too, his grip unyielding. His voice takes on a condescending tone as he speaks, "Understand, Janhvi. You have your youth for the time being, but an old father is lying at home. How long will this dancing and singing sustain you?" His words cut through the tension in the air, his gaze cold and calculating.

Janhvi screams, "Let me go, you are like an elder brother to me!" As she attempts to escape, Harpal grabs her tightly and forces himself on her. Janhvi cries out in terror, but Harpal, with a twisted grin, tries to silence her by pressing his lips against hers, trying to shut her up.

Game up...

Outside, the speeding vehicles of the police, DRI, Wildlife Crime Control Bureau, and the Forest Department come to a screeching halt, quickly surrounding the high walls of Raju Bhaiya's lavish estate from all directions. Within moments, the commandos leap out of their jeeps and begin forming a tight perimeter, encircling the entire estate with practiced precision.

Watching the sudden siege unfold, one of the bungalow's guards, stunned and barely able to whisper, turns to another and murmurs under his breath, "Satyanaash..." (O God! This is the end...)

Meanwhile the bathroom door bursts open with a loud crash, its wooden frame splintering as Jaggu storms in—still clad in his waiter disguise, but now a storm in motion. His eyes burn with fury as he charges at Harpal, who is momentarily stunned by the sudden intrusion.

Jaggu grabs Harpal's shoulder and yanks him backward, breaking his grip on Janhvi. Harpal stumbles but quickly recovers, his expression turning vicious. A wild struggle erupts in the confined space—Jaggu and Harpal locked in a brutal, no-holds-barred fight.

Fists fly. Jaggu lands a hard punch to Harpal's jaw; Harpal retaliates with an elbow to Jaggu's ribs. They crash into the marble sink, knocking over soap dispensers and shattering a glass tumbler. Janhvi, shaken and breathless, presses herself against the tiled wall, watching as the two men brawl like animals.

Harpal, taller and heavily built, tries to overpower Jaggu, but Jaggu's speed and fury give him the edge. With a swift move, he ducks under Harpal's arm, grabs the back of his collar, and slams him against the vanity. The mirror cracks with a spiderweb-like fracture.

"You have no idea who you're messing with!" Harpal yells, still convinced this is just a rebellious waiter.

But Jaggu's rage is unrelenting. He knees Harpal in the gut, sending him crumpling. Not once does he speak. Not once does he reveal himself.

Elsewhere, the commandos move swiftly, surrounding the outer perimeter of Raju Bhaiya's sprawling bungalow. Up on the rooftop and in the watchtower, other armed men try to respond—but the sharpshooters are faster. One by one, those who reach for their rifles are picked off. Their lifeless bodies tumble from the heights—some crashing into the garden below, others slumping against the stone walls in grotesque stillness.

Outside the main gate, vehicles from the Forest Department, the DRI, and the Wildlife Crime Control wait. The reinforced gates are locked tight. No one can enter or leave.

Raju Bhaiya's fortress becomes a trap.

A sudden blast of static cracks through hidden loudspeakers around the bungalow, silencing the music mid-beat. The voice comes, hard-edged and commanding.

"This is Inspector Bhadoria speaking," the announcement echoes across the lawns, the poolside, the grand arches of the mansion. "Your premises are completely surrounded. This is a joint operation of the Police Department, the Directorate of Revenue Intelligence, and the Forest Department."

Inside, glasses freeze midair, laughter dies on trembling lips.

"Anyone attempting to flee will be apprehended immediately," the voice continued, sharp as a blade. "Anyone who lifts a weapon will be shot without warning. We are coming in."

A hush sweeps through the bungalow like a gust of cold wind. The decadent mirage of luxury shatters. Panic blooms in the eyes of guests who had, only moments ago, been soaked in arrogance and wine. Some rush for cover, others whisper in disbelief.

Even before the echo of Inspector Bhadoria's announcement had fully faded, a few of the guards guarding the perimeter begin to stir. Others, hidden in plain clothes among the trees and shadows near the house, reach for the concealed weapons under their shirts.

They never get the chance.

Crack. Crack.

Silenced sniper rounds tear through the night like invisible fangs.

Panic erupts.

People stumble over one another, glasses shatter, heels break and a stampede of frightened footsteps thunder through the corridors.

Meanwhile, amid the violent scuffle in the lavish washroom, Harpal manages to land a heavy blow across Jaggu's jaw. The force of the hit loosens Jaggu's waiter disguise — the wig shifts, the cap flows off, the moustache dangles and the makeup smears under the sweat and struggle.

Harpal freezes.

His bloodshot eyes widen in disbelief as he stares at the face beneath. "You?!" he gasped, his voice cracking. "Tu... tu jail se kab nikla? Kaise nikla?" (When and how did you come out of jail?)

Jaggu didn't respond. His chest heaves with fury, and his fists are clenched like iron hammers.

Within moments, three burly, heavily built bodyguards storm into the washroom like bulls let loose. Their thick necks and wide shoulders barely fit through the ornate doorway as they charge in.

Harpal takes a staggering step back, then spits out with venom, "Yeh bachna nahi chahiye. Ghaat do isko! Maar do saale ko!"(This man should not leave the premises alive. Finish this nuisance once and for all.)

Without hesitation, they lunge at Jaggu from all sides.

Jaggu, agile and wild like a cornered animal, ducks and strikes back, his movements honed from a life on the run. But the odds are against him —four on one, and all trained to kill.

Jaggu, bleeding and breathless, yanks the hand-shower from the wall and whips it around like a flail, slamming it square into one of the bodyguards' faces. The man reels back with a cry of pain, blood gushing from his brow.

The second guard lunges, but Jaggu twists and shoves him hard into the massive vanity mirror. The glass shatters on impact, spraying shards everywhere.

Seizing the split-second advantage, Jaggu pulls the key ring from his pocket and hurls it towards Janhvi with a shout— "Ja! Jaldi ja! (Go! Rush!) Open the gate, the force is here!"

Janhvi catches the keys mid-air, her eyes wide with fear and adrenaline. Without a word, she turns and bolts out of the washroom, sprinting past the wreckage, past dazed dancers and confused guests, her breath ragged. She cuts through the party and the crowd, leaving a trail of murmurs behind her.

Seeing her rush towards the gate, Raju Bhaiya and Mohammad Hanif exchange a sharp glance. Without wasting a moment, they move in her direction, their steps fumbling with intoxication. They are intent on stopping her before she escapes. The party's gloss and glitter had crumbled into chaos, the tension thickening as they closed in on her.

Janhvi, in a desperate move, grabs a beer bottle and swings it with all her might, shattering it over Raju Bhaiya's head. The bottle shatters with a loud crash, splashing beer all over his face. Raju Bhaiya staggers back, dazed, his hand clutching his forehead as he tries to steady himself. Meanwhile, Mohammad Hanif lunges at Janhvi, his hands reaching out to grab her.

In one swift motion, Janhvi pushes Hanif with all her strength, sending him crashing to the ground. His drunken body sprawls across the floor. Taking advantage of the moment, she sprints toward the gate, her heart racing. The sound of her rapid footsteps echoing in her ears as she pushes through the last of the crowd.

Her hands tremble slightly as she fumbles for the key, but her resolve keeps her focused. She manages to unlock the gate, pushing it open just enough to allow the force outside to enter. As the commandos and officers flood through, Janhvi calls out urgently, "Go to the washroom—rescue Jaggu! He's in there!"

She watches as the commandos immediately rush toward the washroom, ready to confront the violence inside and rescue Jaggu, who is still being pummeled by Harpal and his goons.

Finally, the police commandos rush into the washroom, guns drawn and ready. Inside, Harpal and his bodyguards have pinned Jaggu down and are still relentlessly beating him, completely oblivious to the commotion outside. Each blow lands with force, leaving Jaggu bruised and battered as he struggles to defend himself.

As the commandos step in, Harpal, in a moment of desperation, grabs a large, jagged shard of broken glass from the floor and attempts to drive it into Jaggu's neck.

Just as he swings the shard down with brutal intent, a police sharp shooter takes the shot. The bullet hits Harpal's hand with precision, causing him to drop the glass shard immediately.

Harpal stumbles back screaming, clutching his injured hand, as the commandos quickly close in, securing him. One by one, the three burly bodyguards are wrestled to the ground, handcuffed, and dragged out of the washroom by the tactical team. Their resistance is short-lived under the trained precision of the commandos.

Flanked by two officers, Harpal staggers out of the washroom, his hand bleeding profusely from the sniper's bullet, his bravado gone, replaced by grim silence and seething pain.

Despite the savage beating and the searing pain that wracked his body, Jaggu's thoughts remain fixed on one thing—Janhvi. His limbs tremble, and every step sends waves of agony through his frame, but something deeper than pain—an urgency, a fear—keeps him moving.

He drags himself out of the bloodied washroom, leaning heavily against the wall for support, his shirt torn, face battered, and one eye nearly swollen shut. "Janhvi... Janhvi!" he calls out, limping past dazed party guests and shattered furniture.

His eyes scan the chaos—overturned tables, flashing lights, the bark of commands from officers—but he doesn't stop. Not until he sees her. Not until he knows she is safe.

POLICE

Contraband...

The entire bungalow is torn apart by the combined forces of the police, the Forest Department, the Wildlife Crime Control Bureau, and the DRI commandos. The officers move swiftly, room by room, leaving no drawer unopened, no secret compartment untouched.

In a concealed armory behind a false wall, the police uncover a staggering cache—over forty illegal rifles, including high-powered sniper guns, and more than 50,000 live cartridges stacked in crates.

In the lavish kitchen's industrial-sized freezer, the Forest Department and WCCB officers make a grisly discovery: the carcasses and dismembered remains of protected wildlife—chinkara, blackbuck, chital, sambar, and nilgai. Packed between slabs of ice, they also find 171 kilograms of raw bush meat.

The unmistakable hides of rare wildcats are rolled up and hidden in trunks, alongside bags of bones, teeth, horns, and claws in Harpal's hunting room—evidence of a sprawling poaching and smuggling racket.

Meanwhile, the Directorate of Revenue Intelligence opens a locked room and recovers over ₹40 crore in unaccounted cash, stuffed in trunks and duffel bags.

Raju Bhaiya is arrested at the scene, his bloodied scalp still smarting from the blow dealt by Janhvi. Harpal Singh, nursing a bleeding hand and still in shock from the commando raid, is also taken into custody.

Alongside the illegal arms and wildlife contraband, the police uncover yet another layer of the sprawling criminal enterprise. In a hidden study behind Raju Bhaiya's opulent office, they find a stack of handwritten diaries and ledger books. Page after page reveals detailed records of illicit financial transactions—massive proceeds from illegal sand and stone mining operations, flowing directly from Mohammad Hanif to Raju Bhaiya. The entries, complete with dates, coded references, and amounts, form irrefutable evidence of a long-running partnership rooted in environmental destruction and political corruption.

As officers inspect the dining area where the party had been in full swing just moments ago, they find half-eaten plates of cooked wild meat—some still steaming. Among the guests are the two Chinese nationals, caught red-handed with illegal bush meat on their plates. Forensic teams later confirm the meat to be from protected species.

The evidence is overwhelming and damning. Each room of the bungalow tells a story—of wealth built on blood, land ravaged for greed, and wildlife sacrificed for spectacle.

The bungalow, once echoing with music, laughter, and corruption, now echoes with the bark of orders, the clicking of handcuffs, and the hum of justice closing in.

Information from the diaries leads the police to act swiftly. That very night, a special police team raids Mohammad Hanif's warehouse located on the outskirts of the town's industrial zone. Under the cover of darkness and with utmost precision, they surround the premises and storm inside.

Inside the vast, dimly lit warehouse, the officers discover mountains of illegally mined laterite stone and boulders stacked floor to ceiling—far beyond any permissible limit. The entire stock is undocumented and unregistered, a clear violation of environmental and mining laws.

While searching the office inside the warehouse, an officer pulls open a tightly locked desk drawer. Inside lies a worn-out, leather-bound diary. As pages are flipped open, it becomes clear that this is no ordinary notebook—it's a detailed account book, containing hand-written entries of illegal transactions, bribes paid to local officials, coded names, truck registration numbers, routes, and quantities of stone and sand extracted and delivered. Cross-referenced with the diary seized from Raju Bhaiya's bungalow, it becomes a damning piece of corroborative evidence. The warehouse is sealed, the stock is seized, and more arrests are set in motion based on the names listed in the diary.

But even after the successful raids on Raju Bhaiya's bungalow and Mohammad Hanif's warehouse, there remains a gnawing sense of incompletion in the air. Lakhan and his gang members are still unaccounted for. Most disturbing of all, the kidnapped child, Rajiv, is nowhere to be found. The police teams exchange anxious glances, the tension visible in the furrowed brows of senior officers. A sense of dread begins to build—what if the child has already been harmed?

After being attended by a team of doctors, Jaggu, despite his injuries, sits up with visible strain. His eyes, bloodshot and weary, flicker with urgency. "These people," he says in a hoarse voice, "when all their escape routes are cut off, I know exactly where they crawl back to."

Everyone turns to him.

"A place nobody dares to go. Deep inside the forest, beyond the abandoned quarry, there's an old forest chowki—an elevated wooden outpost on stilts. Hidden. Isolated. And easy to defend." Jaggu says, eyes intense.

Everyone in the room falls silent, absorbing the weight of that revelation. The location is unfamiliar to most and dangerously remote. It's the kind of place designed to vanish.

Within minutes, a high-level rapid response team is mobilized—comprising seasoned police officers, forest department rangers, and Wildlife Crime Control Bureau operatives. The mission is clear: find Lakhan, bust the last hideout of the poaching gang, and rescue Rajiv—before it's too late.

"I'll have to guide you," Jaggu says. Blood seeps through his bandages, but his eyes burn with purpose.

Inspector Bhadoria, shocked, steps forward. "You're too injured, Jaggu. You've lost blood. How can you possibly lead us in this condition?"

"You won't find them without me," Jaggu replies firmly. "They know the forest better than anyone. But I know them better."

The paramedics rush in. They check his bandages quickly, an IV needle already taped to his arm. One doctor protests, "He needs immediate rest. He has internal injuries. This is madness."

Jaggu winces but brushes them off. "There's a child out there. If we wait, he might not live to see the sunrise."

There's no arguing with that.

Inspector Bhadoria locks eyes with him. "Alright," he says. "You lead. We follow."

The team loads up. The dark forest is waiting. So are the shadows.

The elevated chowki ....

The elevated forest chowki stands high on stilts, nestled amidst a rugged and treacherous landscape. The forest around is dense and suffocating, with ancient, gnarled trees towering above, their thick canopies blocking out most of the moonlight. The surrounding jagged cliffs form an almost impenetrable barrier, offering no clear path for anyone to approach except one: a narrow, dry riverbed. The riverbed, once a trickling stream, is now barren, its cracked earth hidden beneath a tangled mess of underbrush and twisted trees.

It feels as though the forest itself is guarding this isolated, elevated station, protecting its secrets, and deterring anyone who dares to venture too close.

The team moves in silence, their breaths measured, careful not to disturb the eerie quiet of the jungle. It presses on through the dry, cracked riverbed, their every step calculated and deliberate. The moonlight flickers through the branches above, illuminating their path just enough to reveal the next obstacle—an old, twisted root or a cluster of sharp rocks. They navigate these hazards with practiced ease, their eyes trained on the faint outline of the elevated chowki in the distance, looming silently above them, where danger and secrecy await.

As they continue moving, strangely the soft but distinct sound of a Mujra—a traditional Indian dance and music performance—drifts through the air.

Suddenly, a sharp, high-pitched call breaks the silence—a barking deer, startled by their presence. The alarm call is loud, echoing through the jungle like a sharp warning. The team halts immediately, freezing in place. Jaggu, who leads them, holds up his hand in a hush. "Be very careful," he whispers, his voice barely audible. "Any alarm call could alert them."

The tension thickens in the air as the team holds their breath, waiting for the echo of the call to fade into the night.

Finally, the team reaches the edge of the forest, where the dry riverbed flattens out, leading them up to the base of the Chowki. They slow their pace, moving quietly, keeping to the shadows as they survey the area. The Chowki's silhouette now looms above them, elevated on stilts. A dim light glows from the upper floor, casting faint shadows. The faint, lilting melody accompanied by cruel, drunken laughter carried on the night breeze adds an eerie element to the otherwise tense atmosphere of the jungle.

The police team surrounds the Chowki from all sides. Inside the upper floor of the Chowki, the mujra is in full swing. There's a lot of drinking, mockery, and loud noise filling the air. Jaggu, hearing the chaos, warns the police team, saying, "If you try to climb the stairs, the child's life will be at risk. I'll create a diversion upstairs. On my signal, break down the door and enter."

With grim determination, Jaggu makes his way toward the adjacent Neem tree, which stands close to the Chowki. His hands and feet, though trembling with pain, move with practiced precision as he climbs the tree. He's been a natural climber since childhood, and now, despite his severe injuries and the numerous bandages wrapped around his body, he relies on those long-honed skills.

He reaches the tree's highest point and carefully maneuvers himself to the same elevation as the Chowki. With steady hands and a focused mind, Jaggu edges closer to the window, peering inside to gather information.

What he sees is a dark and disturbing scene. The chowki has been completely overtaken by Lakhan's poaching gang — Pratap, Bhola, and Chimta among them. They lounge on charpoys, drinking alcohol and laughing wildly. The original four forest guards stationed at the chowki have been humiliated — stripped of their uniforms, forced into sarees, and made to dance like mujra performers.

An intoxicated Lakhan yells at them, his voice slurred but filled with venom, "Goli khayega ya nachega? Chal Basanti naach! Tujhe Veeru ki kasam!" (Will you eat bullets or dance. C'mon Basanti dance. Swear on your lover Veeru!) His cruel mockery loosely based on the hit lines of a famous old Bollywood film, fills the air, the force of his words making the guards tremble even more.

Then, in his drunken stupor, he suddenly hurls an empty whisky bottle at the ground. The bottle shatters into pieces, the sound of breaking glass sharp and echoing through the room. Jaggu, hidden in the shadows of the Neem tree, clenches his fists. His heart pounds, knowing that these men are too far gone to reason with. Every part of him screams for action, but his injured body is not cooperating. He grips the tree tighter, his mind racing as he plans his next move.

The guards trembling with fear and humiliation are now forced to dance on the broken shards of glass scattered across the floor. Their feet begin to bleed, but they have no choice — the guns trained on them leave no room for defiance. The once proud forest guards are now nothing more than playthings for these sadistic criminals. Every step they take sends sharp pain through their feet, and the blood mixes with the glass, turning the scene even more grotesque.

Lakhan taunts, slurring his words as he raises his glass in a toast to their suffering. "Dance faster! Dance properly! You worthless fools!"

He and his gang continue to drink, their cheering, whistling and laughter ringing through the room, echoing off the walls like a sickening symphony of brutality. It is a scene of total dominance and debasement — a symbol of how far the chowki has fallen from law and order.

Meanwhile, the police team moves swiftly into action, surrounding the Chowki with a robust net, ensuring that anyone who might fall from the upper story won't be mortally injured. The net is stretched tightly around the base of the structure, offering a crucial safety measure for the impending operation.

Simultaneously, the team's snipers take up carefully calculated positions, hidden in the shadows of the thick forest. They position themselves strategically, ensuring clear lines of sight, prepared to eliminate any threat that might emerge.

Jaggu"s keen eyes focus on Rajiv, the kidnapped child, lying motionless in the corner of the Chowki. His face is obscured by a cloth gag, and his hands and feet are tightly bound. His body shivers occasionally, as if in a semi-conscious state, overwhelmed by the trauma and fear.

Lakhan, his face twisted with sadistic pleasure, strides up to the helpless child. With a mocking laugh, he opens a bottle of alcohol and carelessly pours it over Rajiv's body. The liquid seeps into the child's clothes, dampening him further.

"Chal-chal uthjaa,"(C'mon get up) Lakhan sneers, his words dripping with malice. The rest of his gang cheer and jeer, amused by the scene, reveling in the torment they've caused.

Jaggu's anger boils as he watches the tormenting scene unfold. The pain from his injuries seems to disappear, replaced by a surge of adrenaline.

His gaze hardens; the time for action has come.

With a swift motion, Jaggu swings from one of the hanging branches, using it like a makeshift swing. His body propels through the air, and with a powerful leap, he catapults himself into the room, landing inside with feline grace. The moonlight catches the gleam of the khukri as Jaggu leaps forward, and in one fluid motion, he presses the blade firmly against Lakhan's throat.

Lakhan freezes, his drunken haze clearing in an instant as Jaggu's sharp knife rests on his neck, the cold steel sending a chill down his spine.

"Chimpta, open the door, otherwise Lakhan's neck will be slit open." Jaggu's voice is low but laced with deadly seriousness, his gaze locked onto Lakhan, whose eyes widen in shock.

The gang members, though initially frozen in shock, begin to slowly inch towards the back of the room, fear creeping into their eyes. Jaggu's fury, combined with the sharp khukri pressed against Lakhan's throat, has them paralyzed. They know this is not a man to be trifled with. The forest guards, still bleeding from their forced dance, look on, hope flickering in their eyes.

Jaggu says, "If you try any tricks, there's an entire army outside. Open the door now."

Despite this threat, Chimta, with a clever move, tries to reach for his weapon. Jaggu, however, presses the khukri lightly against Lakhan's neck drawing a red line of blood.

Lakhan screams in pain, "Yeh baawla ho gaya hai. Maar dega. Iski baat sunle Chimpta. Baad me nipat lenge isse."(He's gone mad! He'll kill me! Do as he says, Chimta! We will deal with him later)

But just then, Bhola chuckles and says, "Arrey Jaggu Bhaiya, why don't you take a look over here too?"

Jaggu turns his head and sees Bhola pressing a crude country-made pistol against the kidnapped child's head.

He is forced to release his grip on Lakhan for the sake of the child.

Suddenly, from outside, the sharp blare of a police megaphone breaks through the chaos — a loud announcement echoes through the forest air:

"We are giving you a final warning! The entire forest chowki is surrounded. The wise choice is to raise your hands and come out through the door quietly. Surrender now. Otherwise, we will open fire — and there won't be enough left of you to pick up in one piece!"

Chimta rushes to the window of the chowki to peek outside—just as he does, a sniper's bullet rips through his shoulder. He stumbles, crashing down from the window like a broken doll.

In that split second of distraction, Lakhan manages to snatch the khukri from Jaggu's hand and lunges at him with it, aiming to strike. A brutal hand-to-hand fight rages between Jaggu and Lakhan. Lakhan slashes wildly with the khukri, swinging it left and right. Jaggu evades each strike with agile somersaults, his movements sharp despite his injuries.

Meanwhile the forest guards, who had been humiliated for hours, suddenly spring into action.

Two of the guards lunge at Bhola. In a swift move, they wrest the country-made pistol from his hand. Another guard loops a scarf tightly around Bhola's mouth and throat, muffling his screams as they pin him down. The tide begins to turn.

Then, like a panther, Jaggu suddenly lunges forward—grabbing Lakhan by the throat and twisting his neck while simultaneously locking down the arm wielding the khukri.

The two men are locked in a savage grappling posture, each straining for dominance. Lakhan snarls, "Pratap! Grab the boy!"

At once, Pratap rushes toward the child. But just as he lunges, a loud gunshot rings through the chaos—Dhayaaan!

The second forest guard, wielding a crude local firearm, has fired directly into Pratap's leg. The bullet hits its mark. Pratap yelps and crumples to the floor, writhing in pain.

Jaggu doesn't waste the opportunity. With a forceful heave, he slams Lakhan to the window, then pushes him straight out.

Lakhan tumbles out of the window in a wild spin, crashing straight into the police net stretched below. Before he can even regain his senses, the commandos pounce—pinning him down and securing him in seconds.

Inside, Jaggu, bloodied and limping, lifts the child gently into his arms. He staggers to the chowki door and throws it open. At once, the police force storms in with thunderous boots and flashing torches. The entire poaching gang is swiftly overpowered and taken into custody.

Jaggu, barely able to stand, limps over to Amit Verma. He hands the semi-conscious child over carefully—his breath heavy, eyes glassy.

A faint smile flickers across his face — a mixture of relief and exhaustion.

Then, just as his knees buckle and he collapses to the ground, he murmurs something under his breath. The words are broken, barely audible, but they pierce through the silence like a whisper of redemption.

"Mera prāyaśhchita... poora hua..."(My atonement... is complete...)

Before anyone can ask more, his eyes roll back and he falls unconscious.

Inspector Bhadoria drops to his knees beside him, checking his pulse. The commandos close in. The entire Bavaria gang lies cuffed on the ground, their reign finally over.

But those last words linger in the air like smoke over a battlefield — Atonement for what? What sin had haunted Jaggu all these years?

No one speaks. But they all know: this wasn't just a rescue. It was the closing of a long, painful chapter in a life shadowed by guilt.

Into freedom.. Into love...

Jaggu's mind drifts into a dreamlike stupor, the edges of reality blurring as his body succumbs to exhaustion. His pulse weakens, but his consciousness expands into an endless realm, a surreal world where the past and present collide.

Visions flash before him— He was a boy again, moving like wind through the forests of Central India. The earth was softer. The air was rich with the scent of wildflowers and damp leaves. He ran, barefoot and bright-eyed, chasing footprints, reading trails. He saw the creatures he once adored: the silent-footed leopard, deer bounding in the sun, a sloth bear tumbling in play, porcupines shuffling through the underbrush, birds like painted arrows above the canopy. Spirits of the forest, they had been his friends, companions —until poverty and desperation turned him into their enemy.

He saw himself again, a young man standing at the crossroads, torn between survival and his soul.

And just before the trail vanished into the mist, he saw him again—his blood brother.

Out of the yellow grass—emerged the tiger.

Massive, silent, sovereign.

The tiger walked slowly toward him, each step powerful and certain. It circled him once, and then came close, its golden eyes locked with Jaggu's. The great beast stood still, staring into him with a gaze that held no malice—only understanding.

As if to say, "You were lost. But you found your way back. Go. Love. Live."

The striped monk bowed its head once, slowly, and melted back into the grass.

Then the forest faded into moonlight.

He saw her.

Janhvi.

The only woman who ever truly touched his heart. He had always chosen her as his only and true soul-mate, but she had refused him.

But now… now his sins were washed. His penance paid in blood, in pain, in sacrifice.

She stood beside a tall black horse, her long white dress catching the breeze, fluttering like a flame. She didn't speak. She didn't have to. Her eyes were soft, wet, glowing.

Jaggu stepped forward. She reached out her hand.

He took it.

He climbed onto the horse and pulled her behind him. Her arms wrapped tightly around his torso, her fingers curled into his chest. Her cheek rested against his back, feeling the rhythm of his heart. He smelled the salt of her skin, the jasmine in her hair. She felt his warmth, the curve of muscle under his torn shirt, the hard breath in his lungs.

The horse began to move—then gallop.

They clung to each other, man and woman, heat and breath, sweat and spirit. Her dress billowed around them like smoke. The wind whipped through their hair. The world melted away as they raced faster, faster than the wind, deeper into the silver mountains.

Behind them came the wolves. Grey, snarling, tireless.

But those wolves were not of flesh and fur—They snarled and chased, memories of his past—his guilt, his violence, his shame.

But they could not catch him now. The black horse flew through the night, untouchable, unstoppable—like an arrow streaking through the moonlight.

Janhvi held him tighter. Her mouth brushed the nape of his neck. His hand reached back, touching her thigh. Their bodies, pressed together, moved in rhythm with the horse's stride. Their breathing synchronized, rapid and hungry. Together, they were fire and thunder, riding into the night.

One by one, the wolves—those shadows of his past— fell behind—howling, fading, forgotten.

Jaggu and Janhvi disappeared into the silver mountains.

Into moonlight.

Into freedom.

Into love.

Forever.

Justice and mercy...

In the High Court, standing before the judge, the three children—Aamir, Rajiv, and Anya—bravely identify each of the poachers. Their voices are steady, their eyes filled with the weight of what they had seen.

The entire Bavaria gang are sentenced to rigorous imprisonment under the law. Their crimes were monstrous—they had taken the lives of at least thirty one tigers and several leopards over the years, leaving behind a trail of blood and gore in the forests of India. Lakhan, named the ringleader of the poaching syndicate, is convicted not only for killing protected wildlife but also for the kidnapping of Rajiv and Jayant Ghosh, and the attempted murder of the latter.

Given the gravity of the offenses, Harpal Singh is sentenced with severity. The court finds him complicit not only in game hunting and illegal possession of firearms, but also as a financier and enabler of the criminal network involved in the poaching of critically endangered species.

Mohammad Hanif and former minister Rajpal Singh—also known as Raju Bhaiya—are found guilty of serious environmental crimes, including illegal river sand mining, boulder extraction, and the harboring and consumption of bushmeat and other wildlife products within their private properties. The court delivers lengthy sentences to both men under wildlife protection laws, environmental degradation statutes, and charges of criminal conspiracy.

The net spreads wider.

In an unprecedented international breakthrough, Interpol, working closely with Indian and Tibetan authorities, extradites Dechen Limi and Varad Praja to stand trial at the International Court of Justice in The Hague. Their transnational trafficking network is dismantled piece by piece.

The final nail in the coffin comes from science. A DNA analysis by the Wildlife Institute of India links blood and bones found at the Kaziranga poaching site to tiger skins recovered from Lhasa. The match is indisputable.

This forensic breakthrough becomes the cornerstone of the prosecution's case. For the first time in international legal history, a forensic trail proves how a living tigress, a lactating mother of cubs, was butchered in the heart of an Indian forest and sold halfway across the world.

Justice is served—not only in the courtroom, but in the dark heart of the forest where the tigress once walked free.

Jaggu stands in the dock, his head bowed. His heart carries the burden of guilt. He had been part of the same darkness, walking the same bloody path.

But then, something shifts.

Because of the special appeals made by the police, the forest department, wildlife researcher Jayant Ghosh, and Rajiv's parents—who saw not just the poacher, but the man who saved their child—the court decides to reduce Jaggu's sentence to three years of rigorous imprisonment. His bravery, his repentance, his sacrifice, and his crucial role in rescuing the children cannot be ignored.

The gavel falls.

Justice is delivered. But mercy, too, finds a place in the courtroom that day for Jaggu —the man who turned on his own past.

Holi...

It was Holi.

The sun hung low above the craggy granite cliffs that encircled Janhvi's humble home, casting long shadows across the secluded courtyard. The house was humble in size but mysterious in presence. The earth all around was dry and dusty, cracked like an old palm, yet it held a strange kind of strength, a haunting stillness.

In the center of the windswept aangan (courtyard), a simple tulsi manch stood, bricks faded with age, but the basil plant thrived — green and defiant, like Janhvi herself, quivering in the afternoon breeze. A few goats were lazily tethered to wooden posts, bleating softly, their bells tinkling faintly in the silence of the late afternoon. Janhvi sat cross-legged on the ground. A baby goat nestled in her lap, nibbling at her dupatta as she softly murmured lullabies and stroked its ears. The sound of distant drums floated through the air, mingling with the earthy scent of gulal.

She didn't see him come.

Without a word, two weathered hands reached out from behind and gently smeared red gulal on both her cheeks.

She gasped.

Spinning around, her eyes widened in disbelief.

For a moment, she could not speak.

There he was—Jaggu. Taller somehow, leaner perhaps, but unmistakably him.

Dust clung to his boots, the sun danced on the dried sweat on his forehead, and his eyes—those eyes—looked at her not with the fire of guilt, but with the quiet resolve of a man who had served his sentence and returned whole.

"Jaggu..." she whispered, barely audible, the color draining from her face even as the gulal bloomed on her skin. "You... you didn't tell me..."

"I wanted to see the surprise in your eyes," Jaggu said softly, smiling with a touch of mischief and a weight of memory. "Three long years. You waited."

He stepped closer, but she instinctively turned, as if to flee—overwhelmed.

Jaggu moved quickly, gently blocking her path. "Don't run," he said. "Not from me. Not today."

Her breath caught as she looked up at him again. In that moment, emotions tangled inside her—shock, joy, anger, relief—all swelling together until they burst in tears that spilled over silently. She punched his shoulder weakly, twice, before suddenly burying her face in his chest, trembling.

Jaggu held her.

She shivered — not from the cold, but from the sudden heat between them.

Suddenly Janhvi made a break for it, rushing toward the bucket of coloured water sitting near the Tulsi altar. Jaggu chased her. Just as he reached out, she spun around with a squeal and splashed the entire bucket over him. The water soaked through his kurta, revealing the lean muscles beneath. They both laughed, breathless, dripping with colour and delight.

Their eyes locked. The laughter faded for a heartbeat.

She walked towards him slowly, pulling more gulal into her hands. Jaggu stood still, letting her smear it over his face, his neck.

Then they squatted on the ground. Her fingers trembled as they brushed past his collarbone. His hands brushed against her thighs. He leaned in, brushing his lips against her forehead, then her cheek. Her eyes fluttered shut.

There, under the warm sun, soaked in colours, they kissed — a kiss of reunion, of forgiveness, of passion long held back. Around them, goats bleated, the wind kicked up a swirl of dust, and the tulsi leaves fluttered quietly.

And that dusty courtyard, beneath the cliffs and memories, witnessed their story, which seemed to have just begun again — a dance of love between a man who had returned from darkness, and the woman who had waited with a quiet flame.

Sheopur Tiger Reserve...

On the day of Holi, Jayant Ghosh's face was streaked with vibrant colours — smears of pink, green, and a bold streak of yellow across his forehead, remnants of cheerful villagers who had come by to bid farewell.

Jayant was quietly finishing his packing. His work here was done. The data collected, the camera traps removed, the reports compiled — it was time to move on.

He folded his documents carefully, slid his field notes into a folder, and zipped up his weather-worn suitcase. His laptop, now loaded with months of hard-earned documentation of the forest's secrets, went into a padded sleeve. He paused for a moment, looking around the room that had been his base for so long. The map of the Sheopur forest division still hung on the wall, corners curled. The wooden table bore faint coffee stains and ink blotches from long nights.

Just as he reached for his phone to shut it down for travel, the screen lit up.

"Mr. Verma" — the name glowed on the display.

Jayant smiled. A quiet, knowing smile. With coloured fingers, he wiped a little of the holi dust off the screen and accepted the call.

“Amit Ji,” he said warmly, “I was just thinking about you.”

Mr. Verma's voice crackled through the line, warm and filled with genuine admiration. "Congratulations, Jayant! Kya baat hai. The report on Sheopur Tiger Reserve is nothing short of brilliant."

Jayant smiled, glancing out the window where the sun painted golden stripes through the sal trees. "Thank you, sir," he said with quiet pride. "And now, with the declaration of the tiger reserve, we'll finally see a surge of clean, green tourism dollars flowing into the region. There will be prosperity across the area — real upliftment for the local communities."

There was a pause, and then Jayant added, his voice steady with conviction, "This was the point all along, sir. To prove that a living tiger brings more wealth and honor to the nation than a hundred dead ones ever could."

On the other end, Verma was silent for a moment — the kind of silence that carries deep agreement.

The morning sun filtered gently through the dry deciduous canopy of the newly declared Sheopur Tiger Reserve, a sanctuary born from the relentless dedication of wildlife activist Jayant Ghosh and local villagers. The tall, sparse trees—mostly teak, tendu, and palash—stood as silent sentinels over the parched undergrowth. The air was still, but rich with anticipation. Once a vulnerable patch of forest teetering on the edge of exploitation, it now thrums with new life, protected under the banner of conservation.

This was a momentous day.

It is the season of the 2026 All-India Tiger Census. Amidst the dappled green, we see Jaggu, no longer the man he once was, but reborn. Now a full-fledged forest guard and tracker, he addressed a group of fresh-faced forest guards and rangers with quiet authority, his stride confident and his eyes alert as he demonstrates how to read pugmarks in the soil, how to set up camera traps and how to distinguish a tiger's roar from the leopard's sawing call. His past has forged him into a teacher with unmatched instinct and experience.

"This land is ancient," he began, kneeling to point at faint tracks in the dust, "and the tiger walks it like a shadow. During the heat of the day, they retreat into ravines, shaded nallahs, and the leopards rest in caves in the rocky outcrops. But early morning and dusk—that's their time. That's when the forest breathes with movement."

He tapped the ground beside a dry streambed. "And when you hear sambar calling—kaonk-kaonk—it means the predator is close. Cheetal will bark, nilgai may stamp and snort. These are your alarms. You follow their eyes. These calls can tell you where the tiger is. And remember, the tiger isn't alone here. Sloth bears roam these forests. Striped hyenas. Wolves. You'll see different signs—claw marks on soft bark, dug-up termite mounds, droppings, tufts of hair. Each has its own story. Learn to read it."

A distant langur gave a sudden whoop from the treetops, and the recruits instinctively turned their heads. Jaggu smiled slightly. "Good. You're already learning."

"You don't just guard animals. You guard the soul of the forest."

Far from the group, standing at the edge of a small hillock, Jayant Ghosh watched silently, his arms folded, eyes following Jaggu with a flicker of pride. It had been three years since their fates crossed under darker skies. Jaggu had kept his word—he had been instrumental in bringing down one of the country's most notorious poaching networks. As promised, the forest department had rewarded him with a second chance—an official post as a forest guard in the very forest he was once forced to betray.

His eyes met Jaggu's for a brief moment.

"My work here is done. Sheopur Tiger Reserve is now alive. It's time for me to return to research, to other forests, to new battles. But this place— this legacy—the flag now rests with you."said Jayant.

Jaggu's face grew solemn, but resolute. "I'll carry it with honour, Sir. I owe it to this land… and to the ones we couldn't save."

Jayant nodded. "You were chosen by the forest, Jaggu. Every arrest, every confession, every seized skin and weapon — it was part of the tiger's will. The forest had sent one of its own to clean the rot from within."

A brief silence passed between them, filled only by the rustling of yellow grass and a distant peacock's cry.

At the edge of the clearing, a new wooden sign swayed gently in the breeze:

Sheopur Tiger Reserve Established 2026 — A Sanctuary Reborn

This is was new dawn — for the forest, for its creatures, and for the people who have chosen to defend them.

Jaggu glanced at the trainees waiting for him. "Now, if you'll excuse me, Sir… I have to take my rangers on a field walk. There's a trail we must follow—fresh pugmarks near the rocky ridge."

Jayant raised a hand in farewell.

Jaggu stood straight, brought his hand up in a crisp salute, then turned and disappeared into the tall, waving grass with his team of khaki-clad men. The forest seemed to welcome him, the golden grass parting like an old friend. Jayant watched until they vanished into the wild.

In the distance, a lone sambar stag gave a soft hoot, as if announcing a new guardian of the jungle.

Reborn—Reloaded...

Dressed in the crisp khaki uniform of a forest guard, Jaggu moved with quiet authority through the dry deciduous terrain of the Sheopur Tiger Reserve. Around him, a few fellow forest guards and wildlife trackers followed closely, their eyes scanning the forest floor with reverence and focus.

Jaggu crouched near a patch of grass flattened by a heavy body. He brushed his fingers over the soil, sniffed the air, and leaned in to examine a faint stain near the base of a bush. “Tiger urine,” he said quietly. “This mark is fresh—likely from a territorial female. They often scent-mark territories along ridges or paths near water sources.”

The others listened with a kind of awe. Jaggu wasn’t just reciting textbook knowledge—he was living it.

He stood and led the group deeper into the terrain, pointing out subtle clues: a bent twig, claw marks on a salai tree, a trail of crushed leaves.

He paused as a distant call rang out—sharp and urgent.

“Cheetal,” Jaggu said. “That’s an alarm call. Tigers rarely walk unnoticed. The entire forest speaks when a tiger moves.”

Pressed into the dusty path were pugmarks—large impressions with clearly defined pointed toes. “A tigress,” Jaggu murmured, tracing the outline with his fingers. Then, just behind those, three smaller, lighter imprints—tiny pugmarks, barely the size of a human fist—appeared in succession.

“She’s not alone,” he said softly. “Her cubs are following. Three of them, moving close behind. This trail is less than an hour old.”

He looked up at the trainees, his voice tinged with awe. “You’re witnessing something rare. A mother tigress leading her cubs, likely towards water or a fresh kill. This is life unfolding right before us.”

The group of forest guards and trainees moved in quiet formation behind Jaggu as he tracked the tigress and her cubs. The dry deciduous forest slowly gave way to an open expanse—a sunlit grassland shimmering with tall, yellow grass that swayed in the breeze like a sea of gold. A narrow pug-dandi (foot trail) snaked its way through the swaying blades, barely visible unless you knew where to look.

Jaggu crouched low, scanning the pugmarks in the dry, dusty track with the eyes of a seasoned forest man. His fingers brushed the impressions lightly—large pads of the tigress, followed by smaller, clustered prints of the cubs.

He stood up slowly, face darkening.

"Something is not right," he said quietly, almost to himself.

The trainees looked at him, puzzled.

Jaggu pointed at the trail ahead. "Look closely. Till this point, we had three cubs. But in the pugmarks that go forward... only two remain."

There was silence, the weight of the forest pressing in.

Jaggu walked ahead, eyes scanning the signs, his every movement rooted in intuition. Then, suddenly, he stopped. His hand rose slowly and pointed to his nose.

"Tiger," he said in a low voice. "I can smell it."

The group froze in their tracks. A quiet ripple of unease passed through the line. The scent of musk and wildness resembling raw meat, hung faintly in the air, unmistakable to a trained nose.

"It's coming from the left. From inside the grassland. The tigress has moved ahead. But this... this smell is fresh. It's strong. Close." He added, eyes narrowing.

He looked over his shoulder at the hesitant group. "Something's happened. Maybe a cub strayed."

Before they could respond, he stepped off the pug dandi and entered the tall grass.

The yellow stalks whispered around him as he pushed through, his senses heightened. The others followed, but with clear reluctance—feet dragging, eyes darting, hearts pounding.

One of the younger trainees called out, panic in his voice, "Sir, don't! The tigress could be in there... she might charge!"

But Jaggu didn't look back. He raised his hand in a calming gesture, the golden grass closing behind him like a curtain. Within the grass, Jaggu moved with the precision of a predator and the respect of a devotee. His senses were heightened—ears alert, eyes scanning for movement, nose tuned to the shifting current of scent.

He whispered to himself, "You're close... I can feel you."

Another ranger added, "With cubs, she'll be more dangerous. She won't warn before attacking."

But Jaggu didn't turn back. His instincts were in command now — old, primal, sharper than reason.

The musky scent of tiger thickened, wrapping around him like a warm fog. His steps quickened.

The sunlight filtered weakly through the dense yellow veil, turning the world golden and hushed.

Then Jaggu raised his hand again, halting the group. His body stilled.

His boots sank slightly into the soft earth, but he stood motionless, as if the very wind had whispered something only he could hear. He raised one hand slowly, placing it behind his ear.

From far away — carried on the drifting wind like a secret — came the faint cry of a cub.

A tigress's cub.

Jaggu's eyes narrowed. It was a low, plaintive sound — not the shriek of danger, but the whimper of confusion, of being lost. Of being alone.

"There," he said, voice low but certain, pointing into the denser part of the grass. "Did you hear that? One of the cubs. It's calling."

The others strained their ears, but heard only the rustle of dry blades. Still, they knew better than to doubt Jaggu's senses.

Jaggu turned and entered the thicker patch without waiting. He surged forward, swift and instinctive — like an arrow loosed from a bow. His movements were fluid but urgent, part hunter, part guardian, eyes locked in the direction of the sound.

Behind him, the others hesitated, exchanging anxious glances.

Jaggu pressed on, the cry growing clearer, sharper — laced with distress. As he ran, his boots slipped on loose earth and dry leaves. Suddenly, the ground beneath him gave way — a shallow gully hidden by the grass.

He stumbled, nearly tumbling forward — but years of jungle craft kicked in. With a last-second pivot, he shifted his weight and caught himself on one knee, just at the edge of the pit.

Jaggu's eyes widened in disbelief as he observed the trap carefully. Inside the pit, he noticed a fine muslin cloth covered by dry leaves, a crude makeshift covering. At the edge of the pit, half-hidden in the shadows and twigs, was a tiny ball of golden fur — trembling, frightened, and utterly alone.

A young tiger cub, helpless and exhausted, was repeatedly attempting to climb out. Its tiny claws scraped the edges of the pit in vain, every effort thwarted by the depth of the trap.

Jaggu's heart raced as he watched the cub struggle, its tiny body trembling from exhaustion, foam bubbling at the edges of its mouth.

Without a moment's hesitation, Jaggu unbuttoned his khaki uniform. He swiftly pulled it off and leaped into the pit with the agility of a predator. His movements were swift and precise, almost instinctive, as he crouched down to the cub. The little tiger, though clearly weak and disoriented, was still a tiger at heart. It hissed, baring its tiny fangs, desperately trying to intimidate Jaggu. Its tiny claws swiped at the air, but Jaggu wasn't deterred. He smiled softly, a warm, reassuring smile that was more about comfort than dominance.

"Easy, little one," Jaggu whispered, his voice calm yet firm. "You're safe now. I've got you."

With practiced care, Jaggu wrapped his khaki uniform around the cub. He could feel the cub's body trembling, the exhaustion, the fear still clinging to it. But Jaggu was steady. His hands were firm, yet gentle, as he cradled the cub in his arms, feeling its weak, rapid breathing.

In one fluid motion, Jaggu leapt out of the pit, his body soaring with the grace of a panther. With the cub cradled in his arms, Jaggu turned to his team. "Get ready. We need to take this cub back to the forest department for treatment. It's severely dehydrated, not out of danger yet, but we've given it a chance."

Jaggu turned slowly, his gaze fixed on the pit that the poachers had dug. That pit, where the young cub had struggled, was a symbol of everything that was wrong with the world—everything he will have to fight against. His eyes, though weary, burned with a fierce resolve.

The tribal wedding...

As the evening waned, a jeep rumbles down the rugged path, kicking up a cloud of dust in its wake. The vehicle comes to a halt at the edge of a forest river. The last traces of daylight linger in the sky in brush strokes of lilac and crimson, but the moon is already high, its silver rays dancing across the ripples.

On the western banks of the river, a tribal congregation has gathered in quiet celebration. A bonfire blazes at the center of their gathering, its flames licking the night air, casting flickering shadows on the granite outcrops and dusty earth. Around the fire, a group of men and women dance in a slow, rhythmic circle, their anklets jingling in time with the beat of hand-drums.

From within the gathering rises the haunting strains of an Alha—a warrior's song from the parched heartlands of Bundelkhand. Its melody, ancient and proud, seemed to emanate from the dust itself, as though echoing across generations.

The song carries the stories of valour, virtue and the sacred legacy of the tiger—the noble soul of the forest. In its haunting refrain, the tiger is not just an animal, but a guardian spirit, a warrior, a king in exile whose land has bled and burned. Set to a hypnotic tune, the song draws everyone in—men and women sway gently, children clap in rhythm, and the elders nod in solemn reverence.

The rest of the community sits cross-legged by the river, their faces lit by both fire and moonlight, silently listening, some nodding to the rhythm, some lost in memory.

Mr. Verma steps down from the jeep, brushing the trail dust off his sleeves. Behind him, the three children—Aamir, Anya and Rajiv—leap out with wide eyes, their faces lit by the golden glow of the bonfire across the riverbank. Ms. Aparna follows gracefully, adjusting the soft dupatta over her shoulder, her gaze drawn to the mingling silhouettes of dancers and flames.

Something sacred is unfolding tonight—at the meeting point of sky, land, and water. The silvery river glistens beneath the rising moon, and the air is thick with the scent of wildflowers and woodsmoke. And the Alha soars into the wilderness, a hymn for the land and those who protect it.

The special guests have not come here by accident.Tonight, under the tribal stars and beside the whispering river, they are here to witness a union forged not by pomp and ritual—but by fire, earth, and spirit.

It is Jaggu and Janhvi's wedding. And in the company of forests and friends, of elders and cubs, the vow of togetherness is about to be made—not only between two souls, but between all those who choose to stand with the wild.

From the direction of the bonfire, Jaggu approaches swiftly. Dressed simply, but with an unmistakable pride in his step, he reaches Mr. Verma and bows down, touching his feet with both hands.

"Please come, Sahab. Please come," Jaggu says with emotion in his voice. "You have changed our lives."

Just then, Janhvi appears beside him, her face glowing with joy. She too bends down to touch Mr. Verma's feet, and then warmly embraces the three children one by one, as if they were her own.

Mr. Verma smiles, placing a gentle hand on each of their shoulders.

"Shaadi mubarak ho, Jaggu," he says warmly. "And to you too, Janhvi. May this bond be as strong and wild as the forests you both love."

Jaggu stands tall, looking striking in his traditional tribal angavastra (marriage attire), its earthy colors woven with symbols of his land and people.

His face is ruddy—not just from the dance and the crackling bonfire, but also from the joy he's trying so hard to contain. The flickering flames reflect in his eyes, giving him the air of a forest spirit caught between man and myth.

Anya tiptoes close, grinning mischievously. With a gentle gesture, she places Janhvi's delicate hands into Jaggu's calloused ones, then turns to him with a teasing glint.

"So, Jaggu Dada," she says, cocking her head, "won't you tell us how a monster like you managed to catch such a pretty fairy?"

Laughter erupts from around the fire, even as Jaggu scratches his head, pretending to think hard, before replying with mock seriousness:

"It's a long story. Want to listen?"

Janhvi laughs, lightly slaps his shoulder, and the circle bursts into cheers.

The Mottled Wood Owl, its feathers mottled with the wisdom of centuries, suddenly takes flight from the thick, dark arms of a neighboring Jamun tree. Its wings slice the night air without a sound, gliding gracefully above the tribal congregation below.

From the owl's ancient, all-seeing eyes, a dreamlike vision takes form—the tribal dancers are caught in a trance, their bodies swaying to the hypnotic rhythm of the Alha, encircling the fire like shadows from another age. Sparks rise into the indigo night like fireflies, vanishing into the dark veil of stars.

The owl soars onward, its wings silvered by moonlight, and crosses the river whose waters glimmer like polished mirrors under the moon's watchful eye. The sound of the warrior song becomes fainter, replaced by the gentle rustle of reeds and the distant croaks of frogs.

On the far bank, the grass grows wild and the tall reeds sway silently in the night breeze. And there—half-shrouded in shadow, half-revealed by moonlight—a pair of golden-yellow eyes glisten.

Still. Unblinking. Watching.

Suddenly, the night is torn.

From across the river, from the shadowed bank cloaked in whispering reeds, rises a sound—deep, guttural, mournful.

A roar.

It bursts from the tigress's chest like a storm long held back, echoing across the shimmering river, through the jamun groves, over the bonfire light, silencing the drums, pausing the dance.

It is a roar that awakens memory. Of forests untouched. Of instincts unforgotten. Of everything untamed and untameable.

It rolls across the darkening landscape like a low thunder, stirring leaves, birds, hearts. It touches each listener differently—fear, awe, reverence—but no one remains untouched. For it is not just a sound.

It is the mother.

The tigress.

She stands still behind the tall water reeds, her breath shallow, her golden eyes searching the riverbank beyond the silver ribbon of moonlit water.

She had crossed that river yesterday. She had three cubs then.

Tonight, only two walk beside her.

And so, she calls.

It is a cry — raw, broken, ancient.

A cry wrenched from the depths of a mother's heart.

She calls to the one who did not return.

A cry that rises from her chest like thunder dipped in sorrow. It trembles through the reeds, across the shimmering river, into the clearing where the fire flickers and drums have gone silent.

It is the voice of a wild mother who does not understand why the little heartbeat she carried within her is now missing.

And the forest listens.

The fire hushes. The dancers still. Even the mottled wood owl, circling overhead, slows its wings.

In the hush of that moment, the land, the river, and the sky seem to ache with her

And somewhere near the flames, a man who once crawled through yellow grass hears it — and closes his eyes.

The Saviour...

Seated in the wedding pavilion, Jaggu's ears prick up at the sound. His attention sharpens as he hears the distant, mournful cry. Immediately, he takes Janhvi's hand, his grip firm yet gentle, and directs her attention to the sound. Looking into her eyes, he says softly, "His mother is calling for him. I have to go, Janhvi."

He pauses for a moment, then adds with a reassuring smile, "Wait for me...This time, I'll be back soon."

Janhvi's eyes glisten with unshed tears, but she quickly blinks them away. A single tear escapes, sliding down her cheek, though her lips curl into a bittersweet smile. She squeezes his hand and replies quietly,

"Go, Jaggu, go...I have always stopped you, all these years, but not today." Jaggu quickly unknots his his tribal wedding attire knotted to Janhvi's saree, stands still for a moment, glances at Janhvi one last time, and with a swift motion, he gets up and starts running.

The people around him, watch in stunned silence as Jaggu sprints away from the festivities, disappearing into the night.

Jaggu enters the forest department compound in the dark, unlocking the gate with swift, practiced hands. The sound of the cub's cries fills the air, drawing him toward the cage. His heart races as he moves quickly, the urgency of the situation propelling him forward.

Jaggu takes off his angavastra (the wedding attire) and with swift hands, he wraps the trembling cub in the fabric.The cub lets out a tiny, weak cry, a sound filled with fear and longing. Jaggu cradles it gently, his grip firm yet tender, offering the warmth of his embrace as he whispers soothing words.

The mother's call echoes again, distant but thunderous, reverberating through the forest and across the heavens. In Jaggu's arms, the tiger cub begins to stir. Its small, trembling body holds a sudden charge, an instinctive urgency. Its ears perk up alert to the sound of its mother's distant call, its nose twitches — it knows. It looks up at Jaggu, and for a fleeting moment, their eyes lock—an unspoken connection between two intertwined souls.

And then, without wasting a moment, Jaggu sprints towards the river. In the hushed silence of the night, the riverbank lies wrapped in a dreamlike stillness.. The gentle murmur of subdued waves whispers over pebbles, while fireflies flicker like scattered stars in the dark.

Pushing aside the reeds, Jaggu emerges at the edge of the river, the cub still wrapped close to his chest. His steps slow as he reaches the bank, the pulse of the forest beating quietly around him — a sacred rhythm of life, sorrow, and reunion.

The moment the cub senses its mother's roar, now from closer, its tiny ears perk up sharply. A desperate mewling escapes its throat, growing louder, more urgent. Jaggu pauses for a breath, uncertain, glancing down at the trembling bundle in his arms. Then he lifts his gaze to the dark expanse of the wild river stretched out before him under the moon.

Without hesitation, he steps forward. With a soft splash, his foot breaks the surface. The water is shallow — waist-deep in most places — but it's a true jungle river, unpredictable and alive. The chill of the river washes over him, but he doesn't flinch. He presses forward, the cub wrapped against his chest, soaked and breathless. The opposite bank rises slowly to meet him, cloaked in silver light.

The little cub, tuning into it's mother's roars, lifts its head towards the night. Its wide, amber eyes shimmer in the moonlight, and in the glistening orb of its eye, the moon's reflection dances like a silver ghost.

The air is thick with magic — a hush of anticipation, of something ancient about to complete its circle.

As Jaggu nears the shoreline, the deep, echoing roar of the tigress softens — it becomes a sharp, guttural bark, urgent yet tender, the unmistakable call of a mother seeking her lost child. And the cub, now trembling with excitement in Jaggu's arms, responds with a series of soft mews, high-pitched and yearning, carried across the still night like a forgotten lullaby.

As he steps onto the silver bank, the forest hushes.

Above, a shooting star streaks silently across the sky, as if the jungle itself has made a wish.

Jaggu kneels down in the moonlit grass and gently sets the cub on the ground. "Go," he whispers, "your mother is waiting."

The cub, as if understanding, takes off in bounding strides, vanishing into the tall grass. The moonlight flickers through the reeds, catching brief glimpses of the cub's small, striped form darting forward.

Then she appears.

Through the tall, whispering reeds, a faint glimmer emerges — a pair of golden-amber eyes, glowing like forgotten embers in the wild. They do not blink. They watch, burning with recognition, longing, and a mother's fierce ache.

She emerges from the shadows like a dream brought to life — her powerful form gliding over the ground in silence. She reaches her cub, bends her great head low, and licks his forehead, then his ears, then his entire tiny body. With a delicate grace that belies her strength, she picks up the cub by the loose skin behind his neck.

Before she disappears, the tigress turns her head toward Jaggu. Her amber eyes lock with his — deep, ancient, glowing with something beyond words. A silent acknowledgement.

Then, with a leap, she vanishes into the darkness of the jungle, carrying her child home.

Jaggu feels something shift deep within him—like the final piece of a long-broken soul finding its place.

Then he turns back slowly. His heart is full — of joy, of longing, of something ancient and sacred. He steps into the river, now aglow with moonlight, the ripples catching silver sparks as he walks deeper.

The fireflies shimmer on either side of him, golden lanterns of the wild. He moves forward, waist-deep now, the sparkling waters embracing him like the arms of the earth itself.

Above him, the Mottled Wood Owl glides across the moonlit sky, like a sentinel of the night, its haunting hoot echoing through the silence, circling Jaggu like an omen or a blessing.

As a teardrop glistening in moonlight, runs down his rugged face tracing his weather beaten features, Jaggu stops and turns to look back. The jungle behind him is still, as if holding its breath— veiled in mist, ancient, eternal.

His breath catches — not in fear, but in awe. For in that moment, he knows the truth. The tiger is not merely a beast of the forest.

It is a prayer.

A promise.

A warning.

Sculpted by nature.

Chiseled by time.

And he —just one man wading through moonlight — is its witness.

Into the future...

Many years have passed. 'AI' has taken over. The world has surged ahead—its machines more intelligent, its cities taller, its humans smarter but lonelier, its intrusion deeper into the heart of nature.

Many forests have fallen silent, rivers run choked and wild cries once heard at dusk have faded into distant memory.

The untamed and untameable have been replaced by the cute, cuddly, domesticated and the predictable.

The wilderness, once vast, sacred and impenetrable, has been carved away and violated by the ever-growing needs of an exploding human population.

Yet, in one forgotten corner of an ancient land, beneath the dense canopy of a forest fed by a deep, dark river, whispers of the wild still remain. Here, it is said, wild tigers still prowl—fierce, regal, elusive.

It's been long since Jaggu retired from forest service.

The children — Aamir, Anya and Rajiv— had become old, silver-haired and slow of step, their youthful adventures long behind them.

But whenever they sat together, beneath the shade of an old neem tree or around a crackling fire in winter, their eyes would brighten with a familiar gleam.

They would speak of Jaggu Bhaiyya with a fondness that time had not dimmed.

Locals maintained that the legendary tiger tracker never returned to his village, never claimed the comforts of age and retirement. Instead, he disappeared into the wilderness he once knew so well — slipping into the trees like a wraith.

The tribals spoke of him with reverence. They said he lived for a while in the depths of the forest, near the Dheel's whispering banks—guiding tribal children, helping wounded animals and warning lone rangers of hidden danger.

They said he carried with him not just wisdom, but stories—of loss, of loyalty, of a world once teeming with life.

Then, one day, Jaggu vanished.

The jungle quietly swallowed him up. No one saw him after that.

No goodbyes. No trace.

But legends don't fade easily.

Sometimes, late at night, when the moonlight spills across the treetops and the wolves howl in the distance, villagers whisper of a man riding a black horse, with a woman beside him—her hair flowing like the river wind…

And they say a tiger walks besides them — not of flesh, but of spirit.

They call him The Last Tracker…